Driving Wheel

and

My House is Dark

Two Novels by
Tony Hozeny

First Edition
ISBN 0-88361-033-7
Library of Congress Card Number 74-82345

Copyrighted 1974 by Tony Hozeny

Printed in the United States of America for
Wisconsin House, Ltd. by Straus Printing
and Publishing Co., Inc., Madison, Wisconsin

ACKNOWLEDGMENT

The author thanks Sally Daniels and Mark E. Lefebvre for encouragement and editing, and Cheri Hannay for typing.

Driving Wheel

For Sally

every word is
a whole day

–My baby don't have to work,
    she don't have to rob and steal,
I give her everything she needs,
    I am her driving wheel.

Roosevelt Sykes

PROLOGUE

I ain't ever hated being pregnant like I do today. My ankles been swelling up pretty bad, but this is the worst it's been; about a week ago, when it started, I went to see the doctor and he says Connie, you're on your feet too much, you have to quit your job, the baby's almost here, how much longer can you work anyway, and I go, okay, but I'm thinking how'm I going to get along without a job? Then I remember one of the girls at work, she told me Connie you ought to gone on welfare soon's you found out that boy wasn't going to marry you, but I told her I just don't feel right about it; now I guess I'll have to do it. It's always cold in Milwaukee this time of year, but I ain't ever felt it like this, and besides I always heard your ankles only swell up when it's hot, maybe I ain't eating right or something. Anyhow, bending over them files today I sure knew I can't work after today, seems like I've got so heavy all of a sudden and everything hurts.

Now I got this Medicaid card supposed to get me some pills the doctor says will keep down the swelling. So I rested up at home awhile after work, til I could walk to the drugstore, then I went down the steps; some of the steps are loose and the landlord never gets around to fixing them, I'm kind of scared of them now cause I can't hardly see my own feet.

But when I got outside it was warmer cause it was snowing, and it wasn't too bad long as I walked slow. Better than being in the apartment, it smells musty all the time and I can't seem to get rid of the smell, maybe now when I start cleaning things up more, I been so tired after work I haven't felt up to it. The city looked big and grey in the snow; funny, I never would of thought anything grey could be pretty. When my baby comes I won't be lonesome, won't have time for that. Sometimes I get to thinking I'm too young to be having a baby, but you got to have one sooner or later and I still won't be forty yet when the baby's my age, maybe I'll still understand about things.

It felt good to get inside the drugstore, there were lots of people talking about the snow, and it was warm, and some of the people's glasses were all steamed up. But the clerk told me there was something wrong with the card and I go what's wrong with it, I just got it in the mail and he says you got to have it stamped or validated—what kind of cigarettes you say you want, he says to the man behind me, kind of shoving me aside. I walked over by the door, tired all of a sudden, like I could never make it home, telling myself everything's going to be all right, tomorrow I'll call the doctor; but I notice the wind is blowing strong now and the snow looks like it'll hurt my face.

PART I

I

Jack walked out the back door of the cafe with a week's pay in his hand, shivering as the rain began in Lexington, blowing up hard in the dark Appalachian wind and hurting his face, the sky grey and moving like a coal hopper shaking on a railroad siding:

he saw a child fall down near him, cry out for his family, the father looks over his shoulder, yells get your dog ass up here and turns again, never looking back though the child keeps crying, stumbling way behind on the slick hill; Jack came up and helped the child stand, touching the small wet face quickly and feeling like mixing it up with the father, though he knew it was crazy, he'd lost every fight he'd had since coming east from Kearney, Nebraska, crawled around on cold alley floors for hours more than once, but he wondered if he'd been such a child somewhere in Nebraska, back before the years he remembered, some children's faces and names, maybe from that time, seeming to move now in his memory til he saw other things and lost the feeling; old drunks were already trying to steal newspapers to wrap themselves up in, most of them never getting up again after nights like this one, and he leaned into the wind, knowing only then how sick he was of cities, how they were all the same after the waiting time; he'd thought to go right home but he changed his mind, knowing he'd never get to sleep now and hating the cold too much to keep on outside.

Jack sat down in the bar he'd come to and watched from the window, sensing the rain as it froze and slipped down, turning the snow dirty in the street as cars slide quiet, hit and tear loose like freight cars on a hump, this same scene beginning again down the street by the stoplight, shit, these people call this snow, he thought, remembering his home prairies, long bare snow drifting over sheds and barns til the land moved in the spring, spare houses leaning then like stands of grain as the sun continued, the wheat sky working the blue air down, down in the black soil, and men waiting on the land, telling time by furrows and rain, and Jack,

feeling his own hands raw from broken glass, hot stacks of dishes he'd have to wash again in a few hours, sipped his beer and watched the men slam leather cups down on the bar, throwing dice in time as the floor shakes under the juke box, other men tapping their fingers in rhythm or looking close at women in bright dresses moving around the tables, their legs smoky and bare in the dull light, voices rising as the drinking goes on, men talking about some woman named Stennis, she'd do her own brother if she can't use somebody else, if she got to have it that bad why don't she come on in here, he thought, as he shook his head and walked out, figuring to go home after all:

he saw two men working by the side of a beer truck, pulling down the heavy barrels and trying to get through the slush, their faces red and lined, cold as he'd been all day in the cafe kitchen, choking in the steam rising from the sinks, the ice worse now as he turned into his own street, dark already, the next streetlight three blocks down, houses shaky as old drunks he's seen everywhere he's been, leaning together and leaving spaces to hide alongside their walls, nobody talks to him but they let him alone long as he doesn't look too close, say something about a man running down the street or stretched out on a stoop, somebody's always running down here, even in the winter time;

but now he'd got home, feeling tired and lonesome as he got inside the front hall, he walked slowly up the steps and heard blues off a radio jamming up the walls, people moving together behind the left door on the second floor landing, they've just gotten paid, been going strong since last night and they'll party straight through til Monday morning, sometimes they lay their empties on the fire escape out back and take turns shooting at them, the glass breaking and flying like small birds all over the steel steps, floors shaking now as he turned and kept on up the stairs, wishing some woman were lying up in his room;

he felt the wind near the top of the stairs and stopped, somebody'd broken his lock again, jimmied along the door frame and got inside, cleaned everything out but the dirty bed frame and some old rags, scrape marks all over the floor and coat hangers banging together as the window shook loose in its sash, chipped and covered with frost;

Jack hit the door hard and it slammed back in the room, cracking the wall worse, hard sound of claws scratching now under the paster as he swore, wishing the rats'd come out but changing his mind as he came down the steps, shoved the front door open and got outside, slipping, falling on the slick streets as he ran hard for the station he'd passed on his way home;

the bus, silver as ice in the bare light, carried him from Lexington.

II

The bus was snow grey indiana morning and these were not the fields he
remembered:
    these were city brick shod and sleep, not cold or thirsty, just days
along the road,
    not like they, who even in snow bind were wind of women's voices,
round moving as a woman,
    these did not move, and no sun, not even rain could work them,
they were salt and no mountains came to their beyond, just the ditch of
Chicago;
    Jack looked out,
    remembering Baltimore, San Francisco, Omaha;
    he was cold and close on the bus,
    his hair was dirty,
    his cheeks were dark as his eyes were red,
    his eyes
    fell below the fields and saw nothing, he tried to sleep but could not,
for this was like Lexington mornings and he must wait,
wait for the night to open:
    the dun
of Hammond Gary Chicago, what difference but grey, to look down from
the Skyway, remember Maxwell Street and the rows of empty shoes
inside, the outside men who fingered them, see South Halsted Street and
know the faces would not have changed:
    they would be legless
    dead fish eyes, mouths cut glass rocks
    on Illinois shore—
    and Jack had gone in the first days of last time spring to New York,
maybe
    42nd is the best of streets, a man can stay alive, buy off his hunger
with himself, know in that moment he's not dying the deaths of other men
piled on other streets, just his own,
    but how hard to be fucked by a man whose neck sweat is not
    the work of land and sun but the cross of heat pipes below the streets,
    how hard to be fucked by a man,
    how hard to be fucked in the ass,
    and Jack,
to the skin life of Illinois, north to the cold green not of hands
but of spring coming,
watched the cars, and it was not the first time,
his were not new eyes, he was not tricked by the push of the sky,

his backwinds chased him and he remembered cities and fields,
not the same but no different,
    now he knew but he ran anyway,
    for he had seen these days before.

Thin smoke came up just off the bridge rail, and he'd seen the train
line way below the highway, almost hidden as the snow drifted, changing
the coal yard even as he'd watched shapes thick or slipping off in the
dusk, still smelling the yeast factory miles back on the road as he stepped
down from the bus, shivering, watching the others on the street try to get
used to the cold, their faces red and seamed over, eyes watering as they
waited for cabs or buses, some stamping their feet or just shaking like guy
wires, seeing the cold Milwaukee sky darken and the factory smoke turn
white over the river. He'd felt like running from the cold but he slowed
down, looking for a neighborhood he'd remember having seen in other
cities, get a cheap meal and a bed for a few days til he found work or left
town, at least I ain't broke this time, he thought, feeling himself change
as he remembered other times when he'd been cold or hungry, scared
somebody'd shake him down for a little change, not knowing then how to
get by in cities, see somebody before he saw you and move quick, sleep
anywhere long as you never close your eyes, the wind blowing up hard
now through the streets and around the buildings, hurting him as he
turned and ran for the closest bar, pulling the door shut behind him.
He walked in, feeling their eyes on him and wondering if they'd want
trouble or worse things but letting it pass, they'd maybe wait til he'd
eaten and had a drink; they bought each other rounds, kept their voices
low when he looked over, as if they'd been scared he'd hear something,
their voices mixing with older ones he remembered now, changing slowly
as the night went on like a way freight. He stayed there drinking, felt
good enough to play some country music on the jukebox while he shot pool
with a man named Eddie, who'd said you must of just got in too, still got
that smell of moving around on you, and he'd nodded, thinking of a time
he'd shot pool with some boys in west Texas and won, had to get out of
town fast that time, hearing Eddie say he had a bottle home but shaking
his head as he remembered men like Eddie, knowing they were risky, then
feeling lonesome after Eddie'd gone. An old tune came on and he whistled
along with it, wondering if the old men from home still got their guitars
and fiddles out Saturday nights after listening to the Opry on the radio:
they'd sit on their porches long past dark and he'd stay, listening with the
other kids til they'd all been dragged off and he was the last one left, the
old men would let him sing along then and he'd get sips of their whiskey
til the ten o'clock train came through, his time to go, the sky on those
nights rolling over Sidney as he'd try balancing on the rails, fall off, have
to walk the ties behind the shaky red light of the caboose way down the
track, stumbling, sick maybe over the porch rails, or getting inside, the
times he'd been lucky, and his bed, then, moved like an empty boxcar on a
train all night long.
Now he remembered other things and stopped thinking, new voices
seeming to rise and hold in the smoke as the rhythms changed in the
music, and he leaned over to buy another drink: a girl moved in next to

him and he shifted, feeling their arms almost touch and remembering how many times he'd waited for the night to go down in Lexington, til he'd been drunk enough to promise himself anything, sleep alone then without thinking about it and wake up worse off than ever. The girl seemed to smile, licking the drink off her lips as he talked to her, figuring it might be worth it to buy her a few drinks, though he'd been taken bad, set up a few times by women who'd seemed easy, then had boys waiting when he'd got home with them. She led him to a table she'd gotten earlier, waiting for him to sit down before she did and he felt her looking him over with her fine blue eyes he saw moving in the light, her thighs moving, showing as she pulled up her skirt to sit down.

—You come in here much?

—No, he said, getting tired as he heard her say she didn't think so, she knew most everybody in here, feeling her leg shaking next to his after she'd touched his arm a few times, high already or just waiting for him to make his move, wish I had someplace to stay, he thought, knowing how cold he'd feel outside after all this drinking, after he'd spent enough on this girl to buy a room for the night. She kept talking, leaning on him as he sensed something he didn't want to take a chance on, her eyes changing, checking the door every few minutes, maybe wondering why he'd just kept buying drinks and not saying anything, drifting, even a woman won't do me no good now, he said aloud after she'd gone to the bathroom, her hair touching him on her way out of the booth, making him remember the long time he'd been alone or how sick he'd gotten of trying to pick up women in bars, these same lights hanging like persimmons, the men around him weaving slow as cat tails; he walked out drunk, hating the cold, dry snow streaks over the sidewalk and the clear night dry and thin as the air over Salt Lake in the winter time. He slipped and fell down, but he hung on till he'd reached an old hotel on 3rd Street; then he shook all over as he stood inside, coughing from the dust in the room and shifting his bag, and an old feeling came on him as he stood by the desk, almost wanting to run out again.

The skinny clerk took his money, told him in a strange voice where his room was, seeming to smile as he said these words, as if he'd known something or was just waiting; he walked upstairs, looking back at the clerk once before he got to the top, and the room smelled sweet when he opened it, he saw dirty rags in the corner and two small drops of blood or paint on the floor. The smell got stronger near the bed and he lay down in the draft coming through the old sash, shifting around, glad he'd got drunk enough to sleep soon, sleep, til he felt a hand come for his crotch or wallet and kicked out hard with his legs, choking, tangled in the blanket and getting loose too late, they'd gone and there was nothing in the hall or downstairs; he grabbed his bag and ran back outside.

Now the cold took him like a beating, hurting him inside and making him stiff, scared to stop walking, not losing yet the smell of the room, the feel of the soft hands on his legs, they'd been quick and he'd been lucky to wake up, each car seeming to slow down as it passed him, as if they'd be coming for him now, get him out here on the street and let the cold kill him. He found a cafe and got some coffee, feeling his shaky nerves as he watched two men eat runny eggs with their fingers, the second man's head slipping slowly down into his plate and staying down til the other man woke him and they went out like trolleys, their faces hurt and showing through the glass door of the cafe.

Next door, he got a bottle just as the bar was closing, the cold easier to take now as he followed the street east til he got to a laundromat, looked around and walked inside; he sat on a low table behind the machines, knowing he was hidden from the street but watching the window anyway, drinking slowly for a long time til the lights stopped moving outside and he wished he'd stayed in Lexington or gone south, as he finished the bottle, began to feel it coming and lay down on the table, drunk again, drifting

in the strip of night he saw the dawn, saw the runner and the train, and truck lights clipping the deep side of the highway, the moon crossing behind a train as bells came down from a church like hounds, hound bells, rabbits running from the clang of hounds, guns and shouts, running, running as he shook in his dream, sick of his dreams and wondering why the beginning was always the same.

III

On the second morning, he'd felt the dry cold early, wondering if he'd slept at all, as if he'd only remembered old habits or dreams, roads and white lines coming up fast in his eyes as if he'd been driving, riding high in a truck cab all night long, same long time to shake down the dawn, same sick feeling, his nerves shaky from the whiskey as he moved, stretched and looked around, checking his money before he sat up.

The others were mostly old men trying to wash clothes, dropping half what they carried each time they'd change machines, then wheezing like tarmills as they bent down for grey socks or union suits; they seemed never to straighten up again, though they kept moving til it was time to go, each one quick enough with what a man has left to keep his socks from the wind; he stayed, thinking about the times he'd run from the cops in Chicago when they'd come down to clean up the drunks, how they'd beaten up a man til his teeth cracked like old glass and fell out, the man crawling then, looking for his teeth as the cops laughed or went on to the others, as he'd watched, hidden back of an oil drum and too scared to move, running his fingers over his own lips, the feeling of those days coming on him as he remembered other men he'd known, the way their mouths twisted when they tried to eat, I got to stop this shit, he thought, got to get going.

Now the sun was high and small, shining the west side of buildings and hurting his eyes worse than snow on the plains in winter; sometimes he'd had to stay inside for days while a blizzard howled over the fields and houses, changing them hour by hour, and he remembered sleeping downstairs on a blanket by the stove, scared of the wind but curious as a child is, not wanting it to end, knowing the grandmother was uneasy even as she tried to cover up, singing and baking to forget the wind, the sound of her old voice coming back in a tune he seemed to hear now as he passed a cafe, she'd been singing it the day she'd taken him from the first place he'd been, and he'd known then he'd like her as he stood up on the seat, looking out the window of the old Nash she'd kept as long as he'd known her. Later on, after she'd sent him away, he'd stayed up nights in the orphanage wondering if she'd taken in other children before him, if she'd had others after he was gone, the cold feel of this city coming inside now as he shivered, hearing diesel horns off to the south and feeling lonesome as he thought of Sidney again, the snow piling up by the grain elevator and the brakeman huddled in his shanty, small light breaking out the back window as grey smoke burned straight up on clear nights, sometimes just a shaky dark line if the wind were blowing: and he wondered again why he'd ever left the plains as he walked through this city, as if he'd forgotten the judge and his wife, the big house in Kearney, the way he'd felt when they'd looked at him, the feeling of those days moving in memory as he looked for a job in Milwaukee, knowing a man just moved on when he couldn't find work but not wanting to go this time, he was tired as horses, tired as dreams gone bad to the seasons, and he'd thought to hang on til spring, building a little stake so he'd travel easy.

He walked into an employment office and sat down, feeling sick as he watched other jobless men move in and out of a row of small rooms, most of the men older than he, and he knew the counselor would ask about references, his work record and other things he couldn't talk about, thinking this is bullshit, I ain't going through with it, almost leaving til he remembered how he'd hate to go back to dishwashing or the one day jobs he was used to, shoveling fertilizer, unloading boxcars and trucks alone.

The other men would move out as slowly as they'd come in, some carrying papers in their hands, and he felt worse the longer he waited; then he heard his name called and he followed one of the secretaries into a small room. He lit a cigarette, watching the man closely and making up names and places in other cities, almost thinking he'd gotten somewhere til the man looked at his watch, shifted his papers and handed him three white cards with the names of cafes printed on them.

He spent two days looking, walking in the cold til he couldn't stand it, then going into libraries where he'd learned they'd leave him alone, let him read the want ads or even fall alseep on the soft couches, he was young and he looked like he might belong there. But he'd feel less like going on each time he stopped, never losing the cold, the faces of the men who'd seem almost glad to tell him there was no work; by the second afternoon he was sick of trying, he'd hear trains running just two blocks away and feel like going south, pick fruit if he had to, thinking that way til he remembered the cold boxcar floors, the week he'd spent in a Wyoming jail because he'd got caught last time around, the slick feel of the deputy's hands on his shoulders. So he kept on, so cold he'd shake even when he got inside these places, feeling sure he'd waited too long to leave this city and he'd never get out now; but they needed men badly on the garbage trucks and he got a job late that afternoon, almost falling down when he got outside again but leaning in a doorway til he felt strong enough to make it back to the library.

The city garage was a mile and a half north from downtown, so he took a cab the first morning, not wanting to miss the truck; he worked hard from the beginning, the driver sitting all morning in the warm truck cab and laughing at him and the other man, Rick, as they moved fast, hearing cans clank in the cold alleys, garbage freezing inside the cans so they had to slam them hard on the back of the truck, pull the loose stuff out with their hands; they'd run between houses, stamping round footprint packs in the snow to keep warm, the smoke from the yellow truck almost smelling like the tobacco plants in Lexington; the sun began to help them in late morning, they felt better til the driver'd leaned out his window, laughing, saying he'd just heard it was ten below and getting worse, great day for working outside.

They stopped off to drink beer and play pool at noon; he listened to the men, learning the sound of their voices before he knew their names, voices rising and falling as the bartender washed glasses and set up rounds with one smooth motion of hands, noise of glasses skidding down the bar and pool balls breaking as the men warmed up and got louder, kidding the bartender about his wife or the way he cut his drinks as an old waitress served up sandwiches fast as they could eat them, never smiling once, even when the driver called out hey honey, bring some of that over here, Rick saying then, just loud enough for everyone to hear, to laugh at, some of what, old man, some of what? He'd got his touch after the first game, winning enough beers so he didn't think he'd mind the cold much when they got back outside, Rick getting mad after each game, swearing, running his hands through his hair before leaning over the pool table, and the driver patted his big belly and chuckled, never playing himself but saying every few minutes I can beat this here Jack any day of the week.

He heard their stories later on, after they'd finished working and they sat in the warm truck, the driver remembering the old days and Rick's mostly army talk and women, the thin high smoke coming from the cab stack in the grey afternoon light, the feeling of dusk beginning already as he sipped his coffee and hoped he'd find a place to live soom, lose this cough and sleep in a bed again, knowing then how lucky he'd been last night to get off safe in a bus station, knowing his luck wouldn't hold. He left the truck at quitting time, surprised to find he'd gotten used to the cold and liking the dirty river and the bridge, the water still running after all this time of cold nights and snow, the feel of switch engines rolling in the yard, boxcars swaying from the slam of brakes and couplers as their cold wheels skidded on the icy rails, the semaphore changing as he watched, wondering what this hill would be like in the spring, after the waiting time, when the land and the trees changed under the south wind and birds out low over the houses, as if to remember the old ways before coming down for good:

someone called his name, but the voice was strange, he didn't turn til he'd heard the sound again—Eddie, the man he'd met his first night in town, was walking slowly toward him, weaving a little as he came up, and he saw that Eddie was older than he'd thought, maybe twice his own age, coughing all the time from the years outside, thin summer pants that never stopped the wind and an old jacket, cardboard stuffed in his shoes. He thought what's this man want from me as Eddie said where you been, Jack, ain't seen you around, smiling at him as if they were old friends, telling him this here's my stomping grounds, I just get downtown once in awhile, come on in, let's have a drink on Tommy here—he walked in behind Eddie, knowing again he'd better watch him close but tired of being alone, feeling good to laugh at something Eddie'd said as they got inside the bar.

It was quiet for late afternoon, he could hear the clock and the hum of the beer sign as he sipped his drink, not saying much as Eddie talked about the usual things, saying he'd done time in Georgia, had trouble in lots of towns, Eddie's voice then mixing with his own memories, as if he'd seen his old days beginning again in the mirror over the bar. Eddie told him how he'd come up behind some drunk his first week here and taken a thousand dollars, never had such luck, the goddam fool standing in an alley hollering taxi, taxi—hey, Jack, I got some watches here, you want to buy some cheap; he said no, don't have no use for one, watching the streetlight shift outside in the wind, making shadows on the window frost as he looked out, wished he had someplace else to go besides back downtown, line up at the Rescue Mission for soup that tasted the same in every town, feeling the other men's eyes on him as he took his turn, the looks on the faces of chaplains who'd always try talking to him, tell him change your ways, boy, ask God for help while you still got time, Jesus, Eddie said, they ain't much action in this man's town, you know that, not a goddam thing:

—Ain't much anywhere else either, he said, and he bought another round of beer; he figured Eddie'd been lying about the money but he listened a while longer, not wanting to stay but hating the cold, the doors he'd have to knock on to find a room and the way people would know he'd been running a long time and change their minds about renting to him; he told Eddie he'd see him later and moved slowly outside, leaning into the wind, almost believing it'd warmed up a little til he'd walked a block, thinking about Eddie's stories, days of rail joint miles, twenty years since the war, Eddie figuring he had grown kids in ten states by now, maybe you was friends with some of them, Jack, just didn't know they was my kids, Eddie'd said:

he remembered the way Eddie'd laughed as he watched the clouds move in, cutting fast across the sky as if they weren't as heavy as they seemed, snow coming tomorrow and warming things up, though the cold after the snow would hurt worse, last as long as the winter had been, make the paint crack on these old wooden houses, shingles this old tearing off easy in a bad storm, Eddie was lucky he was inside.

Now he stood on the bridge, hearing a fast freight roll through the crossing as the last light faded in the west and he looked down, feeling all those he'd known swelling and choking in this river, their faces turning like fish in the dark, his own face too mixed with the ripples as hot water poured in from the sausage factory on the other side, moving the faces in the water, old voices hiding like rats under the steam and moving water as he shook his head and hung on the rail all the way across the bridge.

IV

He stood at the window, watching the sun begin covering the rooftops and knowing already he'd hate this room too, remembering other beds with bad springs, cobwebs in the same corners, same bare light only making things darker and dry heat slipping through the walls like bad dreams left behind by the last man here; he took off his clothes and shoes, thinking how easy they'd been to steal, and he lay down on the bed, turning his face from the window and feeling sick, almost afraid to close his eyes—

but he knew he needed sleep badly and lay back, slipping down the edges of old memories or dreams, the night he'd run east from Kearney, the fields seeming to stretch out like women waiting in the darkness, range grass cracking under his feet as he ran for a train, feeling wild and happy as an outlaw, rolling and sliding in strange rhythms or sinking down to hide in the grass, close and quiet as the small animals around him, heavy, still as the dark ground, the grass changing like snow, covering him.

Now he heard trucks and raised his head, knowing only then he'd been asleep as he saw the green walls of the room again and lights flashing outside the window, thinking maybe a snowplow was down the street as he went to the window, and he saw the plow coming in the south end of Pulaski street. He dressed quickly, wanting to get outside so he'd lose the feel of this room and the smell of oatmeal coming up the heat register, almost running down the stairs after he'd closed his door but feeling good, then, to have a key in his pocket again.

The sky was hidden in a mist coming off the river, and warm snow fell easily, sticking to his face and hair as he watched cars move slowly up the hill, the trees hanging white and heavy, their branches seeming to touch the cars passing below; he followed deep tire tracks across the street, remembering the old feeling of walking over a trestle, looking down through the ties at deep water, his feet small enough in those days to slip through if he weren't careful, how Eddie'd told him a man could get killed if the wind blew wrong, never hear the horns or whistles til it was too late to jump off the track, a man on a trestle's got no place to go anyway; Eddie'd been drunk enough last night to go on a long time, the stories getting better as the night continued, as he learned the spaces between Eddie's words, sometimes even knowing what Eddie'd left out or made up but listening closely, as if to remember the name of an old tune, almost hearing Eddie's voice run on again like water in a metal sink, shit, had me two wives once, one in Nashville and the other in St. Louis, used to travel back and forth quite regular for about eight years, get me some money and a piece of ass, but goddam it they found out about each other and I ain't had the nerve to go back since, probably run my ass out of there with a shotgun, ain't that a bitch? There'd been more but he'd forgotten most of it now; he walked east, still smiling a little and liking the feel of the snow, the way it made the street quiet and slowed things down, hearing the telephone lines slapping gently, the cries of birds hanging on those lines.

He passed a laundromat and turned the corner, hungry now and wishing he had some cigarettes. The drugstore was crowded, he heard people talking about the snow as he looked around, wondering if he needed anything else, the line moving slowly in front of him as he shifted his feet, feeling his hangover come on him and wanting to get back outside where he could breathe. The sales clerk was looking at a card a woman had given him and he could hear the clerk saying this card's not properly validated, can't give you these pills, the woman arguing, fumbling in her purse as the clerk turned away from her, going on to another customer as if she weren't there, cutting her off when she tried to speak again. She turned, and he saw she was as young as he was and pregnant, carrying the baby low in her belly and looking tired as she closed her purse with her bare left hand, seeming to look at him then but saying things he couldn't hear, as if she were only talking to herself. He felt something in her half smile, the way her eyes darkened as she turned, as if he'd seen how hard the winter had been for her.

She stood by the door, wrapping her coat around her body and shivering, saying softly it's so cold out, why ain't these cards ever done right? He waited til she'd stopped talking and walked up to her, asking her if she'd like some coffee, watching her smile as she said thanks, except I can't drink it, sure like a coke though; they sat down in a booth by the soda fountain and waited, not saying anything till the waitress came. The girl slipped off her coat and he saw how thin her blouse was, thinking she must be half froze in that thing and wondering what she was like, maybe she had a boy waiting and was just being friendly, passing the time so she wouldn't have to go back outside, make that walk home again. They got their drinks and she started talking, saying she had a medical card from the Welfare Department but nobody'd take it and she'd get pains once in awhile, her voice going on softly as a fire burning down in a pile of leaves, holding him as he seemed to move in the rhythms she'd spoken, feeling himself change and calm down in the sound of her voice, the feel of her hand passing his as she reached for one of his cigarettes. He asked about the baby and she said pretty soon, less than a month. He smiled, knowing how good she'd look after the child was born.

They stayed til the waitress told them they'd have to buy something else, and then he walked out with her, telling her he was working for the city but nothing else, liking the sound of her name, Connie, as he used it the first few times, some kind of young girl's roll still left in her walk, even though her toes pointed outward from the weight of the child. She'd said she lived on Kane Place and they walked slowly, shivering as the wind came up, the snow stinging them now, the sky showing more as the clouds shifted and the afternoon began to go down in the cold air. She leaned into the wind and didn't say much, as if she'd remembered she had somebody else or maybe just wanted him to go. He'd wonder later on why he'd said he had things to do when she asked him in, remembering how she'd looked as he walked on alone, the way she'd told him to come over and visit anytime, feeling good then but stopping himself, knowing she must have something going or she'd show more, seem more alone than she did.

The wind died down again and the sky looked purple from the city lights as he stayed out, stopping at different bars to get the feel of the neighborhood and going out again after one beer, sometimes remembering something Connie'd said, feeling more lonesome than he'd been since leaving Nebraska, before he'd learned to keep to himself and hide from people in strange towns, men who'd come for him in the dark to take his money and men he'd had to turn to when he'd run out of luck, the feeling of those times stronger now as the night came on, trees shaking like old winos who'd scraped up enough for a morning run, spilling their money on the floor and grabbing the bottles with wet hands, the wine finished off before they'd got half a block past the liquor store, down in the Mission in San Francisco, where he'd learned early never to walk the streets drunk because the junkies came down hungry and sick, he'd see them slip into doorways, shivering, waiting for an easy roll til they couldn't stand it any more.

But he thought about Connie again as he walked into a hamburger joint, not losing his bad memories but feeling them change as he wondered about her, wishing he'd said the right things or figured out what she'd wanted, knowing only then how much he wanted to see her again, as if he'd come back home and found somebody grown whom he'd remembered only as a child, as if she'd changed him in those minutes he'd been with her, cutting him loose from something he could feel moving inside him now, and he was afraid. Eddie'd be down at the bar by now, but he didn't want to see him so he went to another place, drinking and playing the pinball machines til he was tired again, glad he had to work tomorrow so he'd have something to do, the time seeming to drag worse than before as he walked home, hearing the sounds of fighting and drinking from houses set close to the street.

Next morning he sat up in the cab as they started off, smelling the driver's cigar and looking down at the river when they drove over the bridge, figuring he'd wait one more day and go see her for sure.

V

When he got to her door, he wished he hadn't come, thinking maybe she don't even remember me, she's probably got her boy with her anyhow; he knocked twice, almost hoping there'd be no answer but waiting, leaning on the door jamb in the hallway and watching the low white sun shine colors all along the spider webs in the window as he listened for footsteps, for the sound of a lock slipping its catch. The door opened and she stood there wrapped in an old sweater, looking more tired and sick than he'd remembered but smiling at him, saying don't mind about this place, it's a mess, as she led him inside, as he loosened his coat and pretended to look around, watching her closely as she straightened things up, as if he'd learn something she couldn't say if he kept his eyes on her. He showed her the chicken he'd brought and she said why thanks, I'll cook this up right away, there's beer if you want some.

He felt the cold hang on in the room as he opened a beer, knowing why she seemed to shiver all the time, her hands shaking now as if she were afraid, maybe because her cough was worse today and seemed to hurt her, sometimes making her eyes water. The late sun came through the window, showing dust on the floors and tables as she picked up old clothes and newspapers, pressing her hands to the small of her back each time she'd stand up, then washing off the table and walking into the kitchen; he followed, wondering why she was so quiet, why he couldn't think of anything to say to her when she smiled, or looked at him, remembering other women who'd asked him questions, never listening to his answers but talking on, making it easy for him to say the right things, Connie asking only if he wanted another beer, you like your chicken fried or baked, coughing as she opened the stove, her face soft now, as if from the fear her voice covered, and he felt himself change and move in the spaces between them, wanting to stay and take care of her even though her boy'd be coming back some time, remembering how many times he'd hoped some woman might come along and save him and almost believing Connie would each time he looked at her. He leaned back, thinking, smelling the baked chicken and watching her moving by the stove, seeing the shadow of the dark strands of her yellow hair on the wall.

She served the meal and sat down, folding her arms across her belly and only picking at the food, saying she didn't drink when he offered her a beer; he started eating, telling her the food was good and hearing her say thanks, ain't no fun just cooking for yourself as he smiled back and began to talk to her, saying for the first time he'd lived in other cities, telling her about the job, noticing then how her eyes shifted, how she seemed to glance at the window as if she were waiting for someone. She looked at

30

him, told him her parents had thrown her out when they'd heard about the baby, she'd had a job til last month but it's been kind of lonesome here since, just wish the baby would come, her voice going on like fire and grass, easing him even as he wondered about her boy, as he listened and talked, knowing she'd changed him and watching her move in the chair, her strange eyes open like the end of a dream. When she poured his coffee, she leaned close, and she smelled good, he could almost feel the way they'd move together, after the waiting time, after she'd known him longer with her eyes and hands, slipping beneath him then like the fast currents deep in a river.

But she looked tired again and he knew he'd better leave, wondering if he'd already said too much to her, feeling cold and empty as he saw darkness come in the windows, as he thought of his own room, then wanted to stay even as he got up and put his coat on. He watched her look away for a moment, then get up and walk him to the door, her hand resting on his arm. Connie's face was close and he saw her kiss him before he'd felt her lips, knowing what she meant by the kiss and feeling scared as he kissed her back, said he'd see her soon.

Now he felt strange as he walked outside, wishing he'd stayed but wondering if they'd have hurt the child, then remembering the feel of her body close to him, the way she'd moved into him without waiting and laid her small hands against his face. He walked toward the bar, figuring to have a few drinks and calm down, talk to Eddie long enough to stop thinking about her, til he could wait to see her again, telling himself I got to be careful with this one as he got inside and looked around.

Eddie was talking to someone he'd never seen, a young man with long hair and nice clothes who was listening closely, the way a man does when he's trying not to show that he's drunk; Eddie said this here's Al, friend of mine, goes to college, and he sat down next to them, letting Al buy him a bourbon, Al laying the money on the table and going off to the men's room.

—Who the hell is this fool, he asked Eddie.

—What you mean, fool?

—Got on one of your watches, ain't he?

Eddie laughed, saying you know them's good watches, hey, listen, he's a live one, all we got to do is bullshit him and he'll buy all night, and Al came back shaking a little and sat down, talking loud, college is a drag, sure, sure, you get an education but you don't really live, you don't learn about life, like you cats; he listened, knowing Eddie'd been right, and he made things up about women, Eddie sometimes joining in, as he'd pretend later on to be in on Eddie's stories, telling Al he'd had women pay him five hundred dollars just to look at it, why, I got me a woman down Texas send me checks every month just so I get on back there once a year, watching Al's mouth hang open from the liquor as Eddie tried to keep from laughing, going on til he was through, and then hearing Eddie tell worse lies; he kept drinking, knowing he had to work in the morning but not caring, the free drinks tasting better as the night went on.

A fight was beginning at one of the small tables behind him, he heard voices rise and wondered if Tommy'd throw the men out or just hope they'd cool down, he'd seen them before, big men from the tannery down under the bridge by the railroad, tough and mean after a few drinks, but he'd always known how to leave them alone; he saw Tommy's hand resting on the bar phone, wondered if Tommy kept a piece under the bar, waiting, then knowing someone must have calmed the men down as he watched Tommy walk slowly toward the other end. It was quiet again and he turned back to Eddie and Al, Al asking him what's going on, looking down when he didn't answer, as if to pretend he knew anyway, Al's face seeming to sag then and go soft, eyes half closing, mouth turning down, saying you know, you guys are great, you know things: and he wondered what Al wanted from them, why Al didn't just go to bars with his own friends, thinking these boys got better ways to spend their money as he remembered the judge telling him get good grades so you can go to college, make me proud of you, the judge's wife joining in at parties, and he'd stood around taking it, always feeling as if they'd loaned him a day's food and clothes and they'd want to get paid back by nightfall, knowing then he was crazy to take up with Connie, she just wanted some man to pay her bills til her boy came back, she wants to take me for a ride, he said aloud, then moved quick as Al slumped into him, eyes rolling, head slipping down on the bar. Eddie moved the money and they used it to go on drinking.

He looked at the clock only then and knew how bad the morning would be, but he kept talking, laughing at things Eddie'd say til they'd both got too drunk for talking. But he couldn't look at Al's face on the bar, the yellow light falling and the stains, dead as a man always seems after he's passed out, let's leave him a little to get home on, he said, hell, he's good for this anytime.

—Shit, you crazy? I'm fixing to clean his wallet before I'm through; hey, you ain't leaving—

—Yeah, some of us got to work, ain't all rich like you, he said, grinning as Eddie slapped him on the back, then looking down as he went out the door slowly, leaning, tired and angry as he remembered how Connie'd tried using him, thinking going to show that bitch as he turned east, toward her house, shaking worse in the cold air from the liquor and slipping on the ice, yelling each time he went down:

he held both rails going up the stairs, swinging back and forth like a light bulb on a frayed cord, sick and weak as he slammed on the door with his fist, almost falling when she opened the door; he felt good seeing her white face, knowing she was scared as she backed away and he moved toward her, saying, give me some my money, goddam it, I'm gone sleep here, don't give a shit what you say, hear me?

—Jack, she said, her voice soft enough to make him hang on, stand still, and listen, watching her eyes move in the darkness, knowing only then what he must look like as he felt his legs shaking under him, Jack, she said, why don't you just lay yourself down on that couch, I'll get you up in the morning.

VI

The garbage cans were heavy and hard to move even in the late morning, and he felt his back straining as he dragged them over the ice, breathing deeply and hoping to shake the hangover; the thin hard snow hurting his face, making him stiff all over:

Rick and the driver'd noticed his hangover early and they'd been kidding him about it all morning, laughing at him when he couldn't keep up and seeming to make him work harder each time they made a run down an alley, though he knew Rick was just good at his job, moving steady, but working faster than he ever could. He smiled at the things they said, knowing enough by now to give some of the same back, then losing their voices as the driver pulled up behind a super market, as he remembered the first time he'd been drunk, he'd gotten port wine from some older boys his second time back at the orphanage, must have been about eleven, he said to himself, thinking about how sick he'd been, the houseparents saying he'd hurt them, they'd done so much for him and now he'd gone and broken a trust, served him right he was sick, their voices slipping back in his memory as he thought of Connie, the way she'd brought him coffee and fixed him breakfast, not making him talk, saying she'd see him later; now he felt he might be wasting his time just hanging around her as he and Rick pulled the heavy packmasters and steered them onto the lift in back of the truck, steadying them while they rose and emptied, dragging them back two at a time, I got to do something, he thought, figure this damn woman out, hey Jack, Rick said, laughing, bet your goddam belly feels good looking at all this shit;

—Yeah, just about the way you feel each week when your fucking car blows up.

—Bullshit, Rick said, you just jealous, she's running fine.

—Sure was this morning, sound like a goddam old bathtub dragging down the street, he said, moving quick when Rick lunged at him, laughing as Rick said, I'll get you, beat your ass playing pool today, just wait and see; they hung on the back of the truck, yelling across to each other all the way down the street, continuing even when the driver stopped the truck in front of the bar and got out.

He hadn't figured to drink today but the driver told him have a beer, you got to get a little hair off that dog what bit you—the driver was right, he felt better as they worked in the afternoon, the snow still falling but not hurting so much now, and sometimes he'd hum an old blues he remembered from Lexington, thinking about times he and his best friend Dave had hung around the freight yard in Kearney, running along the tops of wire bales stacked in a warehouse, climbing up the grab irons of freight cars and sneaking around til they'd get caught and chased off, the feeling of those times staying with him most of the afternoon, lasting til he and Rick were done working and they'd climbed into the warm truck.

The driver's cigar made him cough and he leaned close to the window, knowing he should go back to Connie's but uneasy as he tried to bring back the night, remembering only that he'd met someone named Al, there'd been a fight in the bar and he'd left, but he forgot the rest then in the talk going on in the cab; Rick and the driver were watching a girl walk across the street, the driver saying she works up in the office, I hear she's always asking for me, guess she wants the dick or something, right? Rick started kidding the driver again, kept on as they left the truck, the driver saying you young guys, what do you know, and he heard Rick laughing all the way across the parking lot, yelled out as Rick drove off, losing his own laughter then, his thoughts turning and moving like the bad snow as he walked.

He thought he'd go home first and wait awhile before coming to her, then changed his mind, wondering what he'd said to her, what she'd maybe learned and how she felt now, sitting alone, waiting for him or for someone else. He got to her house and walked up the stairs, she seemed to take a long time coming and he hoped she was all right, but she was just pale when she opened the door.

He said, you want to take a little walk, like down to the bar to get some beer?

—I ain't feeling so good, Connie said, I don't know, but I swear I can't sit in this house any longer; she got her coat and took his arm when they went down the stairs, leaning closer as they got down on the sidewalk, her hand seeming hot as he helped her over a patch of ice, her eyes a little red; he felt as if they were old people having a tough time making it through the snow, as if they'd be run down at the corners if they weren't careful, and he wondered about Connie, she was quiet, breathing hard, as if she'd been running, but she said she was glad they'd walked, the snow makes me feel good, like I'm clean again or something. When they got to the bar, she leaned against the counter while he bought beer, he saw Eddie wave and he led her outside quick as he could, wishing Eddie hadn't seen them together because he knew what Eddie'd say when he ran into him next time. Connie coughed twice, he put his arm around her and she tried to smile up at him, maybe hoping he wouldn't see how sick she was, shouldn't of come out, she said, oh Jack, I feel awful, sagging against him as he held her tighter, hoping she'd hang on til they got home, glad they hadn't far to go; he felt her body shaking as she coughed on the stairs, choking for breath, she ran into the bathroom and he heard her throwing up, saw her come out white and dizzy and helped her into her bed.

The fever took her hard, as her boy maybe had, coming into her one night after weeks of trying, scaring her with his rough hands, her eyes moving now as she moaned and thrashed on the bed, calling Jack, Jack in a high thin voice he'd never heard her use, she was out of her head and he tried to hold her down, hearing her scream and cry devil, the ceiling's gone fall, give me him my baby's got no eyes and he saw the things she'd spoken moving around in the room, howling like the snow outside as they came one by one, as she moved in strong rhythms and he tried harder to hold her down, wishing she'd stop screaming, more scared than he'd ever been as he saw and remembered things he didn't want to think about, kids chasing him down by the grain elevator, hollering after him, yelling who's your daddy Jack, who's your daddy, ain't you got one, these words coming in rhythms he seemed to feel as she kicked at the blankets, as she rolled and moved on the bed; then she made a sound like a small animal dying on a highway and he felt cold—she lay still and slept.

He got a wet rag and put it on her forehead, hoping to bring the fever down, hoping more that the child wouldn't come as he looked around the little room, shaking and lighting a cigarette. He drank a beer, wishing he had something stronger, wanting to leave but afraid she'd get worse, and he wondered what he'd do if she woke up with the baby coming, how he'd even know if her time were beginning. Connie turned over, still sleeping, and said, he's coming, but he felt she meant the boy or the fever, not the child, wondering then if the boy always came back in her dreams even after this long time alone.

She slept for a long time, sometimes saying things he couldn't understand, and he watched her closely, seeing the baby move once or twice in her stomach and feeling worse as his own fear moved like the fears she'd spoken, coming in dark shapes he'd seen sometimes when he'd been alone or dreaming, Connie's face turning grey in the late streetlight, making him think about the grandmother, making him wonder if she were lying with her people in that little field outside Cheyenne, where she'd taken him once to come and pray along with her. It was too dark in the room and he got up to turn the hall light on, seeing her breathe easier when he got back and beginning to think more about the child as the night went on, as the cars thinned out and then stopped going by outside.

Once in awhile he'd fall asleep, always waking up quickly and drinking another beer til the six pack was gone, wishing it were his child coming, feeling he had more right to it than her boy, who'd probably gone running from Connie soon as he'd heard she was pregnant; he wanted to hold the child and sometimes believed he did, wondering how Connie'd be then, whether she'd want him to stay, or leave so she could move close to her child while she waited for her boy to come back. She moaned loudly near morning and he seemed to see the boy moving in her dreams, seemed to feel he could grab the boy and throw him back down the stairs, almost forgetting, or too tired to remember, how he'd believed she'd choose the boy, the father, over him. His nerves jumped each time she moved, once she sat up straight and looked at him, her eyes dark and open, her face hard and still as if her skin had been stretched—then she lay back down and he felt as if someone had just slipped into the room, he kept watching and turning around, trying to see in the dark til she moved and he calmed down again. Now light came in the east windows and he was tired and empty, glad to leave though he was worried about her, and he wondered how he'd make it through a day's work.

It seemed harder to move in the alleys than it had yesterday but he held his end up and drank a lot of coffee, hoping the driver wouldn't tell somebody hey this man Jack, he comes in drunk two days in a row, ain't worth a shit, Rick quiet and strange til lunch time but almost his old self in the afternoon, even throwing rocks at the river rats behind the tan-

nery; he'd bet Rick a dollar he could hit the most rats and almost felt glad
to lose. Later, when they'd finished and were pulling into the yard, the
sand trucks started to roll out the main gate and he heard their tire
chains slapping on the ice, felt something in that sound and listened hard
to the noisy garbage truck so he couldn't hear the chains, thinking, as he
walked toward Connie's, I got to sleep tonight, I'm hearing things, walking as fast as he could so he wouldn't think about going to his own house,
wouldn't remember how scared he'd been last night; he used her keys in
the door and jumped back a little when he saw her, surprised to find her
up and dressed, looking better than she had the last few days but still
pale and tired as she moved around in the kitchen, then came to him and
held on, speaking softly into his chest. He didn't talk much about the
night because she didn't ask, she said only that she'd slept all day and felt
better, I know I must of been pretty sick though; hey, you want some
supper, I guess hot dogs is all I got;

    sure, if you feel up to it, he said, sitting down and lighting a cigarette,
knowing only then how tired he was as he saw she'd come through the
fever, almost falling alseep once in the chair but waking up quickly,
looking at her and hoping she didn't feel worse than she was willing to let
on. The country station played sad songs and sometimes he'd hear her
humming along too, the songs seeming to change and sound better then,
as if they'd never been meant for just one person to sing, though he'd
carried these tunes with him a long time, always feeling the way the old
men had played them together back home but singing them alone since
then, and he knew he'd remember how she'd sat here singing whenever
he heard these songs again.

    You was nice to stay over, Jack, she said as she served the meal, but
he remembered how lonely and trapped he'd felt, not wanting even to lie
down with her but knowing he had to stay, so he said I'm just glad you're
okay now, watching her, feeling something pass between them each time
she looked at him, as if she'd sensed him moving inside to places where
they'd touch and move together, as if he'd shown her more than he'd
meant to; she stacked up the dishes, then said she had a pain and he
helped her lie down, she kept his hand and lay with it close to her breast,
her head on his lap, talking, and he remembered how long it'd been, how
good women feel up close as she said she hated the waiting, she'd wanted
a child for a long time, even since before she was grown—he saw the child
kicking in her belly, felt scared and wondered why she'd let him close to
her like this, don't she know what I got to want now, he thought, then
hearing her say she was tired as she took him into bed with her hand,
curling herself warm against him as he moved closer, his face against her
back, his hand under hers moving along her leg as she shifted in her
sleep, breathing softly, going down in slow heavy rhythms.

    He dreamed then, or lay awake feeling the time move between them,
seeing her skin turn brown as she fed chickens in the barn yard, hearing
their kids running and yelling, throwing rocks at the barn as he came in
from the fields at noon, knowing from the feel of her close to him she had
nothing on under her dress, they'd smell the soup burning on the stove
later on, before she'd even called the kids in for lunch, before he'd pulled
his pants back on and she'd slipped her dress over her head, her face still

and sad now in the winter light as she turned in sleep to face him, and he lay quiet, seeming to hear children playing somewhere outside this room, maybe in a hot barn yard or downstairs in an old house.

Suddenly Connie opened her eyes, leaned toward him and stretched, her breasts pushing up and touching his shoulder; wait, she said, and she got out of bed, young and easy as she walked into the bathroom; she looked different than she'd been in his dream and he felt strange, as if he'd known once what she wanted and forgotten now, not yet believing the reasons she'd gone into the bathroom even as he heard water running, then stopping himself from unbuttoning his shirt as he remembered the baby.

He waited without moving til she came back to bed, wearing only her shirt and smelling clean as new wheat he'd sniffed long ago in the spring breeze, he felt her warm bare legs even through his clothes as she lay back on him, turned her face and kissed him on the mouth, her fingers sliding down his chest, stopping at his belt, loosening his pants, and his hands moved over her breasts, then under her shirt and slid down, his hands moving her slowly as she sucked in air and opened her legs a little, holding his hand between her legs as she turned away from him, her belly still showing the moving child, making him stop for a moment, then lose the fear as she moved against him in a round sideways rhythm, her hand looking for him, taking him inside her as she seemed to open a little at a time, the new feel of her different from her cool breasts under his hands, the soft line of the back of her neck against his face, her hair falling, shaking loose in his face as they continued together in slow easy rhythms till she changed and closed tight around him, almost hurting him, he pushed hard into her, moving her as he slipped down, as she made noises, squeezing him with her legs as he pressed his hands down hard on her breasts, he shook all over, he felt a train smashing into the side of a mountain.

Now she lay close to him for a long time, smiling, and kissing his hand as if she wanted to begin again, talking softly as leaves as he held her and listened, wanting to stay like this and never move again, feeling the good way she'd eased him down, taken him close and left him loose and settled, almost hidden from the cold feeling he knew was beginning again in the darkness, changing as he turned quiet, telling her when she looked up at him, just too tired to talk but I sure feel good, so do I, she said, her voice going on for awhile, then low and drifting down to sleep again. His nerves got worse the longer she slept and he felt he'd have to leave, walk around or drink so he'd be tired enough to sleep.

He moved quietly in the room and walked slowly down the stairs, believing he'd go back home but knowing he wouldn't as soon as he got out to the street, the cold sinking over him like fear, making the snow hard under his feet as he tried to remember how good Connie'd felt, the clear round of night seeming lonely as if he'd never been with her or never known her name, just paid a visit and got what he'd come for. The closest bar was dark and noisy and he was glad he wasn't staying, he spent his last two dollars on a pint and walked back outside, then opening the pint and taking a few quick swallows on his way back to Connie's house. He knew she'd be sleeping, wished he could feel right about waking her up.

VII

In the slow easy time of lying with Connie late at night, he'd begun to wait for the baby, and to ask her questions, almost seeing her with the new child at her breasts, mostly believing they'd hold a place for the child between them, and he stayed with her through the weekend, learning the calm way she had of settling in next to him, feeling her move deep inside him as those first five or six days ran together, as he'd slip down to her each night after work, never wanting to leave her house again, the good feel of her staying with him most of the time, except when he'd lie awake nights after she'd fallen asleep.

Today he didn't go right home after work, he walked instead to the supermarket, sometimes fingering the money in his pocket, her last few dollars, he'd thought to get the groceries and surprise her but he'd felt strange taking the money this morning, as if he hadn't any right to buy food with her money when he'd be eating most of it himself, so he was glad he'd get paid tomorrow; he could see her house to the east as he went by, the low sun shining brightly on the windows and the white eaves, and he wondered if she were watching from upstairs, maybe thinking about him the way he'd felt her the first day in the drugstore, watching her from a distance and making up his mind.

Yellow lights flashed in the corners of his eyes and he saw a tow truck stop down the block, its engine idling noisily, dark smoke rising and shifting from its cab stack as the driver and his helper hooked up a new car and got ready to raise it; he waited for someone to come outside yelling, for neighbors to join the man after a few seconds, all of them swearing and hollering you ain't got no right to take this car—but the street stayed quiet even as the truck pulled away, as he knew he hadn't got used to this neighborhood, remembering how people in other cities seemed to live half time in the streets, as if their houses couldn't hold them or they just felt better moving around outside, making noise and talking together, keeping a little ahead of things that'd catch them if they stayed inside too long, but here only a few old ladies walked up the hill to the Catholic church and he heard only the sound of the cars smearing the snow over the street. The streetlights went on as he came up to the market, a few women waited outside for cabs and he saw a pretty girl checking groceries as he walked inside, wondering how girls in uniforms kept from freezing when they worked close to a door that opened and closed all day long, thinking of Connie, who'd told him she'd been a waitress, and wanting to get home to her; he pushed the cart quickly through the aisles and grabbed a few cans of beans, not seeing Al until he'd almost run right into him.

Al started talking before he could back away, saying I've been standing in this supermarket all day trying to do a survey for psych class, like you wouldn't believe the answers people give you, man, they think you're crazy just because you ask them how they feel about the war; doing your shopping?

Yeah, he said, feeling Al next to him as he looked at the hamburger, thinking might just borrow some of this here, course this asshole probably go tell the manager if I done that, knowing Al was asking him questions but pretending to figure prices, then giving up as Al kept asking how do you really feel about the war, man, what do you think?

—I ain't got to worry about that, he said, bad knee; no you don't understand, Al said, going on about morality or something as he remembered Connie was waiting, maybe wondering where he was and missing the money by now, should of left her a note, he thought, slipping a pound of bacon under his jacket, grinning when he saw Al hadn't noticed and picking up a few more things, he'd tell Connie later on about the bargains he'd found and she'd smile and shake her head at him; Al's voice kept on over the noise from the cash registers, the people pushing each other to get in line, the carts banging together, and he stood in line, not listening but following Al well enough to nod his head once in awhile as he watched the girl, felt her hand touch his as he gave her the money, seeing her smile at him and smiling back. He picked up his groceries and walked outside, hearing Al's voice running on next to him, turning, knowing only then Al had followed him outside.

—I'm through for the day, I guess, Al said. Want to go have a beer? I'm buying.

—No, I got to get home.

—Well, I'll walk up that way with you, nothing else to do anyway, Al said; he shrugged, wishing he'd gotten rid of Al back at the market but figuring Al would have to leave when they got to Connie's, feeling the way she'd come to him, saying she was worried, or just glad he was home, as Al started talking about the girls in his classes, his problems, Oh Christ, he thought, stopping in front of Connie's house, now he knows where I live, standing, waiting for Al to stop talking so he could get away without making it seem as if he had to.

—Jack, Connie said, poking her head out the door, where you been? Who's that you got with you?

—Al.

—Well, ask him to come on in, don't stand there in the cold; he nodded, then turned to Al, saying, look, I'll see you later—sure, man, I understand, Al said, winking at him before going, then whistling off key all the way down the street; she'd already gone back in to get away from the cold and now he walked slowly upstairs, feeling as if he and Connie'd lost something, knowing the easy things between them would change now that Al and Eddie'd found out, Eddie'd say things to hurt her and Al'd maybe come around looking to get next to her, maybe changing her mind with his money or good looks, she'd seen enough of Al in those few minutes to ask about him, why ain't he coming up, Jack, he got something to do?

—Why'd you ask him, I been trying to get rid of him all the way home;

here's the groceries. Don't have to get mad, she said, just wondered, oh, did you take the money that was laying out to get the food? She pressed her hands to her back then, and he seemed to feel as if she were hiding something as she shifted her weight and looked out the window, maybe to see where Al had gone, squeezing her hands together as if she were nervous—he slammed the grocery bag on the table and she turned around quickly.

—Jesus Christ, did you think I stole your money? Get your goddam groceries yourself next time, he said, walking out and letting the door bang behind him, hearing her call but not turning back, almost running down the street as he felt his blood moving and pounding, nerves shaking as his thoughts turned in circles of repeating scenes, he'd beat up Al and the boy, feel their ribs breaking under his feet, their faces changing and softening in the snow, kill them for trying to beat his time—he calmed down only after he'd run the two blocks to the bar, he wanted a drink and he was glad he had enough change for one beer.

He started to drink his beer fast but stopped himself and looked around, wondering if he could touch anyone for a few dollars til tomorrow or get Tommy to give him credit, but no one was in yet and Tommy looked like he was in a bad mood. So he drank slowly, wishing then he hadn't snapped at her, she hadn't meant anything and couldn't have known he was mad at Al, and he began to feel badly about running out, making her wait even longer when she'd been alone all day, goddam Al, he said under his breath, then jumped when he felt a hand on his shoulder.

—Hey, Jack, Eddie said, by Jesus, I didn't know you was getting some of that. Smell just as sweet with that kid hanging up front? Your kid, huh?

—No, he said, looking at his empty glass, thinking about leaving but letting Eddie buy him another one, listening as Eddie told him you crazy, get out of there before she talks you into marrying her, ain't you got a lick of sense, boy, feeling himself get angry again but not showing anything, drinking a couple of beers as Eddie went on talking, changed the subject, had to get me a job washing dishes, ain't that a bitch, going on about how bad the job was and then saying see one pussy, you seen them all, I get the hell out of there if I was you.

—Hey, I ain't in no mood to talk about this shit, he said, watching Eddie's face change and go dark, his eyes flickering as he said don't get smart with me, boy, you hear?

—Ain't nothing you going to do about it, he said, sliding off the bar stool but hearing Eddie swearing at him as he walked out, feeling cold as he turned toward home, looking back over his shoulder a couple of times but moving as fast as he could through the snow, wanting to see her badly even though he'd have to say he'd been wrong, wishing he knew how she'd take it and afraid she'd throw him out, she'd move beyond him the way a bus goes by a man stranded on a highway, making the highway worse then before as the next cars seem to come right at you, missing only because you've jumped back, that feeling hanging on til you don't stand close to the road anymore, just keep walking and hoping somebody comes before morning, and he remembered those nights still as he walked upstairs to her apartment, felt his face change when he didn't hear a sound:

the door was open and she'd already gone, leaving all her things and few lights on, as if to make him think she'd be right back, and he sat down, feeling uneasy as the door creaked in the jamb, cold from the empty house he'd liked til now, hating the thought of his own room after this time with her; he picked up one of his old shirts from the bed and turned around, seeing a note she'd left him on the mirror and reading it twice, thinking, 'already?', smiling then and running downstairs, not even knowing where the hospital was but thinking he'd hitch west on North Avenue, ask somebody, knowing only then she hadn't left him, she was waiting for him with her child and he'd see them soon.

But a train was going by when he got to the crossing, so he stood by the gate, smelling soot and diesel smoke, counting the freight cars as he'd done years ago, the car lights on the other side flickering like semaphores in a fog through the spaces between the boxcars, the wet air and the wind in the night seeming to roll down from the train like hobos when they've just seen the yardmaster's tower, caboose lights going on and off as he looked down the line before crossing the tracks, hoping he'd have good luck with a ride. The neighborhood changed as soon as he'd lost sight of Connie's house and he knew by the faces of the people out walking that he didn't belong here, but maybe they'd leave him alone; he wondered how Connie felt, lying there alone and waiting out the pain for the child, knowing only now she'd have to change to let the child she'd carried, felt moving inside her for so long come out and move in her different ways, the child needing new things she'd have to give though she was tired and lonesome, maybe wanting the boy, the father, to come back and see his child; he hoped she was done with the boy but always felt he was lying to himself if he believed that, he was still thinking about her even as he saw men come out of a bar and seem to move together just down the street, forming a circle that hid or showed two men fighting in the middle, the men around them yelling and moving in closer, almost seeming part of the fight themselves, and he moved quickly then, seeing cars and three trucks as he glanced at the street, ran out and hung on the rear door handle of a mail truck, scared, and hoping nobody'd see him til he'd got past the fight, feeling his luck as the light changed but still breathing hard, holding on for a few more blocks and then jumping off just before the truck turned a corner: he waited only a little while before a ride came, the lady took him right to the door of the hospital once he'd told her his mother was dying.

Inside, he felt dirty and cold as he walked up to the desk; he waited for someone to come but gave up after a few minutes and walked down the hall, figuring to find the maternity ward himself. A janitor was polishing some silver facings above the marble and he asked him for directions, the smell of the polish making him sick as he waited for the elevator, then used the stairs, feeling his head clear in the stairwell. The waiting room was empty, he'd read all the magazines in bus stations and laundromats and he only wanted to see if Connie were all right, tell her he'd wait as long as it took, but the ward door was locked and nobody came when he pushed the bell; now he began thinking as he kept pressing the bell, remembering she hadn't had any money, it'd come quickly and he wondered how she'd even gotten here, feeling worse to think he'd been sitting in a bar while she'd been trying to get to the hospital, then giving up on the bell, telling himself he'd try it later as he picked up a magazine.

Sitting down, then getting up and going to the window, he looked down at this city where he'd lived almost a month, seeing the dark roads and the cars moving west through the slush, other tall buildings and low purple clouds, wondering how long he'd have to wait and wishing there were other men in the waiting room so somebody'd have to come through the door soon, as he watched the clock and smoked cigarettes, feeling hungry and tired, knowing it could take all night though he'd seldom been around babies, the grandmother'd told him she'd been a midwife but he'd only learned what she'd meant later on, after he'd heard stories from the older boys at the orphanage, or told jokes with his friend Dave; he wished he'd brought along a bottle, or had money to buy one, anything to make the time go faster, feeling his dry throat as he remembered Dave again, how they'd stolen the judge's liquor and gotten drunk behind Dave's father's barn, sleeping it off in the pasture, then rodding hell out of the old farm truck, a '49 Studebaker that blew a rod ten miles out of town the one time they'd gotten some girls out with them—they'd talked always about rodeos, or maybe stealing cars, heading east and screwing city women, talking all night sometimes—til one morning Dave took his father's car and drove it off a bridge, and he'd known then he had to leave, remembering now the old riverbed late that morning when he'd come down, burnt blue cloth in the weeds, junk metal and burned outs, empty as the sound of flies buzzing at the broken windshield, he'd gone that night on a freight train, lonesome as he was now in the waiting room, trying to forget Dave and the old times they'd had.

He walked down the hall to stretch and drink water from the fountain, hating the smell, the feel of this place, old people dying all over the halls and janitors mopping up under empty beds, he'd been a janitor in Baltimore but he was glad it hadn't been in a hospital, and he remembered how he'd learned to like the little things, getting outside to sweep up, putting a clean mop on his handle, carrying a row of keys and opening all the doors in an empty building, looking for things inside the rooms; the longer he had to stay alone in this room the worse he felt, thinking about his old days, he'd been shot at twice, maybe taken for a poacher as he'd come across Nebraska on his way west, not even knowing where the bullets were coming from but hearing loud noises seem to fill up the running night all around him; he'd stay close to the ground next time, never being seen, it'd be cold out west in March and the plains would ride out ahead of him, a man might easily freeze, nights like this one, the wind running like a wild plow, no hills or rocks big enough to even slow it down, but he'd make himself dark and small and hide close to the ground like a snake, letting the wind go by without touching him.

He lit a cigarette, leaving those times finally as he thought of Connie hurt and alone behind that door while he waited for a child who didn't belong to him, hoped the women that wasn't his yet would make it through the child's birth, trying the bell again and again, the hours going by slow as muddy water lying in low spots after a prairie rain, as he found himself listening to the elevators, the medicine carts going by, sometimes calling out to nurses and attendants, who'd always say they didn't work in maternity, didn't know anything about Connie. He finished a cigarette and wished he had another one, but he waited a long time before he went looking for the janitor, finding him at the slop sink down at the other wing.

—What, you waiting on a child, I been through that three times, the janitor said, mopping his dark face and handing over the cigarettes; he nodded and the talked for a few minutes before he walked back down the hall, then moved faster as he saw a man in an overcoat head for the ward door, the man pulling keys out of his pocket and loosening his overcoat as he came up behind him;

—Sure, I'm a doctor, the man answered, and this is my day off—hah! Some day off, this is the fourth week in a row somebody's delivered on Tuesday. Why?

—I'm waiting for Connie McLeod, do you know—

—Charity case, right? Yes, yes, I'm going to deliver her now—you won't be able to see her though, too late, hospital regulations—better come back tomorrow afternoon.

He stood there as the door closed, wishing he'd forced his way in but not wanting to take chances with these people, knowing Connie'd have the baby named before he even knew whether it was a boy or a girl.

VIII

Nice of Rick to give me a ride, he thought, as he waved good-bye and started up the hospital steps, remembering last night and getting angry again, feeling they'd better let him see Connie this time; he lit a cigarette when he'd got upstairs, and he looked at the women in the lounge, hearing them talk about the bad times they'd had delivering their babies, the work and troubles they'd have when they got back home, their faces hard and tired, there eyes moving over him as he passed through—he turned down the hall, wondering where she was but knowing he'd rather not ask anyone. When she came out of her room, he didn't know her at first, she seemed too thin and she'd done her hair in a way he'd never seen, but she smiled at him and he held her, smelling her rough yellow hair next to his face, then seeing how pale she was as he stepped back, her eyes dark as if she'd been crying, her arms seeming to shake at her sides; he put his hands on her hips and she made a face, as if she'd tried to cover up a pain.

He said, how you feel, little bit?

—Okay, just tired is all, and still sore all over. She smiled, said hey, you know we got a baby girl?

—I'll be damned, he said, remembering how Connie'd called the baby 'he' when she'd been carrying it, knowing only then he'd wanted it to be a girl; They tell you I was here last night, he said, trying to get in to see you?

She took his hand and kissed it, saying no, but I kind of thought maybe you was, then walking with her legs a little apart as they looked for a place to sit down; she asked him for a cigarette and he showed her the bottle of wine he'd brought, seeing her look scared then as she whispered, they'll throw you out—so he put it away; her legs seemed white and smooth as the stones on a riverbed as she asked him how he'd been getting along alone, seeming to smile as he looked up and told her about the freezing rain this morning, the way he'd had to slap his hands together, get them to hurt so he could go on working, still talking as he remembered this morning when they'd stopped for coffee, the things the driver'd said about the old days, a man just took what he could get, didn't bitch about a little cold weather like you guys, the driver's voice coming back to him now as he thought of Eddie, and of his own time in New York, last winter, when he'd walked around for days and couldn't find any kind of work, always hungry, the hunger seeming to bend the center of his body, making him feel he'd spent his whole life hunched over, hanging on then, afraid to leave til the sun seemed warmer, early in March, and as he'd hitched west, he'd felt that city always behind him, sometimes inside him, maybe til now—her face seemed to show more color as she listened and he felt good just to be talking to her, though he'd notice how she'd seem to look past him sometimes, maybe dreaming of her boy but coming close to him a few times and kissing him, pulling away then and telling him what she'd just remembered, you know what they told me, we got to wait six weeks til I'm healed, ain't that awful?

He said he hadn't known it would be that long, looking at her, not knowing why he felt they'd use other ways but grinning as he saw the look in her eyes, stop it, she said, laughing and whispering in his ear, pushing away the hand he'd slipped over her leg; oh God, she said, looking up at the clock, if we don't hurry you ain't going to be able to see Laurie, just let me get my housecoat. He touched the bottle under his jacket and they walked down the hall together, Connie was in a good mood and he wondered if the other women had been talking, if it were easier for Connie now that he was with her, they all been telling me I'm crazy cause I want to nurse Laurie, she said as she showed her card in the window and they waited for the nurse to push the baby's cart close to them.

Laurie had darker hair than the other babies and he wished he'd given her that hair, she was crying, her face red and seamed from hunger, she seemed to shake all over as the nurse moved away from her; Connie touched her own breast, turning away from him as if she were embarrassed, saying I hate this, why don't they let us feed our babies first so we ain't got to just sit out here and watch them cry, her face changing as he put his arm around her and wished he could see her with Laurie, wondering how a baby would feel in his own hands as he moved his hand over Connie's back. A nurse came down the hall, saying all visitors must leave promptly, mothers, return to your rooms for feeding, he stared at the nurse and Connie looked down at her bare toes, moving into him with her head down and making him wish he could figure a way to stay with her even here; he kissed the top of her head and told her he'd be back later, watching her as she walked back down the hall and wondering how badly she was hurting, hoping she'd take it easy when she got home.

Outside, sleet blew in his face as he held the rails going down the steps, and he changed his mind about hitching when he remembered he'd just gotten paid. He settled back in his seat on the bus to warm up, the smell of wet feet so thick inside that he opened his window and looked out at the small shining cracks in the streets, the telephone wires heavy with ice and holding the light from cars and buses, sometimes seeming to spark like trolley rails in a tunnel; the bus was slow in the heavy traffic and he began to get hungry, thinking he'd go to the cafe on the east side of the river where he and Rick and the driver sometimes had their morning coffee, knowing he didn't want to go back to Connie's house after yesterday, after this morning when he'd felt her house close in on him like the uneasy sleep a man might catch in an all night movie downtown, he'd had to run out to work as soon as he'd been dressed. But the sleet seemed worse now as the bus crossed the river, as he remembered he'd have to walk a mile home now after he'd eaten, wishing then, as he shivered and waited for his stop, that he'd gone right home and drunk enough to sleep through til morning. He got off the bus and crossed the street to the cafe, still feeling the cold sleet melting on his neck even after his food had come, but eating slowly for a change, remembering old times when he'd eaten alone and almost forgetting he'd ever stayed with Connie, as if he'd just now seen an old friend on his way through town and they'd spent a few hours talking before the friend had gone back to work, the baby's face already hard to bring back as he sat and smoked after dinner, and he wondered how he'd wait six weeks with Connie lying next to him the whole time, maybe changing, loving her baby enough so she wouldn't need him anymore, he might find himself remembering her sometime soon when he was travelling west, to South Dakota or Wyoming to hire on at a ranch or fram. The sleet continued outside the cafe windows and he wished he were out of the city now as he had another cup of coffee, hoping the weather would break.

The longer he waited, the worse the sleet became, he could see people sliding badly as they walked by and he figured he'd better leave: but he didn't want to see Eddie and he couldn't go home to the slipping darkness he'd see outside Connie's window, the steady wind he'd hear over the sound of the radio as he'd try to sleep and wait out the night, feeling the old house shake when trains went by, the memories of other rooms and cities coming back to him now as he pulled on his coat and walked outside, walking toward Connie's house but not believing he'd go there yet, then feeling he must be crazy even to think about visiting Al, he'll talk all night and won't give me no peace, most likely ain't home anyway, he said aloud, looking around and seeing he'd been closer to Al's than he'd figured, and only wanting by this time to get out of the cold; he climbed up the outside wooden steps to Al's apartment, seeing Connie's house from the landing and almost turning back.

He wished he hadn't come when he saw how glad Al was to see him; he looked around at the books, the pictures and bright rugs hanging on the walls and the record player as Al said good thing you came by now, Jack, I was just leaving; we can go out somewhere, I guess, but I've got some good bourbon.

—If you was leaving, I—

—No, No, Al said, come on in, I was just going to look for you guys—thought I had a date but she hung me up at the last minute.

Al handed him the bourbon and he took a drink, finding a chair, pulling it over and watching Al put a stack of records on, looking again at the strange yellow and green painting, the small television on the bookshelf and the half-size refrigerator, thinking somebody could come in here and steal this shit so easy, you could hand carry half of it, asking Al then if he had any country music and settling back as Al said I have some stuff here I think you'll like. They started drinking and Al told him about the girl, she'd called and said she had an old friend coming up this weekend; he listened to the music, not liking it much but using it more and more as the night went on, as Al drank fast, got drunk and began repeating himself, telling him things he didn't want to hear but not noticing when he didn't listen, letting his thoughts move to Connie, wondering if she'd be different when she got back home. He heard Al ask about Connie and surprised himself by telling Al about the baby, the hospital and the time he'd spent waiting, I got a car, I could give you rides out there, Al said.

—Thanks, but this guy at work, he takes me on his way home, he said, moving forward in his chair as he remembered Connie'd have to get home from the hospital with the baby and trying to make up his mind whether to ask Al to go out and get her on Friday. Then he heard the song and asked Al not to talk,

the song seemed to go on for a long time and he felt it move in his memory like a train at night, maybe like the sound of a horn or steam whistle far down the track, the music behind the harmonica like rail joints clanking under the weight of the train but soft, as when a freight crosses a trestle, the sound wet as it comes back over the water, a slow freight leaving the sound of crossing bells he seemed to hear now as he listened, as he knew the song was about a woman but he felt a slow freight in the silences, knowing the train better than the woman and remembering the voice of the singer, not the words he sang, thinking of the time gone since he'd heard voices like that, days of eyes open like the end of a dream, silence between words and the cold feeling of quiet, like a woman's body in a dream, as the harmonica came again and the train was farther away, the woman gone, but he heard the voice still as he'd heard trains when he could no longer see them, like tall grass shaking and then gone;

he knew he'd play the song again, after Al had passed out and he was alone, feeling the words and tune merge as if he'd made them up or sung them himself, hoping to carry the tune with him for awhile, though he knew he'd forget the few words he'd learned. He looked at Al only then and saw him slumped over in his chair, he played the song and thought of Connie, feeling the tune drift over the shapes in the room, not wanting to leave but knowing he should go back to the house where he'd seem to hear Connie speaking again tonight, saying she was afraid, her voice cracking, her eyes hot and wide as a fever in his dreams, her face holding in the darkness, then fading and turning old when he woke up—and he'd maybe have to sit up again tonight, smoking and drinking and wishing he could believe she was safe.

The record finished and he went out on the landing, feeling the sleet for a moment before walking down. Laurie, Laurie, he said to himself, trying to get used to the name.

IX

He walked home from work this afternoon for the first time since
she'd gone to the hospital, knowing she'd be waiting with the baby when
he got there, feeling the sun cold and white as it is in March but warming
the ground as the air rose with new smells, wet pine from a lumberyard
down the block and dark foam from the river, the ground losing the grey
feel of morning frost, showing brown where the snow and sleet had
melted, this day like another almost a year ago when he'd stood on a
bridge northwest of Trenton and watched a long B&O freight go by,
wondering if he should slip down the hill by the bridge and try to grab on;
he'd heard stories of men who could walk the roofs of boxcars when the
train was going fifty miles an hour and he'd felt like trying that one time.

He remembered the time in the hospital, the things Connie'd told him,
and he thought she'd feel easy and begin to settle in with the baby only
now, after she'd spent these last days sick and lost in the hospital, and he
wondered if she'd still be as weak as she seemed yesterday, if they'd made
sure she was ready to go or just shoved her out to make room for
somebody else; he walked faster, knowing he should have brought some
things for the baby but thinking he could get what Connie needed later,
since the weather'd probably hold, seeing dirty cars move easily through
the slush on the hill, the strong warm wind blowing yellow and blue diesel
smoke, and remembering horses rearing in the plains wind. But the
weather could change easily, and he seemed to feel the damp cold coming
in the night as he reached the house.

Connie heard his footsteps and she was waiting at the door, he held
her, feeling her small body fit close to his, remembering the clean smell of
the white sun and these last days alone, then seeing Al smiling and
sitting on the couch, hearing him say Jack, glad you're home, we've been
waiting for you.

—Want to see the baby? Al bought her a crib, ain't that nice? Connie
said, taking his arm as he looked at Al and leading him into the bedroom,
leaning against him as they looked down into the crib: Laurie'd squirmed
a little way out of her blanket, so Connie covered her up, making soft
noises and patting her stomach. She's no bigger than a minute, he said,
seeing her now as if for the first time, her face red and wrinkled tight
around her shut eyes, small as his hands and soft as Connie's breast,
helpless, but safe as long as Connie smiled down at her, loving her in a
way he'd never understand, like the sad feeling of a mother for her sick
child, the hours she'll spend just watching, and he held Connie closer,
feeling her kiss on his cheek and hearing her say she was happy; her face
was against his chest and he knew she couldn't see his face.

—I'm happy too, he whispered, touching her hair close to her face and feeling her in the dark bedroom like his dream, the old dream of the days they'd spend together hurting him as he thought of all the things he didn't know how to tell her.

—Sure is cute, man, Al said; hey, maybe you ought to get some cigars.

Connie smiled and Al seemed to fill up the doorway, his face bigger in the darkness, his body bending toward Connie as they walked out of the room, as if Al and Connie'd talked about a lot of secret things this afternoon, learning about each other and moving together while he'd been working, and he saw Al sit down next to her on the couch, wishing he'd never asked Al to bring her home and thinking maybe I should send the sonofabitch looking for cigars on the bottom of the river.

Al knew how to talk to Connie, knew what to say to make her feel good, she'd laugh, watching Al's face as she listened and talked about people she'd known, moving when she talked, her legs showing under the house coat as she shifted around; he watched Al looking at her, remembering he'd seen Al's way of moving in on people, buying drinks or meals, talking, seeming friendly, but he didn't know how Connie'd feel if he threw Al out and he didn't want to start out wrong now, so he stayed quiet, not wanting to talk even when one of them spoke directly to him, hating Al and thinking he might just leave them together.

The baby cried then and Connie got up to get her, the crying strange in the room after the sound of Al's voice, the child shaking her head around, looking for the nipple til Connie helped her find it, making the same soft noises and pushing Laurie's head gently so she could suck: he saw Al shifting around on the couch, as if Al wanted to look at Connie's breasts but didn't dare, and he smiled a little as Al got up to leave, saying he had to study, going quickly after they'd thanked him again for the crib. Connie watched Al leave, saying sure is a talker, ain't he as she shifted the baby on her lap, and he walked over and touched Laurie's head, feeling Connie's breast and the baby's warm body next to his hand, I'm just glad he's gone, he said, turning from her and looking out the window.

—There's a ring around the moon, might rain tomorrow, he said.

—Jack, you ain't made at me, are you?

No, he said, sitting down next to her and holding her close, thinking he'd wait and see what Al was up to, then hearing Laurie sucking with a sound like slow rain, eyes closed as Connie lay back, her hand under the baby's head, he had the feeling of wet land and rain, the land contained in the giving, remembering Connie'd sometimes been like water in his own dreams: but he hadn't seen til now that she'd known the child these months before Laurie'd been born, Connie loving her own dream of the child and waiting, as the ground waits til frost turns to water spreading out unseen, the soil moving, changed by the water; and he'd change, and learn what a father feels, what he does for the child he's been given, and he knew then he'd stay with Connie as long as he could, even if he had to fight the boy.

Connie sat the baby up, burped her, and handed her to him, smiling when she saw he was scared and saying she ain't going to break, don't worry: Laurie was warmer than anything he'd touched, lying in his hands and warming them, trying to lift her head and then laying back in his hands, moving a little, but quiet, as a small animal never is; she cried out sharply and he gave her back to Connie, watching while she nursed and smoothing her soft hair til she was asleep, her mouth hanging open, her body shuddering once when Connie carried her into the bedroom.

—Now I'm going to need these things, you can get them at the drugstore, Connie said, handing him a list and telling him to please hurry, she was going to make supper while he was gone, coming close and kissing him, almost making him believe he'd been wrong about her and Al, though the uneasy feeling hung on as he walked and shopped, getting worse by the time he stopped at the bar; Eddie was drunk, standing by the far end of the counter and coughing into a handkerchief, and he shivered, as if he finally knew how sick Eddie was from drinking and from the long time spent outside through too many winters, Eddie seeming then like the old man he'd seen in the laundromat, waiting, unmoving, as if those men and Eddie'd been beaten by the things they'd done to stay alive, the drafts of the city coming inside them as they waited to get warm again, waiting like men whose train has gone;

he bought his beer and walked out, wanting to get home so he'd lose the sound of Eddie's cough, the feel of Eddie's voice as he told stories about the old days, the scars from old fights on Eddie's arms and face, older voices he wished he'd forgotten came back to him then, making the street loud and staying with him all the way up the steps to her door.

When he got inside he knew Connie sensed something, but she didn't ask any questions, talking instead about Laurie, her own pains, and how tired she was; after dinner, they sat together on the couch talking for a long time, and he began to feel her coming close to him again, moving him as she had in the beginning, as if they'd maybe have to ease down to each other now after the child and the time Connie'd spent in the hospital, the strangeness lasting as they waited and felt each other, as their voices seemed to him to move apart and break off at the wrong places, shifting and mixing til the two sounds changed and moved almost the same, just before she got up to go to bed. He lay down with her, laughing as she told him she'd stay awake, but watching her slip down, her breathing soon heavy and even as the child's. Then he sat up, resting his hand on her bare shoulder, drinking beer til he thought he could fall asleep too.

X

The low sun hit the wet roofs and shined them, he'd heard water running in the drainpipes and sewers on his way over here, and he'd known it was snow melting because it hadn't rained last night; now, as he moved quietly in his old room, he hoped the landlady wouldn't hear him and come upstairs asking for rent. He'd left two paperback books and a pair of pants in the room, and he picked them up quickly, leaving his key in the lock before slipping down the stairs again, feeling good that he wouldn't have to come back here.

It was just past dawn, and he felt strange to walk the streets this early without carrying garbage cans or running after the truck when the driver was in one of his hurrying moods; he wished he didn't have to work tomorrow, thinking he'd like to be out of the city and moving west now that the days were getting warmer, the quiet morning making him remember times he'd fished or swum in the creek outside Sidney, and he wondered what Lake Michigan looked like this far north, he'd seen it only once in Chicago last year, the cold water steaming off the docks from the sewage pouring in, the dead fish almost hidden in the foam along the shore, and he'd thought that lake would kill a man in less than five minutes, his clothes freezing soon and dragging him down, pinning his arms to his sides and making his legs useless. But he'd liked it better than either of the oceans, so he turned east, past the drugstore, moving into a neighborhood of brick apartments and hotels, old people standing in driveways waiting to be helped into cars, these long cars somehow like weddings or funerals the grandmother'd talked about with her friends, often changing or forgetting the gossip she'd begun, making things up the others would add to as they'd leave their own stories one by one, quietly as these cars were leaving now; he used to hide and listen til the grandmother'd catch him and chase him out, feeling wicked from the things he'd learned about people he saw everyday, almost wishing he had someone else to tell.

The lake was shiny as a steel roof when he looked down from the road, the park land rolling under him like plains before hills as he came down to the land's edge, watching the lake water hit the shore rocks and turn back green into pools and currents different from the rivers he was used to, the lake seeming to go on in the blue light toward the middle, never reaching the other side though it might turn and move faster in deep channels far off shore, and he remembered the strong city smell of Chicago as the smells of wet land and moss carried easily on this breeze, making him think of the baby, wishing she were older til he saw Connie in the water and said aloud, ain't no use anyhow.

The lake moved hard against the rocks, splashing him, and he turned away, wanting to go to her and sick from the run of his crazy dreams in the sunlight, the way they'd always change like shapes in a dark room when he tried to lose them; now he walked back toward Connie's house, trying to remember the song he'd heard at Al's, thinking of the words as the tune moved easily in his voice, as he sang and moved slowly to Connie, almost without knowing he was coming, then feeling good when the sound of the baby's crying stopped this tune and continued another, an older song he'd heard Connie humming a few times.

He picked up the baby and handed her to Connie, watching while Connie lay back and spoke softly, but he could hear what she was saying and he smiled down at the baby; he held Laurie when she'd finished and watched Connie get dressed, seeing for the first time how her body'd changed, her rhythms more natural now as she moved slowly around the room, trying on two of her old dresses before she found one that fit. She turned, then, and saw him looking at her, and she laughed as if she were pleased.

—Been a long time since I been stared at like that, she said.

—You just ain't caught me looking before.

PART II

XI

Blue hills, way beyond the Wyoming border: in Cheyenne they are mountains and he had seen them, big and heavy and deep into the winter clouds. Old women had talked with the grandmother and he'd walked around, dreaming of gunfighters and pinto ponies.

Two seasons gone since then, his days were the days of the harvest. It was warm as September can be, and the air was wildflowers and honey bees, corn and wheat and men. The grain elevator stood like himself above range grass and flowers.

A railroad ran above the fields on a ballast roadbed. Jack put his ear to the track and felt the rail moving, clanking under the coming weight; then, it was black and heavy as a mountain, steam like snow spray from smoke boxes and journals, on driving wheels tall as a man and twice as broad, pounding, steel sparks burning grass, steam hiss air brakes, coming clanks and metal, smokestack boiling over in the siding by the grain elevator. It was beautifully dark and sooty its whole long way. Jack loved it, knew each part of it by name as he knew the gullies and gopher holes in the field beyond the railroad trestle. He wanted to ride in the cab behind the boiler, but he did not know how to ask the engineer. So he was glad for one steam locomotive left to see and he sat on a tie piling, feeling the sticky creosote, smelling its good burnt smell.

The workmen had begun to load the boxcars. Someday Jack would wear red bandannas, faded blue flannel shirts open so the hair could come through; he'd have stiff red hands and hard muscles. Or he would be boss, driving the fork lift, pushing his men with whiskey yells as he squirted tobacco juice.

Now he walked on the rails without falling and weeds tickled him. He knew the things of the plains: how to wander far off in fields where grain stood above him and not lose his way, how to hear clouds tell of rain or long heat, how to find old arrowheads in the dark ground. Gophers shook the grass cracking under his feet and the birds flew as he remembered they had, watching the harvest and the sky. In the hollow of the long puddle brook beneath the trestle, Jack rolled mud with his hands and threw at the gophers. There was only the sound of the workers. From here they looked like sunburned cowboys, haying their horses.

But Jack had heard of cities Omaha and Lincoln and Grand Island, down the railroad the other way from the blue hills, farther from him than even they were. Sidney was only a town with a grain elevator stuck in prairies ten miles around. So he spent his time alone by the trestle, stretched out and dreaming. Grass was brown and warm and held him. Down the line, the workers had stopped for lunch, so Jack knew he'd better be getting home.

The screen door banged and a noon fly came in for the butter slab on the table. Jack got good cold milk from the refrigerator and a raisin cookie from the jar on the stove. The man who talked like an auctioneer was giving market reports on the radio. Jack was hungrier than milk and cookies.

—Jack?

The grandmother sat in her hard chair on green cushions, below the china. It was her time to sit, after washing and sweeping and dusting the house that kept them. The shoes an old woman wears were beside her and her hands he had known when sick or scared by night storms lay in her lap.

—Hi, young fellow, the policeman said. Sometimes he came for dinner and told the grandmother stories, he laughed loud and paid for those meals.

They told Jack he was going and he hung on to the cool dry grandmother, the hot room beating him, the policeman standing. She would not hold him and said the same words over and over in a voice he had never heard her use. Her eyes seemed to see only the clock across the room which hadn't worked for two years. Jack wouldn't let go but she was very old and would not take him. He turned his head from the hogback suitcase lying in a sun patch on the floor. Yellow chicken skin grandmother arms pushed him away and he ran but the policeman was stronger than kicks and scratches and his face darker than Hallowe'en fire. The policeman held him now and she said the same thing in her voice of old grasses: he hated her, she'd gone from the screen door before he'd even reached the car.

And the policeman took him, farther down the highway by the railroad than he had ever been, until he could no longer see the grain elevator, through prairies and over rivers that were not his. Hurt from crying dried his throat and he wanted water; the sun through the car windows could not warm him and he started crying again. The policeman said nothing.

Later, Jack asked him, Are we going to the mountains? Is it in the city?

The policeman didn't answer.

XII

In the night, he'd felt her move once as she'd got up for the child, fed her and come back into bed: then she'd seemed to come into his sleep without his knowing, moving through her skin in different ways to the places where they touched, maybe changing dreams he'd had or lost as she moved her thighs and breasts against him, not remembering til he awoke how her rhythms had touched him, eased him, taken him down gently in his sleep. He'd awakened to the sun and crying, to Connie moving back into bed, the child's small mouth and body between them, her mouth on Connie's breast, her skin soft all over as a woman's skin is in some places, different than the sleepy feeling of Connie's flesh against him. He seemed to hear the child's heartbeat against his own, almost in time with the sucking sounds she made, the bed was deep and warm from their sleep and now unmoving bodies, heavy and dry smells mixed with the scent of the baby's skin. Laurie lay for a long time against them, as Connie slept, as he watched the sunlight or sang softly, the child seeming more like his own.

He took her out of bed when she'd finished, so Connie could sleep; he changed her as Connie'd showed him, played with her, and held her close when she cried. Laurie cried for a long time and he walked with her, afraid she'd continue til she woke Connie and wondering at the same time if he'd hurt or scared the baby with his strange body and hands. Then Laurie opened and closed her mouth against his chest and he gave her water from a small bottle, feeling part of the giving Connie'd known each time she'd let her baby suck; Laurie's face was puffed around the longer nipple, he listened to her breathing as he rocked or sang songs he'd learned from the old men in Sidney, the baby seeming heavier as her breathing slowed, almost losing the nipple as her mouth opened, warm and sleepy as he lay her down on her back. He watched her, seeing Connie's face and eyes in her child, then shapes and colors from the boy he'd never seen.

Now, he began thinking of how the boy'd taken Connie and left the child, knowing things Connie'd said or left out and wondering how she'd been with the boy, how she felt now seeing the boy's hair and the shapes of his face in her child; but the child had come to him, Jack, through Connie, changing to his own, as Connie'd come to him, speaking his tongue with her voice, sound and words like memories seeming to come again, he'd felt the sound of their common tongue when she'd touched him, seemed to trust the sound of her body moving in different rhythms or still, her smell mixed always with the sounds she made, the way her hands were and the feel of her skin, her body under his hands. He watched her as she slept, remembered her wrapped around him and her breathing, going down in the night with him and letting her skin move against him, hiding and close in his sleep. Now she seemed closed in her sleep, waiting for his hands or dreaming of the boy's hands, her face different and cold in the light.

Her apartment seemed to close around him then, seemed like his own houses in other cities, no good for anything but dying: he was restless as when he'd walked nights in the beginning, losing then the smell of rats he'd carried with him since Chicago, the smell working in the walls like claws or heat, stronger now as he moved in this room, feeling the lie of the night and morning in the boy he hated as he'd hated other men who'd bound him or made him leave. He hadn't heard her come out of the bedroom and couldn't feel her now, she'd moved in these thoughts and in memories he'd shaped before; she talked now in a strange voice or the one she'd used before he'd known her again, seeming not to notice he'd changed, talking til she'd made him listen, as she'd always done before, she was feeling the morning without knowing the old shapes he'd seen beginning again in the daylight, not knowing he'd lost her in those shapes; she spoke and he snapped at her, pushing away from the table where he'd sat eating, turning his face, turning back only when she said his name: he looked at her, seeming to know only now how lonely she'd been before they'd met, wanting a man, maybe scared to bear the child alone, he'd hurt her again and she was watching him as if she didn't know what to do; he moved against her, feeling as if her skin spoke in a voice he could almost hear, moving against him, the sound of her body through the clothes like her mouth and his skin, changing and holding like the face of the child between them in the night, and he moved his hands over her body til she said no, please, everything's too sore, just lie down with me;

he felt then like wet land under her hands, her mouth moving down his chest, his stomach, and he seemed to turn hot and cold when he felt her mouth around him, holding the back of her neck with his hands, helping her move, feeling her hair in his fingers, her hands on his legs as she moved her tongue and lips up and down and closed him in her mouth, making his skin stretch and tighten as she called rhythms like water, feeling them in her mouth and his skin, rhythms he could hardly stand til he felt them sink into him, settling him, and he lay still now, her warm dry face in his hands.

XIII

He remembered only yellow fire burning in spring dust, the sky seeming red above the fire, sometimes still red beyond the sheave line, and there must have been older children around the fire, keeping the young ones, like himself, from getting too close: these things he shaped now in memory, out of the fire that seemed to continue as it had then, when shifting wind or smoke had made his eyes water and a girl, older than he, had washed his eyes, he'd felt kin to the girl and the others, hearing songs he was too young to sing or remember, but he'd liked them, he'd heard the girl singing in a voice he seemed to remember now; nobody'd cried or got hurt, the older children hadn't laughed or shoved the younger ones as they'd done at other times, they were singing or staring at the fire, sitting close as kin or old friends, not minding the younger ones: the night had been cold, and dry as this one, he'd shared his blanket with a little girl who'd kissed him later and giggled, her face seeming the same now as the one who'd washed his eyes. The houseparents had taken him in with the others his own age and he'd been sleep, though he'd wanted to stay out with the older kids, they'd maybe be telling ghost stories, maybe they'd talk to him; he'd wished then there'd be other fires, but there never were.

He'd been walking in the night, after Connie'd gone to sleep, after he'd held the baby for a long time, feeling her warm against his chest like the fire he remembered now, til she'd slept and he'd put her down, covering her, knowing then he'd never get used to the quiet way a child sleeps, as if he'd trusted the feeling too much, thought it would last like fire or warm skin: the fire was gone, he felt like he'd lost a week's pay in a poker game or left his last ride in the desert, nothing to do but sing songs for good luck, keep on moving.

Some nights, he could talk to the bartender or the others; city men spent a lot of time alone, but once in awhile they'd have a few drinks and seem to miss being neighborly, they'd remember things their fathers had talked about when they'd met down the road or in town; they'd hunched shoulders too, stuck their hands in the pockets of their jeans, spitting wish juice instead of tobacco and listening to stories their fathers told, talk of rain and corn, tractors, prices: now they'd been drinking, become their fathers, talking of things they remembered in this city, Milwaukee, a town after a few drinks, talking in names that sounded to him like towns or prairies, and the bartender knew their drinking as well as he knew their stories and names, they waited for him in his house down the road, come to help him get his work done and maybe he'd help them tomorrow, they were neighbors, they all knew the same things. He listened and he could tell his own stories, he'd known the land close in his own time, learned to wait on the land the way their fathers had; they waited for cars or houses now, talked of women and jobs as the land hung on in their voices, hidden behind the words like a train in a siding; he heard songs he remembered from home and they moved like the land in his memory, names of prairies and towns, the voices of neighbors in a bar waiting on the land for things to change:

he sang with the songs and drank til he saw his man, felt drunk and wished he were sober: Eddie was coming toward him, smiling, and he felt himself tense up, remembering how Eddie'd sworn at him and wondering if Eddie were still angry, the child's skin coming back to him, the small foot he'd touched, and he felt lonesome, trying to get back his nerve; things seemed to slow down and stop as he lost the voices of the other men, as he felt himself watch Eddie closely, knowing again the risk he'd sensed in the beginning, waiting for Eddie to make a move of some kind.

Eddie said, Hey Jack, let me buy you a drink.

—Got one. Sit down if you want to.

Then the other voices seemed to start up again, settling easy as they'd done before, he loosened up as Eddie talked about the job, his voice almost mixing with the others, saying he wouldn't take this shit much longer and a lot of other things, mostly rambling but making some sense, and he saw Eddie was lonesome, he might get mad but he'd never turn down talk or free drinks for long. He felt his own anger leave him then, figured to listen and talk as he always had but he drank his one beer slowly, letting Eddie catch up, sure Eddie'd know how to get behind him and roll him in the night if he wanted to, and he had to be ready, the other continued, using voices friends used with each other, feeling loose enough to talk of no good sons or wives who wouldn't shut up, saying they'd worked the same jobs for years and never got treated right, goddam foreman get told one of these days. Eddie swore, used the same word they did but Eddie's voice changed, sounded different from the others as he heard them settle like dirt in old houses, their own houses maybe. Eddie bought another round and looked at him.

—I'm fixing to leave this town pretty quick. You still want to get out west?

He said he didn't know and thought Eddie sounded tired, his face older as the light from the beer sign passed, as he swore at his job, the town, coughing hard and slapping his chest; Guess you living with that woman you got, Eddie said.

—Yeah, that's what I'm doing, he said, and Eddie laughed, but he knew what Eddie meant and wasn't angry, he felt sad as Eddie talked about the war and how it had been to come back, saying sometimes he wished he'd stayed in but he'd hated it then, come back everything was different, guys taking jobs they wouldn't piss on before just because they'd up and married the first piece of tail they could get their peckers into and had a mess of kids, course that's just about what I done except I didn't have no kids: he let the talk come, thinking of Connie, she'd make it all right, have his kids and still look good, love him maybe long as he wanted, long as he could hold her;

he heard Eddie say been doing this a long time and it ain't getting any easier, and he remembered Eddie's stories, each place Eddie'd lost a tooth or almost got killed in his sleep for a pair of shoes; Eddie'd lived only as long as the other men in the bar, they'd got heavy and he was still quick but his hands shook on the glass, his eyes were old, seeing times behind him in the bar mirror, quiet as smoke or highways at night. Now Eddie began talking to someone else and he knew he had to leave, feeling strange, sick almost, even in the night air, knowing Connie'd maybe be awake now, nursing the baby in that lonesome house, wondering why he'd been leaving her alone nights, going out while she slept. The feeling of Eddie's slipping time stayed with him, he knew she was good, as only a woman is, wished he could take her down and love her, feel close as her own skin and know he was good to her. Sometimes he'd felt that way when they talked, her face open and moving like the body he trusted and her strange eyes, til she moved beyond him in sleep, changed into dreams, making him wish he could come inside her, change her dreams to his own and make her forget everything she'd known before she'd come to him.

His chest jumped as he sucked in air, he'd been walking too fast for his thoughts, thinking he'd known for a long time Eddie was dying, one more winter like this one would kill him sure if he had to live outside, Eddie was too old for the jobs a man gets when he's moving around, except 'pearl diving', maybe: he slowed down, seeming to feel steam and hot water, the sound of coughing and spit, sometimes blood, bottles rolling on the floor or street, always cold in the steam and the steam was gone, slip and fall a few more times and maybe get another drink, one more ride downtown; he didn't move, remembering the old men in Sidney as they took it easy, waiting around with friends and going down to die in the place they'd been born, lay down some time like grass after a hard rain, even the last one gone wouldn't die a stranger; he remembered Eddie, saw him, heard him say doing time's the only thing worse than winter and the words seemed to hang and fall, hang and fall as he heard them again, again

he seemed to drift then, almost remembering the way the fire'd warmed him but forgetting as he watched the sky clear off, the clouds shifting, good night for travelling if a man had somewhere to go, Wyoming, he thought, nights like this didn't ever want to see no sunrise, walking, the night better and soft, never see sunrise and all the stars: the door felt good as he remembered hard things he'd kicked along, sounds almost like tracks way down as Al opened the door, the light uneven in Al's eyes and the shapes inside seeming thick, as if they'd been milled or cast: it was a song he knew, some old blues, and he sat down with a drink in his hand, smiling, drifting slowly over the shapes like the song, Al's voice seeming now to clang like a broken bell in this smooth room and song. He thought of Connie but it passed and he looked out, hearing Al's voice only sometimes, losing it in the song or in places where his thoughts moved or drifted, shapes or songs or memories spreading, drifting

he seemed to lose the feel of his pulse and lungs, something was draining out of him and Al's words had a strange sound, as if Al were making up his thoughts or words as he went on, though he sensed the sound of Al's voice continuing without hearing the words,

and he felt himself seep like water into something dry, sand or old hard riverbed, drying inside as his juices seeped and dried in the sun, as if these shapes were part of a furnace or mill and they'd waited for him to change as he was changing now, waiting til he was ready to be worked or cast or used, it seemed easy, then strange to be thinking as he slipped and drained, dried or bent; a thought or memory seemed to come from below him, somewhere in the drying, strange as rain in these parts, I don't know what the hell he's been talking about, I don't

—Like you and Connie, man, Al said, I mean, that's different, you seem to—to really understand each other, like it's real, and the baby, do you—I mean, does it ever—well, does it matter that it's not yours?

and he saw then this long space of Al's voice, like headlights so far down the road you weren't sure you'd really seen them, you'd been waiting at night on a cold road and now the ride came, too soon almost, you still felt as if you were waiting, Al's voice like the bright headlight close to you or the sound of crying, he'd been shaken from his sleep by crying and he'd gone to the baby, remembering the feeling he'd had when he'd gotten Laurie to stop crying; and he stopped, now, and looked at Al, thinking Jesus Christ man ought to know better than to ask a stranger shit like this.

—Ain't sure, most times, how I feel about that, he said.

—Do you want to talk about it, man?

That's what they do, he thought, Al and his fucking friends, they all sit around talking this shit to each other like a bunch of goddam old women; he felt his nerves get tight as they'd been with Eddie, turned away and heard Al going on about some friend of his, he's been going out with a married woman, bad scene because he feels guilty about her kids: he couldn't lose Al's voice this time, the nerve jumped and he saw Connie, wanted to go to her, feeling bad now for leaving her alone while he sat here bullshitting, think I just better leave that bottle where it is—then Al said, I saw Eddie the other night and he says he's leaving town. I tried talking him out of it but I don't think he really listened—wouldn't tell me why—

—You tell me why, he said.

—What? Oh you mean, why he's leaving—well, man, I think—

don't matter what you think, there ain't any reasons, he thought, he laughed to himself as Al went on, feeling sad as he remembered Eddie's face when he'd asked him to go along, he knew now he was going home and he told Al he was tired, stood up and felt himself moving as if his anger had pushed him, as if he'd turned in some way to come back and felt easy from the turning, strange from the liquor he wished now he'd never seen, walking fast, the wind seeming to hurt him as he kicked a stone to the gutter: he remembered Connie as she'd been in the beginning, dry and cold as a scared bird but hard, like something that's lasted a long time and started to crack, stone siding or wood. He heard water and ran over the bridge, some pain coming in his chest and burning as he remembered the beginning, the things he'd seen in the river, sewage coming in and hot splash moving the ripples, the sound continuing up the block, almost til he reached the house:

he was running, hoping the liquor would blow off him and leave him alone, trucks going by long as houses, get on back like sitting on a front porch back home with the old men, running, thinking he'd have to spend some time with Eddie before Eddie was gone, they'd maybe both be worse off next time—he was tired, breathing hard up the stairs, as the one light swung slowly and seemed to fall

she'd been waiting up for him, crying, even her hands were red, dry as the brown paper laid by the lamplight: he held her and felt his own body shaking, feeling her seem to bend into him as he tried to speak her crying, his shaking nerves, yeah, he said, I know I got to stop this.

XIV

He'd come home drunk and tired, the feel of the dirty rain still on him, knowing these steps, and the wall he leaned on, from memory, coming up slow: he hoped she'd fed the child already and gone back to sleep, but maybe he'd find them now, Connie tired, rocking slowly, the rhythm begun inside her with the child and continuing now as she held Laurie close as skin, feeling the giving as the child shared; he felt like a stranger, trying to get by in the darkness, the light from the window dim and shifting over shapes he'd remembered before and forgotten now, as if she'd maybe changed the room around so she'd hear him come in.

Then he saw her and hung on, she stood by the bedroom door, some light showing her body through the nightgown dark as a woman he remembered but couldn't place, long time gone, some old store he'd found and pried a board loose, slept it off inside down on the floor, cold as a flatbed the next morning.

He felt the light in his eyes and lost her as she moved, her words soft or running til she came close, as he remembered now he'd heard her say these things other nights, her voice thick as he seemed to choke, felt himself fall down on the floor, his voice coming loud and broken as he pushed her away, and crawled: he could hear her, feel her next to him and knew she'd try to help again the way women always do when a man's helpless or sick, coming too close so he's got to beat on them to get them off: floorboards seemed like grab irons, sideways and things going by as he felt her coming, following him like men who'd done for him when nobody was around, should have been long gone, the floor rusty as old spikes when the sun got to them, worn from inside and cracking—

He pulled himself up on the bed, turning like wheels, sound of flat car brakes when the wheel wears down coming like a dream, seeing her face for the frist time as he felt himself move, saying things that came back in the walls, calling her—

she seemed then to come into his flesh like pain and heal him as she came, as he felt her close and quiet, taking him down in the night and hiding him, covering his flesh with her own as she stayed still and changed him so he'd sleep, as he wondered when Eddie'd head out, the room kept going and he remembered, knew it was coming again.

XV

This morning, he woke up before the child and looked out their window: the sun came down slanting off the east roofs of houses and the sun came in to Connie, sleeping on her side with her hands between her legs, her eyes moving behind their lids, her face soft and safe in her dream; other women he'd known slept with their faces hidden like shadows on glass, shadows gone.

In the sun, the roofs seemed to slant again, as if they'd moved and the sun stood still, and he felt a good hot day coming in this morning wind, maybe they could take the child outside. Then he looked back at Connie, her face, her hair hanging over the bed a little, and something hurt him: it was like waking on the plains, he'd felt dew all over his body and known then he was changing inside, moving in strange ways to things he couldn't understand, that road, that morning like the time just before dying when it's too late to use what you finally see, as if people always die in the morning and you couldn't let the time rest, had to keep moving; once he'd come over Iowa and it was cold enough to freeze, he'd felt like an old man, cold and weak in the daylight, same light now, just a different time of the sun.

He turned and stopped thinking when he heard small sounds in the crib, and he went in; Laurie smiled at him for the first time and he laughed, rubbing her stomach and making noises as he picked her up, moving, feeling again the morning sun he knew would last; she was holding her head up, still smiling, and he choked a little, feeling sad in the warm light but happy for the child. Connie stirred, then he saw her come into the room rubbing her eyes and slipping down one side of the night-gown with her other hand, he'd seen her go many times for the child in half sleep, seeming not to move on her own but drawn only by the sound of crying, feeding Laurie then as if dreaming.

She kissed him hard, the child sucking between them, held in their arms as she held him with her mouth, and he felt something rising in Connie as she changed again, as if she'd known in sleep what he'd seen on the slanting roofs and sun, remembering now as she continued with the child, and he saw how much she'd come to know him in a month's time, come inside him and stayed,
growing in him like seed, round and deeper than the sliding places he'd touched with other women, and he seemed to feel all of this now as she kissed him, as he said, why don't we take Laurie outside today? Her whole body changed and moved then as it always did when she was happy, as when he'd come home from work and she'd have the baby with her, she'd be singing, cooking his meal, and sometimes he'd sneak up behind her,

watch her jump when he grabbed her.

Now she gave him the child and moved around the kitchen, putting on coffee, frying bacon as he watched her move, played with the child, glad most of the waiting time was gone and remembering how he'd never thought they'd last this long; Laurie waved her arms, seeing the colors on his shirt, and he smelled the bacon, and Connie when she came near him;

—Think I'll wear a dress when we go out, she said, that'd be nice for a change. You want eggs?

—Yeah, but just bust them, I'll eat them with my bare hands.

—You stop that, she said, laughing, and she turned back to the stove as the sun moved higher, coming through the top windows and down, opening on the little smile she had, and on the baby's hands; he saw his cigarette smoke moving in the room the way she'd move, all bright colors and slow, sounds turning wet and quick, her skin the same shade and moving close to him; she looked at him then, seemed to see his thoughts and blushed a little, pleased, coming over to serve the food, and he wrapped his hand around her bare thigh, moving up til she squirmed away, her face turning red from the smile she'd almost hid.

The baby was almost asleep when he put her in the carriage; Connie pushed the carriage and he walked beside her, she was warm and smooth in the bright day and he seemed to see white lights in her hair, the line of her body through the cotton dress, sun on her legs and arms; he was proud of her for looking so soon as if she'd never had a child, for not getting wide or lazy. She talked to him in the soft voice she used when they were happy, said it sure was nice to be outside again, and she'd like for them to get out of the city, the land was so pretty in the spring: he felt better hearing her talk this way, almost forgetting the fights they'd been having, the way he'd been coming home lately, the good things between them seeming stronger now. They'd got as far as the hotels near the lake, old people stood bent over, talking, waiting for doormen to help them get to their cars, and he saw them, remembering old men he'd seen wrapped in newspapers as she came closer, pressing her cheek against his arm, her eyes showing him his own face, and he pulled away, sometimes he'd seen her look like this and want to hurt her again, and now he felt the day change and go wrong, memories running like freight trains as he pushed the carriage, the steel handle the same feel as a drawbar or grab iron, sometimes running his hands over brick walls they passed and then looking down at his hands.

Connie was quiet, he thought she looked tired, maybe they'd walked too far, and he thought of the morning he'd come down here, there'd been no one in the park and he wished it could be that way again, the land rolling in on itself, empty as the hills of Idaho southwest of Yellowstone; Connie smiled only when people looked down to see Laurie, throwing shadows across the carriage as they did, and then she turned and walked over to a bench. He saw her legs and wanted to touch her all over, thinking of the sounds she'd make if he did it slow, seeing trees they'd hide behind and remembering they'd brought a blanket as he slid his hand over her leg pushing her dress up a little.

—Don't you act like nothing's wrong, she said, keeping her lips tight together. A minute ago you were pushing me away.

—Jesus, little thing like that ain't worth—

—Ain't a little thing, happens all the time—and you ain't very nice about it, either.

—Yeah, I know how much you like Al, he talks his damn fool head off; and that sonofabitch come over all the time when I ain't around, you think I don't know? Talking better be all he's doing.

She looked as if he'd hit her, saying he didn't have any reason to be jealous, she'd never let another man touch her, Al's real nice, that's all, and he said, yeah I'll just bet you know how nice he is, seeing her face change then as she got up and walked away, heading for the trees and people, back toward the houses she'd said nobody lived in, they were kept up too nice, and he saw the birds, the sky seeming to roll over the trees and lake, yellow or blue as the sun moved in the trees, as Connie moved between the light and trees as a child would, watching the ground and walking slow.

Laurie cried out and he saw she was hungry, looked back and Connie was gone, so he pushed the carriage, calling for Connie as he ran, the baby screaming now, he heard the rattles he'd hung on the carriage, the rough path bouncing Laurie as she cried louder, almost choking; Connie turned and stood, coming back as she'd heard her baby, her anger still dark in her eyes but passing as she took Laurie, making gentle sounds that seemed to go on like blue water in the lake, all sound the same. She said why'd you come running after me that way, scaring Laurie, you know I'd never leave my baby, and he said he was sorry, trying to tell her he'd had Al figured out from the beginning, then stopping as he saw that Connie wasn't listening, she seemed more and more inside the baby til he told her he hadn't meant what he'd said about Al, he was just scared to lose her:

she said, sometimes you sure don't act like you care if I'm here or not. I can't stand it anymore, Jack, you got to stop saying things about me you know ain't true.

He touched her hand, hoping she'd say something, but she turned back to Laurie, bundling her up and laying her back down in the carriage; they walked down to the lake, he skipped stones, and the wind blew her dress and hair as she fretted over the baby some, wrapping Laurie in the extra blanket, seeming cold herself by the water and the sound of stones, squeezing her upper arms as she stood waiting; when he came up to her, he put his hands on her shoulders, but her eyes were quiet, not moving when he asked her if she'd like to go, as if she didn't understand, or had to see first what he wanted her to say. he knew then what he'd done, felt her close quiet look still as he tried to hold her cold body, as strange now as a different woman would be after this time with her, and he heard their voices, seeming to mix together as the same sound for the first time, as he tried telling her he knew he'd been wrong and she tried to make it all right, speaking sadly, her eyes the same as they'd been that day she'd waited for him in the long hall by her hospital room. He took her hand, and they walked as the sun crossed, seeming to move now almost like water as he used both hands to push the carriage up the hill, sometimes looking back over his shoulder to see her coming up behind him, her white legs showing when the dress pulled, her arms crossed in the chill and some red on her skin, the dress folding loose over her breasts.

XVI

Clouds came across the early sun, the air was thick and he knew the cold feeling was coming on him again, as if it had never left. He loaded cans and tried to think, sometimes hearing Rick and the driver, Rick saying something about a drunk who'd tried to make time with the girls they'd been with, his buddy'd finally had to beat up the old man, going on then to what they'd done with the girls: he was sick of the same talk everyday, sick of the way the garbage blew up in their faces like flies, and he almost wished for winter again but kept still, Rick was swearing enough for both of them.

His thoughts seemed to turn and run; he felt as if he finally knew a good woman when he saw one, and Connie loved him, or said she did, he'd seen himself in the long cold fall ends and winters when a man might make things with his hands, or play with his children, sit up late with his wife, most things worked out by then, and sometimes she'd seemed like the woman she'd be then, mostly when they talked together, when he touched her as she slipped and held, kissing him the way she'd done in the beginning, the secret way a woman always begins, showing more slow and dark as water streaks, some light at the wide ends. He remembered her face and hands, her body he trusted in the dark but couldn't hold when he'd get lonely, or scared she was leaving him, maybe she was waiting for another man even now as he worked and tried to feel the words she'd use to calm him down.

He didn't feel like drinking at noon, he kept to himself and watched the pool games, the men talking and the glasses slipping down the bar, sounds mixed and seeming far away as he remembered the feed mill in Sidney, and the railroad men he'd met from time to time, weeds along the rails and cinders dry as the sound of leaves, dirty as his own hands from this job he hated now and wished he could quit. But he'd known he'd give up these things before the baby's been born, they were his family now, though he hadn't got them by himself, and they'd be easy to lose, like most things.

The driver said they'd see some rain before the day was out; he hummed an old tune and didn't think much, losing the talk around him as the cans clanked, remembering diesel horns he'd heard up close, the noon whistle from a Baltimore factory in the sound of this truck grinding up the garbage; he and Rick worked fast now to knock off early and kill time with the six pack the driver kept in a cooler up in the cab, he moved quick as he could but Rick had long arms, Rick slammed the cans hard on the back of the truck with one quick move he was still trying to learn. They'd feel the beer then because they'd run hard and sweated, the driver

70

laughing at them as Rick cussed him out, and he knew the company sometimes sent men out to check and they'd be fired sure if they ever got caught, the three of them jammed together, high from the beer and the smell of it in the cab, Connie'd say most times, when he'd get home, you smell like you been drinking all day—he knew she'd be asleep now, with the baby, but soon she'd be up to start supper, and then he thought he'd like to take her out, not to the bar but to some place she'd like to go, if the woman downstairs would watch Laurie.

—Hey, what's the matter, the driver said, that girl you got giving you trouble? I keep telling you, you just got to let them know who's boss, ain't that right, Rick?

Rick said don't listen to him, he ain't seen it in so long he's forgot what it looks like: he wished the time would pass so he could get home, see if she'd be waiting, maybe they'd talk it over again and things'd come out right this time, he'd been wrong to leave her alone nights, they'd been happy till he'd started coming home drunk, passing out sometimes before she'd said a word, and he didn't remember now why he'd ever gone, each night the same til he'd got sick of his own talk, and Eddie's, the liquor, the way she'd look when he'd come home cold and hidden from her, just hoping she'd leave him alone.

He left the city garage in the rain, running between the lights and backed up sewers, feeling blind, his face hard as the rain came down, and he wondered what Connie was doing, he could almost see Al coming up their steps, hollering 'anybody home?' and Connie coming to the door, smiling at Al, her arms folded across her breasts, her smooth legs a little apart, til he'd get home and she'd change, never seem quite the same each time Al left her, she'd fret more about little things or hardly say a word, leaving him with Laurie while she finished making supper. But when he walked up the steps, she came to him alone, her body warming him as he touched her neck, feeling her hair fall uneven in his hand, 'ain't got time to mess with it now,' she'd said after Laurie'd been born, he like it loose and fine, the way it fell in different ways when he touched it, and he moved his hand now to her waist, feeling the smooth skin under her shirt, remembering what he'd felt in the day, how he'd wanted her for himself and wanted to make it all right, her face seeming strange as he felt her fingers moving down his chest, drawing lines and circles around him, as if he'd forgotten how her eyes darkened sometimes when she'd get lonely, and he heard her say it's funny, I been waiting for you all day, now you're here and I wish you'd leave again; he said I been thinking about you all day, but she was looking over his shoulder at the rain, the flat sound of the drain pipes and the tin roofs below them mixing with her voice, as if she'd spoken from across the street,

sometimes I swear I don't know what's going to happen to us; she smiled in a way he'd never seen, saying I always thought I would of got married by now as she moved to the window, tapping her fingers on the glass, her face hidden behind her hair as the rain darkened, the last light slipping like an old wheel on the wet street. He felt she'd be leaving soon, taking the child and going out in the rain, as if she'd figured out more than he'd ever shown, knew he wasn't worth keeping. She turned from the wet glass where she'd waited or looked out, her hands turning and close, saying you're all I got Jack, just you and that baby.

—You just don't worry, little bit, I'm going to take care of you, he said, wondering if she still wanted him to stay.

—I hope you can, honey, you got to.

They turned; their room was dark as rain makes an afternoon, leaving nothing to shine or move, splashing the windows, thunder shaking the house til they felt they'd lose it, I hate storms, she said, standing cold and stiff even as he touched her arm: he said maybe we got to do more things, we ain't hardly been out of this house since Laurie's been born.

—The two of us ain't been out alone at all, she said, but please, let's not go to that bar where you always go.

—Anyplace you want. You think that woman'd watch Laurie?

She said she'd go down and ask her. He watched it rain harder, the lightning strange as a movie house in a suburb, and he saw cars moving slow, their drivers scared as kids before a storm til their mothers take them in, the children's voices rising higher as the wind gets stronger; Connie came back and Al was with her, they looked happy, and Al was looking at Connie in a way she never seemed to notice but maybe felt, he was sure she knew what Al was thinking and wanted him thinking that way; he felt how badly he'd he like to stop Al from grinning, maybe bounce his head on the sidewalk a few times.

She said Al's come over to ask us to the movies, ain't that a coincidence, and he knew she could turn from him as easily as she'd done in the park: he sensed Al between them, seeming to protect her, maybe knowing what they'd been through and figuring out how to use it, and he remembered now the way Al had moved close to her the day she'd come home from the hospital. It sure is, he said, and he watched her face, her body seem to lighten as she moved easily in the kitchen, getting the food ready; he saw Al's eyes on her, heard Al say he'd love to stay for supper.

Connie sat between them at the table, but she took his hand, her fingers smooth and quick as she told Al this is the first time me and Jack been out together since our baby's been born, Al saying the movie's really supposed to be funny, and I know a bar close by where we can get something to eat afterwards. He touched Connie's leg, wishing it were bare, seeing her now as if she were standing by the bathtub, drying herself slowly, saying she liked the breeze on her when she felt wicked, letting the wind on her, moving as sap comes to the sideways mouths of maples, as swamps sink, drain into mud, riverbanks flood slow and fall down, the earth moving in water rhythms and slowing the water down; and he'd seen himself slick and hurting against her when they hadn't been close, when she'd said things that'd made him angry as he'd been when he'd first gone running from the land, as if his fingers still hurt from the dirt he'd dragged, as if he'd hung by his feet from the back of that first train: her fingers stole over his leg like outlaws, looking to take him along, and Al was a crow, circling always, waiting.

He wondered what Al was thinking, tried to learn from his eyes and the way his hands twitched, thinking maybe it's good Al sees us like this, he'll think twice before he makes his move. Her smile worried him, he remembered he hadn't trusted her in the beginning when she'd seemed to move back in dreams or memory, now she was maybe moving to Al with a smile that seemed to hide her so Al could come close to her with what he'd learned; she picked Laurie up when she heard her crying, and he made sure he kept watching Al as he moved next to Connie to help her with the baby. Laurie fussed and cried, as she always did when they changed her, and he talked to Laurie, feeling Connie close to him. Al said, maybe there's a pin sticking her.

—Not hardly, I ain't put the pins in yet; hold her legs up, will you Jack honey?

—Yeah, he said softly, now you watch them pins, and she laughed to herself; he looked around the room as he held Laurie, the walls and crib seeming dirty next to her new skin as Al's voice continued, as Al laughed at his own jokes, and he thought maybe I'll paint this room bright colors, Connie could make some curtains; then he heard the rain die down, the smell of the air wet and cool, thick enough to taste, he and Connie finished up with the baby and he watched her gather Laurie in a blanket, then walk small and young with the baby over her shoulder, almost as if Laurie were her little sister, not her own child. He and Al looked out the window, Al leaning easily on the sash, sometimes pushing the hair out of his eyes, talking about the movie, and he said, how's your car been, ain't you been having some trouble with it lately?

—Well, you know, actually, considering how old it is, I haven't had too much trouble at all—just the usual shit—it gets me around.

—I work with this guy, he's got one of them new cars with all that racing shit on them; he sure drives hell out of it, too, he said.

—Yeah, Al said, laughing a little and scratching his head, that's a little sad, I think, you know, man, people who try to show off with their cars.

He laughed too, thinking of what Rick would say if he heard that, and stopped listening as he saw the clouds move, opening over the city lights and closing dark, the way the land looks at night sometimes when you've been driving too long, the room feeling close, filling with the smells and creaks that come later on, the sound of Al's voice thick as the room. He wished Connie would hurry.

She shivered a little, coming close as they walked and sitting against him in the front seat, her leg warm under his hand, Al continuing on the other side of the windshield bar, the square radio and the dashboard chrome shining as the light came in, but he lost Al's voice in the low noise the car made, hearing only things Connie'd answered, and she'd been quiet most of the time. They were driving west toward the hospital where Connie'd been, he saw some kids moving together on a corner by a warehouse, and he heard Al say it's a damned shame those black kids don't have better places to play; he looked back again, thinking, they ain't playing, buddy.

The light seemed the same, the screen shifting, showing her face as he'd seen in the car, sometimes different, as if she'd been someone Al was with, her hair hanging and dark, quiet, dressed like girls Al had told him about: Al laughed at the movie but she shifted around, pulling at a strap under her dress, there was nothing going on with these people in bed and he wished he had Connie now, she'd move better than this girl, I wouldn't have none of the problems this man's got, feeling her come close then, saying low we ain't too old to make out in the movies, do you like this movie, I can't figure it out half the time; you kiss good, he said, remembering the sky moving in the cold light over the river, how he'd walked or they'd gone together and slipped down, never like that before, the way she'd said things and taken him, holding him as he held her now, keeping her close and hoping she'd never leave, wishing he'd just opened to her in the beginning and never asked questions inside himself, as he thought maybe a woman's like travelling slow, you're all right til the land starts changing and you see you got to start all over again.

—Do you want to get something to eat, Al said when they came out of the movie; that bar I told you about's only a few blocks away.

—Yeah, I need a drink anyway. You going to have one, little bit?

—If you do, she said.

—They have really fantastic hamburgers there. We used to have lunch there all the time when I worked for the parks department last summer.

—I'm cold, said Connie, pressing his arm tighter as they walked inside, maybe feeling the way these men stared, the women dressed up in jewels turning to each other, laughing, their voices filling the room like smoke or music he'd heard when he'd washed dishes in cafes, drifting and becoming thick til they'd sat down. Connie leaned on him, the other voices seeming to quiet, Al's voice only continuing, saying they'd probably been staring at him for his long hair, he'd gotten used to that lately,

—They're such a drag. Oh, by the way, you really look nice tonight, Connie.

—Why, thank you.

—Did you like the movie, Al asked her; I thought that man was fairly real, like I've felt that way before.

She leaned toward Al, saying she wasn't sure and listening as Al's talking went on, as Al looked into her eyes, maybe so she'd hear him better: he drank the whiskey fast and wanted more, knowing what Al was doing but not wanting to watch or listen, watching instead the people who were dancing, they were drunk and bumped into a table, spilling an old man's drink. The old man walked out, and he heard him say I never tolerated nastiness in the oil fields and I'm not about to start now, and Connie seemed to move across the table with her face and hands, leaning as she talked and shifting her body in that way she had of listening he remembered only now; she was telling Al not to take it so hard, there'd be others, and he thought wish I'd of said no and just let her get mad, now I got to listen to this asshole all night: Al looked down, saying he'd really loved that girl and couldn't understand why it hadn't worked out, he'd done his best to please her, given her what she wanted.

—Sometimes a girl wants somebody that tells her what to do, so she don't have to figure it all out herself, Connie said.

—Yes, but Connie, you have to really feel that way to convince someone, you have to believe in it. I'm no good trying to impress people, not—you know?

You lying sack of shit, he thought, but he sipped his drink, trying not to get mad, telling Al with a straight face he ought to try his luck downtown, like Rick did: Al said thanks, but I don't think I could stand that.

—You got to give it time, Al, you just ain't over this other girl yet, Connie said, her voice strange in these hard shapes around them, the lights, the shiny bar where the others laughed and tried to sing, making him wish again he'd stayed home and let Al go out with her, maybe she likes listening to this bullshit: he felt sick and tripped once, saying he was going to the men's room, then getting out in the night and breathing hard; he watched trucks get down the road, marker lights dull in the fog, remembering how you'd never see those markers on nights like this til a truck was nearly on top of you and you'd jump back, feeling the wind suck you in, see those wheels and wonder how you'd feel dragged down the road, better off dead. He finished the whiskey and threw the glass, the sound cutting and breaking like a face in a river, lights dim and held in the fog as if the poles were down and the lights had floated, rising slowly as he'd come near, and dropping down again, and he wondered where Eddie was, what he'd be talking about now.

They'd caught up to him, their faces seeming the same til Connie came closer, holding his arm and asking if he'd gotten sick; she felt good and he wanted to stop thinking, something hurt him, he said, I just couldn't take it in there no more, let's go home.

XVII

She said we ain't got nothing left that's clean, I guess I'd better do the wash: he looked up at her, remembering the last time she'd tried carrying the baby and the clothes to the laundromat, coming back so tired and stiff she'd had to lie down with Laurie for two hours; he'd come in from work and felt the strange quiet in the house, asking why ain't you got any lights on in here when he found her in the bedroom, her face tired, though she'd tried to smile, saying I'm all right, ain't nothing to worry about: no, he said, I don't believe you're ready yet, thinking maybe he'd been letting her do too much on her own, she wasn't strong anyway and he was scared her body'd rip open again, she'd have to spend another long time in the hospital, or worse; just fix me something good for when I get home, he said, time I done something around here.

He picked up the bags, came down the stairs and walked east, wishing the laundromat were closer or the day better, wondering why he'd begun to feel uneasy again, the quiet between them getting worse these past few days when he'd come home from work, her eyes turning and moving around the room as if she were restless, or afraid; he'd thought about other women a lot when they'd fought or he'd lain awake feeling her next to him, wanting to touch her but knowing he couldn't because she needed sleep and this long waiting time. He sorted the clothes, some of hers stained from her blood, and wondered if she'd ever heal.

It didn't matter to him if he were drunk, most times anyway, he'd sleep easily and forget the sense of her skin moving in sleep next to his, but she'd asked him to stay home last night and he'd gotten angry, saying things to hurt her til she couldn't sleep, she'd talked and cried most of the night, crying even while she nursed Laurie. These clothes seemed too small for even a baby to wear, and he knew then how small she was, how much she'd need a father soon who'd do more than just stand around, Laurie'd wake easy then, scared if she saw him drunk in the dark hallway outside her room.

He loaded all the machines and they rattled against each other; he lit a cigarette and picked up a magazine, turned then and saw a girl wearing a short skirt come into the laundromat, and she looked at him once before she began sorting clothes. Holding the magazine in front of his face, he watched while she bent over to load clothes, showing more of her legs each time and seeming to look back at him once in awhile, as if to see if he were watching, not hiding the smile on her face; she had long soft legs, he could feel the way she'd wrap them around his ass, moving like three women at the same time and maybe laughing all over when she'd finished, her face seeming to know all these things as she smiled again, crossing her legs as she sat down.

But he knew this girl would need time, like all women, he'd have to talk and move right so she'd know how to lead him on, like to fuck her right here, up top them machines, he thought, then feeling he'd better leave when she looked at him again, unsmiling, her face calm and closed in a way he'd learned to hate in other women, making him uneasy or angry, and thought he'd visit Eddie, they could drink a few beers while the clothes dried.

The street was grey and thick as those rooms below him in Lexington would be after a party, and Eddie's hallway was dark, heavy with a smell he remembered but couldn't place til he'd reached the top of the steps, forgetting Eddie's room number and knocking on the door to his right, seeing scratches on the jamb as if the door had been jimmied a few times; the television set seemed to get louder when he knocked but he heard someone coming, the handle turned and rattled.

—Jesus, he said, when Eddie opened the door.

—Yeah, I got rolled last week. Some shitheads. Done happened again, Jack, I got fired before I could quit. Come on in and have a drink.

He walked in, taking the bottle and seeing other bottles on the floor, as clean as if they'd already been washed out, Eddie'd started early or just hadn't bothered to stop, and he smelled wine, strong and heavy as old clothes or cigar ashes, saw fine dust all over like the end of a sand storm as he tripped on a rug and sat down, hearing Eddie tell him I can't sleep nights as they passed the bottle back and forth, Eddie taking long fast pulls, coughing sometimes, saying them bastards at work, they think a man's drunk if he's had two drinks;

he felt strange, holding the bottle, listening to rats or mice crawling in the walls as Eddie went on, as he remembered how he used to save up a quarter for the cowboy movies on Saturdays til the judge had let him go alone and he'd seen other movies, they made him think of the girl he'd just seen. The wine was sweet and thick in his mouth, like the first wine he'd stolen, hadn't tasted anything like that since or ever been that sick again, ain't this a bitch, Eddie said, just as broke as when I come here; by Christ I'm getting out of this goddam town tonight.

Eddie was more drunk than he'd ever seen him and he knew Eddie'd talk, so he stayed quiet, feeling something start to go in himself as he remembered a red covered bridge in Indiana, the fields stretched out and leaves changing as they fell, the cracked road warm and split from last year's snow falls, the sky like living things close up, but he knew he'd only notice the river under the road if he went back now, and Eddie'd just be counting the miles.

—Just want to get someplace warm again. You know I ain't had a woman since I come up here, you believe that shit? Course you ain't got to worry about that no more, Eddie said, telling him how easy it used to be to get a piece of ass, didn't even have to pay for it some times, Eddie never says nothing but what he don't mean something else, he thought, he tried to remember what he'd felt in the beginning when Eddie'd said he had a bottle, why don't we kill it, let's hustle some pool make some beer money, I can tell by how you hold that cue—

—Listen, just listen, I want to tell you something, you're all right,

Jack, you know that? No, from the heart, listen, you know what I mean —here, take my hand on it, go ahead.

He took Eddie's hand, felt veins, rail joints he'd run under his own hands, the feel of early spring when the ice cracked, shook the rails again til they'd come back up on the ties with the weeds, the sun smooth and hot in his eyes in those days; you just take care of yourself, hear me, he said.

· —Don't you worry about it, old Eddie knows what he's about—got me a friend down New Orleans, he likes me, he's going to set me up, you know what I mean?

—Yeah, right, that's good, he said, reaching for the bottle, watching Eddie's eyes seem to move in memory, dark bridge bottom slick green and deep cracks, the same water running as Eddie's eyes, Eddie's face red as a fish in the sunlight til you turned him over and saw his belly color, and he wondered if Eddie'd ever fished, strung flies and cast lines with old friends a long time ago, all of them talking soft in the quiet morning;

—Yeah, I like you, I could use a boy like you, Eddie said, moving toward him with a smile he wished he'd never seen,
remembering now what he'd known in the beginning, before he'd got soft living with a woman, Eddie came closer, saying know what you got to do, ain't your first time.

—You just drunk, Eddie, you ain't making sense, only thing you need is money; no, he thought, only if I got to do it to stay alive and there ain't no way, the lights, smell of men close as this room, pale and sick, and Eddie moved closer, circling, the room seeming smaller as he watched Eddie coming, he felt his nerves jump when Eddie smashed the bottle, seeing glass chips, the long neck stuck in Eddie's fist as Eddie came waving the broken end, saying I know how to get your money if I want it, ain't what I'm after right now, come on—

—Put that thing down, he said, moving back and hearing the wall, the wet floor scrape of glass, the sound of Eddie's feet dragging as Eddie coughed, and said I'll use this thing now if I have to, come on—then Eddie swung the cut end close to his face, he kicked Eddie and watched him go down on the wet floor and bottles, Eddie rolling over once and holding his stomach, and he heard the noises Eddie made as he threw up wine and rolled on the glass smeared on the floorboards, he felt the room get louder, sensing the street as he opened the door,

—Take the goddam money, he shouted, he threw it at Eddie and it scattered and stuck to the floor:

Connie said, honey, I got something for you, she pulled her dress over her head, seeming to move more slowly, her hands, he tried to feel her mouth, her body moving all around him as she led him down, coming over on top of him with the new weight of her breasts, the pull of her thighs; his heavy slow fingers seemed to stick to her skin or slip by her as she moved in a warm, steady rhythm, taking his heaviness as her skin slipped over him: it took a long time, she touched him and waited, making gentle sounds in his neck and arms as his dreams ran in the light or morning, kicking at garbage, beer cans the same flat sound as the early street, drainpipes where the water ran before her; he waited for her hands, her thighs to move around him as he watched his body lie to her again, she moved him and moved against his dry skin til he was strong snough to come inside her, and she took him easily, he moved then in rhythms she'd formed early, his face against her breasts as her fingers moved like living things in his hair, some sweet taste of wine still in his mouth and he wondered, waited for her fingers to come down to his wet face.

XVIII

The stiff prairie wind came close to the ground, and Jack knew the long thin clouds would stay higher than the sun for the rest of the day. He was out early to sweep the driveway before the guests came for dinner; the fields seemed almost red now, as they had been in summer, the dry short grassed blowing the same way, north to south, as the birds were gone and he remembered the way they'd flown. Out by the mailbox, he watched a car go down the road toward the highway. It was a new Buick, the first one he'd seen.

Jack walked back to the garage, wondering when the snow would come. He remembered a blizzard from the first year he'd come, how he'd helped the judge shovel the car out the next day, how they'd put chains on the tires. The chains had seemed to break the snow up softly, then they'd clanked later on over the wet road. Now he smelled this new car and circled it, putting the broom away without touching the car at all.

The guests would come soon in big cars, mostly new or a year old. Last night Marge, the maid, had started cooking around six and he'd watched her from then on, smelling the pies and remembering their sharp taste. He'd forgotten those people, or almost believed he'd be lucky and they'd stay away just this one time.

—My, my Jack, don't you look nice!

It was the judge's wife and he looked at the bracelet she was holding.

—What's the matter, you forget what day this is, she said.

—I was just sweeping up, like you told me to, Jack said.

Her eyes seemed to look through him, even past the walls of the house.

—Never mind that now, she said in a low voice, and he saw the red mark on her cigarette as she laid it on the ashtray, should have been done with that sweeping two hours ago. Now go get cleaned up, for God's sake! She stopped looking at him and went back to the bracelet, feeling the roundness of the silver links, almost seeming to smile at them. Jack eased himself around her chair; he shivered going up the stairs. He turned on the faucet and looked down at his hands.

The water was cold and he let it run a long time, looking at the sunny fields through the bathroom window til he saw cars pulling into the driveway. The guests got out of their cars and walked two by two, huddled in their coats, their faces even redder in the wind. Then he could hear their voices, the heaviness of their feet in the hallway, and he knew he'd better hurry. She was calling him again, her words sounding different up here than they would from the stairway, where the others would be moving around, waiting for their drinks.

—You know my foster son, the judge was saying as Jack came down the stairs, Jack, shake hands with Mr. Toomey here. Mr. Toomey's on the school board so mind your p's and q's!

Jack took the man's thick hand, heard the judge breathing behind him; the man said now sure was a fine thing you done for this boy, Cliff, by golly. The judge leaned back on his heels, smiling, using the voice he kept for company or friends. Jack heard Marge call him from the kitchen and he was glad he could leave. He wiped his hand on his pants once he was sure the judge wasn't looking.

—Take these out and offer them to the folks like I showed you last time, okay? Marge said, smiling, breathing close to him when she talked. Jack had heard that she like to go down to the bar and drink a little, she'd talk about the judge and his wife as if they were friends of hers. He could smell her now as she filled up his tray, see the dark veins in her arms and legs. The tray was heavy and he could feel his hands sweating; the crackers were sliding around.

—Oh, thank you, dear, the judge's wife said, and she took his arm the way she liked to do sometimes, usually when she was telling her lady friends how well he was doing in school, how much the judge had helped him. Then she let go and he moved away, hearing her say, oh yes, Jack's quite the little helper, you know.

Sometimes Marge would talk about the son she'd lost in Korea; she'd pour herself a drink and sit down, resting her feet on the stepstool. Jack liked those times best when she'd talk slowly, her eyes a long way off, because he'd see her son before him as he saw himself, proud in a new uniform with lots of ribbons and medals. He wished she'd talk now but she was busy in the hot kitchen, and she looked tired as the men in the feed mill. Sometimes, when he lay in his bed at night, he would dream of being one of those men, almost feeling the smooth prairie, the soft cold grass he and his friend would walk through on summer nights, the sky seeming to change or cover the sound of their voices. Marge was watching him, so he grabbed the rag on the counter and started working on an old stain.

—Jack, come on now, please, we ain't going to let those people wait, are we now? No sir, Marge said. He walked into the dining room with the silverware, remembering the right order as he went along. Their voices were louder now and he heard the judge laughing, saw him waving his arms. There was a young girl he hadn't noticed before, and he sneaked looks at her as he moved around the table. She looked nice and Jack wondered if he could make friends with her. Maybe she'd like to go for a walk later on. Her feet swung a few inches from the floor and he could see the shiny spots her stockings made on her knees.

Now he felt the guests moving close around him and he tried to finish without touching them. The low voice behind him made his throat feel tight; the judge's wife had called Marge aside, but Marge was looking down and he could only hear the voices of the guests. Someone said judge, now why don't you tell us about that Legion Hall speech you made last campaign—gee, that was a humdinger! The judge led them to the table while he talked, changing a few of the words Jack remembered, maybe so it would sound even better to the others who'd heard it before. The women smelled of perfume as they came up behind the judge's wife, and the judge had his arm around the girl. She was small and her hair was bright in the low afternoon sun that came now through the window, shining the silver and the white plates. Jack thought he could maybe kiss her once the sun was down outside. He wished he could sit next to her while they were eating, but she stayed by the judge and he walked back into the kitchen.

Marge seemed angry now, and he wondered what he'd done wrong, but he was afraid to ask her. He took each tray and set it down carefully, watching the girl all the while. Why thank you, one of the women said, as she took the cranberries—Yes sir, Jack's just like one of the family, the judge said, continuing his story when he saw them all lean forward again, waiting to listen. Jack heard the words rise and fall each time the judge moved his right hand.

Dusk was coming over the fields, making the kitchen yellow and dark at the same time. Jack sat in the kitchen with Marge, and stayed quiet while she ate. She said she was sorry she'd snapped at him, and she asked him to climb up and get her some whiskey. Her hands lay on the table; Jack saw brown spots by her knuckles and looked at his own hands. The talking had died down in the other room and he heard only the sound of forks against the white plates, small creaks in the chairs. Marge told him she was tired and he knew she'd be leaving soon. After all, she told him, I got Thanksgiving dinner of my own I got to cook for my husband.

They went out together when they heard the talking begin again. Jack cleared the table while she made coffee and brought it out to the front sideboard. He washed the dishes, thinking of the girl as he worked fast and wondering what her hair would feel like up close. Maybe she would be different than those girls at school, who seemed to laugh or whisper each time he walked by them. Jack could see her sitting with the women til Marge closed the kitchen door and took off her apron. You almost done now, Marge said; just make sure you keep the booze out where they can get it. I'm going to smoke a cigarette.

Later on, he took out glasses and buckets of ice, wishing the girl could have stayed til he'd got done. The women were talking now about Christmas or their husbands, and he brought full whiskey bottles to the men in the dining room.

—Hey, boy, Mr. Toomey said, the judge said to send you into the den; guess they want some brandy. Jack smiled and thanked him; then he went back and got the best bottle down from the shelf. They were talking inside as he came close to the door of the den; he could hear a man's voice saying yeah Cliff, going to be another tight election race, maybe you better raid that orphanage again. The judge was still laughing when Jack came in and set the bottle between them.

XIX

Sharp tannery smoke drifted on the skyline down river, and he smelled the smoke as he and Rick walked outside to the car, as each smell carries longer than usual on a clear day, even in the early morning, and he'd been glad he'd come to work sober; Rick put on his sunglasses, started the engine, and took off hard, saying this ain't such a bad way to make a little extra money, you'll like it all right, and he nodded, wondering how he'd take to two jobs at once but knowing again what he'd begun to feel only in the last few days, it was time to have a house of his own where he could live easily with Connie and Laurie, settling down like other men and saving his money, maybe buying another house or some land later, some of the men who came into the bar had talked about that to Tommy, saying they'd made money that way. He sat quiet as they drove on, sometimes looking out when Rick pulled hard into corners, once seeing a child's sudden face move like deer in the Big Horns at night, thinking don't know what else I could of done with Eddie as they passed an office building and headed south onto the freeway; he heard Rick saying they ain't particular about who they hire, just so a guy knows how to work, but he was thinking of the way Connie'd taken her time til he'd got used to her again, she'd stood for a moment with her hand under her breast before coming into bed, moving slowly til he kissed her and then seeming to shudder, her stomach shifting as his hands came down, touching her til he slipped under the hard bone again, can't even think straight when she's like that, got to be careful, he thought, wondering how far Eddie'd gotten, hard telling if you didn't know how somebody was travelling.

A railroad yard stretched out below the road, and he saw the long grey line of smokestacks and factories, knowing this was the way he'd come into Milwaukee and remembering the roads he'd used to get to other towns, all these roads seeming the same in his memory and he wondered why he'd ever thought things would change as he moved on, why Eddie was heading south only to see the same scenes beginning again outside Nashville or Birmingham, and he felt as if he'd changed on the bus ride from Lexington, as if he'd been tired and cold enough then to know he'd have to hang on here, learn how to get by quick because he might not make it out of town this time, and he shivered, pressing his back against the car seat as Rick pulled into a warehouse yard.

He stood still while Rick called out to someone, watching the sun seem to hold and burn straight down the steel sides of buildings, beginning to wish he hadn't come here with Rick and shading his eyes to see the highway, hearing the voices around him only sometimes as he tried to think again of the money he'd make, the things he'd buy Connie and their children; but he felt better when the man said, Rick'll break you in the first week or so, til you get the hang of it. Cans of wax stripper were piled in the doorway next to a pickup truck and he remembered he'd worked on floors before, wondering what else they'd have him do, how tired he'd be when he got home nights, as he listened to Rick and his boss talk awhile, waiting til Rick said they should go before he signed the paper in the boss's hand.

—Is this guy all right? he asked Rick when they got back to the car.

—Yeah, but he's kind of a sneaky fucker, you got to watch him. He settled back, watching Rick cut lanes without ever slowing down, getting inside big trucks and out again quick as a match flicked from a window, Rick saying he loved the way the car shivered and broke loose when he stood on it hard—well, I been pedaling pretty damn fast over her, he said, grinning when Rick swore at him and lighting a cigarette, his legs stretched, his hand hanging out the window shaking in the wind like a rabbit's ass in a gunsight, and he remembered the dark smell of the spring ground, dirt road bent down the line and cross rails yellow as dusk when the men came home with the rabbits they'd killed, waiting for the women to cook up stew they'd eat later on with home made bread, licking the grease off their fingers and drinking coffee, he'd hear the men say the judge done these fields a whole lot of good just by himself, best shot in the county, the judge standing close to them by the fire, smiling, cocking his western black hat back on his head and tossing the rest of his coffee in the fire, as if there were plenty more where that came from, and he seemed still to smell those fields, the stacked bales by the grain elevator, even as Rick let him off, as he walked up the steps hungry for some of that stew, wondering what she'd say about the job.

Laurie was crying, and he saw Connie trying to lay out a dress pattern on the floor; sure glad you're home, she said, this baby ain't given me a moment's peace all day.

—Just got another job, I mean I didn't quit my old one but—

—Great, she said, talking loud over the crying as she picked Laurie up, you ain't hardly home now as it is.

What the hell's the matter with you, he thought, as he heard her go on, saying she hadn't got much sleep, hate it when Laurie's like this, Jack when you going to fix that back door, take her, will you—

—Jesus, one thing at a time, he said, Laurie crying louder at the sound of his voice, making his nerves jump as he went into the kitchen, he slipped the case off the lock, hearing Connie start supper behind him as he picked at the latch with a small file, the baby over her shoulder still screaming, her rattle of pans like bottles rolling and banging together, that sound mixing with Laurie's crying and making it worse, and he was glad when a spring fell into his hands, the coil split at both ends, knowing that he could leave for awhile.

He said he'd be back soon and closed the door, feeling better in the late breeze, the afternoon light moving like dark places on the sheet when Connie moved and slid along him with her wet skin, wonder if Eddie's really gone, he thought, remembering how he'd touched her and seemed to feel the veins in Eddie's hands, the smell of a hotel room three flights up the brightest street he'd ever seen and the faces of the men who'd wait outside the movie houses all night long, seeing Connie's face now, the hurt look she'd always have in her eyes those times he'd pull away from her, the sound of her voice coming back to him, it's all right if you don't want to say nothing, Jack, I understand: then he felt himself changing as he stood for awhile watching new cars come down the ramp of a truck trailer, thinking of how he and Dave used to talk about driving trucks across the country, not knowing then how a long ride in the cab shook you damn near to pieces, funny how a man could get sick of anything if he did it long enough.

After the truck drove off, he walked north half a block, hoping Laurie'd calmed down and looking at the clock as he got inside the key shop. The locksmith tried to talk him into a new lock, saying a new spring would just snap quicker because the latch was probably worn, but he thought ain't got to last but a couple of months, saying he'd just take the spring and another set of keys, remembering, as he watched the locksmith grind the keys, how he'd sharpened the judge's hunting knives on a whetstone, so the judge could skin rabbits and make it look easy when friends came around.

He took the keys, paid the man and stepped outside; then he saw someone walking ahead of him and stayed behind, knowing Al's walk; Al was singing part of a song he'd heard often on the radio, singing the same words over and over in a slow calm voice:

> Trying to make it but I'm losing time,
> I got to bring you in, you're overworking my mind

can't carry a tune in a wheelbarrow, he said to himself as he turned off, thinking he'd like to make love to her when he got home, Al would knock on the door just as he was slipping it in, she'd giggle, say we'd better answer that, then tell him in a strange voice she'd been kidding as he moved away from her; Al would stand outside for ten minutes, then go downstairs slowly as a man waiting for one last chance: he and Connie'd take a shower together before they started, or afterward, they'd rub soap on each other and she'd shift like cold water when he moved his hand under her, saying I just got to get you clean, Connie; he thought suddenly he'd take her out for dinner, she'd feel better if she got out of the house, anyways, he said aloud, I got a feeling Al's planning on coming over tonight, we ain't seen him for a few days and he's just got to spoil the peace and quiet.

He came upstairs and told her what he'd planned, and she seemed happy when she took Laurie with her to see the woman who lived below them; the spring slipped easily, but he checked the lock a few times before putting the case back on. In a few minutes Connie came up the back steps and tried the door, saying Nadine says she'll be glad to watch Laurie for awhile, I put her to sleep already, guess I better take a bath and get ready.

—Can I watch?

She smiled at him, saying I thought you wanted to go out as she walked into the bathroom, and he heard water running as he put the tools away, opening a beer so he'd drink one less at the restaurant. He'd changed into some clean clothes by the time she'd finished, and he watched her run back and forth half-dressed through the apartment, putting the food she'd made back in the refrigerator and sometimes brushing her hair with her free hand.

—Laurie should sleep for a couple of hours, I just nursed her, she said, slipping a dress over her head, sure I look all right?

She said it was nice to be going out as they crossed the street, as the sun slid down the roofs, seeming to move with them; he squeezed her hand, wishing she'd cover or hide him as they walked, as if his old days seeped in the small space between them, touching them like the wind through the trees after it's rained, but she felt strong in his hand and he wondered how much she'd guessed about him, what she'd learned on her own and planned for them. He put his arm around her and she smiled half to herself, half to the warm evening, a small breeze blowing through her hair showing her neck down to her collarbones as she told him how much trouble Laurie'd been today, the dark houses quiet as lights went on in their kitchens, showing families moving around inside, and he thought I'm glad we ain't living on the first floor as he slipped a half step behind Connie so he could watch her hips moving, looking at her smooth legs and believing only then that she'd healed.

The restaurant was dark, except for small red lights around the walls, and he had to squint to see tables and chairs. They took a corner table, the colors changing on her dress as she sat down, her skin seeming dark and warm as he listened to her talk about things they'd known together, her voice like an old tune, or grass outside a fire; the waitress brought drinks, and took their orders, and he knew he'd have to begin telling Connie what he'd done, wishing he'd left things alone as he remembered how she'd been when he'd got home, as she smoothed her hair back and stopped talking, seeming to look around the restaurant as if she were waiting for somebody. Now what about this job, honey, she asked.

Ain't much, ten hours a week, he said, I figure we can use the extra money to save up and buy some things.

—Like a car? she said, as she took one of his cigarettes; then put it back and picked up a bread roll.

—Yeah, or a house, take a long time, but we ain't doing nothing by paying rent, he said.

She smiled at him, her eyes seeming brighter than they'd ever been as he went on, telling her he'd like to learn a trade, buy a house outside the city so they could grow things in the summer, and her eyes opened wide as they'd been the first time he'd ever talked to her, maybe wondering what he would say but quiet, waiting to give him time.

He sipped his beer, thinking I should ask her now, but there'll be time to talk about that later and I ain't in no hurry, his dream coming back then, the way she'd smile as the kids played in the barnyard, as he came in to her and she let the food burn; now she ate slowly, her fingers shaking a little.

—You ain't got to worry, little bit. It's just took me a long time to make my mind up. You ain't never pushed me.

—Sometimes I have. But not about this, she said; she touched her

neck and seemed then to raise her head so she could look at him.
—I know, he said. You sure you want to go on with it?

She pressed his hand to her face, letting his fingers move down the clear skin of her neck, blinking her eyes a little but smiling back at him, saying food's getting cold and moving her fork in the beans, Jack I—

—Mind if I join you? Al said, coming over to their table and grinning down at them, and he wondered how long Al had been sitting in the restaurant, watching them and waiting, biding his time for the right moment to come over and invite himself to sit down. He looked at Al, and then at Connie, shoving his chair back a little.

—Uh, Al, most times it'd be all right but we got some things to talk over right now, she said.

—Oh okay. Well, I'll see you later, then, Al said, walking slowly back to his own table, his friends raising their voices to call the waitress over; he watched Al, then turned back to look at Connie, as if to make sure he'd really heard her tell Al to go away; she lit one of his cigarettes, half hiding her smile til he said something and then blushing, and he leaned forward in his chair, touching her wrist, saying next time Al comes over to our place, see if you can sweet talk him into letting us have his car this weekend, we'll go out and look at houses: she giggled behind her hand, looked over at Al, and nodded her head.

In the morning she told him Laurie'd been awake most of the night, I tried everything, so tired I'm about to fall over and I got to take her to the doctor today; he took Laurie and walked her til she slept, laying her down easily in her crib and feeling, as always, that she'd wake up unless he did it just right. Connie looked as if she were almost asleep when he got back into the kitchen, he sipped his coffee and she stared at hers, resting her head in her hand and yawning, and he saw her walk back toward the bedroom after he'd kissed her goodbye.

XX

Connie sat close to him in the car, sometimes moving her hand over his knee while she sang to the baby, or talking to him as he looked down the road, driving slowly to get used to Al's old car, remembering Dave's pickup and thinking he'd better be careful; Connie seemed to change when they passed an old storefront on their way out of town, staying quiet for awhile and then saying my daddy had a store once but it went out of business, he wouldn't talk to nobody for weeks: he nodded, waiting for her to go on, remembering families who'd left for Omaha or Lincoln when their farms had given out, their old cars hanging low in the rear from the trailers they pulled, broken toys jammed against chairs and trunks, and the children scared and quiet behind the car windows, as if they didn't believe the good things their parents had said about the cities, maybe even knowing their mothers were lying when they'd said we'll all be coming back soon to visit, you'll see your friends again, and he wondered if he'd know these old friends if he met them now, their faces changed as other faces he'd carried with him years after forgetting their names.

Laurie cried and fussed, and he watched Connie rock her as if from habit, shifting the baby on her shoulders, knowing only then that Connie hadn't said anything for awhile and wondering if she were thinking of her family the way he'd sometimes seen the grandmother's face moving in his memory, feeling only that last voice she'd used, the way she'd looked shoving him out the door behind the policeman, he'd lost the times before that when she must have played with him, or seen to his needs, or been kind. Connie's dark eyes were moving now as if she's been one of those children, and he seemed to feel what she'd been like as a child as he watched the land roll under the new grain, then stretch out in seed corn in brown rows like the spaces between boxcars going west, changing to sand somewhere west, though a man got so used to fields running off beside him he'd never notice the sand til he'd gone a hundred miles past Mitchell, South Dakota.

The radio scratched a little but the country station came in and she sang along with the tunes, as if to herself or only to the child, continuing as she bounced Laurie on her lap, those small feet sometimes pulling the hem of her dress, showing her legs as the blanket hid or uncovered them white as she'd be all over at sundown, the sunlight seeping from the child's face as Connie held her close, Connie's eyes fixed on the land as she swayed a little when the car went over rough spots in the road, and he remembered he'd seen her face like this nights when he'd come home drunk, felt her quiet, maybe lonely as she was now and waiting for him to talk. He drove on toward Delafield, slowing down on the rough two lane road because the car rolled badly on curves, misfired as he drove up steep hills behind trucks and wished he could throw a chain out to their trailers and get pulled along, feeling uneasy as she stayed quiet, as he watched the land rising in stands of trees thinning out toward the road, and he tried to think of Laurie running between these trees, growing up with small animals so she didn't seem strange to them, the animals telling the child scent as they stood hindfooted on half sunk rocks, the grass cracking as Laurie chased them and laughed, her little brothers maybe trailing behind her;

He said, Connie, what you thinking about?

—Nothing, just this house we're going to see; course I wish I could get this little one to sleep, she said: he looked at her, trying to figure out what to say to get her to start talking, then wondering if she felt this way when he stayed quiet, and he heard Connie going on about Laurie now, can't think what's wrong with her, most babies go right off to sleep in cars, well, must be she's wet, Connie said, pulling diapers from the bag on the floor and laying Laurie down next to him on the seat, Connie's hair falling and hiding her face as she pinned the diapers, as he felt the strange quiet of this land inside the road noise and breathing of the child, remembering the times Connie'd calmed him down and wishing he knew how to make her seem like herself again, feeling then as if it were too late and he'd lost the easy, open times she'd given him til now.

—Well, it's kind of pretty from the outside, she said, as they pulled into the yard; if you just get the buggy out, honey, I'll see to Laurie while you look around.

He went around to the back of the car and opened the trunk, losing Connie in the sun on the side chrome as she got out of the car, then looking down as he pushed the carriage and seeing roof shingles on the ground, the barn down the yard half charred from an old fire; the porch felt shaky under his feet and Connie rang the bell. A woman let them in, and Connie talked to her in that easy way she had with strangers, smiling at the woman's kids and letting the women hold Laurie while he walked around inside, the walls and floors feeling solid, probably held up by barn beams. He went upstairs and saw what he'd figured from the shingles outside, the roof leaked in at least three places and the ceilings were stained, chipped badly; in the basement, he checked the furnace, the water softener and the pipes, spending a lot of time and wishing he knew more about houses, nobody trying to sell you something is going to tell you the truth, he thought, hearing Laurie crying again as he walked upstairs, looked the kitchen over, then stood in the living room while Connie and the woman talked about diaper rash and the croup. She thanked the woman and he took the carriage down to the car, looking around once more as he closed the trunk, and then sliding in beside Connie, driving slowly back to the road

—You like it? he asked, after they'd gone about a half mile; it's built pretty solid anyway. He saw her face just before she turned away, remembering the feeling he'd had that day in the park, when she'd seemed to wonder what he wanted her to say.

—What'd you think, little bit?

She turned back then, seeing his face and smiling at him, saying well, I think it's laid out kind of funny with that little kitchen up front, be hard to clean cause there'd be so many extra steps, why that woman told me it takes her all day just to get through it; she stopped then, and asked him why he was smiling.

—Nothing, just never would of seen them things myself, he said.

—I sure couldn't look at pipes and what all like you did, she said, laughing as she held Laurie up to her breast, asking him to close the window, and he watched her settle back, closing her eyes and rocking a little in the same rhythm as the car; he wondered how she could sleep, thinking of the times he'd stayed awake on all night truck rides, watching truckers drink coffee and wash down pills while his own fingers jumped on the truck stop table and he smoked too many cigarettes, not trusting the pills, feeling sure the truck would crash if he went to sleep. He drove on, used to the car now and hating to give it back to Al, thinking sometimes about the house, don't matter about this extra job, ain't nobody going to give me a loan anyway, feeling then as if he should have waited til he had some money before telling Connie his ideas, but he was still glad they'd gone out looking.

When they got home, Connie woke up, and she carried Laurie slowly up the steps so as not to wake her: then they went into their bedroom, where the breeze came in best off the river, and lay down on the bed, feeling the afternoon sun warm in the window, the sounds from the neighborhood finally opening below them after the long winter quiet he'd never gotten used to; Connie raised her knee, as if to let the breeze come in under her legs, and she lay with her head a little higher up the bed than his, bending a little toward him when she talked.

—It's kind of scary looking at houses, she said, pressing her fingers down on the hand he'd laid on her leg; is that how come you been so quiet, he said, feeling his hand, though unmoving, shake a little on her leg as she said yeah, that and some other things I was thinking about, but then I figured ain't no sense going over things that've happened a long time ago; he listened while she went on talking, mostly about the house they'd seen, remembering all of a sudden that he had to go to work as a song about a truckdriver came on the radio, as Connie stopped talking and listened, asking him what's a 'Sweet Georgia Overdrive'?

—Just a gear, he said, not knowing himself.

—You got to go pretty soon, don't you?

He nodded, feeling her edging closer even as he turned to kiss her, rolling on his side as she touched his face, letting his hands come down over her breasts and seeming to sway then, as if calling to a slower rhythm, and she had fine hands, her skin felt slippery and his own hands were smooth against her as he came down to her, moving in the same slow rhythm and feeling then as if he'd never touched her before, as if he's waited for her in some dream and remembered who she was only now, his flesh along her flesh, the feel of her mouth and hands, her smell seeming to change or darken the rhythms which hid or uncovered him as she moved along him with her breasts, as he heard the sounds she made and moved his fingers under her dress, knowing by now the way she liked to be touched and feeling she'd move for him soon, as her mouth turned quiet and her rhythms changed, he slipped down to her and moved inside her like water and stones, kissing her hard as her hands shook or returned to his back, feeling her feet move down the back of his legs, then the hard push of her legs around him, her wet mouth, his flesh shaking like hard rain and still.

And the night seemed to come slowly, as it never does in winter, then going on like mist in the early morning, changing to darkness only after he'd mopped the floors and turned out the lights in the office building near the lake; he walked north, following the road along the lake, feeling the stillness she'd formed in his body lasting even now, after he'd worked three hours, and he remembered how she'd smiled and said I'll be waiting for you when you get home.

XXI

The other day I was making hamburgers for supper. Laurie was lying in that little seat we bought her, sort of on the kitchen table, and all of a sudden she gave out with a scream. I jumped, dropped the pancake turner behind the stove. Well, you get used to doing for yourself so I was trying to move that stove, and Jack come in from work; he got real mad at me, he says you ain't got to do them things now, you got to be careful, ain't you got no sense? So he takes and puts his arms round that stove and picks the whole thing up so I can get the pancake turner, and this little mouse runs out and he jumps like he's scared half to death, not like he's just surprised. He starts going on about me lifting things again and I go, oh, Jack don't be silly and he yells no, I don't want nothing happening to you, you do what I tell you, hear? Then I see he's real serious and I'm acting just dumb, is all, so I tell him I'm sorry, and feed him; seems he ain't hardly sat down before he's got to get up and go to work again.

I got to thinking then; he's so quiet and you got to watch for them little things, you wouldn't ever think he'd be scared of mice, course he ain't very big and you wouldn't of thought he could shove that stove either by himself. I really jabber some time, I believe I've told him about everything that's ever happened to me, like I done with Bill, but Bill just got bored. Jack, he listens though, but it's funny, it's like he's never heard of anything like I'm telling him, and there sure ain't nothing spectacular in any of it.

He don't talk though. I try to get him to sometimes and he says, oh there ain't nothing much to tell, and just laughs, his face gets real serious though—it's like he's been in jail or something, he should know I wouldn't care even if he would of been. I can feel him getting scared sometimes when we're just out walking. He's real gentle with us and all but it don't seem like there was anything gentle in his past.

Like with this job; I go, you ain't got to do this, honey, I'm happy just being here and he says no, don't want Laurie growing up down here. He ain't drinking like he used to either, I didn't think you'd ever get a man to change but he says he done it for me, he ain't got time for that drinking now.

Course it takes a long time to get to know a man, and I sure did guess wrong on Bill. Bill wouldn't of done nothing for me. Thing I'm waiting for now, I almost got so I like it, even when I'm lonesome, is it's kind of nice to have Jack coming home twice in one day, he's so tired he's real settled by the time he comes in, tonight I'm just going to start kissing him soon as he gets in that door.

XXII

The landlord's car drove away from the house just as he was coming home from work, so he slowed down til the car had rounded a corner: Connie was still giggling from fear or relief when he got upstairs, telling him she'd heard the landlord talking to Nadine downstairs in the hallway, good thing you ain't got many clothes, Jack, Connie said, cause I ran around like crazy throwing your stuff in drawers.

—What's that sonofabitch want? We already mailed him the rent, he said, wondering if the landlord would call the cops, make them leave if he found out Connie were living here with a man, and he heard Connie say, nothing, I guess, just wanted to snoop around is all, hey you got any money, can we go to the store, feeling her close to him, then dark and quiet as if she'd really been scared, but seeming calm as she picked up Laurie and they all went downstairs; she pushed the carriage, saying she hoped the rain would hold off, and he walked next to her, feeling they'd be all right as long as the landlord didn't get the cops into it, thinking he should ask Al for the car again this weekend and look around in the meantime for a way to get a loan, as he heard Connie tell him Laurie'd hung on to her rattle for the first time today, course she dropped it in a couple seconds but still, that's pretty good.

When they got inside the store, he put Laurie in the shopping cart and Connie pushed it slowly through the aisles, checking the prices on all the goods and asking him to get the meat, and as he leaned over the meat counter, glancing from that angle at the mirror above him, Laurie seemed to be standing up, and he looked again, knowing only then that she'd grown, as if he'd thought she'd always fit in the crook of Connie's arm—she's going to be grabbing everything now, your easy days are over, he said, smiling at Connie poking her elbow—Oh Jack, grabbing a rattle and dropping it right away don't mean nothing, she said, pushing the cart into the line, then making some joke about the way he was staring at the checkout girl, shaking her head when he pretended he hadn't noticed, but squeezing his arm as they walked out of the store.

They'd got halfway home when it started to rain, he took his jacket off and laid it over the carriage and they ran, hearing Laurie begin to cry as the rain came down hard, Connie seeming scared, talking to the baby while he pushed the carriage and then picking her up when she saw the lightning, holding her close to her breast and running past the last few houses as the rain opened around them, as he came behind with the carriage and felt the sound of Laurie's screaming come into his body and move slowly down his spine; Connie was inside holding the baby, trying to calm her down and crying herself, so he wrapped a towel around them and told Connie to sit down, getting dry clothes for her and Laurie while the crying went on and seemed to mix with the rain outside like the sound of men or horses caught in a flooding river, he'd heard stories from the old men in Sidney long ago and seemed to see now the wide nostrils of the horses, their swollen eyes, and the faces of the men who'd slipped under the water a few times already, hearing the thunder above the house as he held Connie, as she shivered as she always did during storms, listening more to the crying than to the things he was saying to calm her down, as if the crying changed everything to lies and he'd somehow been removed from Connie and the baby, Connie maybe not believing he knew what she'd felt in the rain, though he'd been with her the whole time.

When Laurie stopped, he felt as if he'd gotten his voice back in the quiet, taking the baby then and saying you better get out of them wet clothes, Connie, still feeling shaky himself as he talked and laughed with Laurie, as if he and Connie'd both seen how helpless Laurie was, and had felt helpless themselves, Connie's face in that rain the same as it had been the night she'd had the fever, but changing now as she finished dressing, looking down in his lap and seeming to know only then that Laurie was fine; he looked outside as he changed clothes, the sewers backing up, filling the streets with water, and he heard Connie soothing the baby as she changed her into dry clothes:

sometimes, when he'd watch Connie feeding or changing or playing with her baby, he'd wonder who'd done those things for him; he leaned against the window, still watching them, hearing someone in the hallway and knowing it was Al even before he opened the door.

—Mind if I come in, man, Jesus, it's wet out there, Al said, standing in the light, the rain still running from his long hair, least it ain't the landlord, he thought, seeing Connie look at him before she waved Al in and trying to be friendly himself as he remembered they'd need Al's car again soon; we got wet too, he said, you want a beer?

—Maybe some coffee? Connie said.

Al said, I'd rather have coffee, so he opened a beer for himself and put the hot water on, sensing Connie's eyes on him when he walked back into the room, losing at last the feeling that she'd take up with Al anytime she had the chance, remembering how he'd fought with her about Al but knowing now she'd never have held Al close as a woman holds her dream of a child and a man; Connie'd opened and moved toward him, not Al, she'd lain down next to him and lasted through the bad nights, seeming to take the way he'd felt inside her, as if she'd known even then he had to let the old days run out first; Al's voice continued through dinner, and he wondered how any man could talk so much about himself as he half listened, half watched the rain beginning to slacken outside, the air cool now and coming in a draft through the windows, he closed them so Laurie wouldn't catch cold.

Al stayed long enough to drink two beers and to talk about people not understanding each other, did we really understand Eddie, man, Al said, I mean really, and he thought Eddie'd probably be all right long as the weather stayed warm, since Eddie'd gone down to a friend in New Orleans, though he'd thought Eddie'd been lying then about that friend; then he asked Al about the car, and Al said he had to go out of town this weekend. They talked for awhile and Al left, he read the paper while Connie finished up in the kitchen, wondering if he'd be better off buying a car, even an old one, they could go for rides and get out of the house more often; he set Laurie on the floor and watched while she kicked her feet, Laurie smiling as if she knew him, used to the sound of his voice and the feel of his hands, easier for him to calm down now than she'd ever been and he'd begun to feel less and less as if she were another man's child. He watched Connie while she nursed her baby, sometimes tickling Laurie's feet or touching her soft back skin, then watching her sleep for a few minutes after Connie'd put her down.

Later on, after they'd made love, Connie talked to him, saying she loved him, her fingers moving across him, her voice seeming to call to each late sound in the streets outside, the cats or dogs, the people talking loud as they walked by after the bar had closed, and he lay with his arm around her, sometimes feeling the old shapes of the running time beginning again in the stillness, most times forgetting everything he'd known before he'd met this woman, she'd changed and lasted with him longer than he'd ever believed she would; he let the night go down easily, feeling in the morning as if he'd gotten some sleep for a change.

But even the first few hours working were wet and hot, the sun grey, the sidewalks bright as they'd always be after you'd been drinking in the afternoon, knowing you'd better go on drinking or you'd pass out the first time you sat down; when they sat in the cab that afternoon, Rick told him the next job was way out on the west side and asked him if he'd need a ride, Rick swearing at the boss and saying bastard's got his goddam nerve, I worked that place last year and it's a bitch.

He and Rick stopped at the bar together, and when he got home he was tight, but Connie just laughed at him and said Nadine came up earlier and asked if we'd like to come down for barbecue chicken, that is if you ain't too sick to eat; he tried to slap her on the ass but she moved away too quickly, he felt the late sun come in the windows and seemed to see her naked each time she passed, as he took Laurie and felt her squirming on his lap as she grabbed for his shirt buttons; sort of figured you'd be mad, he said.

—Not when you're home, I know you working two jobs and you got to get a little drunk sometimes, she said, taking Laurie to the sink to give her a bath as he got up and walked to the window and looked out at the neighborhood, the shapes of the old houses making him think of the time he'd passed through Philadelphia, seeing junk cars all over the streets, people stripping them down in broad daylight, some of them sitting on the curb and passing a bottle to each other, or to the man working on the car, and he'd been glad he wasn't staying, though Baltimore and Lexington hadn't been much better, he'd always felt he'd get rolled in Baltimore and one night two men dragged him into an alley, taking his first month's paycheck and knocking out two of his back teeth.

After Connie'd finished, they took Laurie downstairs, and he met Nadine's boyfriend Ray, who talked mostly about the job his old man had gotten him at American Motors while they waited for the chicken, the two women talking, holding each other's babies and taking turns cooking as he and Ray started working on a case of beer. They sat at the table when the food was done, Laurie and the other baby sitting on their mother's laps, too young still to knock food or beer bottles off the table, and the air seemed hot and yellow as the late sun as he went on drinking and watched Nadine moving around in her tight green shorts, she was heavier than Connie, and taller, but he almost thought he'd like to sneak downstairs and pay her a visit some time. Ray got drunk soon, staring off across the street, his cheek muscles moving as he turned tense and quiet, and he saw something coming in the way Ray was looking at Nadine.

They started arguing, so he and Connie took Laurie and went upstairs, Connie telling him that Ray had beaten Nadine up a few times, and he sat next to her on the couch while she nursed Laurie, listening to her as she told him other things about Nadine. Then Connie paid the bills, after Laurie was asleep, and he drank the last of his beer and tried to read one of the books Al had left by mistake, but he gave up after a few minutes and told Connie he was going to bed: he lay down, feeling his stomach clench like a fist when Laurie cried out just as Connie was coming into the room, the buttons on her blouse already loose.

XXIII

It seemed to him then as if he'd worked all night and the dawn should be coming up now, but it was only eleven and he looked around as he came in the house, feeling overtired, restless, as if he needed some time off before he could sleep.

He'd cashed his paychecks earlier, they'd eaten fast to get down to the bank over lunch, and he set the bills and change on the table for Connie to sort out next morning, they could maybe talk about how to save a little extra: she was sleeping, turning over as he made a noise in the room, the light falling then on her face as he wondered how she could trust him, how he knew that she did, Laurie's breathing always the same, deep and unmoving, as if she'd just nursed and gone down, maybe growing even now as he looked at her, touched her hair and remembered the first time he'd seen her, the way Connie'd walked, how she'd hurt more later when she'd had to watch Laurie cry for food,

—You just get in, Connie said, her voice thick as she took his hand, kissing it as he bent close to her hair, saying I got to wash up but I'll be right in to bed;

—I'll stay up til you do, she said;

he walked into the bathroom, rubbed soap on his hands, shivering as his sweat cooled stiff under his shirt, feeling the small ache of his nerves close to his skin as he watched the water run for awhile, the house seeming then like his own worthless quiet, he was always hiding no matter what she'd say, no matter how many times she'd prove him wrong; the light fell again when he opened the door, seeing her, thinking he'd better not wake her up again and wishing she'd sit up, come outside with him somewhere til he calmed down. He bent over and she turned, kissing him back as she slept.

The night air made him shiver and he fingered the money, not wanting to start this again but feeling as if a few drinks might help him just this once, the wind strong and wet as it'd been those first few days of spring, when Connie'd come home and he'd moved in with her, she'd taken him then as if she'd known and wanted him from the beginning, as if she'd seen how he needed her, and he felt the rhythm of her sleep close and quiet around him even as he walked, wishing now he'd lain down with her instead of going out for a drink, the night dark, quiet, like the few minutes before a fight when everything slows down and even the first swing seems to hold for a long time in the air—the way those men in Chicago had done for him without making a sound, almost unmoving til he'd come by and they'd jumped him; the cold air hit him as he got inside the bar, knowing Eddie was gone but looking around for him anyway, almost feeling one of these men would turn around, call to him with the voice Eddie used when he was ready to talk:

he'd learned their names by listening, the way he'd done in Baltimore, learned and watched the sound of their voices seeming the same no matter where he'd been, the strangeness going as he slowly learned about these men, as Tommy'd been doing for twenty years, never setting up anyone til he knew for sure what that man was drinking, and he wondered again why he'd come down to sit in this cold light when he should be home with Connie, waiting for sleep in the still feel of her face against his skin, remembering how the warmth of the bar in the winter time lasted almost all the way home, time now for the men to begin setting down their glasses and turn slowly, as if they hated the thought of getting back home, each one wanting to leave last, though they'd argue with each other night after night, these men, acting like friends only sometimes while their women waited at home, the old feeling coming on him quiet and still as he watched them circle around another man's woman, hoping she'd make a move so they could talk next day like the driver did after a bad night's drinking.

The woman shook her ass in the chair, waiting herself as she watched them gather around her, flashing the rings on her hand like a miner looking to spend his first paycheck in town; she looked at him and smiled, showing her bad teeth, and he remembered she'd come in with these men and got treated almost the same til everybody'd been drinking long enough to know she was waiting for something better than just her old man coming to get her—Connie's waiting for me, she'll move close when I come into bed, hold me while she sleeps ain't no reason to be out here, he thought, drinking faster, the mist falling outside as the lights changed like a man's eyes showing things too late, knowing then why Eddie'd maybe been running, thinking wonder how long it's going to be before I feel like these men and ain't in no hurry to get home—the woman was dancing now, seeming to look at him each time she moved, her skirt pulling tight as she swayed and rocked, sipping a drink with her free hand each time she passed her table, the men looking on the way Eddie'd watched him and Connie come into the bar the first time, as he'd wanted the women in other bars to shake it for him, sit down so close there'd be no time or reason for talking, just get someplace quick—these men kept quiet now, taking turns to get next to her: he started drinking shots with his beers, drifting as in half sleep, as in early morning, when the dawn seemed to drain down in the smoky sky as he'd wait for the sun to get up high as their window, come in and show him Connie's face, as he saw this woman in the mirror, losing her quick in the other faces and wondering where she'd gone, light in his eyes and the way his legs felt telling him how drunk he was as he grinned at the woman and she saw him, pulled her skirt up to sit down;

drifting, shivering in the night as he tried walking and seemed to feel the city come inside him, the wet streets close in on him, can't get home without a ride, he thought, feeling the run of his crazy dreams as he hung on a mailbox, then a few lines from the tune he'd heard that night at Al's, when Connie'd been in the hospital, and he just got by long enough to climb in the cab of a truck and go on, drifting, almost hearing what the truck driver said as he shivered, leaned back, felt the road moving out a long way past their home, out to Nebraska in long smooth lines like the plains before the harvest, then the haystacks bright in the sun like white stones in a creek, each town holding one light on all night long in case somebody came passing through;

sometimes if you looked close on a clear night you'd see those lights from way off and remember how the towns looked, how a man could feel hidden for days, as if he'd only moved in his dreams, soft yellow grass cracking as he seemed to walk again, hearing crickets, and small animals looking for food, blinking as the moon ran white off the low sides of hills in the sand country, near Valentine, the sky drifting and changing as the stars moved, as he'd watched them sometimes to fall asleep by a roadside, hearing truck tires whine and moan, whine on, then quiet and drifting as night hawks, drifting

he felt the hard springs rumble over split concrete as the lights hit him, the trucker laughing, saying I reckon you need some coffee, boy, I sure got to have some to keep on tonight:

—Yeah, I'd like that fine, he said, looking around and feeling strange as the trucker said how far you going, we been making damn good time, why we'll make Minnesota inside of two hours.

XXIV

The high semaphore dimmed, almost moving in the night. Boxcars seemed to contain the fog close to the ground, though Jack could see it rising in the streetlight, changing the shapes in the freightyard. He knew tank cars were being pushed into the siding by the refinery, but he saw only the cab of the switch engine. On the wet rails, the steel wheels of the cars moved easily, quietly. Jack missed the smell of diesel oil and jimson weed, the sounds of the highway a mile off. The feed company sign, under the streetlight, drizzled like dark rain down the side of the building.

Last summer, before he'd had to go back to school, he and Dave had come here often. They'd drink the pints Dave would steal, or talk about hopping freights out of Kearney. Now, in the strange, shifting quiet of the freightyard, he almost believed he'd come to a new town, or returned to an old one, maybe Sidney. Jack moved his hand over the split tire facing of the warehouse dock, liking the fog and the stillness. The closed night held him, then seemed to open out as he remembered stories he'd heard about small town women who hung around truck stops or rail diners. He lit a cigarette and wondered what was keeping Dave.

The smooth face of the judge showed sometimes in the fog, almost like the headlights of a stalled car. Jack shook his head and looked down. It was past time to leave Kearney. Far off, church bells rang out of tune, then marked the hour.

When Dave called out, Jack didn't see him at first, because he'd thought Dave would be coming from behind the warehouse. But he heard noises over by the tie piling, and then he saw the streetlight shining on Dave's wet black hair. Come on, Dave said, got to steal me a rotor off somebody.

Jack slipped down from the dock, and followed, wondering why Dave seemed jumpy. They'd stripped cars together many times. When they got back into town, they found an old Plymouth, and Dave quietly opened the hood. The night had turned cold and Jack shivered as he waited for Dave to finish. Fucking distributor cap won't go back on, Dave whispered; leave it, he said, here comes somebody. Their shoes slapped loudly on the wet street as they ran, Jack could smell liquor on Dave's breath and he was afraid. Later, after they'd hid in an alley and checked the street a few times, he said, why the hell you stealing parts for your old man's car?

—Listen, Dave said, don't make no difference if you ain't eighteen yet, I can't stand this shit no more; I'm leaving tonight in my old man's car—you coming?

Jack looked at his friend, knowing they'd be caught before they'd gone ten miles, they'd be sent up for sure this time. Everything going to be great, just you and me and lots of women, Dave was saying, but Jack did not believe him. He remembered only that nothing had changed much since he'd had to leave the grandmother. I don't know, he said, I got to think about this, we was planning to leave next month.

They argued for awhile, Dave telling Jack they could ditch the car if they needed to, Jack saying I never want to see this fucking town again once I leave, can't see getting dragged back. They stopped in an all night cafe for coffee, and Dave took the rotor out of his pocket and rolled it around in his hands. Look, Dave said, seeing as how you got to think it over, I got to get the car anyway, give me an answer when I get back.

—Okay, Jack said, but watch that goddam bridge on your way back. He walked to the door with Dave, then watched him run up the street til he lost him in the fog. It was too bright in the cafe, and the waitress looked tired as she cleaned the spoons. Jack sat down, sipped his coffee and tried to think. One of the letters in the neon window sign sputtered, then went out.

XXV

The hills changed in the sun, almost moving as he stood on the wayside grass, feeling trucks go down the line, the sound of Connie's voice coming back to him in the smell of grass, the hot feel of the early wind, the gentle rolling land; she'd get up with Laurie and see the empty bed, walk all around the house holding the child close, remembering he'd told her he was coming to her in a little while, the child crying then without knowing why her mother's body shook: Connie'd be waiting, hoping maybe he'd just gone to Al's and passed out.

He'd been feeling now the way he'd slept on the ground, unmoving through the early dawn since the trucker'd left him, knowing then the sharp air running on the empty land, cars rolling and the steady whine of trucks taking him down in dreams of women he'd believed he'd find, as if he'd begin again each time he moved on, like roots under the plains til the snow melted off, remembering nothing but one highway or spring or fall. This morning he wouldn't hear the child and Connie came back to him as a winter nights stays on inside even after you've found a place to sleep, the way she'd feel when she'd finally know he was gone for good, and she'd have to raise Laurie alone; but he'd walk east down the highway, tell her he'd gotten too drunk to make it home and ended up just this side of the Minnesota border, knowing then he'd made some choice by leaving and he'd just be going again soon if he went back now, though he'd wished she could hold him all that time they'd been together.

He moved now away from the sun, hoping he'd get a ride to the next town before the state cops came by, his body aching as he felt the land wide as the plains, yet mostly hidden from his eyes in the small hills seeming to empty into him as if they'd been waiting to roll down like the quick slide of river mud during a hard rain, rising with the water til the sun rose again, the way Connie'd lie next to him or he'd feel her smooth back against his chest, remembering how he'd known she was strange to him as she moved under him the first few times, as he'd tense up each time he'd felt himself sinking, wanting to be held more but afraid til he'd lie behind her, kissing her back and shoulder while she sang softly, or said she loved him, never been like this with any man, ain't you always known how I can't even talk when you come close to me? He'd smiled and turned, feeling how easy she could take him, keep him close as she kept the child, her voice closing soft around them as her body always felt in his hands, her face pale now as if lit by a streetlight, and he walked even farther down the road, not wanting to ride or go anywhere.

Bells rang, making his head hurt as he closed the door of the cafe; he ordered coffee and sat down, thinking of the beginning when he'd gone to a bar to get off the cold street, sipping beer then while the men watched him, feeling glad for the money he carried but hoping he'd be inside before night fall, before other hungry men came up to smell a stranger wandering around in the wrong places: these men looked him over as quiet men will in a small town, only moving their eyes across to each other as if they didn't need to speak, they'd be watching, a man could be hunted out just as quick up here as on the plains, they'd only have to wait til he gave out or moved into sight, as he'd moved low that night with buckshot whistling behind him, scaring out the animals and almost falling sometimes:

he seemed to feel then the open empty plains lying west of him, the slow beat of the sun as he'd walk off lost in the high range grass, the waitress here and the others, the men drinking coffee slowly and mopping up their eggs falling behind him like Lexington, St. Louis, Milwaukee, like the small rise and fall of Connie's breasts when she slept, her mouth open a little as if to take him inside if he'd only move, hold himself back from the plains falling north and south of the highway, and he heard them talking around him now, kidding the waitress by her first name, her face sometimes as Connie's would be in a rainy afternoon light, easy or scared in the same way that turned his muscles inside as a long fever turns a man weak and reaching; he gave her the money and went out, hearing the voices behind him and a few cars rubbing over the street as if they were trying to sand it down.

He walked around killing time, remembering how he'd thought a town this size was a city til he'd come east, wishing now he'd never gone running from the land but knowing again how the judge had kept pushing him til there'd been no chance of staying, where everybody'd seemed to know all about him and he'd felt himself grow scarce as trees, bent over and turned back no matter what he did, seeing now those faces he'd thought once he'd forgotten as he sat down thirsty and hung over worse from the coffee, wanting to keep on even as Connie seemed to move beside him, asking why with her strange eyes, seeming to look through him or back through the other side of his body, her hands reaching as if to clutch him, as if she'd believed all along he had something to give her: he saw birds cutting over the slow open streets and lawns, flying faster than city birds, seeming to glide without moving in the late May sun as he walked, feeling the cool shade trees, the smell of chicken turned on open spits; he fingered the money in his pocket, almost worried til he remembered he'd left Nebraska with two dollars and a pack of cigarettes, getting inside Chicago with spare change—he'd hung on with one day jobs til he could leave again, do worse in New York—

they'd been watching him, yelling words he couldn't pick up as he looked over, thinking of the boys in west Texas, or Rick, they were sitting around the gas station, their motorcycles shining together like the white lights in Connie's hair, the sun showing blue around their faces as they seemed to be coming for him with chains, knives in their strong hands, talking loud and pointing; he crossed the street and walked fast, running when he got past the corner and cutting behind cars and houses, trying to see them over his shoulder til he knew they'd stayed back, they'd have got him by now if they'd wanted him. He sat down on a park bench and held his head in the sun, almost dreaming of this town, La Crosse, and the

plains on the other side of the Mississippi, the grain beginning to swell
and push through the soil, rising and drying in the sun as it'd rise uneven
in the fields on this side, til the harvest, leaves would burn in piles on
early fall nights when you'd first see your breath, feel your eyes water til
you'd got used to the smoke waving in and out like fall trees in the mist
and making the mist darker as it rose, as he'd smell it clean and dry,
burning straight up, his eyes clearing as he'd rake on more leaves, feel
the warm fire under his hands:

years ago he'd sat with the grandmother on her porch while a house
burned down the street, asking her please let me go see as he smelled the
hot smoke and heard the wood crack and fall; she'd started coughing and
led him inside where he'd watched from the window, almost feeling the
fire touch the glass and slip through around him, good thin smoke drifting
like cooking smells from the big iron stove—he'd heard the screams of a
woman then, the bright flames seeming to follow someone he could almost
see running from the house, the sky red and white covering the town and
closing in like a sandstorm; the grandmother'd pulled him away and sent
him upstairs, and he'd heard later the woman had died on the grass:

now he wondered how that woman had saved her children, maybe
carrying them out one by one but not getting out quick enough that last
time, the child, safe, running from his mother's screams, the strange
smell of that night moving back now in the sun as he remembered Connie
and the child, the steep wooden steps she'd be coming down alone with the
child in her arms, trying to drag the carriage behind her, maybe still not
believing he'd gone from her, and he felt his own breath catch, tried to
stop the smile coming to his lips, the shaking in his face as he shut his
eyes tight, feeling Nebraska come into him like waking from a three day
drunk, he'd been crazy to come out here, to sit back quiet as each day
moved along itself and back on nothing but a day's work and the still land
holding in the sun, remembering how he'd thought time spent with a
woman could change everything, even men like the judge and the wide
plainsland turning to sand or hills he'd see after all this time, after
moving east to find women or a better way to make a living or go on
living, can't travel with a woman and child, but you shouldn't have to, he
thought—he knew he'd better start drinking, get some food in him, so he
walked back downtown to a bar, knowing he'd remember her again later
on but trying not to think as he watched a baseball game on television,
the men seeming friendly, calm as they talked or made bets, second
guessed umpires or managers;

they'd live up here or he'd find someone else to get along with, there'd
be time to settle down or keep on moving, Eddie'd been wrong, just hadn't
quit soon enough, he thought, staying, drinking for awhile and getting
out, feeling good inside as the sun moved over him, he'd come out here to
cross the river, the bridge over the river far over the town always like the
sun crossing behind him; he got up to the bridge, looked down from the
rail, feeling the water move a long way south, a man would float down
easy as a long train ride, though the river let you look south, or north, and
remember, see yourself the day before up on the waterline, rolling on
down; the wet air felt good and fresh as he stood high, the wind drifting
around him til he felt close in his chest, she'd be waiting to find someone

else now, he turned, almost going back to her as he wondered how she'd
be with another man, using her fingers on his body and lying quiet as
she'd always done, taking a stranger into her before he'd hardly been
gone, someone who'd stay longer, maybe love her and Laurie better than
he or the boy had; he knew now what she'd say if he went home, how she'd
feel later getting over her tears:

and he stood on the south side of the bridge for a long time, feeling
easier as he watched the Mississippi slap the banks, run deep in the still
channels down river and seem to slip like a woman around the islands
where a man might fish for a few days, though the water was dark, almost
red in the sunlight, changing from rivers he remembered, the taste of
fresh fish skillet fried, the few times he'd had it; he crossed the road then
and waited for a ride, knowing nobody'd be crazy enough to stop on a
bridge but still not moving til he felt the sun low on his face, the
afternoon beginning to go down as he reached the other side and tried
again, not thinking, only waiting quiet and tense as he sat close to the car
door while the man drove fast, breathing heavy from his liquor and losing
rubber on each curve, each grade seeming the last one they'd make as
each curve seemed worse, and he shut his eyes sometimes, wishing he
could jump out or stop the car, the man looking at him, laughing as he hit
the shoulder and cut the wheels hard to get back on the road, saying take
it easy, we'll make it, in a thick voice dying out in the road noise, the
gravel, wind blowing like a siren and shaking the car; the man's hands
were sweaty on the wheel but he drove on faster than Rick ever would on
a road like this, the hard sound of tires whining worse than a hound
caught in barbed wire, the sky getting black off to the west;

the rain started hard as they drove under the clouds, the car shaking
worse on the slick road as he tried to read the signs, prayed for a town to
come up soon, thinking goddam drunk's bound to get me killed as they slid
fast into a bad curve, fishtailing, sprayed gravel and clang of a lost
hubcap wheeling off somewhere—

he screamed at the man slow down or I'll kill you you crazy
sonofabitch, then he saw the man's eyes as the man pulled over and
stopped quick, skidding, throwing him into the windshield. He got out
swearing, standing in the hard rain saying I'll be damned if I'll get in
anything that ain't a truck again no matter how long it takes, the rain
making him cold and empty, wishing Connie'd be there to take him in.

XXVI

Now this last truck moved off south and he was worse than cold standing by the side of the road; he'd got soaked last night and woken up half frozen in some Minnesota field, carried the chill all day long and tonight, got to get inside somewhere, he thought, almost feeling then the slow way Connie'd move after she'd had a bath, turning, seeing her now as he'd seen Minnesota towns last night, sometimes changing the sky as if the dawn were coming;

out here, he'd watched one light way off out the right window of the high cab, the light seeming after awhile like many towns all over the dark plains, though he'd known even then there were no towns or people but he'd made believe, maybe dreaming because he was tired, Connie moving too in his dreams til he'd almost felt she was in another room, waiting for him with hot coffee, a shot of brandy maybe to stop the shivering, the light burning now like the moon out their window on clear nights, a town a mile or so off, and the clear silent sky made him afraid as he'd been in cities when he'd heard only his own footsteps, the small clicks of traffic lights, maybe the breathing of a man who'd gotten to a doorway first; he remembered and felt cold inside, dreams or memories coming back in his chest as he saw them running off the wide, dry fields between towns thirty, fifty miles off:

I can't go back, she ain't ever going to take me in again after this, he thought, knowing then there was nothing out here, no one in South Dakota he'd ever known, though he'd been up here years before and knew this whistle stop by name, Presho, maybe there's a switchman's shanty I might break into, these words sounding strange as if he'd never spoken in the quiet air, she'd make it all right, ain't nothing to worry about but how to get on back to her, he thought, wondering how he'd got so far away, how he'd ever got along before he'd known her, drifting, trying to make up his mind about staying in one place, then going on to someplace else he'd never seen, never thinking twice or caring, never before having someone to remember, she'd be back there even after he'd forgotten what she'd been like, he'd maybe think someday he'd only made her up, her baby and her fine hands, the way her legs sloped down smooth from her body where he'd first known the child, first seen things in her eyes and been scared; he almost turned to go back the way he'd come, til he seemed to see her eyes or hands out before him and he shivered, remembered how he'd once thought a man didn't need reasons, he'd always just know when it was time to get going again—

he turned, seeing another light unmoving off to the north and then moving, as he heard the clanking wheels over rail joints far off, coming

106

closer, and he saw himself as he'd been on his first trip east, lying close on a flat bed, looking out a boxcar door that morning, the train light circling now toward the center as all the prairies seemed to roll down into the train. He stopped walking; then he felt he might be losing time as he watched the train coming, thinking if I run now, if I make it across I was bound to go on, but I'll go back if I see the train coming and I stop this side of the tracks, he ran, losing the fields in the light, losing the sound of his own voice

in the strip of night he saw the dawn, saw himself running and the train, and truck lights clipping the deep side of the highway, wind blowing up around him in the moonlight as he felt the dark small animals, rabbits or ground squirrels come down from the loud noise on the ballast and ties, the rail bed getting light now as all the cities he'd lived in seemed to stretch out over the plains behind him, come inside him like a flash flood, mud and slipping land moving the way faces move in a river at night, he was returning to Connie, or going farther west, feeling the train would choose for him as he came on, knowing now he wanted to go back to Connie but running hard anyway, breathing out her name as his foot slipped on the rail, as the light bore down on him, not making it

PART III

PART III

Well, when I don't see him that first morning I just go down to get the mail like always, thinking maybe you boys got too drunk for him to get home and he'll be by later, tell me he's sorry or something; there wasn't nothing in the mailbox so I go back up and Lord here's all this money on the table and a little note saying how we got to save more money this month and couldn't I figure a way? I kind of laugh to myself then, I guess I made some joke to Laurie about her daddy making good resolutions and feeling so proud he's got to go celebrate right away, and I don't think no more about it til he still ain't back the next day. Why don't you sit down? You want some coffee or something? You look like you ain't eating right, you know that?

Al said he would just like coffee. There were dirty dishes in the sink and he could smell them; he seemed to be aware of every small noise she made in the kitchen. If only it weren't so hot, he thought, if only I'd gotten some sleep. Her housecoat stopped at her knees and he looked at her when she bent down or leaned over to wipe off the counter. Connie said it was hot and pulled at the housecoat just above her breasts. He sighed, lit a cigarette, and looked down into his coffee.

—So what you going to be doing this summer, Al? Got a job?

—No, he said, exhaling before he continued. I think I'll go to summer school. Up in Madison.

—Oh, she said. She sat down at the table across from him. He hoped she was disappointed.

Sometimes I walk Laurie across the North Avenue bridge, over to that park where Jack and me went once. She's a good baby most times, she don't cry much, but I got to take her out during these hot days or there's no getting her to calm down. Jack used to just pick her up and kind of whisper in her ear when she'd fuss, quiet her down right away. That don't work for me, though, so I go for walks, which I like anyways cause it's a pretty time of the year. When I get to the park there's usually mothers there with their babies, and sometimes we sit around and talk. You can learn lots of little things that way, like what to do when your baby gets gas or you can't get her to go to sleep. They're all different; some of them get colic and others you can't seem to get any food in them. You get to thinking sometimes nobody but you has any trouble, so you feel better hearing about other kids.

Course you get a bunch of women together and they're bound to start talking about their husbands. Sometimes they talk about in bed, which is pretty funny, except I try not to laugh. I just talk like I still got Jack with me, don't pay to let nobody know your business. I think Nadine knows all right, but she don't say nothing about it. Funny, my parents ain't ever seen Laurie, they don't even know if she's a boy or a girl. I used to feel bad about that, but I come to think there ain't nothing I can do about it if they don't want to listen. They seemed to change after they found out about how I was pregnant, or maybe they think I done something to make Bill leave, they weren't so bad when they thought he was going to marry me. But I been thinking about them a lot lately, since Jack's been gone I got to do something about money, what he left me's almost run out. And I can't ask anybody about it, sure don't want to go back down the Welfare Department again. Anyway, sometimes when me and the other girls are talking like this I get the strongest feeling Jack's going to be home when I get there and I can't hardly stand how slow I'm walking with that buggy, it seems to take so long to get back.

Some nights, he used to come into bed after working late and I'd play like I was asleep, just to see what he'd do. First few times I couldn't do it cause I'd start giggling but later on I got so I could lay still long as I wasn't facing him; he'd whisper Connie, Connie and pull my hair and poke me, all the time laughing real soft, like from way back in his throat—then he'd run his hand over my bottom a few times til I couldn't stand it, I'd turn around and he'd be laughing at me. Wished I'd of woke up that last night, I can't hardly remember him coming in to talk to me.

Now, when it's real late at night and I can't sleep, I look out and the moon's way over across the river, so bright you'd think it was headlights, maybe he's going to pull up in front of the house in a new car, maybe he'll be walking, I can always see men walking down there under my windows, hear their footsteps for a long time after they're gone. Jack could of told me he was going and I would of minded a little but I know a man's got to get off by himself sometimes, think things over and get his mind clear. I used to get the feeling toward the end there he was trying to get it straight whether he wanted us to get married. But most nights I sleep all right as long as nothing wakes me up, like a storm, or this same dream I been having over and over, makes me so cold I got to put on a nightgown when I get up, drink something to calm myself down:

there's a carnival, bigger than any one I ever seen, can't seem to get to the end of it and the music don't fit with the way the rides are going, all the blinking lights are on, the sun's so hot I'm dizzy, like I just got sick on a ride; all of a sudden, there's Jack standing by the penny arcade, I yell at him but he don't hear me, he looks back though, like I'm someone he can't place, his lips are moving. Then I just lie there scared to death, knowing I'll never get back to sleep; oh, I guess I might drop off later on, but by then Laurie's getting up.

There ain't no way of stopping that dream from coming back, I'm used to having him around and I guess I think about him too much. You ain't going to mind sitting home with a baby when there's somebody coming soon to talk to you, but now I ain't got nothing else to do but think about him, I still keep waiting for him every night til I remember he's gone. I think Laurie misses him too, he was good to her, but I don't figure she's going to know him when he gets back, it's been three weeks. Jack was good about helping, too, I been finding this out from the other girls, sometimes they come over for coffee, or we take all the kids down to the pool. Laurie likes the water, though about all she can do now is splash a little when I hold her up; she smiles and makes noises at the other kids. It helps pass the time but I get bored just talking to women about the same old things.

They're all real nice, though. This girl Rose says to me the other day, why don't you and Jack come over for a cookout one of these nights and I go well Jack, he's working two jobs and we don't hardly have time to go out. So she says I wish Jerry would do something like that, he's the laziest man I ever seen. I kind of nodded, said that was too bad or something, and when I was walking home I felt like crying. Something's happened to him, he should of been back by now. Every day I think it's going to be today and when it ain't I get more worried, I just know he didn't run out on me, he ain't that kind of person. Course maybe he's got himself another woman. But I remember when he come to the hospital, looking scared for me but something else on his mind, I could tell what it was but he didn't know how to ask. He's like that about most things, I figured out pretty early you can't push him, you got to just let him make up his mind, long as it takes. It was like that when he moved in here with me. After awhile, though, we began to know a little more about each other and things went along easier.

Then the other day I get a card in the mail, I was so excited I couldn't hardly breathe, but it's just from Al, telling me he's coming home to visit and he'll look me up. Al's funny that way, who else'd send you a postcard when he's only eighty miles away? He used to talk when he came over like nobody I ever heard, about himself and the things he was reading, and the more he'd talk the closer he'd get to me on that couch. I'd keep one eye on him, the other on the clock, and long about 4:00 I'd put on a fresh pot of coffee so Jack could have some when he got home. It'd be getting dark already; I remember them short March afternoons when I first come home with Laurie, when I wasn't used to her yet and having a hard time. Jack was quiet then, real sweet and all but kind of holding himself back, like he wasn't sure what was going on between us, how he'd got hooked up with me and a baby anyway. Course it's hard when you're sleeping in the same bed and you can't do anything, sometimes I'd feel worse than I do now. I begin to feel like I did when I was alone, except I ain't got that big belly and ain't half sick all the time; I wouldn't of wanted a man then anyway, after what Bill done. But after I quit working, it was hard sitting here all day with nothing to do, getting lonesome. Laurie gives a person plenty to do, so that's changed. But the house has got that same musty smell, even now in summer.

The awning was soaked through, and water dripped down on Al's head as he walked out of the drugstore. He opened a pack of cigarettes, took one out, and carefully closed the foil wrapping. When he moved his arms, he could feel his shirt sticking to his sunburned back, and his legs were stiff and tired, almost numb, from the long bus ride. Al had watched the cloud front changing all the way from Madison, the grey clouds receding into purple, sometimes revealing the blue spaces in between. There had been no possibility of sleep; he'd had too many things on his mind. The sunburn reminded him of an unpleasant afternoon he had spent aboard his friend's cabin cruiser. They had gone swimming in the middle of the lake, and afterward his friend had gone below deck with the girl they'd picked up. Al had lent his car to his friend this weekend, so the friend and the girl could go to Lake Geneva.

But Al was thinking about Connie as he walked through the rain, wondering why he was coming back to see her. He'd never enjoyed listening to her talk about the baby; she would repeat funny things Jack had said and carve at the frost on the window with her fingernails. But he'd liked the way she'd listened to him, she'd get up to bring him coffee or food but she'd never lose the thread of the conversations: yeah, I'm listening, go on, she would say, as he would hear her rattling the coffee pot on the stove, or opening the refrigerator, her movements having an unconscious rhythm, or pattern, and he was never sure whether she knew he was watching her. He remembered now the way she had said that one word, 'yeah', and the sound of her voice in his memory seemed to enclose those wet spring afternoons, the way she walked and her pretty, common face, the dark silent looks Jack had given him. Al was glad it was raining, the rain made Connie seem more familiar to him. In one of these houses, down the hill in this grey streaking rain, Connie was waiting for him, and she was alone. But his back hurt and stung under his wet shirt, and he was cold. He stumbled into her dark hallway, looking once at the street and realizing it was the same as it had been in the spring.

—Why, Al, she said, smiling at him when she opened the door; I didn't know you was coming up this weekend. Come on in and dry off.

He thanked her and walked into the apartment. Connie had a scarf tied around her head and she said not to mind how things looked, she was cleaning up. As she pushed the carpet sweeper, Al watched her closely; he was almost positive that she wasn't wearing a bra, and he tried to sneak looks inside the places where her shirt opened between the buttons. You want a drink or some coffee, she asked, all I got's bourbon. Bourbon is fine, he said, wondering if she were wearing anything under her shorts. Her breasts were nice, he had seen the top part of them a few times when she had nursed Laurie.

Connie came back with the drinks and asked him what he was taking up in school. He told her about his economics course, looking at her quickly when she bent over to pick up a rattle. He wondered if it would be more real with her, or more violent. And he'd have to tell her he didn't love her after it was over.

—How are you, Connie? I mean seriously, are you all right?

—Sure, she said. You like it up there?

—I've been having some trouble studying because the weather's been so beautiful, he said. The drink was strong and he realized he'd better go slowly. She had lit a cigarette, seemed now to be watching the patterns of the rising smoke. The apartment was more barren than he had expected; he saw a pile of dirty baby clothes and tried to estimate how long it had been since she'd done any laundry. She must be really depressed, he thought, to let things go like this. How's Laurie, he said, not knowing what else to talk about.

—Oh, she's fine. Jack ain't going to believe how much she's grown; I can't hardly believe it myself.

Al shifted in his chair, trying to decide what to say. Connie went on cleaning, picking up newspapers and dirty clothes and carrying them off together in her arms. She called out to him from the kitchen, asking him why he hadn't told her about all the wild times he was having with his new girl friends. He laughed then, found himself telling her how lonely he'd been, he was sick of school because it shielded you from the real experiences in life, he said, you know what I mean, like there you are and everything's happening around you, but you're not involved, none of it touches you. When she brought him fresh drinks, she smiled at him, and he began to believe that her smile meant something; he relaxed, thinking this is the way it used to be, only better, because Jack's not around to spoil everything.

The sun came through the smeared windows, and Al knew he was a little drunk, because his eyes held her in the action she'd just completed, lagged behind her present motion of dusting, or bending, or walking; so she seemed to circle around him, even when she stood still. Her tight shorts separated her legs almost unnaturally, making them appear as if they were constantly opening; he felt, as if with his hands, each slight movement her breasts made under her blouse. As she was wiping off the table next to him, he looked sideways and saw her breast clearly through the buttons; he could reach for her and she would bend down to him, her mouth tasting dry in the first minutes, her teeth hurting his lips. Now she crossed in front of the window and Al shifted again in his chair. Connie, he said, did you ever think of going on to school?

—Why would I want to do that, she said, laughing, then moving the radio so she could dust under it.

—Well, for one thing, you'd meet a lot of people. And besides, after you got your degree you'd be able to get a really good job, make money, you know, build a new life for yourself.

Connie looked as if she were about to say something, then shrugged and went into the kitchen, and Al heard her running water for the dishes. I'll wait until she gets back, he thought. He felt thick and clumsy when he stood up, and he stumbled a little on his way into the bathroom. Out the window the wet roofs of the houses were shining in sun, and they hurt his

eyes. The houses were all the same, heavy and ugly in the streets, and Al realized for the first time how much he hated them. He looked at a fashion magazine and thumbed through it quickly, putting it down because he didn't like any of the models; a vague feeling came to him, as if he'd been involved in some long inner conversation which had nearly come to the point of resolution. But it was a few minutes before he realized this, after he'd already forgotten the feeling, and he seemed to remember only its passing. He sighed and splashed water on his face, hoping to feel sober again. Connie called out to him, but he said he was all right, she could make him another drink. As he opened the door, he heard her emptying an ice tray and he thought he could smell the liquor. He walked as carefully as he could back to the couch and tried to speak slowly
—Do you get out much, Connie?
—No, I ain't got the time, really. I ain't been doing half what I should around here as it is.
Al took a long sip from his drink, looked away from her and told her he wished she could meet some new people, have some new experiences. Oh, she said, I been meeting lots of people; but before she could go on he finished his drink in one swallow and cut in on her—you know Connie, I hate to say this, I really do, he said, looking into her eyes, but maybe you should realize that he's probably not coming back.
—How come you say that? Connie said, calmly, as if they'd been talking about the weather; but he felt she had been shaken, so he said, well, I've known people like him before and they just can't seem to face the responsibilities of settling down.
Connie cleared her throat and got up to check on Laurie; she had apparently heard a noise. When she came back, Al couldn't decide whether she was angry or whether she was thinking about what he'd said. So he continued to talk about Jack, hoping she would understand his meaning. The clouds had moved in again, and the room was dark now, making her seem smaller as she sat motionless in her chair, facing him, and yet seeming to look past him. She lit a cigarette and said I don't want to talk about this stuff anymore.
—I only bring it up because I care so much about you, Al said; I'd rather not see you hurt.
Her toes wiggled, her hands were clasped under her legs: the times he had imagined her and Jack in bed together came back to him now, and he felt as if she'd sat up in bed afterward, like this, looking down at Jack, her knees under her chin, her hands joined under her bare thighs. Al slid sideways on the couch, laying his cigarette in the ashtray, and noticed the small rise between her legs. He shifted again, thinking over things he had said to her this afternoon and then, suddenly, understanding the feeling he'd had in the bathroom. He started to say something, but stopped as the baby cried out, I went into the bedroom and picked Laurie up and just kind of leaned on the door for a moment, and when I come back Al's sitting there with this blank look on his face, mouth hanging open a little, but not like a person who's surprised, and I was glad I'd brought a blanket to wrap around me and Laurie while I nursed her.
—Maybe when Jack comes back, we can all go on a few picnics if you ain't up in Madison all summer.
—Yeah, that'd be nice.

My House is Dark

For Warren Fine

When I come home,
My house is dark
And my thoughts are cold.

—Carlos Santana,
"Evil Ways"

PART I

IN THE COLD CENTER OF WYOMING, near Rawlins, heading east, I watched a cloud front thicken ahead of me; I turned on the car radio and found out it was snowing in Cheyenne. And the waiting for those clouds to turn into a blizzard was like the waiting we'd been doing, my wife and I, for months, but no one would make the first move.

I could think about my wife now, without anger, as she slept near me in the front seat; Ben was sleeping restlessly in back, his bottle probably leaking somewhere under his legs. In sleep her face was vulnerable again, as it'd been when we'd been getting along, before we'd had Ben; she moved, her face flickering from the reflection of snow flakes in the early dawn light. She'd been hard for so long, hardly ever crying or raising her voice even though we'd argued viciously and coldly about Ben and the long weeks I spent away from home, the other women she rightly suspected me of having. I reached my hand out to touch her face, then stopped myself.

She'd been calm on this trip until I'd become irritable and spoken my fears, the half dreams I'd had in the long night of driving alone, I'd imagined the three of us broken down on the road a hundred miles from any help, Ben crying from hunger and she and I trying to keep him warm, uselessly, we'd all freeze soon enough in Wyoming. I'd said Ben made us vulnerable and she'd gotten angry, telling me that she and Ben were getting through this trip much better than I was. But she didn't understand the whine of the transmission bearings; she was unconscious of all the circumstances we'd be helpless against. She'd complained about Ben the whole time we'd been in San Francisco, some vacation, she'd said, we can't even go out, I could just as well be sitting around home. I'd said the trip was her idea, not mine; Ben hadn't bothered me, even though he'd cried a lot; but I could never be that calm around him now.

What I remember best from that trip is the snow: the road looked blue under the snow streaks, especially near Medicine Bow, where it was two lane, the snow was worst here and the clouds were as black as the mountains I'd come to hate, there was lightning, and sometimes thunder. My transmission was louder because the snow cut the road noise and I hoped the clamp I'd made out of a coat hanger would hold my old radiator hose on. I saw cars and pickups off the side of the road, men standing around, looking off to the west for help to come: you get used to the motion of a car, figuring miles by time and believing you'll hold that speed—then the car breaks down and you might as well be walking to the store for a pack of cigarettes, taking your time on a Sunday morning, only now maybe you've got to walk a hundred miles, you can't fix the car, it's useless but you still have it, can't just leave it by the side of the road. Three patrol cars were sitting where a truck had gone into the ditch, the trailer frame was sprung, the trailer body bent along its side as if you'd twisted it like a washrag; I'd seen the truck a few hours earlier when I'd stopped for gas, it was a brand new Peterbilt, blue with bright orange stacks and chrome tanks; when I saw the truck in the ditch, I hoped the driver didn't own his rig. But the color scheme wasn't what you'd expect on a fleet truck, and I imagined the years that driver had saved his money, maybe this was his first run on his own, and I'd seen him run his hand carefully over the fender when he'd been in that gas station.

The snow was down to flurries when we reached Cheyenne, though the sky was overcast and cold down in the plains; by the time we stopped for breakfast and gas outside Pine Bluffs, Nebraska, I was too tired to think, I was shaky from the coffee and my nerves, believing it was wrong to stop and eat, sure you could get off this long black road only by dying, my feet were turning into wheels and my body continued the road rhythms, closing my eyes I could still see the shoulders out the sides of my eyes. Ben banged his spoon, chattering and laughing, and Nancy and I looked at each other. She said, you know you've really ruined this for me.

Ain't my fault, I said. I never wanted any part of this. Middle of winter, and you want to go to San Francisco. She shrugged, as if to brush me off, and I wished I had a four hundred gallon tank and forty hits of speed so I could drive and drive and never stop again until we were back in La Crosse. But she had to have another cup of coffee, had to waste more time. I saw her hard tired face and I remember thinking I'd be losing Ben soon, some other man would raise him, but I couldn't feel anything about that. Out the window of the cafe, the wind was blowing dust over the smooth black road. I want to drive when we get back on the road, Nancy said, I always get stuck with Ben.

—We'll see.

She blew a stream of smoke toward my face and whispered, what's the matter, don't you trust me? You run all over with the band but you go crazy on a little trip with me; what's the matter, can't you talk either, she said, aren't I worth talking to?

—You don't know shit about it, I said. Ben started to cry. I told her to do something with him, he needed something, she was his mother and I didn't know what was wrong with him.

She ground out her cigarette. You do something with him, she said.

Our manager had a tour booked for us, and we went out two days after I got home. For the first time we were getting occasional gigs opening up for name acts, it made us feel good and we could tell it was going to happen, after four years we were about to make it. We were tight, everything moved and jumped together, and we came downstairs after the gig in Baltimore knowing we'd blown the lead act off the stage. There were already some girls in the dressing room; we were getting high, waiting for the party.

Suddenly Nancy walked in carrying Ben, I'll never know how she got all the way to Baltimore with him, and she looked around at the girls, the wine bottles and the bags of dope. The other guys stared at her stupidly. I was so high that I started to laugh, but there was something in her face that I knew, even then, would never break, never end; and when she opened her mouth, I got the feeling that she'd thought over those words for a long time.

—Here, you take him, she said, handing Ben over to me, glaring when I almost dropped him. You just see what it's like, I hate him and I hate you, you've wrecked my life, you bastard. Her voice was so quiet that no one else heard her, though the room was quiet, and I knew the others were listening; there had been nothing but polite interest in her eyes, as if we'd been talking about music or the weather. But Ben started to cry then, and if I'd thought this was easy for her I changed my mind, she wavered, because I was high her legs seemed to tremble crazily as she turned and walked out. My son was still crying and squirming on my lap, I could smell wine and I was aware of the dressing room lights, the concert noise upstairs. Nothing was moving me, not Ben's crying, not the fear I barely understood in his face; I seemed to see Nancy still standing there, repeating those same words over and over again.

All night I held him through that crazy party, he went on crying and I was too wasted to understand or comfort him, in the morning his ass was bright red because I hadn't thought to change his diapers; I had never changed his diapers in my life. After I'd put him on the bed I just sat there, he lay there crying against the music, the people, drunk, shouting and pushing amid broken glass; and I sat there, drinking and smoking, staring at him until I passed out.

Almost a week later I sat with him in a rented room in Baltimore, reading the want ads, beginning to fully understand what he and his mother had done to my life. I looked at him and I hated him for his helplessness. The band was in New York with a new guitarist; they'd got a review in the *Village Voice*.

Now the first winter Ben and I have been alone is coming, but winter in Baltimore seems to be just an extended fall, or maybe early sping in reverse. This bar is two blocks from home, a block from the shoe store where I work, in a neighborhood just north of downtown, an old people's neighborhood, though some students have been moving in lately. When I first moved into this apartment I was surprised that the neighborhood was 'integrated', I'd only been in northern cities; down here I'd see black and white people talking in buses and cafes and on street corners. But all the laughing and jiving is as empty as the silence in the north, nobody really gets along; sometimes, in this bar, you see them having drinks together. Then you see how the white people look at each other when they're alone again.

The counter is U-shaped and the men are across from me, the old women are on my left, talking, as usual, about their dead husbands; Libby is saying, well Ruth, of course there weren't no money for dry cleaning in them days, so I had to take and press my husband's grey flannel trousers myself, right there on the kitchen table. From across the counter, I can hear the old men talking, mostly about the jobs they had before they retired, sometimes about wives or grown children. In this neighborhood the talk is always the same, in this bar or on the front stoops during the summer, in the grocery or liquor store before dark. I like it down here because it reminds me of home, the old people do everything slowly; Baltimore is like the ocean I saw in San Francisco, never still, changing too fast, making too much noise.

When I can get someone to watch Ben at night I come down here to drink, and, from habit, to listen—I used to write songs out of the things I learned in bars. Once Jake, who's here off and on all day, told me about marathon dances during the depression: joined one once but you bet I dropped out pretty quick, he said, them people was just killing themselves, I seen plenty of them keel over and try to get right back up again. But Jake also says he's got Cherokee blood, that he used to have a farm out in Arundel county, once burned down an old barn for the insurance money so he could buy a new tractor. He was putting his coat on now, and he waved as he walked out. I looked up at the clock, figuring I had time for another beer.

The sun through the doorway fell on the old women, making their nylons bright, and the cribbage games had started across the counter. I drummed my fingers on the counter and sipped my beer; than I drank it all in two swallows and walked back home to get the car. I have an old Chevy, worse even than the Ford Nancy and I took to San Francisco. On the way to the day care center, I tried to remember if there was any food in the house. I've been reading books about nutrition lately, trying to figure out a balanced diet for Ben, because I don't care at all about eating and I realized a couple of months ago that I'd been feeding him whatever was lying around, sometimes just a piece of bread with margarine. So I have to remind myself now to cook something for him every night, and I have to eat it with him because he thinks it's no good if I won't touch it.

They'd been tearing up the street by the day care center, the bulldozers, steam shovels and dump trucks were parked at strange angles so the traffic slowed up to get around them, and the sun on the steel plates over the street made me think of times I'd fished on the Mississippi in the early morning. I parked illegally between the steam shovel and a pickup, and walked into the day care center. Ben ran up to me, shouting daddy, daddy pick Ben up, and he banged hid head against my thigh. July stood behind him, her eyes moving from the back of his head to my face; she seems to have taken some interest in Ben and she tells me the truth about him. She told me was really beginning to adjust, she straightened her hair with her hand and I could see her breasts move under her tee shirt; I stopped myself, again, from asking her to come home and have dinner with us. Ben's head under my hand was warm and sweaty, he'd grabbed my pants leg with both hands and was rocking sideways on his heels. Julie said she'd been taking him in to watch the older kids use the toilet and he seemed very interested; she suggested that I might try to talk to him about that. I nodded, realizing I'd been hoping for six weeks that Ben would magically learn to use the toilet by himself. We said goodbye, and Ben and I talked about bulldozers and dump trucks on the way home.

The apartment is small, kitchenette, bathroom, and one big room with a Murphy bed; Ben sleeps in the corner, his toys are under the crib. He went to the window to watch the cars and buses going by, and I stood behind him, feeling, as I often do, that he just pretends to be happy for my sake, that I drove his mother away from him, and she'd have done a better job with him than I'm doing. She and Ben would have learned about each other seriously, patiently, not as Ben and I had come to know each other. But it's better since I've had him at the center, I can learn from Julie and she's always willing to talk to me.

These last few months I've been playing gigs at the coffee house up the street, and I always take Ben with me, the people are good about watching him while I'm on the stand but I can't help feeling that a coffee house is no place for a little kid, I can't really be sure how those people are treating him, and I wince and make mistakes when I hear him cry. But I have to do it, I walk around that store humming tunes all day and it drives me crazy; once a week, now, I can remember the old days and they've almost stopped bothering me.

We had liver and onions for dinner and Ben wasn't impressed. Afterward, he helped me with the dishes like he sometimes does, he stands on a chair next to me and washes his plastic bottles and dishes, finishing them, usually, by the time I've washed the other dishes. When I turned off the water he screamed and cried and I tried, like a fool, to reason with him, you can't reason with a child any more than you can reason with yourself when something happens that you can't understand. I never believe I can get him to stop crying, but a car backfired and he ran to the window again. Then it began again when I changed his diapers and got his pajamas, he kicked and screamed and I had to hold him down, after all this time I can't seem to get his clothes on him without twisting his arms and legs; so this happens every night, until I'm done and I ask him if he wants to read a story.

He comes to sit with me in our one big chair and I read to him, he asks about the pictures, turning back to see some car or somebody crying, his face intent as he listens, singlemindedly, to the words; I want to hurry it, want him asleep so I can be alone. But then I hang on to the sound of his heavy regular breathing, there's a stillness in here that even the cars and people going by outside doesn't affect, there are roaches in the kitchen when I turn on the light and all the things I remember scatter through that stillness, I lose the sense of continuing that Ben has given me, a sense I never had alone, or with Nancy, sometimes I drink and always I forget how to conserve things, I have to conserve this time with Ben.

I think back now of those first few months, unable to believe they've ended, feeling they'll continue in Ben for years; Ben hadn't even words to tell himself what he felt, had no word for me and cried mama when he was tired or hurting. I'd try to explain his mama was gone, hold him clumsily, misread his crying; once, in the middle of the night, it took me twenty minutes to realize that there was no hole in the nipple of his bottle, twenty minutes of talking, holding him, handing him a bottle he'd try to suck on and then throw down. The high breaking sound of his crying would make the back of my neck turn stiff and cold, I'd remember how easily he'd calmed down for Nancy, feel he was crying only because she was gone. All through that rainy spring I dragged him wherever I went, to cheap hotels before we found this apartment, through three weeks of job hunting. The employers would be hearty, or pitying, especially when Ben got restless and cried, or ran around their offices. His nose ran from the cold he couldn't shake, and his diaper rash was raw from the greasy food he couldn't digest. The sound of his crying continues now as I think of those morning bus rides, the inside lights blinking each time the tires hit a bump in the road, the hard, helpless faces of the riders and the looks they gave his dirty clothes.

By the time I got a job I'd learned enough about Ben to know he needed a routine; he'd miss even this crazy way we'd been living, and his confused fears would begin again. I had to leave him with an old lady down the block who must've needed money bad because she complained every night when I came to get him; every night he'd be crying when I got there, and her contempt would shake whatever I was hanging onto then. Every morning I'd drop him off and he'd cry, I'd have to make myself leave and I hated the time I forced him to spend with a woman who might hurt him, I kept trying to think of another way and I'd make mistakes while I was working. When I think of it now, I don't know why I didn't just go on welfare or something; but welfare never even occurred to me, it was as if I'd never even heard of it.

But once I began working I stopped being angry at him—if he was vulnerable, we both were, it wasn't his fault. I began needing him, looking forward to the nights and weekends we could spend together. We'd talk, or, really, I'd talk, and I'd play with him, and as I calmed down he seemed happier, I missed women only at work, and once I had to wait on customers I didn't miss friends at all. But at night, if I got drunk enough, I'd call out to Nancy as if she were in the next room, remember holding her, and imagine her with another man—first hating her, then loving her, and loving her was worse because it was useless. I'd go in and look at Ben, touch his head, feel, again, that there was some reason to go through this.

In the last part of May I met Ron and Sharon, who live downstairs. She acts for a repertory company, and I liked her immediately, but it was hard to keep talking to him about sports. When I told him about the band, though, he began bringing his guitar up and asking me to play for him, said maybe I could teach him some 'licks'. The guitar was an old three quarter size Gibson and I'd play it even while I was talking, it was ridiculous that he owned such a good guitar. Ben would run around, or talk to Sharon. When he'd take the guitar back down, I'd feel a loneliness I couldn't shake for hours.

At the end of the month they had a party and I went downstairs; I felt guilty for wanting to go, but I stayed three hours, checking on Ben every half hour. There apartment had large wall hangings and pieces of pottery and sculpture, painted milk cans and stone crocks in the corners; by the time I'd been there awhile, all these things seemed to move like dancers; the women, mostly, were dancing—in this time alone with Ben I'd forgotten how much I wanted a woman and I thought they must be able to see me staring at their breasts and crotches, it was as if these parts of their bodies were moving separately. I couldn't talk to anybody; Ron passed some smoke around and all I could see was Nancy in that dressing room.

He kept asking me to play but I stalled him because I hate people who wreck parties by playing; once I started, I played and sang as loud as I would've onstage, playing as if I imagined a whole band behind me, and they listened. I stopped, afraid of the old good feeling, relieved when I heard the conversations start up again.

A woman I'd been looking at most of the night was standing next to me when I put the guitar down. The woman was Julie and the first thing she told me was that she worked at a day care center; she thought Ben could get in even though he wouldn't be two for another month. I remember that I believed, immediately, that she'd love him, help him through this; maybe it was the softness in her face, the same softness in her face that made me think her marriage was fragile, and I didn't want to break in on it—all through this time, I felt sad and envious whenever I saw married couples, especially the ones with kids. Her gestures kept me away from her, but her voice was warm; she was the first person I'd met in Baltimore who didn't ask me how I'd come to have custody of Ben. She walked upstairs with me the last time I checked on Ben, and promised, before she left, to call me about the day care center.

As I've gotten to know her, through talking about Ben, I've begun to hate her husband, mostly because he exists at all but partly because he makes me believe I was a shitty husband. He makes me blame myself for what's happened to Ben, for what I've done to him.

Friday night I stopped off at Ron's to borrow the guitar. They usually come to see me play, and they're both good about watching Ben, especially Sharon. They weren't home but there was a note for me telling me that the door was open, which I thought was stupid of them; somebody else might come by who'd be interested in their stereo system. I took the guitar upstairs to practice some before the gig, running through scales until my fingers stopped hurting.

Ben likes to come to the coffee house for some reason, maybe the music or the people; at least twice a night he climbs up on the stand while I'm playing, he dances and the audience loves it. Jesus, they're a serious group of people, and I suppose I should be grateful for that, but it makes me want to laugh, all of them listening cautiously to the blues, as if they can't really dig it but think they ought to discover it. But everything's different when you play alone, you notice a lot of things that you wouldn't have time to see if you were playing with a band.

After dinner, I felt the cold nervous energy begin, and I knew it would last until I got up on the stand. Ben played with his blocks while I scraped the dishes, and then he came running in, saying daddy, Ben make house. He'd arranged his blocks in six flat rows; I'd been building with him for months but this was the first time he'd tried it alone. Though I wanted to remove myself, let my nerves build, I felt some relief playing with him, laughing when he giggled and kicked down the houses I made. I got him dressed and we walked to the coffee house, we'd get there early enough so that I could check the sound equipment; I've never understood why the other acts don't bother to do this, the mikes are old and they feed back unless the sound levels are adjusted exactly. But this is a good place to play, the red tin walls have flower patterns in squares and the relief of the patterns is emphasized by yellow floodlights, the tables are old, carved and solid oak and you can smell the coffee heating on the hotplate near the stand. There is no liquor in the house, so I'd brought along a pint and I started working on it, giving Ben money for the juke box to keep him occupied. He can put the money in himself, but he needs me to push the buttons; he knows this juke well enough to have favorite songs, 'The Weight' and 'Domino'.

By quarter to nine, I was dry and shaky all over and Ben was restless, he had a tantrum because I wouldn't buy him another coke; but Ron and Sharon came in, and she got Ben quiet by drawing pictures for him on a napkin. There was a real crowd tonight, and I let myself think they'd come for me, not the cat who follows with Simon and Garfunkle tunes done badly—not that it's worth doing those tunes well anyway. At nine fifteen, I got up on the stand, going through the little routine I use to get my guitar tuned, pretending I'm tone deaf and asking a member of the audience to sing an E note; someone always falls for that, and the laughter loosens me up. Then I look around, making a few bad jokes; I was glad to see that my favorite couple had come in and were sitting right in front of me, as usual; this cat cannot keep his hands off his girl, he's always reching around her back to cop a quick feel or sliding his hand between her legs, whether or not she's wearing a skirt; she always has this unreal smile on her face, like someone who's released a loud fart in a crowd and is trying to pretend it was someone else. Behind the mike and the guitar I felt alone and comfortable, as if I were playing on my front porch and would never play anywhere else; you can talk and jive the people when you can't see them, they want you to move and holler those tunes so they can watch, feel your difference, they won't listen to a man who seems the same as they are because he'll ask them, in some way, to share what he's going through. I started out with Jimmy Reed's 'Take Out Some Insurance', letting them get warm enough so that some of them would clap their hands. When I got to the harder tunes they moved in their chairs and I could smell their noise and smoke, I imagined the things they hoped, I hoped, they'd do to each other later on. Tonight they called out for tunes they'd heard me do before and I moved through those tunes, fighting to keep them mine and so quieting the audience down, risking intimacy only with Ben, who'd feel me up there but wouldn't understand that feeling. Somebody set a glass of water onstage just as I was finishing my first set, so I went backstage and mixed it with my whiskey, letting the drink go down slow and pulling hard at a cigarette. The second set moved down to the slow tunes I always ended with, I'd see separate faces between the light and the smoke, there was a lot of quiet talk now and my couple up front had their hands in each other's laps.

When I was through I waved at the applause and came down, grinning at the Simon and Garfunkle cat and his uptown girlfriend; Sharon was holding Ben and he looked tired, his mouth hanging half open as it does in sleep, but she said he hadn't been cranky or difficult. I picked him up, glad to feel his body between my hands, because by bending over him I have those first few moments after a gig all to myself, those moments when I let the energy go loose and try not to think about how long it's going to take before that other musician has to warm them up for me. Softly, I sang one verse of 'Walkin' Blues' to Ben, the river and ocean verse he always asks for.

—I just want to tell you I really enjoy your music, said a woman's voice, and I looked up; she was wearing a tweed suit with a bright scarf around her neck, her mouth was wide in her thin face and her mouth changed around every word she spoke, so that later on it'd be hard to remember her face, her hips were wider than you'd expect a slim girl to have, and her bracelets jingled as she twisted a handkerchief in her hands. I thanked her, introduced her to Sharon and Ron, and invited her to sit down for a drink. She looked surprised when I poured some of the pint into a glass of water for her. Ben was squirming on my lap so I let him down, and she watched him curiously as he ran off to visit others in the crowd. She leaned forward to accept the match I held for her cigarette, she said she taught English at the Peabody Conservatory and asked me if I played full time. I'd started to tell her about the old band and was at the point of letting her know that I wasn't married when I heard Ben crying, he was throwing a tantrum in the middle of the floor. I picked him up, hushing him as I talked fast to the girl, asking her to leave with me, saying we could have a few drinks after Ben was asleep. She said she was with someone, then asked me if I'd be playing next Friday. I nodded as I put Ben's jacket on, watching her, dropping my eyes to her crossed legs just before I walked out with Ben. When we were home, I remembered that I hadn't even asked her name.

A shoe shipment was waiting when I got to work, so I spent most of the morning in the back, ticketing the shoes and putting them away; most times I like this, because I don't have to wait on customers when I'm stocking shelves, but today it would've been better to be out on the floor, I'd have been able to forget about the bills I owed, the two hundred dollars still left on the guitar—I'd taken a big loss when I'd sold it, and we'd used the money to live on. Tomorrow I had to take Ben to the doctor, and he hates doctors, cries and kicks and I have to hold him down, feel the doctor's contempt. Nancy'd paid the bills, made the appointments; I'm only now getting to the point where I can remember to do these things, and I hate them.

I bumped into a stack of shoes and knocked them down; I'm always clumsy back here, I think of pieces of songs, can almost see them written out, and then we get busy and I lose everything. It was time for lunch; once a week I go out, taking the full hour, and usually I bring a book along. I punched my card, put on my coat and went out; the dampness blew off the bay, settling between the buildings and making the sidewalk cold, but as long as the wind was up I knew it wouldn't rain, or sleet. A police car pulled up next to me, its red light on, and I almost started running; another cop came out of a liquor store, holding a man by the arm. The man was dragging his feet, his eyes were open wide and staring, his lips were dry enough so that I could see the cracks in them when he passed. People began to gather around, but the cops made them move on; I ducked my head and walked in the middle of the crowd, wondering what the man had done, why he'd tried this early in the day.

As soon as my eyes adjusted to the bar, I saw Julie, and she waved me over. She was smiling as I came up, but her eyes seemed to look past mu shoulder; I sat down, looking at her legs, I'd only seen her in pants before this. She said she'd just finished a child development course today so she was celebrating, the course was a drag but she'd make a little more money now and her husband would like that; I'd always believed she was a happy person, but seeing her out of the center made me feel some strain she didn't usually show; her voice had the same warmth, but was missing a rhythm, and she looked tired, more made up than usual. It was strange to see these signs and remember that I'd ignored them in Nancy. I wondered if Nancy had talked to anyone; maybe her friend Karen had seen the trouble and asked about it; you can't talk about your marriage until somebody asks, and I almost asked Julie.

But through these months anything we'd said about ourselves had moved quickly to Ben, as if he were the only safe thing between us. Now, as we ate, we talked about Ben's toilet training; she said I should try, this weekend, leaving his diapers off except when he was asleep, and if it worked out they could try it during the week. She said everybody liked Ben, laughed when she told me how he'd run naked when she got his diapers off, hollering 'no diaper on'. She leaned forward as she talked, moved around in her chair. The buttons of her blouse separated when she stretched; I felt, suddenly, that her husband made fun of her whenever she was enthusiastic. I wanted to take the afternoon off, ask her if she'd come home with me, but I felt I'd just make everything worse. She had to go to work and I left her at the bus stop. By the time I punched out, I'd imagined and re-imagined a whole scene, changing the conversation as I went along—Julie'd come to my gig alone, stay with me and we'd make love three times; she'd say she wanted to leave her husband so she could take care of me and Ben.

Ben and I were walking up the front steps of our apartment house, we'd just got back from the doctor's and he'd finally stopped crying; I turned, saw the girl I'd met in the coffee house, and called out to her; she stood below us on the sidewalk, her hair curling under her scarf in the drizzling rain, her leather bag turning a dark red. She said she'd just been coming home from work, so I asked her if she'd like to come up for a cup of coffee. She touched her forehead, looked down the block, and said well, okay; she walked behind us up the staircase and I let her into the apartment.

Something came over her face when she walked inside, but she covered it up quickly; she stared at Ben awkwardly, as if he'd surprised her. When I'd gotten his coat off, he started jumping on the bed, which I'd left down and unmade this morning. I asked her to sit down, she was so stiff I wondered why she'd wanted to come up; even when I brought her a cup of coffee, the tension didn't leave her face. Ben came up to her, put his hands on her knee, pointed to her, asking 'what?'.

—Ben, this is—'Carol', she said—He took the name, practiced a few times; then he came into the kitchen, pulled on my leg, whining for a story or a game. Carol walked into the kitchen, and she tried to talk to him as you would an adult. And I was angry at him in a way I'd never been before, without knowing why; I asked him if he'd like a cookie and he took it, ran into the other room, climbed up on the bed and started jumping on it again.

Carol gave her fingers another twist and talked about her day, mentioning a few students who were giving her trouble, and I watched her, fascinated by her mouth, her expensive clothes, enjoying her nervousness.

—You live here alone? With the baby? she asked. I told her I did, not knowing from her face whether that relieved her. But I'd become used to being alone, and suddenly I could feel her loneliness fighting within her, she couldn't fake calm and I began to like her. I coaxed her into staying for dinner, and though she kept saying she had to leave, she was still drinking coffee and talking when I put Ben to sleep. Because I was so glad to have someone else in the apartment, I wasn't tense; but I felt that might be making things worse for her. She began now, slowly, to relax, to talk about herself, and as she did her voice became stronger, soon she was asking me questions about playing and about Ben. Her legs were long and she sat with her elbows on her thighs, sometimes gesturing with her hands; she took off her bright scarf, and her hair rose in tight curls around her head. I answered her questions cautiously, speaking only of my life in Baltimore; when she asked if I'd been to college, I changed the subject. I thought of the two women I'd slept with since I'd been in Baltimore, the way they'd been phony and careless around Ben.

Carol wouldn't be back, she needed an approach from me that I couldn't understand. But I thought about her a long time after she left, the way she'd moved in the chair, her thin white wrists, the tight skin over her forehead. I repeated her phone number to myself as I lay down, I knew she'd be serious and concerned if I got to know her, I wondered if she'd ever relax, what she'd be like in bed: and there was a feeling of memory about her, as if I'd known her before, as if, already, she could affect me like an old friend. I listened to Ben's breathing; we'd lived, continuous and unchanging, since we'd come to Baltimore, and maybe I'd suddenly begin to live apart from him if I took up with a woman; and I realized, even through all his crying, that I believed Nancy's leaving had changed only me. But Ben was older now, he'd learn about any woman who came around, or left suddenly.

A man down the street has a five year old, and the kid spends his time outside on the weekends, mostly alone; I've kept track of the man's girl friends, swearing I'd never do that to Ben. But I needed someone to talk to, someone who'd be around all the time.

And it really began the night Ben got sick. When I picked him up at the day care center, Julie said he'd been sluggish, but he didn't have a fever. After we'd been home an hour, and he hadn't eaten, I saw him dragging his feet, his head was hanging to one side, his cheek was against his right shoulder. He whimpered when I asked him, what's wrong: all better; he said. His head was hot and the pulse beat near his temple seemed stronger. When he began to cry, I picked him up, trying to get him to tell me where it hurt; he held his stomach, touched his ear and his head, and he lay limp and hot in my arms, his hair matted over his forehead. He began to quiet down, motionless as he always is when he's sick, uncomplaining, wanting only to be held and looking up at me as if I can explain this to him; but when he's sick he asks nothing, though he says 'what?' fifty times in a normal day; it's as if he knows there's no reason for him to have to feel this way.

I remembered the medicine, carried him to the refrigerator, and took out an empty bottle. And I'm stuck, I can't leave him, can't take him out into the cold, it's useless for a child to be sick, why can't he tell me what's wrong, I can't help him, he doesn't know, why can't they be born talking, or learn before they can crawl? Ron was gone, I called another friend and there was no answer; I cut an aspirin in half, put it in sugar water and tried to get him to take it, but he knocked it away with a spoon. The second time he took it, and as I washing off the spoon I thought of Carol, I called her. She said she'd come right over, I handed her the medicine bottle when she came to the door; she was back quickly, I gave some to Ben and put him in bed. He fell asleep but I knew he'd be up off and on all night, I hoped he'd be better in the morning because I had no sick days left.

Carol was making a pot of coffee. In her old clothes she looked softer and more relaxed, so I asked her if she'd stay for awhile, in case I needed anything; she said she would, with a half smile on her face I couldn't read. But I hardly noticed when she set a beer in front of me, I was staring at Ben in the crib, listening to his choppy breathing, he moved around restlessly but I couldn't see him in the darkness under the drawn shade; he could have pneumonia, or polio, everything starts with a bad cold and a fever, I have no insurance, I wished he could give me what he had and get well himself, I knew he needed sleep, I was afraid he wouldn't wake up. Carol put her hand on my shoulder; he'll be all right, she said—but that's not the right thing to say, is it?

—It's all right, I'm just glad you're here.

She said she'd been thinking about me when I called; I looked around, only half listening, noticing this room as if for the first time; These grey walls held the shadows, the high ceiling diminished the light, rounding off the four upper corners of the room, and it would be like this outside, a city at night always feels darker than a town, city buildings limit and deepen the darkness. And I could imagine Ben a few winters from now, it'd be dark when he got home from school and this apartment would be empty; when it was really cold, he'd have to stay in here until I got off work.

Carol was talking about a man she'd broken up with a few months ago, and I was aware, because she'd disturbed the silence I'd gotten so used to, that she was here, sitting across from me, rubbing her fingers over the table top. She said something like, 'it must be hard trying to bring up a child by yourself', and I began to tell her what had happened, I found I could tell it flat now, without bitterness, without blaming Nancy or even thinking much about her, feeling the inevitability of Nancy's leaving after what I'd done. Carol didn't listen quietly, as I'd expected; she asked how I'd felt leaving the band, if I'd heard from Nancy and did she come to see Ben, did she regret leaving him.

I told Carol that Nancy'd gotten a job in Chicago as a buyer for a department store, that she'd come to see us on a trip south last summer and it was terrible. Ben began to cry, and I was relieved, I didn't want to think about Nancy's feelings—and I felt Carol hadn't had any business asking. I picked Ben up, wondering how Nancy'd felt when he was sick; he was whimpering, breathing heavily against my face, and I asked Carol to bring the medicine; she touched his face and said we should take his temperature—then she seemed to tense up, seeing how sick he was. If Nancy were here she'd know what to do; but we'd never shared Ben, I don't know how she felt about him, what they were like together; he'd had her for a year and a half and now he'd had me for almost a year. Ben's temperature was almost one hundred five; he didn't even fight the thermometer; I poured coke into a bottle, shaking the bottle so that the carbonation could escape; then I gave him the bottle and I could hear him sucking.

Carol stayed the night, without my having to ask. While I was seeing to Ben the second time, she lay down on my bed and fell asleep. Ben awoke twice more, and between those times I lay down next to her, not touching her; her face was grey and tense, or that was the way her face looked in the light against the grey walls.

But Carol was a stranger, childless, here only because she might feel things for me, things that hadn't anything to do with Ben. How could I have left Nancy to deal with Ben's sickness and bad times by herself, how could I have said, come on, that happened two weeks ago, when she told me Ben had fallen down and had needed four stitches in his chin? I went to the phone to call her, something I'd never done, to tell her I was sorry and to ask her what I should do. But she didn't answer, she must have been out making it with somebody. She hadn't written, we hadn't talked since last August and I'd told her then don't you ask me a goddam thing about Ben until you're ready to do your real job, which is being his mother. She hadn't written, Ben was sick, she was with another man. What a goddam bitch she is. I said aloud; I stayed up, feeling Ben would make it if I didn't go to sleep.

In the morning Carol woke up with Ben and me; she looked at the clock, said she'd have to leave now or she'd be late for work. She reached out her hand, hesitated, and touched Ben's shoulder. I'll stop back tonight, see how things are, she said; can I get you anything.

—Coke and beer, I guess. Thanks for—for coming over.

After she left, I changed Ben's diapers. He felt cooler, and he ate the applesauce I gave him. But I called the shoe store to say I wouldn't be in, and the boss reminded me that I'd lose a day's pay. Ben looked through the toy box, struggled with something, came when I asked him if he wanted a story.

—Yeah! he said, jumping up and down, making me know he was all right.

Down in the neighborhood on Saturday morning, the sidewalks and street were wet and the sun hung between the buildings, keeping the sidewalks in warm shadows. It was an Indian Summer day. Ben ran ahead occasionally, stopping to wait when he was about fifteen feet in front of me. I'd gone to bed angry at Carol, though she'd come to the gig and taken care of Ben, because she'd left right afterward, saying call me tomorrow. I'd lost patience with her hesitations, and by the time Ben and I reached the grocery store I'd decided to talk to Julie next week, or go back to the way it'd been. Things had been simple with no woman around, I'd forgotten how much time you have to waste thinking about somebody you've just met. Ben and I had to do this alone anyway.

The grocer is a small man; he sounds like he's from eastern Europe and he's nearly incomprehensible until you get to know him; we agree, usually, on the weather, though I like snow and he says it's bad for business; then I put Ben in a shopping cart, pick up the canned goods, the grocer goes behind the meat counter, cuts up what I want, and we walk together to the check out, where he'll complain about politics, or the supermarkets, or tell me about the books he's been reading. But today he didn't wave when I came in, he silently got out some pork chops and I had to wait by the cash register for a few minutes. When he came up he looked down at Ben and said, you know, I have a son once, but in the war he die. He leaned against the cash register and began telling me about the concentration camps, rolling up his left sleeve to show me his number. It was blue, like a varicose vein, and very hard to look at. He said he weighed seventy eight pounds when he came out of Dachau. I looked away at the rows of soup cans, then back at his smooth flesh, trying to lose the image of what he must have looked like. I touched Ben's head, and I said that it must've taken a lot of courage to last that out. He looked straight at me, his voice rising, pulling me tight against his memories.

—Courage? What courage? When my son die, I want only that, to die; you got nothing for to kill yourself with, not hairpin, not razor, nothing! My wife, she tell me to pray, Josef; I say I pray to die, you hear? They take my son, six year he was and they—the doorbell clanged and a woman came in; he bent down, kissed Ben on the forehead, his tears stopping in the choking sounds of his throat. My eyes were hot, still dry until I looked at Ben—why man crying, Ben said. Peas, you ask? Josef called out. To the left Mrs. Rasmussen; I squeezed Josef's shoulder, I dropped all my money trying to get it out of my pocket. He looked at me, and at Ben, and he turned away to get a candy stick; Ben took the stick and ran to the door, hollering let's go, daddy, let's go. Josef and I looked at each other, and his smile was nearly a wince, he whispered, take care of him, for the love of God! I nodded, and I opened the door for Ben and followed him out.

I didn't care how warm it was now. Ben was running ahead of me and I called him back in a louder voice than I'd meant to use. I kept trying to tell myself that it didn't matter, Josef had survived and that was the main thing. And I knew I'd have to call Carol, I knew what I'd think about if I stayed alone with Ben. I wondered if Josef's son had died in the summer. I carried Ben up the stairs to our apartment, minding neither his weight nor the weight of the grocery bag, feeling the reassuring squeeze of his legs against my stomach and back. As we passed the landing I could hear Ron's stereo; he was playing 'Another Side of Bob Dylan'. Ben ran down the hall, not wanting to come into the apartment yet, and I called Carol. She asked me if I'd like to take a ride to a park north of Baltimore, but the tone of her voice was as if I'd had to argue her into it. I almost told her to forget it, but by the time I'd made some sandwiches and gotten Ben's things together, I was glad to be leaving the apartment.

We took her car, a year old Volkswagen, and Ben sat happily in his car seat in the back, pointing at cars and trees and, as we left Baltimore, he squealed at the occasional horses, and I wished Nancy and I had done things like this. When he got restless, I'd turn around and make faces at him, or tickle him. Carol talked about things that didn't seem to interest her, and I didn't say much, still thinking about Josef, wishing I'd known what to say to him. Carol was wearing a pair of jeans that fit low around her hips and some kind of knitted top that didn't cover her stomach; often, she'd try to pull it down to the waistband of her jeans. I thought for awhile that I needed to tell Carol about this morning, then changed my mind; I'd dealt with worse things than this by myself; she talked about a Hemingway biography she'd been reading, and when I said I didn't like his books she began to give me reasons why I should, telling me about themes and symbols; though I didn't really understand, I listened because she cared so much, her eyes were large, her face serious, her voice strong and definite.

The park land was covered with leaves, there were natural piles under the biggest trees and Ben jumped in them, he and I rolled around, wrestling and laughing while Carol looked on, tugging at the shirt under her jacket. Once, when we were walking with Ben, our hands touched and she surprised me by squeezing my hand; she let got as if to apologize for the gesture. I put my arm around her, she started to lean her head against me, then stopped and yelled look at all the birds, Ben! They'd been rooting for seeds and they flew up at the sound of her voice, Ben chased after them, laughing and waving his hands.

There was no one else in the park and we walked over the warm rough ground until Ben asked to be picked up; we sat on a picnic table, Ben next to me and Carol across from us, and when he pulled on my sleeve and pointed to my cup of wine, she said, you're not going to give him any, are you? Sure, I said, holding the cup so he could sip it. He made a face and said, no good. He takes wine, I said, but this way he don't think it's anything mysterious. She shook her head and the look on her face irritated me, because single people know so much about kids until you ask them to watch your kid for an hour, then they're not so eagerly responsible and they seem to forget all their vast knowledge. I shouldn't drink so early, she said, I feel sort of light headed; she laughed to herself. Ben was beginning to look tired, I knew he was tired because he threw a tantrum when I told him we were leaving. The edge in my voice as I struggled with him and tried to reason with him was making things worse, but I couldn't control it; I resented Carol for looking on disapprovingly. But he stopped crying as soon as the car was moving. She drove fast, staring straight ahead; when I touched her leg once, to get her attention, one corner of her mouth twitched and she moved her knees closer together. I don't need this, I thought; but when I imagined her dropping us off and driving away I remembered Josef, I felt a tightness in my throat. Carol, I said, pushing my words out, really afraid I couldn't finish what I was about to begin, Carol, why are you so tense?

—Do I seem tense? Are you tense? she said, still looking at the road. Ben was pointing, hollering what? what? so I turned around. Tow truck pulling a car, I said. I'm sorry, Carol said, smiling quickly, then turning her face back to the road. Everything had shifted since I'd met her, I didn't like the time I spent wondering about her, the way she seemed to hover in the apartment even when Ben and I were alone. But I didn't care about that now, I wanted her. I said, carefully, that she seemed to have something on her mind, she'd think about it awhile and then remember she was with me.

—Yeah, there's a lot of things I'm thinking about, mostly school, she said, I believed she was lying, there was something she didn't want to admit. The tension in her face as Ben began to howl and whine relaxed my own; she looked as if she were waiting only for that moment when she'd get rid of us. Yet I didn't think she could stand any longer this sense of something hanging between us.

—Can you come in for awhile?

She nodded, got out of the car and followed me upstairs. Ben took his bottle and for once he seemed to want his nap, he fell asleep quickly. She walked back and forth in the kitchen, her arms were folded over her breasts, pulling the top further up. She'd unsettled me; I didn't look at her, went instead to the refrigerator and took out a bottle of beer. The refrigerator motor kicked in, making the room vibrate. I felt I had to start it and wished I knew how. I sat down, told her she confused me by seeming friendly, then circling away from me. She crossed her legs, lit a cigarette, and said, well, you know—when I do see you you're all wrapped up in Ben or music or something. She must have thought she shouldn't have said anything about Ben, because she held her hand up when I started to speak; No, I don't mean that, I understand, about Ben I mean, she went on, but I need—no, I—she looked around, as if to collect her thoughts, and I got up and looked out the back window. The old black woman down the block was out on her fire escape, taking down the clothes she'd hung up this morning; I hadn't thought it was warm enough to dry clothes. Carol said, I don't think you're listening to me. I turned around, said I could see what she meant but she made me uncomfortable, never relaxing, never really seeming glad that she was with me.

—I've been waiting for a sign from you, I guess: her voice was low and tight, but I could tell she wanted to talk, she'd go through with it. I came away from the window, remembering conversations my wife had tried having with me, I'd cut her off by saying I didn't want to hear her bitching.

But this was different, more like the slow awkward conversations I've had with men who've been my friends, we've always had to get drunk to talk. I'd never had so much trouble talking to a woman. She seemed about to speak, but never did; her legs were up on the third chair, motionless, her left hand lay between them. She finished her cigarette, asked me for a sip of beer. She got up and stretched; then she dropped her arms self-consciously, and she walked over to the window. She looked out, resting her elbows on the sill: I came up behind her and put my arm around her waist, unprepared for the unbelievable feel of her skin; she was trembling, or it was my hand; her hair against my neck felt like a warm dry tongue, unsettling me further, come on, I said to myself, it's just her hair. There's one of my students, down there in the alley, she said: I kissed her hard, her arms came up and she squeezed, hurting the back of my neck, I moved my fingers under her shirt, hung up on the skin of her back and she kissed me again, I could feel her teeth through her lips, Josef's voice came back, fell away through her kiss, I moved my hand over her breast, my hand was numb except for the part of my palm where her small nipple rested, her arms stayed tight around my neck, I felt the muscles of her thighs against mine, her stomach muscles shook once under my hand. Then she pushed me away, took off her pants and slowly unbuttoned my shirt, smiling and shoving my hand away when I reached for my own belt. When I was naked she raised her arms so I could pull her shirt over her head, I moved my hands slowly over her breasts as I pushed the shirt up, my mouth was dry, I blinked my eyes: but we made love slowly, I wanted to touch her and she moved her whole body against me, she kept my hand between her legs for a long time, her eyes were closed and she was relaxed in a way I'd never expected her to be, so that I was surprised when she moved and reached for me, she took me into her a little at a time and breathed out a tight stream of air when I was inside, she began to move hard against me, almost raising my body as I pressed down, there was no style, no cover for her need, she was not like the others, I could feel her coming beneath me, and I was filled with a crazy sense of flying.

Her skin was red from my whiskers; she said, through half-closed lips, you ought to shave more often. She asked me not to move, and her fingers moved slowly over my back, holding me, making me light and sleepy. She said I'd better come out. When I'd moved off her, she rolled away from me and put the knit top back on, saying she was cold.

—Jesus, you've got a marvelous ass.

She turned red, her face bright, her eyes not secretive; I want to look at you, she said, and she sat up, her knees extended, her feet under her. I put my hand on her thigh; she was smiling, telling me I was good in bed. You too, I said, meaning it, but this moment of choice had come later to her and she was more sure of it than I was. There'd been a stillness about Nancy toward the end, we'd let our bodies go and try to follow them, we were unable to say anything afterwards. But Carol, naked and relaxed in front of me, running her fingers over my chest, made me feel we'd been together for months; at the same time, I couldn't believe she was here with me like this. I kept touching her skin, I kissed her; I felt it'd be all right as long as we didn't talk about it, or get out of the bed. I touched her nipple through the knit fabric, watched it rise, and she smiled, brushed her face against me, said when can we do it again? Ben called out, like a memory, Ben wake up, pick me uuuup!

In the morning I heard thunder outside, saw the dull light beginning to fall on the bed sheets; Carol's face was hidden under the covers, but her arm lay extended between us. After those months of waking alone, her arm seemed, until I was fully awake, to be my own, yet separate, as when your own arm falls alseep and seems to move by itself.

I moved carefully out of bed, heard Ben stirring and looked down at her; she'd changed the sense of this room, and I didn't think I could go on living here if she ever left. She'd keep things clean and I'd get used to good meals again, she'd hold everything together, as Nancy had done. Ben called me, and I turned around; he was trying to swing his leg over the crib bar. Most mornings I want to make these first moments last, when he gets up, he yawns and lays his head against my shoulder, protecting me from the real beginning of the day, but this morning I couldn't hold onto that feeling, so I started making his breakfast; now that Carol was here all my days would be complicated as soon as I opened my eyes.

Ben chattered the words he knew, as if to make sure of them again, and I turned the radio, heard the last bar of the guitar intro to Rod Stewart's 'Maggie May', slapped my hand on the refrigerator in time to the first two drum beats. I sang along, and flipped Ben's egg over; as I was putting it on his plate I remembered Nancy, realized I knew only the circumstances, not the reasons for her leaving. If I knew the reasons, maybe I wouldn't make the same mistakes with Carol.

—Carol wake up! said Ben; she was standing in the doorway, wrapped in one of my shirts, which came almost to her knees, and the sleepy smile on her face continued even through the thunder outside. I kissed her hesitantly as she brushed past me into the bathroom. Ben got down from his chair and tried to open the door, and I told him, feeling embarrassed, that Carol wanted to be alone in there. She told him through the door that she'd be right out. I felt like I was in a restaurant; I was watching Ben, hoping I'd be able to give my attention to Carol when she came out.

—Guess I'll have some coffee, she said, sitting down; I put the kettle on and sat down next to her. She was trying to show Ben how to play patty cake, and he was laughing, happy even though he couldn't get the words or the timing right. She stopped abruptly to put milk in her coffee, and he started to cry. Why is he upset? she said.

—Well, see, you have to give him some warning when you stop a game.

She nodded, said she wished it weren't raining outside. We moved into the other room, taking our coffee, and while Ben and I built houses she talked; she said she'd almost gotten married last year to a chemistry student, but she'd seen toward the end what he wanted from her; he was 'passive and disorganized', needed somebody to look after his bills, his clothes, his car, his books and papers. She said he wouldn't stand for arguments the last few months, he figured everything was settled and had already begun introducing me as 'my new wife'. I was surprised, at first, that she was telling me all this; I thought maybe she wanted to make up for asking about Nancy. Leon called me a selfish bitch when I broke up with him, she said, 'nobody does this to me' and all that crap; you know.

Whatever she was remembering made her stop talking. When she looked at me again, Ben was trying to push me over, and I was pretending he could. You know, she said, a lot of people think I'm hard to get along with. I don't think so, but, so many people have . . . she didn't finish. The conversation was making me uncomfortable, I didn't want to know all this, the only important thing was whether she could get along with me. And I felt she was waiting for something from me, she'd judge me by how close I was able to come to it. I said, well you're sort of tense all the time, and maybe people get the wrong idea. She said it was hard to relax, there was so much she wanted to do. She began telling me about the scholarship and the high school tennis championship she'd won, the pressure she'd felt from her parents because she was an only child. I tried to imagine her as she'd been then, as she talked I saw her hair turn limp, saw the sweat on her brown legs running down from her tennis dress, her hand tight on the racquet, smiling at the person she'd just beaten but shaken up and exhausted inside, or maybe feeling she'd evened something up, maybe having envied the other girl for dates or clothes or friends. She was quiet, and she cleared her throat; she'd gotten to me, I hated the people who hadn't liked her. She spoke slowly, as if she were thinking aloud, I guess I like you because you're different from all that, the men I meet are under this pressure and I know all about them, they bore me right away.

—Well, I didn't make it, is all. I mean, I wanted something too, it's just—

—Circumstances, she said, making me forget what I would've said. Then she leaned forward suddenly, and said, tell me about the band, what was the—what kind of music did you play?

—Couple of years ago, I said, it was all this psychedelic bullshit and we were playing it because it was around, and people wanted to hear it, you know? Then we heard Santana, and what the Band was doing, they knocked us out and we got a conga player and a horn man—it wasn't Latin, except a little bit, it was mostly rhythm and blues but it was harder than that, it had this—I can't explain it really—it was like it jumped, lot of back beat, you know, but it just used to feel like it would go on by itself once we got it started, like we weren't playing it, the energy was moving it along, or something—I mostly was listening to the Memphis stuff and writing like that.

—So it's not like you play now?

—No, nothing like it, I said, you need a band to be playing what I'd like to play. There's other bands doing that shit now.

I put the last block on about the fifteenth house we'd made, and Ben, laughing, knocked it down with his foot. I grabbed him, tickled him, sneaked his pants off while he was laughing and started putting on his diapers. Carol said she'd get his bottle ready; she brought it back, looking at me, giving it to him when I nodded. I wondered how I was going to explain to him that she was moving in with us; he'd been mostly shy around her so far, and she seemed awkward, guarded—but I was changing already and it bothered me, I was tense, I'd be short with him if he asked me too many times for a cookie or a glass of milk. Now I put him in his crib, he smiled up at me and touched the hand I laid on his stomach, and I knew I didn't want anyone to get in the way of what he needed from me. Carol was already making me feel things I could barely remember feeling for Nancy, I didn't want to see her lonely, as she'd been in the times she'd told me about, I kissed Ben, left him sucking his bottle, sighing rhythmically.

She was sitting down in the kitchen. I came up to her, and she put her face against my stomach, I reached into the shirt and put my hand over her breast. She kissed me hard, but she was thinking about something else; she lay quiet when we made love, she was gentle but she hardly moved. I felt relieved to get up from her, and I rolled over, put my hand under her leg she'd raised. After awhile she said, I've got to get back and correct papers. When I didn't say anything she told me she'd been thinking, since last night when I'd asked her, about moving in with me, and she'd decided she'd better wait until she felt more sure.

—Well, I don't know how the hell I can see you then, I can't get out of here.

She told me not to be angry, she just felt it was too early. She spoke earnestly and carefully, asking me to understand, and I nodded my head as if I did. But when she left I felt I'd been used, made up my mind I'd wait until she called me, I wouldn't make a move toward her.

Tuesday night there was a three car collision in front of the house. Nobody was hurt but they sent three police cars and I was afraid the sirens would wake Ben. I'd never have noticed the accident if Carol had been here; I was sure she'd never call, or come back, and I wished I weren't waiting for her, wished I'd forgotten her. There was no liquor in the house, I was sick of the radio and I'd read all my books; I was lonely enough to call Ron, but as I went to the phone there was a knock on the door and it was Carol. I couldn't show her I was glad to see her, and I wondered why; she said she'd been to a department meeting, the kind that go on and on and don't settle anything, she'd volunteered for a curriculum committee to get it over with and now she wished she hadn't; they'd had the first committee meeting tonight in a bar, and she'd had to keep moving out of the reach of one of the older professors without offending him. She wondered aloud if you ever got used to the paperwork and the meetings, none of it seems to bother my 'learned colleagues', she said, but I think they all died five years ago. She didn't usually talk like that, and I laughed; I could see she was high. I told her she should make up excuses if she didn't want to go to those meetings, but she said she wasn't any good at lying.

—You got to pretend you're not lying, believe what you're saying. You, know, tell them you're writing an article or some bullshit, they ain't going to check.

She said she wasn't sure; I could see she was thinking she owed the job something, she talked about her principles and the difficulty of finding another teaching job. She kicked off her shoes, sat back on her spine and put her feet up, and she picked dust off her suede skirt, brushed off her shiny blouse, reached under it and skillfully took off her bra, laid it on the table, saw me looking at it, and turned red. I laughed at her; she took my hand, leaned forward and asked me how I'd been, smiling at me in a way that made me forget she'd been gone for two days. I told her Ben had not had a single accident since I'd taken his diapers off during the day; she saw me staring at her, tried to tell me to stop, and started laughing; well it's cold in here, that's why, she said. Hey, look what I got, she said suddenly, reaching into her jacket pocket and pulling out a nickel bag- —you got any papers?

—No, we'll just tap the tobacco out of a couple of cigarettes, I said. It was unbelievable that she had some, it was one of the things I'd given up when I'd got Ben and I wondered how it would take me; I used to smoke numbers like cigarettes. Jesus, he's asleep, I said to myself, and besides it's free; I made two and we passed them back and forth. She inhaled seriously, as if to make sure she was doing it right; as she swung her arm back she knocked her purse over and started laughing; I can't find my barrette, she said, and we laughed harder, my ribs felt like air compressors and I imagined iron lungs on wheels roaring down the street, all these cats using mirrors to drive them backwards like bulldozers. She thought everything was funny, she said I sounded like I was ten miles away. Wow! she shouted, standing up, extending her long arms and trying to spin on one leg; she ran into the bed and fell across it, laughing so hard that she couldn't move—help me up, she gasped, and as I grabbed her hand I had that beautiful slow second of knowing what was going to happen, she pulled and I fell down with her.

We kissed slowly; I could feel her breathing, every give or resistance of the bed, I pushed the blouse away and kissed her breasts, she put her hand in my hair and lay still, I moved my tongue over her for a long time, my mouth dry and leaving her skin dry, I could hear the clock and I thought about the cars going by outside; she pushed and struggled with her skirt and nylons and I tried to help her, there wasn't any strength in my arms; she laughed softly, I pulled the nylons down her legs, kissing her thighs, I could smell the soap she used, feel her legs shaking next to my face and I moved slowly over her, felt her tight, then releasing under me, her breath sharp now, hard against our slow moving bodies; she lay still as sleep, and she whispered something I couldn't hear, I came our of her and she rolled on her side and I moved into her from behind, holding her breasts tight, moving slowly to make it last.

When I didn't feel her move I came out of her and I saw that she was falling asleep; I dressed quietly, put a jacket on and went out. By the time I reached the bar I was no longer high; I drank for about an hour, getting depressed thinking about Ben and my old suspicions; I'd left Ben with her, what if he'd awakened? When I remembered him, I swallowed all of my last drink in one gulp.

In the morning I had a headache, mostly from the beer, and I had to shake Carol to get her up. She smiled at me, hugged me, maybe not feeling my body's resistance; she said she'd move her things in after work tonight. Good, I said, kissing her; I couldn't feel anything. She looked at the clock, her face changed, she ran into the bathroom and I started breakfast. Ben woke up, and while I was changing his diapers I smelled the bacon frying and remembered waking up to Nancy's cooking; I'd expected, without knowing it until now, that Carol would have already been up to make breakfast. Ben stood up without looking and banged his head on the drawer I'd left open; I swore at myself, then picked him up and kissed the spot he'd hurt, and Carol called out from the kitchen that she'd like to go to the Chinese restaurant tonight, we could talk about her moving in.

—I don't know, Ben acts up in restaurants.

—Come on, please we can keep him happy.

—No, look, what's wrong with talking here?

—Oh, all right! she said; she was making an egg for herself and she'd set the table. Egg! Egg! Ben howled; I made him one, told him not to cry, and I could see Carol's fist tense up on the table; when he knocked his plate over she looked irritated and turned away. Later on I'd learn that she was always nervous before her first class, but now she made me angry. I've got to go, she said; she banged her knee on the table, and swore. She kissed my cheek and ran out.

—Bye, bye, Ben said, but she'd already closed the door. The food tasted sour to me, but he was eating it steadily, sometimes dropping pieces of his egg on his lap but always picking them up. I dressed him, shaved, and drove to the day care center; each time we stopped at an intersection I could almost feel the oil leaking from the split main seal in front of the transmission. Some mornings he looks younger than he is and I hate to drop him off, though he's stopped crying when I do; I think of the old woman then, or someone like her, and I know this is the best place for him. But I wish I had a wife who'd be his mother. It was Julie's morning off; if she'd been there I might have asked her about Carol's moods. When I got back in the car, the feeling passed, I knew how stupid I'd probably feel after a conversation like that. For a change I was glad I was going to work, I needed to be busy today.

Three months ago, midway through my second gig at the coffee house, I was backstage drinking whiskey and trying to calm down, the set hadn't been going well and it was the first time Sharon and Ron had watched Ben, I could see they were having trouble and it was bothering me. As I bent down to light a cigarette, I felt someone come in; he said, pointing to the whiskey, let me have a hit on that, man, and I passed the bottle over, sondering what he wanted. He took a drink, put the bottle on the table, and he said, hey, what I'm saying, what I want to ask is, uh, can I come up and blow one? On the piano, you know? I was suspicious, but it took me back, I'd wondered around years ago with my guitar, sitting in with anyone who'd let me, sometimes making an ass of myself, like the time I thought I was good enough to play jazz, but learning; when I said, 'sure', his dark face opened without giving anything up, he said, yeah, thanks, and we passed the bottle back and forth, the cat was fingering a pair of sunglasses, I could see his pink palms turning over in the dim light and suddenly I couldn't wait to get back onstage: he'd managed to ask in a way that made me feel he was good, making me know, also, at that same moment, that there wouldn't be any bullshit, he wouldn't try to upstage me, he knew it was my gig. As we were finishing off the half pint, he told me he could play anything, as long as it was blues, and we agreed on 'I Can't Quit You'. When we got out into the light I saw that he was taller than I and well built, the light made his bright blue shirt almost green, I could hear his heels as he went to the piano; he put his hands on the piano, they looked bigger and more relaxed.

I introduced him to the audience and we got into it, and after twelve bars I knew he was good, he had a light, fast touch with his right hand, like Otis Spann, his left hand was a whole rhythm section: and I felt something I'd missed in this time of playing alone, when you play alone you do only what you can carry, only what the auidence will stand without much rhythm, and you get sick of listening to yourself; but there was Marcus coming in behind me, surprising me because I'd forgotten but making me feel right because he played all good notes, I remembered hearing 'Shop Around' on scratchy Detroit stations, and trying to get Little Rock and Chicago, Jerry Butler, The Impressions, even Little Walter's 'My Babe' way back when I was a kid, the Shirelles and the Drifters, I remembered the blues and I remembered when we put the other mike on Marcus and we sang 'There Goes My Baby'; I felt the audience fall away like people finding beds at a party, Marcus and I played for each other, giving each other the tunes you usually can't share, letting them spread out between us, but not letting them off the stand.

We heard only the hand clapping and the applause, when I'm alone I can practically figure the conversations. We didn't say one word to each other during the set, I'd begin a tune and he'd come in and our riffs would fall together by instinct. When the gig was over I re-introduced him and the audience clapped loud and whistled, forgetting themselves. Beautiful, he said, we squeezed each other's hands, rubbed each other's hair. I took him over to the table, and before Ron could be impressive and liberal I told him I had to leave with Ben, asked him to come along. He looked down at Ben, some people feel things in children, they're waiting to be surprised but they don't have expectations; he said, what are you, I ain't ever seen anything like you, and Ben said I'm a baby—Marcus said, no, you're a tiger, man, I'm going to show you how to be a tiger. But his girl friend waved him over, he looked uncomfortable and walked to his table; I watched his hands moving, cutting the air between their faces. When he came back to my table he said, sorry, man, can't make it, another time maybe. I wished I weren't with Ben; I told him on the way home that I was sick of being controlled by him. Then I felt terrible, partly because I knew he couldn't understand.

I've been hoping Marcus will come around again, every Friday night I look for him.

Ben and I walked to the store alone after we parked the car; Carol had asked me to get some sauerkraut for dinner. There'd been about an eighth of an inch of snow and some of it remained in the doorways and gutters. The walks were dry, Ben's red boots made a sloshing sound as he went along.

This was the first time I'd seen Josef since he'd told me about his son; he looked down, mumbled hello when I came in. As I was checking out he said he was sorry, he always talked too much. He waved me away when I told him it was all right, I understood—he handed me my change and as I walked out I realized he'd gone against some standard of his own by telling me. My reaction meant nothing to him.

Maury, the five year old down the block, was tagging along behind his father and some woman. Maury had no hat or mittens; he stopped to talk to Ben but they walked on ahead and he had to run to catch up, they never even looked around. Ben squeezed my hand as we crossed the street; he said he was cold, reached out so I'd pick him up. When I wouldn't, telling him we were only a block from home, he sat down on the sidewalk and cried. But as I was getting angry I thought of Maury, and I picked Ben up in my arms. I wanted to kick Maury's father's ass, and that feeling was stronger each time I saw him.

Carol came in right after we got home, saying she didn't feel like cooking, asked if I'd like to go to the Chinese restaurant. I told her I'd made a special trip for the sauerkraut, and I'd have to dress Ben again, he was already hungry and he'd be cranky at the restaurant. I was thinking that she hadn't cooked anything since she'd been here.

—Oh, Ned! Don't be like that, he'll be all right. You don't feel like cooking, do you?

She'd go by herself if I said no, so I put Ben's jacket on him. I couldn't beg her to do something for me. But I saved the feeling up, knew I'd be angry later on.

It was colder now but Ben was happy to be out, and I almost forgot that I don't think it's worth it to take him to restaurants. As we passed the hot dog stand, the dry meat smell hung in the air, stronger than the diesel fuel the buses burned and the smell of dirty cement. Carol said, you know, I hate hot dogs, but if I'm hungry all I have to do is smell something and I want it, even liver.

In the restaurant, we sat down toward the back and put Ben in a high chair; I wished I could relax, but he had to be watched, seen to, he interrupted conversations and he had no patience; at the same time I hated the restaurant, I wanted to let him run around and break things and I wished I wouldn't have to care what he did, that nobody would care if he made noise or spilled things. Carol was in a good mood; she didn't even argue when I said I didn't want to get a babysitter for the gig tomorrow night. She'd got her students interested in a discussion of *The Sun Also Rises*, she said, they were 'bright kids' but, usually, all they thought about was music. I half-listened, helping Ben open the crackers the waitress had given him, so far he'd been quiet and he was doing well with his soup. As she put food on our plates, and as I cut Ben's into small pieces, Carol told me how much she'd hated being a waitress, the way people had stared when she'd leaned over to wash off the tables, the bosses who'd told her to raise her hemlines and to stop wearing tights, the other waitresses, who'd never talked about anything 'intelligent', just boys and clothes. She reminded me of my friend Ernie, who'd told me once that uneducated people have it so much easier than we do, they're happy because they don't have to think, they just accept things. But it wasn't worth arguing about; besides, she had reasons for everything.

Our waiter, when he came by to ask if we'd like another drink, stared at Ben with the sort of detached curiosity some people have when they watch a freak show at a carnival; the other customers looked up when Ben banged his spoon, or made noises, and I wondered what they'd do if he got really upset. But he continued to be happy, he looked around at the people and played with his food, asking me what it was but otherwise not interested in it. A woman had come in the store today asking for white shoes, because she was getting married; when she looked at herself in the mirror, she blushed.

—How come you're so quiet?

—Tired. You been wearing me out, I said. Carol touched my hand and laughed. When she laughed, my whole chest turned over, shoving my throat into my stomach. I knew she'd take all her clothes off when we got home, and she'd put on her long robe, I'd see her skin between the buttons. Ben was restless now, beginning to whine, so we got up from the table, and while I dressed Ben, Carol went over and paid the bill. I'd said I didn't want her to, but she said come on, I'm working, you know. Ben and I walked out ahead of her, but she caught up quickly and took my hand. She looked even smaller now in her grey fur coat, her skin darkened immediately in the cold. She said, I like living with you, I've never lived with anyone else before. I squeezed Ben's hand as we crossed the street, and I said I think of it like it's my first time too.

—But you really ought to trim your moustache, there's things hanging from it, she said, laughing again—but I was sliding away from her laughter, wanting to join in but feeling removed, as if she were across the street and Ben were much further away than my hand could reach.

He didn't fight when I changed him, but he wouldn't go to sleep; every time Carol and I started talking, he yelled out for something, and giggled when I came up to his crib. I wanted to hit him, I said goddam it, all you have to do is to to sleep, can't you even do that? He started to cry then, catching the tone of my voice, and I held him, suddenly angry, believing he was jealous of my time with Carol. But I calmed down as I held him;

he and I had been evicted from the first place we'd lived in, last March when I was broke. I'd wandered around with him until six o'clock, found a cheap hotel which was noisy and stuffy, there were cockroaches in bed with us, and I'd known then, finally, that I couldn't live my life unplanned anymore, I'd gotten a job two days later, and set up a routine we'd followed since then; but now that Carol was here my old hatred of having things organized was starting to come back; I didn't know why she wasn't taking charge of the house, why she wasn't making things easier.

Now, as I lay him down again and patted his back, I wondered about all the things he couldn't tell me, wondered how he was taking to Carol. I touched his head and went back to the kitchen. Carol was twisting her hands together. I knew she'd ask me, what's wrong? and I hoped she wouldn't. She said I seemed angry; I told her there were certain things I expected of her and she wasn't doing them—Ben needed attention from her, I needed the cooking and cleaning done so I'd have some time for myself. She spoke quietly; she brought up her job, her favorite subject, and said she had more to do at night than I did. She'd moved in to be with me, not to turn into a housewife. But this is silly, she said, this is a small place, we can work on it together. Do we have to think about it all the time?

—Look, things like that don't just get done, you have to make yourself do them.

She said it was all in the attitude you had about work—then she changed the subject and told me this wasn't easy for her, all three of us had to adjust to each other. She got up and walked into the kitchen, and I heard her telling me it was just going to take some time. I followed her, took one of her cigarettes, and lit it; I said I'd expected her to see what needed doing, I'd mostly been concerned with Ben's adjustment, not hers. She looked sad; she said she was uneasy around Ben, she didn't want to move in on him too suddenly, didn't really know how to get close to him, or even if she should. I saved that up; she was taking an easy way out. We talked around it for awhile, and by the time she was tired we hadn't settled anything. It was the first night we didn't make love; I'd been waiting for that to happen and I was glad to get it over with.

The next night she said it was cleaning she hated, not cooking, so things looked like they might settle into a routine; maybe she was getting ready, in stages, to take charge of the apartment. But she irritated me in other ways; I'd come home, sick of talking to customers all day, and want to read the paper—she'd want to talk. If I came home complaining, she wasn't sympathetic, as Nancy had been, she'd ask why I didn't find another job, since I hated this one so much. With Ben she was friendly, but uninvolved, as a friend might be; he continued to take all his conversations and troubles to me, and didn't much notice her comings or goings. She was just somebody who slept in daddy's bed. But at the same time he was more demanding, and it was hard to watch Carol do nothing but turn the pages in a book. Though she wouldn't do anything, I felt she disapproved of the way I handled him.

Every few days she'd go back to her room to get her mail; occasionally she'd go over there to study, and I hated that; but I knew we'd have to spend hours talking about it so I figured I'd wait until she calmed down. Her nervousness came out in strange ways; once she told me I was taking her for granted, that I'd already stopped 'working on the relationship'. I told her she was crazy, and kissed her on the cheek; she pulled away and stomped out of the room. That meant I had to talk to her; she couldn't make love if we didn't talk first. Afterwards, she'd lean against me and I'd feel her happiness and it all seemed worth it, we'd talk about things we believed, make plans to stay together and buy a place in the country; she said we should live on her money, she knew I was going crazy in that store, how badly I wanted to play music. That made me embarrassed; she was moving into some place inside me that Nancy'd never touched. I'd feel it only when we made love but it kept me with her and it scared me, sometimes I'd lie awake half the night, wondering if I'd have to pay for loving her, sometimes I think you can only get away with loving a child.

Tuesday morning, she put her hand on my arm as I was getting out of bed, and said I don't have a class at noon today, come on home and I'll make you some lunch. I began the morning suspicious of her motives, maybe she was trying to soften me up, though that didn't seem like her, but soon I just wanted to see her, I felt as if we were two kids from different schools being truant together. I ran home, thinking I'd get there first, but when I walked in she'd already started the soup and hamburgers. I'd almost forgotten the way she looked when she smiled, even now it was difficult to remember her face when I was away from her, I'd remember the feel of her hair against my ear when I kissed her. I wanted to make lunch for you, because I think we've both got to be more patient, she said. I thought I'd been patient enough, but I didn't say anything. She put my food on a plate and we sat down together.

While we were eating she talked about Thanksgiving; she said she'd promised her parents she'd come up, but she thought she could get out of it. I said I'd rather stay here, maybe have some friends over after dinner. I ate slowly, tasting the food for a change as I thought of the bologna sandwiches I carried to work everyday; she kept looking at the clock.

—You got to go somewhere?

—No, she said, just wondering how much time we have before you have to leave. It took me a few seconds to realize what she was talking about, I still hadn't got used to the way her moods changed. She touched her breast for a moment, smiled again, and I said, about ten minutes.

—You know, she said, reaching under the dress she called a pinafore and pulling her stockings slowly down her legs, a few years ago this boy asked me up to his apartment for a 'quick one' and I thought he meant a drink, so I said I didn't drink. We lay down on the bed, she threw her leg over mine and I moved my hand over her ass. What happened? I said, looking down at her. I didn't go, she said. I kissed her, she loosened my pants with one hand and I almost laughed, I still had my tie and my shoes on, she put her hand between her legs for a little while, put my hand on her, I pushed the skirt aside as she reached for me; she wrapped her legs around my back and rocked sideways, squeezing me tight inside her, I pressed down on her covered breast—when we were finished she said I like it sometimes when you can't hold back.

—Yeah, me too; it's more—nobody's thinking about it, you know?

—I guess, she said, tickling me, and shoving me off. You'll be late. She came to the door with me, as she kissed me I put my hand under her dress again, holding her tight even as she stiffened. She said, you're not fair; she kissed me again, saying drop by anytime honey, long as it's not working hours I'll fix you up.

As I walked back to work I had the same feeling I'd had the night we'd gotten high; she'd had it too easy, you just can't do whatever you feel like doing. While I was working I began to believe it was time to say, now look, if you're going to live here there's just some things you've got to do. The thing I wanted from her was a feeling she'd give to my home, something I'd always expected a woman to know how to do. I looked at the clock; she'd be teaching her last class now, but I can imagine her mornings:

she walks in early, for her first class, then sits drumming her fingers on the desk top, waiting for the bell, and she lights a cigarette. Her hair is clean and shiny, her clothes pressed, her jewelry is always silver, rings, bracelets, earrings; she wears only a little make up, but I have never seen her without any, except when she's first come out of the shower; her stomach stiffens, then seems to bloat, she's learned never to eat anything before this class, she has to know whether this is to be one of those days when none of her sentences comes out right, when she has to restate half of them, though the students won't notice anyway; they are recovering from hangovers, or falling asleep, or coming down from getting high last night—today they're asking questions about the final exam, three weeks away, showing more attention than they will in ten minutes, when she'll be explaining the uses of the subjunctive—she expects this, no longer resents it: one of the students she's mentioned, who bullshits and wheedles in class and tries to look seductive when he comes into her office, is trying to get the exam questions out of her; she brushes him off, she's tired of all of them, but her energy begins to move within her, she begins to work hard, enjoying herself even though she hates grammar, and she gets them through the lesson:

in her office, she makes coffee, she will drink five or six cups each day and always has trouble sleeping; she lights a cigarette, relaxes as she never can at any other time; her energy has to yet build up again; her dress is too tight, she's run her nylons again, but her lit class, the only one she really enjoys, is coming up next: while she sits in her office, if no one comes in, if she's not correcting papers, she might be thinking:

Ben's hyperactive, he hasn't got enough to do. Ned spoils him, he's too indulgent, but he's impatient too, there's no consistency. Ned says he wants to play music again; then how come he doesn't have any ambition, how can he stand that shoe store?

If I start taking some responsibility for Ben, Ned'll let me, in fact he'll take advantage of me, and I never wanted kids, I don't like them and Ned wants to be taken care of.

I'll bet that's what she thinks; I'll bet she doesn't understand any better than that.

Ben wouldn't leave me alone while I made supper; I was thinking about what Carol had said, that she'd make supper if I'd clean. He pulled on me, whining and crying and hitting, so finally I took him into the other room and made him sit still in a chair; I listened to him cry for awhile, and then I went in and gave him a stalk of celery, after that he settled down, he asked questions and played with his dump truck, and I wished I hadn't gotten angry at him.

Carol was in the bathroom, changing her clothes; she tries not to let Ben see her naked, though I don't think it matters—maybe she doesn't like the questions he asks her. When she came out wearing her tightest pair of jeans, I slapped her across the ass. She said, I've told you before, don't do that, it reminds me of when I was a waitress. She's wierd about that period of her life, I could've expected this, so I shrugged; she sat down across the table from me, opened a book, and began reading. Ben shook his head at the baked fish, threw himself around in his chair; he knocked his food off the table. While I was cleaning up I asked her why she had to read now, we hadn't seen each other all day. She said she just felt like reading. Ben pushed his plate away, then dragged it back and began to pound on it; it was a metal plate. I shouted, goddam it, shut up, will you?

—Ned! Don't talk to him like that, you'll hurt his feelings.

—Since when do you know so goddam much? All you ever do is ignore him.

She said, oh, you're a perfect parent? Nobody can tell you anything? We said a few more things to each other, and Ben looked from one to another until his face softened as it does when he's about to cry, he said, mad? mad? The clock radio turned itself off, and it seemed very quiet. Carol got down on her knees and began telling Ben in her most professional tone that it was good for people to express their emotions, he slapped at her, hit her arm and she looked shaken, then angry

—He's not going to understand that shit, I said; I picked Ben up and held him tight, but Carol had a look on her face I didn't like, it was as if she were waiting for what I'd say to Ben so she could tear it apart. I whispered to Ben, led him into the other room to build with his blocks; I could hear the pages turning in Caroll's book again. I helped him build a garage, glad he'd finally gotten into his cars and trucks, they were the first of his toys that I'd been able to enjoy. He kept asking me about the wind, which was moving the window sash; I told him it was winter now and kissed his head, forgetting about Carol but not losing my anger, and I, wished there were something to say to Ben, we hadn't better fight in front of him anymore. When we'd fought, Nancy and I, I'd walked out of the house, leaving her to see to Ben, who from about six months would always cry when we were fighting; but I couldn't walk out anymore, not without Ben; I have nothing to replace him, I could lose him, anytime Nancy might change her mind. He asked me to read him a story, so I read him *Gwendolyn the Miracle Hen;* I changed his diapers, got his bottle and put him in his crib; I didn't tell him to go kiss Carol goodnight. When I was sure he was asleep, I walked back into the kitchen.

She was still reading, but she put the book down as I came in. Just to be in the same room with her made me angry, but when I saw she was calm it unsettled me so that I forgot what I was going to say. You know, she said, very quietly, I've been sort of depressed all week, and thinking about it—I guess we're not ready for this, at least I'm not.

—Less'n two weeks, and you want to give up, I said, folding my arms over my chest, moving my head back on my neck; the teakettle whistled and she got up to turn it off. I took one of her menthol cigarettes; her calm worried me, I felt she'd be unshakable if she'd made up her mind. Now she lit a cigarette, and said she wasn't happy, we weren't moving toward anything, she felt she was pushing me to change things I didn't want to change. I remembered the way I'd felt when she'd talked about moving, when she'd said I should change jobs; I said I'd changed all right, I'd found out what a bitch it was to live with her. Don't you see, that's just it, she said, still not angry; I felt I'd been tricked, she'd made it seem as if we agreed we should split up. She stood up again, rubbed her hands and walked around the room. You know sometimes I hate looking out this window, she said. It's too soon, she went on, I think we've got to have some time apart.

—That's such bullshit, you just want to run away from trouble—you're always hanging back anyway, you want things easy.

—No, I don't!

—Yes you do, sure as hell you do—all that stuff you said, last week, it don't mean shit, I shouted; she looked down, held the table with one hand, said she hadn't been lying, she loved me, thought we'd destroy that love if we didn't have some time apart to think about it.

—All right, get out, but don't come back, I'm sick of this shit, I said; even after the way she'd been tonight, I didn't think she'd do it, thought she'd been trying to con me into something. But she got up and began to pack a suitcase, looking hurt now, not looking at me. Then just before she left she told me to call her if I wanted to talk.

—I won't, I said, fighting back the thing in me that wanted her to stay. I took a beer out of the refrigerator, nodding at her when she said good bye. I was glad I'd bought a pint of whiskey this afternoon—as I drank I kept looking around, imagining she'd never lived with me, trying to get the old feel of Ben and me here alone. I was ready to sleep, but as I get into bed I remembered a time when I'd been collecting for my paper route, a woman had paid me, closed the door, and I heard her say to her husband, Herman, if you ever say anything like that to me again I'll slap your face. I'd wondered what he'd said, what her face looked like, I was scared but I pressed my ear to the door, trying to hear something that would make my understand; I knew now her face must've looked like

Carol's tonight, when she was packing the suitcase. I was too angry to sleep well now, and I swore at the things I remember.

She wasn't in bed in the morning; you always think of empty beds at night but they're worse in the morning, because you know another night's coming. Ben woke up; as I was changing his diapers he said, where Carol is?

—She's at work—do you want some applesauce?

I didn't want to go out for lunch; Carol's leaving made the sense of Nancy strong in me again, Nancy was something I could hold to so I wouldn't think too much about Carol, wouldn't spend all my time angry:

When Nancy was seven months pregnant, we drove up to Minneapolis for a concert the Band was giving at the Guthrie. She'd sent away for tickets because she knew I'd never get around to it, even though I wanted to go, and she'd arranged for us to stay overnight with a friend of hers in Stillwater. I drove slowly, and we stopped often. We talked about the baby, or wondered aloud if the concert would be any good; a lot of studio bands aren't worth a shit live. The day was bright, cold after the week of spring rain we'd had, and I saw patches of snow in culverts and on the low ground, sometimes under split rail fences. Nancy sat with her arms folded across her stomach, and I remember feeling that that gesture didn't seem to be like her, usually her hands moved all over when she talked; she spoke mostly of a kind of hesitant excitement about the baby, a fear that everything would change between us. I said it'd make things better, knowing I'd talked her into this, she'd been unsure that she wanted a child—but I felt it was private now, between her and the child, something she'd have to get through on her own. Nancy was quiet about things, determined not to slow down; we were trying to get the house fixed up before the baby came. She hadn't bought maternity clothes, because she hated them; she'd put panels in her oldest patched up jeans; she'd carried the weight well, and stayed thin, the only strange craving she had was for fresh asparagus, she'd eat it almost every day with Hollandaise sauce she made. So I never knew, until later on when she started nagging at me, how sick she'd felt most of the time. Carol would have complained constantly, looking for special treatment.

There was a way we had of looking at concert crowds, some day they'd be coming to see me, some of them I'd probably played for already. Nancy and I believed we knew more music than anyone else in the audience; we felt the others had come to make the scene, to see some names. But when we walked into the theatre, it was suddenly hard for me to believe I was special, I was embarrassed to be with a pregnant woman; Nancy already felt unattractive, so I didn't let on, but I kept sneaking looks at the young girls, was glad we had some gigs coming up. People were passing numbers every few minutes, but we ignored them, we had better stuff; after the house lights went down Nancy opened her purse, took out a bag, and rolled a few.

Taj Mahal came on alone, playing blues and ragtime things like I do now; it's hard to open up when the audience is waiting for somebody else, but he was strong enough to get over on his own, he got the people singing and handclapping, made them listen; on that last tour, when we were opening up most of the time, I remembered what I'd learned from watching him.

The Band didn't bother with a stage show, they just played and they were better than their records, good enough to make you sick if you played yourself. Robertson drove them, like Steve Cropper drives the MGs, and when I listened to his solos and dug all that tight energy I realized what shit I'd been playing. They weren't wasting anything, it just kept moving, every instrument was a rhythm instrument so the solos were contained and given room at the same time. Nancy was listening as closely as I was, but she was hearing more of the whole sound, not primarily the guitar, as I was, and I knew she'd have things to tell me when we got back outside, ways our band could get better.

After it was over, she said why don't you go backstage and show them your songs? Maybe they'd want to help you. The way she believed in me made me uncomfortable, as if I didn't deserve it because I'd looked at the young girls. If I'd come with the other cats, Bill would've forced himself backstage, wouldn't have cared if they'd be interested or not, but I hate it when people hang around us after a gig; besides I couldn't see myself dragging Nancy back there, what would I say to them? So I told her they were too good, I wasn't ready and she smiled and said okay, I understand.

On the way to Stillwater, she laid her head against my shoulder and fell asleep. Her legs were open, her belly was nearly resting on the seat. I drove through Minneapolis, still hearing the music, suddenly wishing we weren't having the baby; already, she didn't feel well enough to come along on out of town gigs so I was beginning to step out, but I always played better when she was there. I should quit and stay home, I said aloud; but we had a booking agent now and he was getting us five and six night gigs in Iowa and Minnesota and Wisconsin, we had to take those gigs to make it, I wanted to make it.

You understand, don't you Nance, I said; she stirred, moved out of the light. The way she believed in me then is the hardest thing for me to remember now.

The next night I took Ben to the bar, because I didn't want to go right home. Julie'd surprised me by saying she had a leftover casserole I could maybe use, she was bringing it over around nine. Ben's come to the bar enough so that the bartenders know him, they give him olives and cherries, don't charge me for his cokes. When people he knows from the neighborhood come in, he runs up to them, and they talk with him or buy him something he probably shouldn't have, but we never have sweets at home anyway. He calls Jake 'cousin' and Jake always tells him, 'that's a lot better than grandpa.' Today two secretaries came in and sat down next to us, and between their friendly comments to Ben I heard them talking about a party they'd both attended—she was so bombed, first she'd be making out with Michael, but he says he's got strep throat so she turns around and starts making out with Chris, it was the funniest thing. They were talking a little too loud for the place, and both of them seemed to realize this at the same moment, they finished their drinks quickly and walked out. We left right after they did, we never stay long because I feel uncomfortable, the wind was blowing against us, up Chase St., and when we'd walked a block Ben wanted to be carried: as I bent over to pick him up, someone pulled loosely on my sleeve.

—Hey buddy, I ain't got no place to stay, he said: he had no teeth, his face was shapeless except for his eyes, which cleared off and receded alternately as he spoke. I said he knew where to go, the Rescue Mission was only three blocks, but he shook his head, saying I ain't got no liking for sleeping with drunks, and he belched. Then he pointed his fingers at me, and he said you don't want your kid to see me, ain't it? You don't want him knowing a guy gets down and out, right?—then his voice changed- —just for the night, all I'm asking.

I shook my head, still holding Ben, watching the man; he didn't look sober enough to try anything but if he did I'd have to hang on to Ben and use my feet, I'd only have one chance. But he seemed to give up, though he laughed in two short bursts before he wandered off. When Ben asked me about him on the way home, I didn't know what to say.

—What? Ben said, pointing at the man.

—Some guy, I said, telling myself there's some people you can't take chances on, but I seemed to be lying, I was shaking, almost hearing the laugh again. At our front stoop I looked back and I could still see him, he'd stopped a well-dressed couple and wqs waving his arms; I'd never known a bum to stop a man with a child, or a couple, he'd got over the fence you put up for people like him, he dragged you in.

I was glad to be home, until I thought of Carol—I turned on the radio and played with Ben as noisily as I could—it was good she hadn't involved herself with him, he'd only asked about her once, but I hated her more for that than for anything else. The radio stopped playing suddenly, but this time the alarm knob hadn't moved, and when I turned it around I saw that a tube had burned out. Ben stamped his feet, yelling 'radio on, radio on', and I tried, uselessly, to explain that the radio was broken, he went on crying until I started to read one of his books in a very loud voice; he crawled up in the chair next to me, but I was angry at him now, bored with the story, Carol had changed the balance and I wished I'd never asked her to move in. You know, you got to stop yourself from depending on things, not wanting them to change, especially bitches, I said to Ben, after we'd finished the story—look at the snow coming down, see how it's covering the bottom of the window. He wanted to see, so I picked him up and took him to the window, he tried to touch the snow through the glass, and looking down I saw Julie get out of her car and come across the street. I'd planned to put Ben in bed before she came, but I changed my mind, I knew he'd like to see her. Julie played with him in a relaxed way he hadn't known from other women, and he seemed happy to go to sleep, knowing she was there.

It was easy to talk to her, after Carol, we talked about Ben's progress with the toilet and started on the six pack she'd brought over. She laughed at lot, said it was warm in the room a few times, and then she pulled her sweater over her head, let her white shirt hang out of her pants. Our chairs seemed to move together as we talked, as we gestured our hands began touching, she was easy with her body, teasing, prolonging this ritual we were involved in and yet making me feel she had some other, unconnected urgency, that she was doing this for some reason. She was close to me, I laughed at something she said and without thinking I ran my finger over her covered breast. She caught my hand and put it against her breast, stood up, weaving a little, bent over and kissed me. We got out of our clothes, I pulled the bed down and she lay on top of me, I moved my hand over her ass, she squirmed away from me; we could not move in the same rhythm, she seemed to want me to slow down, then to start moving all over me as soon as I did, she'd take my hand off one part of her body and put it on another; Julie was not thin, but now she seemed all bones and shoulders and teeth, her muscles were tight and she was weightless, sometimes shutting her eyes tight as if she were trying to think her way out of this; I was getting angry and I wanted to get it over with, she turned on her stomach and said 'hurry' with a passion I knew she didn't feel, and the edge in her breathing made me feel sad. She was crying before we'd finished, so I knew we'd have to talk but I didn't mind, either because it was Julie, or because Carol had changed me in some way I hadn't realized until now. She sat up. I put my arm around her and her body turned stiff, but I pulled her against me, made her lie down with me under the covers.

She told me that this was the first time she'd slept with anyone else since she'd got married, she said she was ashamed of herself, she'd used me. I said I didn't believe that, I'd wanted her since we met. She half smiled, blew her nose, and said her husband had a girl friend, he'd said he and Julie should have an open relationship, they should sleep with other people if they wanted to and he wanted to, he'd even had the girl over for dinner, which Julie'd cooked. He keeps telling me he still loves me, he says this is healthy, Julie said, and tonight he's out with her so I came over here. I was going to tell him all about it and make him jealous.

—I wish you'd told me all this stuff before.

—You wouldn't have slept with me probably, she said—well, now I don't know what to do.

I felt I had to say something, so I told her she shouldn't do things she didn't want to, especially sleep with someone, I thought of high school waitresses taking their break, smoking, waiting for their boyfriends to call, their faces looking even younger each time the phone rang, I thought of the times I'd had Ben in cafes and I'd envied the people who could sit quietly and eat without interruptions, until I'd remember that my life didn't seem to exist before I'd gotten him; there was another life, with Nancy, before we'd had him, but nothing in between. I asked her if she wanted to stay with her husband, if she thought he'd change.

—Do you?

—I guess you got to find out.

She said I know, I really just need somebody to talk to; she began to get angry at him, to tell me private things, what he was like in bed, how he treated her when their friends, his friends, came over, and he thought the day care center was a joke, a 'little hobby' to keep her busy. I was uncomfortable, wanting her again in spite of what she'd told me, her hand lay on my stomach, her legs were wrapped around mine, her breast fit into the hollow of my shoulder. Then she sat up, her back longer and white in the light from window, she lit two cigarettes and handed one to me, and I knew I'd miss her long hair when I felt it against my chest again. She had the ashtray balanced on the blankets, right above her stomach, we smoked the cigarettes and she was quiet, so I didn't say anything.

After she'd put her cigarette out, she lay as she'd been before, with her hand on my chest now, and she said, how'd it happen that you got Ben? If you don't want to talk about it that's all right. I told her; she said she couldn't believe I'd done those things but if I had I was a real son of a bitch; it was different from telling Carol, Julie hadn't asked any questions. I wished she didn't love her husband and then, no longer making sense to myself, I wished she were Carol. Julie moved her hand down my chest to my stomach.

—Julie—

She put her hand around my cock and left it there. I want it to be right, she said, moving one finger over my balls, after this I'm going to get up and go home but I want it to be right, we know each other now.

Friday night Marcus showed up at my gig, and he was alone; in the second set he played piano, and afterward he came home with Ben and me. I felt good when I put Ben into bed, I was glad there was only the two of us and I was proud of him for getting by as well as he did. In the first few days after Carol had left I'd been hard on him, half-believing he'd caused her to leave until I realized he'd had nothing to do with it—but it's easy to blame things on a child, because he can't act on his own, can't take responsibilities. I'd begun to think of Nancy again, felt maybe I'd learned enough so that we could get together soon; after Carol, I appreciated Nancy so much that it almost hurt. Ben said daddy, kiss and hug; and I pulled the blanket around him; I leaned over the crib to kiss him, felt his hands pull gently at my hair. Marcus had already opened a couple of beers by the time I got back into the kitchen. He was staring into his glass and tapping his right foot.

—Hey, I'm glad you could come by tonight.

—Yeah, well, man, he said, I've been having some trouble with my old lady so I split for awhile. I said everybody had trouble with his old lady; he started to laugh. As he looked around I felt he was taking my while life in, he'd listen to what I said about it but he'd figure the rest out for himself, not feeling the need to ask questions. His voice was soft but it made you listen, he seemed to choose his words but it wasn't as if he'd rehearsed them; he'd gone to school in engineering but hadn't found a job, so he was an insurance trainee, hoping something else would break before he had to commit himself to the insurance company. He told me about the blues clubs back home in St. Louis, and he said he'd taken piano lessons for nine years as a kid but hadn't played much the last few years. When he asked me how it'd been to tour I found myself telling him the truth, neither bullshitting him nor pretending to experiences I hadn't had.

We talked about jobs we'd had as kids, and he began to talk; Marcus had a way of using his whole body to tell a story, he'd use his face and eyes to show how the characters in the story looked, changing his tone of voice to each of theirs as he talked, his hands would be moving always, he'd spread and close his knees:

One of the worst times, man, was when I was in college in St. Louis, I was doing this janitor thing to get through, you know, working at this hospital and shit—well, like this one semester I got mono and that laid me up two weeks—when I got back to work I saw it wasn't cool, but I didn't think nothing of it, see I'd been working there three years and always done my shit. So one morning, man, I came in six o'clock and there is no time card for me, so I find this supervisor cat and he says well, they were going to call you, you're fired. Naturally I raised hell and then the Man come in and I got on his case, told him he's a fucking racist and it's lucky students couldn't join the union and this shit—well he sent one of his boys to get the security cop so I split, which was stupid man—if I'd been cool, I wouldn't have said nothing to him but gone to a dean or some labor board, I might have got some shit out of it—but he was a hard fucker, wouldn't even give me an advance on money I had coming.

Marcus leaned back, opened another beer, and we talked that one over for awhile; I told him about the times we'd been paid off in bad checks, once we'd given away a thousand dollars worth of equipment. Marcus sat forward in his chair, listening, smiling for both of us, for the times we'd been idiots. But I could see he was getting ready to go, he knew enough to go home and straighten things out with his old lady, and I wished I'd tried to make Carol stay, or Nancy. No, just Nancy, Carol wouldn't have stayed anyway. Before he left, he said he'd come by next Friday, maybe with his old lady. I realized, as I got into bed, how long it'd been since I'd talked to a man: when I talk to some man it's got to be easy in the beginning, I haven't got the patience to give things time, I've never wanted to talk to Ron since the first time, when he told me I could use his guitar. But I listen to what he wants to talk about, and he and Sharon have asked us down for Thanksgiving dinner. I don't want to be alone on Thanksgiving.

It'd turned warm again, probably in the fifties, when I went down the next morning for the mail. I was restless and I tried to think of someone Ben and I could visit, I knew, unwillingly, that I wanted to see Carol, but she hadn't called. Most of my anger was gone, I felt miserable, wishing she'd stayed. And so I called Marcus, felt relieved when he didn't answer. Ben was eating the last of his egg, which I'd cut into little pieces; his head was bent so that his hair raised in a tuft, showing the back of his neck. When he's quiet I wonder, always, what he's thinking about, if he remembers Nancy. I felt closed in tight in the apartment and I remembered the house Nancy and I'd rented outside La Crosse, we'd been told we could buy it and I remember how we'd felt those first few weeks in our own house, before I'd gone on the road. We painted all the rooms and cleared everything out, she was pregnant but she worked as hard as I did; every night she'd cook up a big meal and the other cats in the band would come over and we'd play quiet stuff, sometimes she'd sing with us and she always made sure we had beer and things to eat while we were playing.

The first time I ever gave Ben a bottle was about two months after that, the night I got home from the tour. We'd fought, hadn't settled anything, and Nancy'd fallen asleep but I couldn't; she'd read ghost stories when she was pregnant and I'd said I didn't believe in ghosts, but she'd talked about it so much that I was jerking my head toward every noise in the floors and walls that night, as I sat up and got high so I could sleep. Suddenly Ben cried out, and I stiffened, looked toward Nancy but she didn't wake up, I swore at her but I didn't want to deal with her so I went in and got him. The whole bottom of his face moved as he sucked on the nipple, he'd trap the air and I'd have to take the bottle out of his mouth and squeeze the nipple. My arms got hot under him, the more relaxed he became, the heavier he got, and finally he let the nipple drop out of his mouth. I got into bed, being careful not to touch Nancy, listened to Ben's breathing and fell asleep.

—More applesauce, daddy, Ben said; I wondered how many times he'd had to ask me. No, he would've started to cry soon enough if I hadn't heard him. After I filled his bowl I went to the window, and I decided that I'd take him down to see Chesapeake Bay, we hadn't looked at anything in Baltimore and it was a nice day. He was excited when I got his coat and hat out of the closet, I laughed when he said 'oh boy!' and waved his arms, ran to the door, stopped, came back and said, indignantly, too cold, jacket on. On! When we started off I realized I'd forgotten to look at the map, but I figured I'd have to run into it if I headed southeast.

But I couldn't find the bay; we got caught in slow traffic on the far east side of Baltimore and I was lost, the neighborhood around us looked rough and it seemed as if the morning had turned to dusk, shutters and store fronts were boarded up and the people looked desperate, or afraid. It was getting time for Ben's nap and he was cranky, I was at a stoplight swearing at some out of town driver when I heard a loud banging under my hood, a rattle like the quick worsening of some sickness, and the oil and generator lights came on; I knew what it was, I steered the car toward the right, the engine gave out and the car coasted just far enough to reach the curb.

I turned to get Ben out of his car seat, trying to hide the little shake in my voice as I told him we'd have to get a taxi, or a bus: I heard a tapping at my window, there were three men standing on the driver's side of my car; when I tried to roll up the window the rest of the way, the man in front stuck a small knife between the window glass and the door frame. I locked my door. Ain't you a long way from home, he said.

—I ain't getting out.

—You ain't got no choice, motherfucker, we can come on in just as easy, he said. I swore under my breath, I had no chance with Ben, but when I looked at the men again I knew I had no chance anyway. Ben started to leave his car seat when I opened the door, but something in my tone of voice must've made him stay. It was right around noon, there were cars and people all over the street as the men made a tight circle around me, shoving me up against the car door. They were all big, all wearing wide-brimmed hats and leather coats, one of them wore an earring; I was afraid to look at their faces. One of them patted me down quickly, took my wallet, and looked at me with a smile on his face, his head moving as if he were high, they're all high, I thought. Ain't you got no sense? the man with the wallet said—hey, I'm talking to you, boy. He seemed only to tap my stomach but I lost my breath, and they started laughing; in some horrible center of my mind I could hear Ben crying. The third one, who hadn't spoken, reached in through the car window, took the keys, shook them an inch from Ben's face, opened the car door and slammed it as hard as he could. I'd never heard Ben cry like this; they were still laughing, bumping asses and slapping hands, the front man said hey, I ain't talking shit, let's cut this jive ass hippie motherfucker. I'd told them I'd got lost, my car's engine had blown a rod, and remembered how I'd always heard you made it worse if you showed your fear but I was shaking uncontrollably, I said please, you got my money, don't mess with my son, hating myself for the whine in my voice, and for their laughter.

—Oh we ain't got to do nothing to that little fucker, we just allow him to watch and leave him, the front man said. I remembered the small knife hidden by his hand.

—No, just let me take him and we'll go, please, I said again. The front man hit me in the mouth, that's right he said, get down on your fucking knees, you going to have to ask us nice, he said. He shoved me against the car, I bounced off and the other two hit me in the stomach, I couldn't get up, Ben's name moved in my mind, seemed to become a memory, his crying as far off as my head seemed from my body. Hey, pigs, one of them said; the front man pulled me up, said he'd cut us both if I tried anything, if I didn't make it look good, I grabbed the fender, rolled off, and got Ben out of the car, he was near choking from his screams and the wool hat I'd tied too tightly under his chin. I wondered if the other people would finish me, but they didn't even look. None of the taxis would stop, and when I saw my own face in a store window I knew why. I stumbled, and looked back; they were stripping my car and passing some smoke around. Ben was getting heavy; I stepped out into the street and a taxi stopped; when I got in he told me I'd better not be pulling some shit, he'd only stopped for the kid. He asked me what had happened and I told him until he seemed too interested, almost enjoying it; I held Ben tight, kissed his head, rubbed him, tried everything to stop his crying and the deep shake that moved through his whole body.

When we got home the driver waited until Ben and I came down with the fare, we got back into the house and I locked the door, took Ben's coat off, gave him a bottle and rocked him, trying not to think. Ben made the driver stop, and I'd had it backwards, they'd maybe have killed me if it hadn't been for Ben; but they've got my wallet my address they might come back. I found some cigarettes, poured myself a drink and let Ben's shaking go down into sleep, it was the first time he'd ever fallen asleep in my arms. It was hard to get up from the chair, I was stiff all over and my ribs hurt when I put Ben in his crib. In the bathroom, I put some diaper rash ointment on my face. Then I went in to look at him, hoped he'd forget what'd happened; I had to get him out of the city. We could go back to La Crosse; I hate La Crosse. I leaned over the crib again and kissed him, it was as if I wanted to make sure he was really there. The car is gone. The apartment was completely still, except for the street noise from outside and I remembered, I saw Ben's face in the car again and knew I'd never forget that, his fear had spoken as if I'd left him on a street corner and he'd been crying after me, when I'd got out of the car he'd had nothing to hold on to. The crying I did then hurt my ribs, my stomach, the tears hung and itched on the ointment, the worst possibilities of that scene became real, making me forget we'd made it, we were home. I almost called Carol; then I felt sick for even thinking about it. I stood by Ben's crib a long time, touching his back in his sleep, trying to prove to myself that it was past, it was over, I hadn't lost him.

Ben and I walked down to the drugstore to get a paper, as we did every Sunday morning. It was overcast and a cold rain began falling on our way home, I hate this fucking city, I said to myself. Ben looked up and opened his mouth to catch the raindrops with his tongue; twice this morning he'd said daddy have owie? and I'd struggled to tell him, mostly evading him, saying, without much conviction, that he didn't have to think about them, they were like the wolves, foxes and witches in his fairy tale book. The only change I noticed in him was that he was holding my hand instead of running ahead; when he asked me again on the way up the apartment stairs, I told him, finally, that they were scary men, that I'd been scared, that they'd hit me because they'd wanted my money and our car. I felt then, though I couldn't be sure, that I'd relaxed him.

I always read the comic strips to Ben, and then I let him put them on the floor, he tries to read them on his own and then has a good time tearing up the paper and scattering it. We sat in the chair reading Major Hoople, and when I heard the knock at the door I hoped, or pretended that it was the pipes knocking. The knock came again and I jumped, unsettling Ben from my lap. I whispered to him to be quiet: we heard footsteps walking away. I was shaking so bad I couldn't stand still; it was like that first instant of falling, your mouth opens, your heart stops, the first instant repeats itself endlessly, lives on long after you've fallen. It took me three tries to get Carol's number. Her voice on the phone made me feel better, though I had to talk for ten minutes to get her to come over, I said I'd been wrong and that I wanted to talk. I couldn't bring myself to tell her what'd happened, felt, somehow, that she wouldn't come over if I did. When she hung up I told Ben she was coming, and put some coffee on.

I opened the door, Ben said 'hi, Carol', and I moved toward her with my arms out. She was about to resist, but I saw her take in my face, she said Oh God and came to me, hugging me so tightly that my ribs hurt. Her face, when she stepped back, opened up in a way I could never have believed if I hadn't seen it, she looked as if she might cry, her face was that vulnerable and yet strong, she could take care of me. Let's have some coffee, she said. She picked Ben up and kissed him, something she'd never done, and he said oh, oh Carol come back, waving his hands and almost dancing in her arms. You know, she said quiet y, I missed him, that sort of surprised me.

I sat down because I didn't think I could stand, I was afraid to tell her; but I began telling her, leaving out only the part I was ashamed of, that I'd begged them not to hurt Ben, hidden behind him, really, because

I'd been asking them not to hurt me. Her face changed constantly as she listened, she blinked her eyes; I was seeing it all again, and I had to stop talking. She rubbed my head as I looked down at the table. Ben, who'd been quiet, got down from her lap and climbed up in mine—it wasn't until then that I really believed he was all right. I said, finally, can you stay until he goes to bed; so we can talk?

—Yes—I didn't expect this—let me;—well, yeah, she said.

She walked over to the closet, and pulled her dress over her head; I remembered Julie suddenly. Carol took out her blue jeans and an old shirt. If I ever run away from home again, she said, remind me to pack right. My hands got warm, remembering the feel of her skin, but I didn't touch her; and then it seemed to me she was showing me she wanted to be here by getting undressed in front of me and Ben. I was sure, though, that she'd forgotten Ben at that moment, her gestures were awkward but she went through with it, struggling to seem relaxed as she reached to hang up her dress; it was familiar and it felt good, her awkwardness was the first thing I'd noticed about her, I'd grown to like it, though I'd forgotten about it while she was gone.

There was tension between us, maybe only because we needed to talk; she seemed to get rid of hers by cleaning up the kitchen; whatever she did, though, she did by choice, I knew the cleaning was not automatic, probably it had almost nothing to do with the fact that the kitchen was dirty. Ben and I played with his trucks and blocks. She watched me take Ben's training pants off and struggle with the diapers.

She asked me how he was doing with it; I said I thought he was a little confused; he'd only learned to urinate in the toilet, he still used his diapers at bedtime.

He didn't want to go to sleep, but I didn't mind much; when she was gone, the old closeness had returned between Ben and me, the old sense of trading and using each other's cells, brains, feelings. I wondered if I'd ever know my life was no longer split between a woman and Ben; he was going down to sleep, and I couldn't wait to get back into the kitchen, didn't think I could stand it if she left again.

Ben's way of going to sleep is to bounce his head up and down on his crib mattress, and he sings 'ah, ah' in the staccato rhythm of his bouncing, you get used to the rhythm and sound and you notice again only when it's stopped. She came up to me, put her hands on my chest, took my hand, and we sat down. I lit a cigarette and opened a beer. Look, I said, I know I was—

—Just a minute, I forgot what I wanted to say—. The teakettle whistled. She turned it off, poured hot water into her cup. The thought that she was about to get up and run out of the room made it hard to breathe; I squeezed her hand tightly, jarring her, her muscles tensed and I couldn't look at her. She said, barely able to get the words out, that she'd never seen anyone hurt like this, and she squeezed back, took me into her arms. Her curly hair scratched against my face, all the crazy months I'd been alone rose in me, I felt myself drying out, the pressure of her body was the only thing I could feel. She was calming me down, and I knew I shouldn't lean on her like this, but I didn't want to move. Finally I leaned back, put my cigarette out, tired, waiting for her to talk.

She said it was easier now that she'd seen I needed her. I was still shaking, but I hid it by getting up and pulling down the shade in the kitchen. I was afraid of what I'd already shown, like a man who tells a friend a secret and then worries for days that the secret got back to the wrong person. If I asked her to stay, she'd say no, tell me she had work to do, or that it was too soon, she'd come over only as a friend. She was thinking now, probably making more sense than I could; what do you want, she said finally; it seemed she put her cigarette out only so she'd have two hands to wring together.

—I guess I want—I want you to stay, I mean if you won't leave again, if you're going to leave—

—I don't think I can promise you that, she said, going on to tell me she'd never liked permanent things, not even jobs, and she didn't want to be a housewife, and I already had a child we'd have to look after—but I want to work this out, she finished, there's something about this—I want to try it even though we're going to have trouble.

—Why?

She fumbled with a shirt button that'd come loose; she said, we will, everybody does; nobody really knows how to have a relationship.

I looked at her, not understanding what she meant; I asked her why she wanted us to be together if it was going to be so hard, and she said it was worth it, she felt close to me, it'd be different with us, we'd share things, we wouldn't 'slip into a conventional relationship'. I didn't want to argue, I didn't care what the terms were anymore. I remembered how hard it'd been not to think about her, the loneliness I hadn't let myself feel came back to me now.

She talked about Ben, she said she'd been bothered because she hadn't seen where she fit, she'd never wanted children and she did not want to be Ben's mother. But I like kids; maybe I could be his friend, she said, in a way I'm—well, I don't know anything about him yet but, you know, you don't have a car anymore—I think I'd like to take him to the day care center, and pick him up. Again, I remembered Julie; I told her it might be rough at first, and she said she knew that, but this time we had to believe that things would be all right. Putting my hands on her shoulders, I felt good; this was something she could do on her own, something I hadn't expected of her.

In the middle of Thanksgiving morning Julie called to invite us over for dinner; I felt like I had something to hide, talking to her in front of Carol; I told her we'd been invited to Ron and Sharon's. When he heard me say Julie's name, Ben said 'Julie, Julie' so I let him talk to her for a few minutes, got the phone back. She sounded unnaturally cheerful, and I wished we were going over there. We hung up; Carol and I were figuring out a budget, dividing up the responsibilities, and it scared me to see how efficient she was. I remembered this morning, when I'd got up early and then realized I didn't have to work, the grey light through the window had been falling on the legs of her white pants and she was lying on her side, only the back of her head showing out of the covers. I'd touched the dry hair with my fingers, pulled the covers away, saw her calm face and moved her nightgown slowly up her thigh, I'd put my hand on her ass and she'd thrashed away, pulling the nightgown down in her sleep. Maybe she was like Nancy, you couldn't touch Nancy without moving brutally through her dreams, but I didn't think so, Carol had other reasons, I'd seen them in the way she was organizing my life; I was coming out a little better off than I had alone. I had trouble with Ben yesterday, she said, he cried and I felt like an idiot—this girl Julie had to come and quiet him down. I told her Ben sometimes cried when I dropped him off, and said she had to make it clear that she had to get to work but that she was coming back.

—She seemed surprised when I brought Ben in. Did you ever go out with her?

—No, she's married.

—Will you bring me my housecoat? It's cold in here, are there any windows open?

I held it for her, and when she'd gotten it on she leaned back against me and I put my arms around her; but I knew she was curious about Julie, probably the way Nancy'd been curious about other women. She changed the subject. So far she'd been able to deal with Ben's interruptions, to give him attention; now she looked as if she were losing her patience. He was cranky, as he always is in that last hour before his nap. Carol didn't make the instinctive responses I remembered from Nancy; but I wondered now about those instincts, it seemed as if Nancy'd taken care of Ben from books, or from things she'd heard from her own mother. I remembered the routine she kept to, the excuses, the impatience with herself. She'd been sad the day we'd bought Ben's crib, had a strange depression the night her friends had given her a baby shower; I'd figured pregnant women just had wierd moods once in awhile. Potty, potty, said

Ben; I took him in, pulled down his pants, and held his penis for him, teaching him to aim. Carol looked on for a moment; then I heard her walk into the other room, she came back with clean diapers, plastic pants and pins. The quiet in the house made Ben's howling sound like an echo; I felt as if I hadn't anything to do with this, was only watching. We put him in his crib, and when he was asleep Carol said she'd like to take a nap too.

I sensed that she was uncomfortable about meeting strangers; I said they were nice people and she said, listlessly, that she knew that.

As I walked out of the apartment I knew I was making too much of Carol's fears; it was as if I were afraid she'd leave as soon as she felt any strain. The day was cold, unusually dry for Baltimore, reminding me of home, the way Nancy and I would split up holidays with each set of parents; her birthday was on Thanksgiving, I forgot about it the first year and I drove around all Thanksgiving morning, pretending I'd gone out for cigarettes, trying to find an open store. I got cigarettes now, ducked into a doorway to get one lit; I wanted to get home so I could see if she were still there.

We went downstairs after Ben's nap, Carol looked around quickly, her hands tense at her sides as Ron opened the door. She was polite, though unapproachable; only I would've known she wasn't relaxed. Sharon was worrying over the turkey, she said she was a terrible cook and this was the first turkey she'd ever tried. Carol watched, listened, I saw her shake her head a few times; when I saw the way Ron could calm Sharon down, I envied him for what he knew about Sharon, the certainties he seemed to feel. Sharon had set the table, but now she decided it wasn't right, and even during the meal she kept taking things off the table and bringing other things in from the kitchen. She laughed and made faces at Ben, pretending she was a gorilla or a bear. Carol ate quietly; she'd told me once she hated small talk, and I could tell she was uncomfortable with Sharon's mobile face and theatrical hands. I remembered Nancy's way of putting people at ease and then I wondered why I was thinking so much about Nancy.

When Carol and I were alone for a moment, she asked me about Sharon; I was bouncing Ben on my knee, and I said Sharon was an actress; oh, that explains everything, Carol said; I didn't like her patronizing tone and I asked her what she'd meant. But Ron came back in from the kitchen then, turned on the football game and sat down on his chair; he called Ben to him and Ben ran up and climbed on Ron's lap, Ben loves television. Sharon was still in the kitchen; I knew Carol didn't like football but I didn't think she'd want to help clean up; yet I felt strange because Ron obviously expected me to watch the game with him. I started cleaning off the table, told Sharon I'd help though she said I didn't need to, and we went into the kitchen.

Sharon tied an apron around her waist and it pulled her dress up; when she noticed she said I couldn't have any, the cheesecake was for later on, with coffee. She had a way of making even an old joke sound as dramatic as any part she'd ever played, and I started laughing. She asked, talking very fast, was the dinner all right, how come your girl friend's so quiet, does Ben always eat so much, are you living with that girl, is that why we haven't seen much of you. I said Carol was always quiet, and told her, making up my mind to see more of her and Ron, that I'd been busy at the store because the Christmas rush was starting. I started drying the dishes; she scrubbed the roasting pan, told me about the play she was in, Coward's "Blithe Spirit": oh, Ned, I'm so excited, I can get you free tickets if you'll come, it's in two weeks, I got the part of Ruth, it's the best thing I've ever done and it's really a bloody challenge.

—You mean it's a violent part?

She hit me on the arm, would have hit me again if she hadn't been laughing; she told me all about the other actresses, the director and the actors. Ron always calls them a bunch of faggots, she said, he says all actors have to be faggots, I wish he wouldn't say that kind of stuff. Yeah, I said; she got out two bottles of wine and we went back into the living room.

Carol and Ron were having a converstaion about mind control or psychology, something boring, and I thought, she would be into that; but she was relaxed now, and seemed to be enjoying herself. Ben sat quietly on Ron's lap, still watching television, his mouth parted, his eyes fixed, and unblinking; he'd been very good all day. But he asked me why all the big men were hitting each other; Ron assured him, with a lot of generous praise for football and for all other sports, that everything was all right, it was just a game. I squeezed Carol's hand, and she smiled at me.

By the time Carol and I were ready to leave, the four of us had finished another bottle of wine and we were all tight; Carol promised Sharon, convincingly, that we'd have them up for dinner soon. While I was weaving around, trying to get Ben ready for bed, Carol told me she liked Ron, but that she thought it was disgusting that Sharon needed so much reassurance, and she went on about all artists being that way. I wasn't very interested in all this, so I just nodded; as I was putting Ben in his crib she suggested I call Marcus. He said he'd come over in an hour, and he'd bring some smoke. Ben didn't want to go to sleep, and just before I lost my patience, Carol said, let me try. It seemed as if he fell asleep even before she'd returned to the kitchen. She said she's told him she was going to take him to the museum tomorrow, and when he asked what a museum was she told him that was a surprise. I smiled, touched her cheek, and she told me not to get sentimental, she just wanted to see if he were old enough to 'appreciate art'.

I've got to get out of this dress, she said. She stepped out of the dress, complaining then that her bikini pants were loose, falling off.

—You should wear them all the time, I said looking at her and smiling. Come on, she said, I saw you looking at Sharon—she's beautiful, isn't she?

I touched her back, moved my hand down under her pants. But your ass is enshrined in my heart, I said, pulling her tight against me. Marcus is coming over, she said, this is ridiculous.

—We'll put a sign on the door.

—Do not disturb?

—No, one dollar admission.

We lay down on the bed, the smile on her face showing, for the first time, her vulnerability; beneath her self-containment, which you'd think of as cold, she was afraid, and she'd learned to protect herself; but in that smile was the reason, though I couldn't have named it, why she'd come back here, it was a tired look, as if the tensions of meeting Ron and Sharon had worn her out; her breasts were small enough so that they almost disappeared when she lay flat, but now they rose and filled out under my mouth, her back arched slightly and her fingers were cold on my shoulders, I had the feeling we were doing this instead of having some long, awful conversation, I felt the violence and suddenness behind her moving fingers, behind my own sudden memory of walking through this room alone, listening to Ben's breathing; there was a beautiful dry feeling to her skin and my mouth felt good against it, my own sense of control, which I'd always had with other women, slipped away and I was almost afraid of the strong sense she had of her own body, different from what she'd shown when she'd sat at the dinner table, her legs crossed, her eyes cool and steady, but just as strong and deliberate as the feeling she'd given then; sex was not something I could ever do to her, her own rhythms were too sure, she was moving even as I put my head between her legs, she turned her hips and ass under my mouth; now she raised me and led me into her, I rocked over her, following her, she seemed to raise her own body with her hands so she could squeeze me tighter between her legs, I stopped feeling, knew only that my legs and back had turned numb.

She opened her eyes and held me; she said I think about making love a lot but I never think about this, how much I want it when it happens. I shook my head, not understanding; I said whenever I thought of her, I knew I wanted to make love to her.

Now we were going to talk; each thing she did was seperate, nothing slid on into anything else; Nancy used to just lie back, smile at me and tell me she loved me, but I guess even that was habit at the end.

—Well, I love making it, I said; her body moved slowly and fit next to mine. She asked me if that meant I'd do it anytime I could and I nodded; she said she had to think about it, make it into a choice. Then she started talking about the ways people have of controlling each other, mostly through sex, wives kept off balance by their husband's interest in other women. I thought of how I'd sat with Nancy in cafes and looked constantly at other women, especially in those six weeks after Ben was born; she'd just sit, looking with me, jealous, hurt, not saying anything. Carol said, now, that people shouldn't be jealous, that each relationship is unique. When she talked like this I'd wonder about her, she sounded too sure of herself, too different from the other women I'd known. She was always surprising me, making me react to her. I got out of bed, felt her finger move over my ass as I did, and went to the refrigerator; I brought her a glass of ginger ale, took a beer for myself, and she handed me a lit cigarette. She asked me if there was something wrong; I said finally, that it sounded to me like she wanted to protect herself, even in sex; especially in sex, she said. I had something to find out; I told her about a woman I'd met once and she'd had to get drunk, needing sex but not wanting to admit it, she'd insulted me, tried to make me as helpless as she must have felt herself to be; I wouldn't sleep with her, I'd said, "I don't want to hurt you," and she'd said, "I hate men who say that." Carol didn't say anything; she put out her cigarette and lit another one. Then she pulled the sheet up over her breasts.

—That's the whole thing, she said, as calmly as if she'd thought of it; you have to make choices, that woman couldn't. Suddenly I could feel Nancy in the room, I wished I could get down and apologize, beg her to take Ben and me back. I imagined the scene, running down the conversation, and it might as well have been Carol who was in Chicago. She sensed this; she told me that whenever I was quiet in a certain way she figured I must be thinking about Nancy. Too many things had happened to me in the last week; I told her she was right, then felt the bad things between Nancy and me come back, the boredom and the fights, her nagging at me for money or help. Carol said all the men she'd ever been with had had somebody they weren't quite over. When she started crying I knew I had to remember this side of her, stop being afraid of her. I held her, told her I loved her, remembered saying that to Nancy before we were married, and felt, finally, that it was all right to say it to somebody else.

I got home from work Friday night still tired from the day off. It took me a moment to realize that Julie was sitting in our kitchen, talking to Carol, the two of them talking and keeping Ben busy. Julie's breasts showed tight under the white leotard; her hair, usually pulled back for work, was hanging down, changing her face, bringing out the softness even more. I kissed Carol, surprised at how hard she kissed me back. Julie was tense now; you looked at her face and always wished she could cover things better . . . I picked Ben up, he yelled "daddy, daddy," and slapped the sides of my face; I asked how he'd been at the museum.

—Uh, he's a little young, Carol said, I spent most of the time chasing him—ran right into a museum guard. She laughed then, stood up and rubbed his head. She told me he'd called it a "nuzee", and that Julie'd come over shortly after they'd got home.

—Things are worse? I said, looking at Julie; she nodded, and Carol told me Julie's husband wanted a divorce and refused to discuss it, he was staying out nights with his girl friend, getting ready to move in with her. You can stay for supper, right? Carol said, looking at Julie with a kindness she rarely shows. She'd seen how badly Julie needed company. I wondered if Julie'd told Carol we'd slept together, I wished I knew what they'd talked about, I'd never expected them to be friends.

Julie continued talking through dinner, more patient and sympathetic than angry; I'd have thought Carol would argue with her, but she didn't, she listened, making Julie know she could say anything. I did the dishes; Ben was restless, probably vaguely expectant, some part of him feeling that tonight was the night we always went to the coffee house. I could tell he liked having Julie here; maybe she would stay and Carol could come with me to the gig.

When Marcus walked in, Ben screamed and ran to the far wall, his crying had the edge I remembered from that day in the car and I looked at Marcus; no, no, Ben cried, pointing at Marcus, hurt daddy, hurt daddy! Carol tried to pick him up but he ran from her, ran toward me and backed up again, still pointing and crying; Julie watched, tense, trying to figure out what to do. I picked him up, he struggled, I told him Marcus was my friend, he played piano at the coffee house, he wasn't one of those men, but Ben hid his head against my shoulder, his body shaking from his cries. I talked softly, repeating what I'd said, and I heard Carol introduce herself, and Julie, ask Marcus to sit down. But Marcus didn't move from his place by the door; he looked as if he wanted badly to leave, but felt he should stay. I waved him over, asked Ben to look at him; Ben shook his head, but I could feel him quieting down. Marcus looked at us, hesitating, and I told him what had happened in East Baltimore; he shifted his feet, said he'd better leave. I said no, please don't, I got to get Ben through this, he'll be all right. Carol was not in the room; when I set Ben down, he ran into the kitchen and I heard her talking to him. You want a beer? I said, and Marcus nodded; I went to get it, to give him a minute alone.

In the kitchen, Ben clutched my leg, and I touched Carol's face, her eyes were wet. I bent down, I said Ben, daddy wouldn't let those men come again, Marcus is daddy's friend, daddy's friend—can you come see him? Ben took my hand and we walked back into the living room; Julie handed Marcus the beer, Marcus looked at Ben. Ben said, not hurt daddy? daddy's friend?

—I'm your daddy's friend, I didn't hit him. Who are you, are you a tiger? Marcus said, grinning.

Ben laughed. No, silly; Ben, Ben, he said, pointing to himself. Then he looked up; Hi, Marcus, this my car, he said, holding up a plastic Ford; Marcus looked at it, and gave it back, and rubbed Ben's head. Carol exhaled loudly, and we began talking, she watched Marcus and I leaned back, sipping my beer. She said she was tired, had a cold, and thought she'd stay home with Ben tonight; she asked Julie if she'd stay for awhile, and Julie nodded. I felt strange, this would be the first time Ben hadn't come to a gig and I was worried, I hoped he wouldn't get upset again. When we'd finished our beers, I kissed Ben and told him to be good, I told Carol we'd be back right after the gig and she walked to the door with us.

Neither of us said anything until we'd almost reached the coffee house; as I opened the door, I said, Ben'll be all right; he said there's some bad dudes over there, about got myself killed over there once. Then he surprised me by saying, I didn't know what to say in there, I mean he was scared, man. I nodded, telling him he couldn't have done it better, Ben remembered the tiger thing. He laughed, shook his head, and said looks like you the one going to have problems now, my old lady split on me.

—Carol split; she just came back.

—She got to have what you got, man?

—Yes, Yes, I said; I walked up to the stage, and Marcus got himself a cup of coffee; together we set up the microphones, then he pulled the pint bottle out of his pocket and we sat down. It was different, familiar, sharing the old nervous feeling, wanting to get on right away, afraid you'd back out if you stayed around drinking too long. Ronnie, the waitress, sat down with us and we gave her a few hits off the bottle when her boss wasn't looking, she asked about Ben and I said he was sick. She told us a new club was opening up the street, we might get a gig there if we moved fast. People were coming in now, so she took one last swallow, stood up, smoothed her skirt, and went off to seat them. A few people came up to us, maybe because Ben wasn't with me, just to say hello; but one, a tall cat with long blond hair, pulled up a chair and invited himself to sit with us, he talked on and on though we didn't say anything; man, I really dig the shit you cats are putting down, like I really dig blues, man, it's so heavy—very far out shit, man. I knew what was coming, but Marcus looked shocked when the cat pulled out a harmonica and began playing along, very badly, with the tunes on the juke box, he hadn't enough sense to stop playing even when Stevie Wonder's 'For Once In My

Life' came on. When he asked the inevitable question, we told him he was a very far out harp player but we didn't think we could work a harp into our act; then we went backstage. Marcus was laughing; when he put the bottle down, I said, that's some far out shit you're putting down; we shoved at each other, slapped each other's hands, still laughing.

We were loose tonight, Marcus felt like singing and I liked filling in behind him, we played louder and harder than usual and I wanted that rhythm section, I could hear a back beat in my head and I played to it, using the bass strings to fill in the rhythm, and Marcus seemed to feel it too, his left hand was heavier than usual. The blond cat sat right in front of us and he was pretending to nod out, he wore sunglasses and he kept trying to talk to a girl across the aisle; I felt great, people were dancing though there was no dance floor, the Simon and Garfunkle cat looked disgusted and I hoped he was.

We left right after the second set, and on the way home Marcus said we should see about the new club. I hesitated, told him I didn't see how I'd have the time. Can't your old lady watch Ben, he asked; I told him I didn't think she knew him well enough yet; I said I had to spend time with Ben, told him for the first time about my wife and my old band, said I'd made myself give up music when Ben had come to live with me; but I miss it, I said, that's why I do this. He nodded, thinking over what I'd said.

The conversation continued as we got inside the apartment, Carol was sitting alone in the living room and she leaned foward when she heard about the new gig. Well, one thing we got to do, I said, trying to slow things down, is get you some money at the coffee house.

—Well, what I'm saying, man, it ain't the money, I want to play.

Carol asked what we were talking about; then he said I should think it over, he might do it alone if I didn't have the time, I could sit in with him as he'd done with me. Then, as if he'd sensed Carol was nervous around strangers, he began to draw her out, asking her direct questions I wouldn't have thought she'd answer, but she seemed to enjoy talking to him about her job, especially when she discovered that he, too, was convinced that all administrators were assholes. Mostly, I listened, turning the idea of another gig over in my mind, wondering how Ben would take to my being gone another night, he couldn't go to a club with me; and I remembered the reasons I'd decided, last spring, that I could never take music seriously again, it'd be too hard on Ben. Marcus stayed until nearly one, and after he left she said I didn't seem very excited about getting another gig.

—I could've had gigs anytime if I'd wanted them, I said; I picked up the beer bottles and took them into the kitchen.

I suppose you don't want to talk about it, she said. I came back in, told her there wasn't much to talk about, I didn't want to leave Ben another night, did she want to watch him if I did?

—Did you ever hear of babysitters?

—He sees enough strangers, I said; hey what'd you and Julie talk about?

—She's having a bad time, she really blames herself, Carol said, it makes me furious at her husband, but, you know? she just can't get mad at him. Then she looked up at me, I could see how upset she was; she said it wasn't worth it to get married, she hated to see people hurt because they thought they should stick it out. I felt bad for Julie, she'd been like Nancy in some ways; it made me think of myself, and I said I thought a marriage could work, if two people really tried.

—But that never happens—somebody always gets—I would've, the same thing would've happened to me if I'd married Leon.

I thought it'd be better to talk about Julie instead of marriage. I told Carol you get used to having one person around, somebody who really knows you; I still want to ask Nancy when I have a decision to make, I said.

—Yeah. But then if that person goes, you're still dependent; it isn't any good like that, you have to know how to leave before that happens.

—You sure know how to do that.

She shoved herself back from the table and stood up; she sneezed, then she shook her finger at me, you think we'd still be together if I hadn't left? Oh, forget it, I don't feel good enough to argue.

Something told me I should push this, but an old instinct, the one that had taught me to avoid fights, was stronger. I said okay, let's talk about this gig. She nodded, saying, as she put out her cigarette, that she shouldn't be smoking anyway. She said she'd thought I'd want to play any chance I got. I told her I'd stopped in at the record store tonight, as I sometimes did on my way home from work, and my old band had an album out, all tunes we used to play; I came so close, I really wanted to make it, I said, I'd have to play every night and go on tour to make it now, same as I did before, how can I do that to Ben? Besides, I don't even *want* to leave him.

—Can't you just play because you like to?

—No, it's—I don't know how to explain it, these gigs are never going to mean anything, I'll never go anywhere with this shit.

She blew her nose and said we could talk about it tomorrow, she was too tired now; that surprised me, but I didn't want to say anything to change her mind. As we got into bed she told me she liked Marcus, asked if we'd talked further about Ben. She looked very young with her red nostrils and flannel nightgown. No, I said, he knows I know the same thing would happen to him a lot of places. It's always going to be fucked up like this.

—You know what your trouble is? You don't have any hope. You don't think you can even change your own life, she said. She sneezed, blew her nose, and said she wasn't being critical. I'll never take these cold tablets again, they make me too drowsy to think straight, she said.

I remember my first gig with that band, a bar in Cuba City, Wisconsin, five years ago; that was before I'd met Nancy, and I wasn't serious yet about playing. The bar was long and narrow, with a low ceiling; there were pool tables where you might've expected a dance floor. When we came in, a woman of about fifty was shooting pool, she wore a red hunting cap over her slicked back hair and her wool pants bagged out of her cowboy boots. All night long, she drank beer and never had to pay for a game, the men would lose, get disgusted after a few games and walk back to the counter to drink with their friends. The juke played while we were setting up, mostly standards and country tunes, and I remember wondering why we'd been hired for this gig. Customers began to come in but they would've come in anyway, they barely noticed us. While Bill, the bass player, and I were testing the microphones the bartender came up and told us to play loud and fast, he had a girl dancer coming in and his customers would want to see something. As he walked away I looked around the bar again at the silent, middle aged men in their heavy coats, their half drunk beers and empty shot glasses in front of them. Most of them had not moved since we'd come in.

So we began our first set cautiously, using country material we'd never have played anywhere else, and we were wrong, couldn't loosen up or work together. The girl danced on the counter top, she wore a black fringed bikini, the pants cut low enough so that the top of her ass showed, she moved in the same way for every tune, the same bored smile on her face even when the customers near her would reach up and run hands lightly over her legs. Bill watched her the whole time he played, and he made a lot of mistakes. Come on, let's ask her over for a drink, he said, when it was time for our break.

She came over to our table and sat down. We heard the juke box again, a younger group of men with motorcycle jackets had come in and they were standing in front of the juke, looking around, talking loud. No one looked at them, but I got the feeling that all the customers knew who they were. The girl was older than I'd thought and her hair was stiff and golden, there were childbirth scars on her stomach which showed through now that she'd sweated off her body makeup. She bent over often, giving the top of her bikini a little shake when she lit cigarettes, and she kept her knee against Bill's leg; but what I remember best is her face, her cheekbones were high and solid but I felt that they'd been broken and reset themselves harder and thicker, as healed bones do, even though her face was unmarked and smooth. And I've seen that face since in the faces of other people, ruined, average, defeated, all these faces so similar as to be unrememberable, not crumpled or scarred, just formless, especially around the eyes. She and Bill were talking about La Crosse, where she said she'd been once; then she leaned toward me and said, her voice even flatter than before, look, I'm tired, could you fellows slow things down? Please? I'm really tired. She smiled at all of us then, showing good teeth, and she patted Frank's knee before she walked back up to the bar.

While we were getting ready for the second set I told Frank, the drummer, we should alternate slow tunes with fast ones, that the girl did look tired and she had all these people to contend with: he told me I was crazy, that there weren't many gigs around and we couldn't blow the ones we had—she was a dancer, she was getting paid. But Bill and Gene and I said that we didn't want to play here again anyway. One of the men who'd come in on our break yelled out, hey what the hell's taking so long! You forget how to play? We heard the laughter even as we started; we played every other song slowly, though we could sense the feeling change in the bar, the leather jackets were milling around, shoving each other to get near the girl, and they got loud every time we slowed down. Take it off, take if off, they shouted, and the older men joined them, we want to see some pussy. I felt the whole bar watching us between stares at the girl, we couldn't hear ourselves under the low ceiling but we could hear always the men in the bar, I can't remember any of the songs we played.

Halfway through the set, I started a slow blues and the bartender came over, shoved his face into mine, and said you play like I told you or I ain't paying—tell them, he said to the girl, hey, you, get over here. The leather jackets had come around to hear, the girl looked at the bartender and at them, felt their hands on her and told the bartender, she'd tried to get us to play fast tunes, but we'd said we'd play what we wanted. Somebody turned on the juke again and the girl went quickly up on the counter; the boys up front moved closer to us, shoved me aside, and began to play with the equipment. They knocked microphones down as if by accident, played with the drawbars on the organ; the customers were laughing because one of these boys was singing over the microphone, along with the juke box. He swung the mike stand around suddenly and smashed it into my amplifier, then they were pushing and shoving us and they began to smash up our equipment; some of the men in the bar came over to help, I was on the floor near the drum kit and Frank was yelling come on come on, there were sparks and a lot of noise, we sneaked out the back somehow and got into the truck.

All the way home Frank swore at me in German, so angry he was spitting and choking; Bill and Gene sat silent and I thought about the girl and the smashed up equipment. Frank didn't talk to me for two months.

A few days later I stopped by Ron and Sharon's to see if one of them could watch Ben after he was asleep. Sharon seemed tired and listless, but she said she'd do it; she told me that she was spending so much time at rehearsals that she hardly saw Ron, and he was angry about it.

—Sure you're not too tired?

—No, it's okay, Ron's playing cards tonight anyway.

When I told Carol what I'd done, she smiled, and said well it's about time. She told me there was a movie she wanted to go to, that she was going to go herself because she'd figured I wouldn't want to. I began looking forward to it by dinnertime, and by the time Sharon came up it was easy to leave Ben; I wanted to go out with Carol.

The movie theatre was way out on the northwest side, so we took Carol's car. The Baltimore street map didn't show any easy way to get there, so we got hung up in the Monday night traffic. Carol swore loudly at the other drivers and used her horn a lot. I sat quiet, thinking of the early months, I'd bought a stroller for a couple of dollars at the Mission Store and used to spend most Sundays walking Ben, thinking, trying to use the walking to calm myself down, getting hung up instead on something worse than regrets or memories; when she went away, all the things I'd never wanted to think about came back to me. I'd had her to hang onto, and then I had nothing, and I had to see what I'd done. Through that whole time, I never really entered this city, though I was walking in it, most of the downtown was as strange to me as these suburbs.

Carol talked about a conversation she'd had with the other woman faculty member, the things both of them were expected to do, make coffee and serve as part-time secretaries. I hadn't seen until now why this kind of shit, which she mentioned so often, bothered her so much; but I remembered that we'd had two road managers on the last tour, and they'd done the setting up we used to have to do ourselves. I knew how I'd have felt if I'd been the only musician expected to help with the equipment. If I wanted to be a secretary, I'd be one, she finished. She parked the car, and locked it, something I'd never have done, and we held hands walking into the theatre. One of the letters was missing on the marquee; it said *They Shoot H-rses Don't They?*

I couldn't remember the last movie I'd seen, but this wasn't like any of the others; this movie cut me off, even from Carol. It was like a crazy person who wouldn't let you alone, who followed you around all day long running down all the terrible things that had happened to him, until you began to believe they'd happened to you. I forgot what Jake had said about marathon dances, hadn't thought much about them until now, but haflway through the movie, when the actress was kissing a dead man, I knew how it was coming out and I almost left. I thought of Ben when I saw the pregnant woman trying to dance, trying to pick up pennies. When the movie ended, I felt as if it would always be playing in my mind, I'd never get rid of it. We walked out, and Carol's face was stiff and felt pale even in the darkness. She handed me the keys, and as I drove off I realized she was shaking. Let's have a drink, I said; she pulled the coat tight around her.

In the light, I could see that the movie had done worse things to Carol than it had to me. The waitress came over, we ordered, and I asked Carol for a cigarette, calling her Nancy by mistake; she didn't even notice, handed me the pack, and put her face in her hand. I knew she had to talk, I knew we had to say something but I kept seeing movie scenes. I promised myself I'd begin when we got our drinks but she was already crying, her body jerking and shaking because she wouldn't let the sound come out. She squeezed my hand until I felt it itch and turn hot; her shoulders shook and moved her breasts together. Carol, I said.

—I know, I know, it's just a movie, she gasped, crying harder. The waitress stared when she brought the drinks but she went away quickly. I felt something returning and I began to forget the movie, Carol was more important. Nobody was ever nice, she said, God, that woman in the shower, there must be some—I lit a cigarette and gave it to her; the news came on the bar television, she felt for her eyes and took off her false eyelashes. Stupid things, she whispered, I'll never wear them again.

—I think, I said slowly, maybe we got sucked in, it's like you die if you stop dancing, or—

—I always thought people could make choices, that everybody was responsible for whatever—she rubbed her eyes, smearing the light makeup. She was still holding my hand, I kissed her and felt her relief, I was something she knew about. Let's go, okay? she said.

She drove fast, turned the radio up. I knew her well enough to see that she was thinking, but that it wasn't getting her anywhere. She said she wished she could forget all about it, but she felt there was something in it that she needed to learn. I didn't think I could stand it, she said, I wouldn't live—why didn't they all just kill themselves?

—I don't know, most people try to go on, I guess.

—They're crazy then, it's not worth it, she said, as we got out of the car. I paid Sharon a couple of dollars, thinking she might need it, and Carol went into the bathroom. I'm going to take a shower, she called, you want to take one with me?

I took my clothes off and walked into the bathroom. She stepped out of her jeans, looked at me, laughed, and said, already? She turned the faucets on, and we got in, I rubbed her back, thinking of only one thing, I expected her to resist, but she didn't; she turned around and began, slowly, to wash me, she rubbed up against me and kissed me hard. I don't want to go in the bedroom, let's just lay on the floor, she said. The steam was coming up and we tried to get comfortable on the short floor, I felt closed in but I came into her anyway, tried to move with her; suddenly she said, angrily, get it over with, I can't move; I can't move, she said, beginning to cry. I lay cold and stupid on top of her, eased myself off and wanted to get dressed, I was embarrassed. She was still angry; she said couldn't you tell, why didn't you do something? I remember the times I'd thought she was an absolute bitch and I said look, it was shitty for me too, what about that?

I was more surprised than she was that I'd said that; she stopped crying, looked at me, something seemed to fall into place in her mind but she didn't let me in on it. She put her arms around me too soon, she said she couldn't read my mind, she needed me to tell her when she'd made me angry. You just sort of—you—you fit in or something, she said, I never know whether you do things because you want to or because—I held her, told her she was right. But I didn't tell her I knew she'd leave if I ever really got angry at her.

—Is there anything else I've done, you know, that you haven't told me about?

—No, I said.

She smiled, and I tried to smile back. You know, she said, I really believe we can make this work, it won't be like other people.

—Yeah, I said, I think so too. I helped her get up and we went on into bed. She turned on her side, hugged my arm and went to sleep that way.

Not thinking Carol and Ben were home yet, I slammed the door and threw my coat over the chair. From the kitchen, Carol called, what's the matter with you? Ben came running, I picked him up and walked into the kitchen, told Carol that sometimes I'd like to blow up that shoe store.

She shrugged, went on cooking; she was making some sort of a chicken dish and I knew it'd take me a long time to get through these dishes. I sat down and picked up the paper; Ben pulled on me, ripping the paper, and I slammed the paper down and snapped at him. Carol wheeled around; she said if you hate that job so much, quit, but stop bitching about it. I walked into the living room, cleaning up a little, swearing to myself; she's never had a lousy job, she was a waitress at a goddam country club and you'd think she'd been shoveling fertilizer the way she talks about it. Ben hollered, pulling on me; this time I knelt down and told him I was sorry for yelling at him, I asked him if he'd help me pick up his toys and he said okay, daddy.

While we were eating she said I had 'alternatives', if I'd take them, I could look for another job or I could stop working altogether, we could live on her salary until I found a job I wouldn't hate.

—Yeah. Then if things don't work out and you split again, I'm stuck here with Ben and no job.

She started to cry, I felt my jaw drop, my throat get dry; I remembered how, as kids, we'd always make fun of anyone who walked around with his mouth hanging open, we'd ask 'trying to catch flies?', laugh at the person and run away; now I felt, horribly, that I was going to laugh. Don't cry Carol, Ben said, looking at her anxiously, putting his hand on her knee; she looked down at him and cried louder. He began whimpering; I told him it was all right and went over to Carol, but she pushed me away.

How can you—I told you I was coming back to stay; maybe I'm difficult sometimes but I'm trying, and you just sit here doing nothing, shaking your head at me, 'sure, sure', as if I were lying; I can't stand it!

—You mean you want to leave again, you can't take it when things get rough.

—No, you bastard, she said, fumbling through her purse; I got her some toilet paper. Ben climbed up on my lap, I rocked him slowly, kissing the back of his head. I told her I was sorry, hadn't meant to hurt her feelings, I was in a rotten mood. She said I was the only man who'd ever listened to her, she felt she could tell me anything, but I didn't seem to care what happened, and she wanted the best for us; I need a man who's doing something he likes to do, she said, otherwise all you've got is me and

I can't take that kind of pressure.

—Daddy, book, book.

—Not now, little guy, we have to talk. I've got Ben, I said to Carol; she said sometimes I think you use him for an excuse. I wanted to pull away because she was pushing me but I sensed, unwillingly, that she was right. I moved my chair closer, reached awkwardly around Ben and put my arm around her; she squeezed my hand and told me to think about this, to maybe try the new gig for awhile, she'd help Ben get used to it. Come on Ben, I'll read you a story, she said. I got up to the dishes, realizing he'd been quiet the whole time we'd talked, I'd forgotten him, hadn't appreciated his calming down. He followed her into the other room and I watched, reaching to turn off the faucet and sticking my hand under the hot water instead. I didn't want her coming back in so I swore under my breath, the water covering the sound. But as I washed the dishes I heard her reading, had an idea that she acted no differently to him than she did to me, Nancy'd made a real separation. I couldn't tell what the idea meant, didn't know why it'd come to me.

In the next few days, the feeling of what Carol had said continued, though I forgot the words she used, I sensed changes in her I'd never keep up with past this winter but when I thought of spring coming I knew, suddenly, that I couldn't go through another spring alone; I wondered why she was with me even as I felt myself move toward her like a man moves toward liquor when he's confused, and I tried to remember what to do, though the old life with Nancy had stopped making sense, losing its reasons as what I'd done then became clear.

I imagined the home we'd had, the new refrigerator Nancy'd probably left standing by the side of the house, or worse, left with the new people; I saw Ben's crib and the toys he'd had then and I remembered the first day we'd come back from San Francisco, she'd refused to get up with Ben and I yelled and argued until I was afraid I might hit her. I gave up and took Ben for a walk in his stroller, he squealed when we passed our car and I wondered whether he recognized it. As we came in the door Nancy looked at us, and something passed over her eyes; she said you'd better get used to it, you're going to be taking care of him a lot more when you're home. I'd said that was her job, I was making the money. She shrugged, and agreed with me, I should've known something was wrong then but she turned friendly, that night was the last time we made love. In the morning she told me to have a good tour, she was convinced I was going to make it this time. But, probably because my way of getting ready to go out again was to forget all about her and Ben, I hadn't thought of this until now; and the memory of that day took away the last shock I'd felt when she'd come to Baltimore with Ben.

As I wheeled the last crate of shoes in on the handtruck I thought of Ben, imagining what it would be like to grow up mostly alone in this city. If Nancy'd come back he'd have a mother to come home to, and I'd help her with him, I'd want to.

The first time Ron and Sharon had watched Ben, last August, I'd gone downtown and picked up a woman because I couldn't stand it anymore; but I was too drunk to do anything, I said some things to hurt her and she'd gotten angry and called a cab; her leaving then was like Nancy's shaky walk alone from backstage, she'd even looked like Nancy, the only one of Nancy's faces I could remember was that hurt angry face she'd given me that night in Baltimore. Now I thought of Nancy's smiling face on a photograph I had at home, but hadn't looked at since we'd split up, and I wondered why I hadn't tried to stop her from leaving.

I am afraid of Carol. I didn't know my wife at all, don't remember how I felt, only some circumstances, some things she told me. Ned, you look a little down at the mouth, the boss said, slapping me on the back. What you need is a little poon. I'll take you down Baltimore Street sometime.

—Oh, man, you know I can't afford that—my kid needs new shoes.

He laughed all the way back to the front of the store.

For two days Ben didn't mess up his diapers, he kept saying no diapers, no diapers, so last night I'd let him sleep in his training pants; he's done it all by himself, I told Carol, and she smiled down at him: He looked confused, not understanding what he'd done to please us, but happy anyway. Carol told me he'd stopped crying, Julie held him up to the window each day so he could wave good bye, and that had calmed him down. Julie really knows kids, she said, I usually hang around for about ten minutes, just watching her, and I always learn something.

—Yeah, Julie's great, I said, but I was thinking about the gig last night. Carol had come along and we'd gone to a party afterward, she smiled at the attention Marcus and I were getting, not resenting it as Nancy sometimes had. She told us she'd never heard us play better; we talked to her about the idea we had of getting a whole band together. I was hung over now, and tired, her hair was dirty and she hadn't got dressed yet, but I felt the old excitement, the old desire to make it. Last night, I'd never stopped being on stage, even at the party; Carol thought I was funny, and she'd dealt easily with the hustlers she'd run into. We'd been touching each other all morning, we were holding onto a tension that wouldn't break until Ben took his nap, we held on because we could feel the high edge still coming off last night.

—Tummy hurts, Ben said; I realized, suddenly, that he'd been dragging around this morning. I felt his hard stomach, and something came to me, I asked Carol how long it'd been since he'd taken a shit, and when she didn't know I called Julie.

—Goddam it, I said, he's constipated, it must be he knows enough not to go in his training pants. I set him on the toilet, and told him to push. No, hurts, he cried; I tried talking to him, but he cried and squirmed off the toilet. I gave up and put some diapers on him, told him it was all right to use them. He whimpered and touched his stomach; I wondered how I could've been so stupid. Carol looked helpless; she was relieved when I sent her to the drugstore. I walked with him, trying to think, afraid I'd have to take him to the hospital. She came back with a children's laxative, and we gave it to him, but the label said it wouldn't work until morning. Carol's face was like the face Marcus had shown that night, tense, unwilling, but staying because she felt she had to. You want to hold him? I asked. She shook her head, then took him from me, rubbed his back and talked softly. We got to do something, I said, can you think of anything? I ran out, remembering the year I'd spent as an orderly, and came back with some suppositories.

Ben and I went into the bathroom. Carol shut the door. Ben kicked and screamed as I shoved the suppository into him; he tried to run out of the bathroom when I stood him up. I could see it wasn't going to work; I heard Carol walking back and forth and I imagined her tension, wished Nancy were here to do this, or Julie. Ben, I said softly, come by daddy.

—No pository, he screamed, thrashing in my arms, he'd been crying for so long that he was completely out of control. I held him, letting him kick, and told him as calmly as I could what I was going to do; he relaxed a little, but I knew he'd scream as soon as I touched him. The bathroom was hot and small, too bright; don't kick, I said, it's going to hurt but try to be still and—I broke off, not knowing what else to tell him; I turned him over gently and used my little finger, I could feel the suppository, I had to force myself to pull gently, it began to come out so I sat him on the toilet, he was still crying but he pushed; see see it feels better, I said, talking in order to breathe. I held him steady; then he stood up and it ran down his leg and onto the floor, he looked scared, tried to step away, but I told him it was all right. He stopped crying, and smiled, he said his tummy felt better and I put some diapers on him. Carol opened the door, and when she saw him her face got some color in it.

—How did you think—of—

—I don't know, I said, shivering. She said she had to get out for a minute. Ben and I stood by the window. We watched her cross the street and go on down the block. I was angry at her for leaving, and for being helpless. But she came back with some licorice for Ben, and she took him in to read a story. I could hear her voice get stronger as she read, I could hear Ben's questions. My hands were still shaking. I took a beer out of the refrigerator, and went in to listen to the story.

I got off work a little early Tuesday by saying I was sick; when I walked in Carol handed me two letters—one was a check from the insurance company, most of the premium I'd paid two days before the car had fallen apart, and the other letter was from home. I told Carol we'd gotten a gig at the club for the Saturday night after Christmas, we'd stopped over there on my lunch hour. Marcus knows the cat, I said, he made his money dealing to college kids.

—Say, you ought to use this insurance money to buy a guitar.

—Can't buy one for this, but I sure can put a down payment on one.

I picked up the other letter, skimmed through it; my parents wanted Ben and me to come home for Christmas, they'd pay half the train fare; my mother asked me if I were taking Ben to Sunday School, and I read that line aloud; Carol said, laughing, all mothers ask that. Then she turned quiet, looking up at me when I laid the letter down. I was thinking of home, the long cold fields turning to hills near the river, the rising bluffs on the other side, the big hill my family's house was near, we used to grab the rear bumpers of cars and slide all the way down; I wished it were time to take Carol with me. She'd been giving me advice since she moved in and I'd gotten angry, or tolerated her; now, for the first time, I felt I needed to know what she was thinking. I stood up and went to the window, the sun would be going down soon, the clouds were coming and I felt the dampness, back home it was cold and dry, they'd had a foot of snow already. Carol, I said, they want me to come home for Christmas —uh—I think I better. Is that all right?

—No, she said. She lit a cigarette. But I guess—are you going to see Nancy? If she hadn't asked, I'd never have thought of it; but nothing was settled, officially, about Ben. I was afraid that Nancy'd change her mind. When I told Carol this, she seemed to stiffen; I hate waiting, she said, I won't wait just to find out you're not coming back. I won't be one side of some half-assed triangle, either. I told her I wanted to stay with her and hoped I was telling the truth, I wondered how Nancy'd affect me this time, she'd got to me, through Ben mostly, last summer. Carol put out her cigarette and told me it was time to get Ben, she said she'd like to be alone so I drove to the day care center. Before I saw Ben I went into the office, borrowed some paper from the secretary and wrote Nancy a short note, telling her to call me if she couldn't come back to La Crosse for Christmas. I bought a stamp from the secretary and put my letter in with her mail.

In the playroom, Ben and two other kids were pretending to be leopards; Ben got up in a few minutes and ran over to Julie, who'd just started a story. He saw me, but he didn't want to leave yet; Julie finished the story and came over to me, and we talked about him a little. She was wearing bib overalls and she kept her hands in her pockets, scuffing the rug with her heel as she talked. She looked miserable, but she told me they'd gotten some things settled; she'd talked him out of the divorce, told him he could live with his girl friend for awhile and she'd wait. I felt she was being too easy on him, he was an idiot to throw her away, he had it made. She said she really liked Carol, and she was glad we were together. It seemed strange to me that she'd say that; it was as if she were giving me up. She put her coat on, saying she'd see me later, and I dressed Ben. On the way home, we had to stop for a train, and as Ben asked me where the caboose was, where the driver was, I hoped Julie wouldn't go out and get hung up some other asshole.

I could tell from Carol's face that she'd made some kind of a decision; she said she wanted me to write to Nancy. I said I had already, and she said good, I want you to get this settled, but you call me collect as soon as it is. I'm going home too. What if you can't get off work?

—I'll quit, I guess. But I feel better about it now that you—

—Okay, but I don't want to talk about it until it's over, she said. She looked angry. During dinner I told her about Julie, becoming more disgusted with Julie's husband as I talked.

—He sounds just like you used to be, she said gently, then covered her mouth.

I hated her for saying that, I called her a bitch and pushed away from the table, ready to leave, as I would've done if she'd been Nancy, but remembering Ben, and, for a quick second, hating him too. I just meant, she said, still calmly, that it was getting to me, it sounded hypocritical for you to—

Jesus Christ, I know what I was like, I shouted, and Ben started to cry; I'm going to spend the rest of my goddam life paying for it! Let's take a walk, she said; I agreed before I'd even realized what she'd said. Ben stopped crying when he saw his jacket come out of the closet and we walked without saying anything. The heavy air smelled raw, wet, it was like the first spring days back home, in April, when it's cold enough to remember winter but the sense of its easing is stronger than the memory; Baltimore had only confused me, except during the summer, and I didn't care what winter would be like here, I'd lost my curiosity about cities and I didn't want to know anymore about Baltimore than I'd already seen, these few blocks around home, the mile drive up Charles Street to the day care center, the road out of town.

The man behind the drug counter always forced his laughter, always looked tense; twice a day the cops came in, had lunch and left with something, and once a day somebody came running in with packages wrapped in brown paper, usually in the morning. I got cigarettes, and, just as if I'd been alone, I thumbed through the stack of tabloids; he carried the kind where the girls had impossible breasts and faces, they all had their tongues out, wore garter belts and sat with their legs spread. Ben ran through the store, but I didn't do anything; Carol called to him, I heard the edge of her voice, and I was glad. I was tired of talking, tired of all of her goddam 'insights'.

On the way home, she said she had this thing about wanting to know the truth, when she sensed a contradiction she had to say something immediately. She was easing up by admitting this, but this was all she'd do, if I didn't pick up on it she'd turn cold and pull back. But she went on anyway, telling me she didn't think I liked her very much, that I was only hanging on to her because nobody else was around. When she said that her face was hidden, she was looking down—I felt myself change and put my arm around her, saying I wanted to be with her, that she shouldn't worry about Nancy. For once she didn't say oh, I'm not jealous; I had an old feeling, it was like the days when Nancy and I'd been close, no matter what else was going on, being together was separate, had its own way, separate and truer than everything else. Carol said we'd have to talk a lot before I left, and I nodded, not really knowing how we could talk about this.

After Ben was asleep she helped me make out a budget, drew up a list of things she thought I ought to take. Then she said she had to correct finals, that she had a book I might like called *Division St. America*. I got through fifty pages of it, liking it, thinking about the people as I did, but I knew I'd probably never finish it.

The tap beer was flat; the old boys across the counter were quiet, they weren't even playing cribbage. Ralph, the bartender, told me Jake had died over the weekend; his landlord had found him this morning. I bought a shot to go along with my beer, looked at the bottles behind the bar and could see Jake hoisting Ben up onto his lap, Ben's face sticky from the sucker Jake had bought him.

I heard the high voice of a child I recognized, Maury from down the block, he was running through the bar, bumping into people, tugging at their sleeves; most of them ignored him, and he was obnoxious, but it hurt me; I told myself that was stupid, I'd seen Maury enough times to know how he was. His father was in the back, sitting with yet another woman I'd never seen; I sucked in my stomach, remembered Nancy, the train ride was three days off and it was coming too fast; Maury ran into the pinball machine and screamed, he held his head and ran toward the back of the bar. I sipped my beer, and then heard crying behind me, Maury was coming back, still holding his head, going toward the bathroom. The feeling came on me again, stronger even than it'd been the other times; I knew I should leave but I followed Maury instead. He was sobbing like Ben would, trying to reach the faucet. Maury, come over here, I said, but he hung back; I remembered times I'd gotten almost angry at Ben because he seemed to be sick, remembered thinking he's got to go to the center, I can't stay home from work. I picked Maury up, wet a paper towel and wiped off his head. It was time to leave; I gave Maury a pack of gum and he stopped sniffling, he used both hands to open the bathroom door. I wondered if I could bring up two kids; but once, last summer, I'd seen Maury outside and I'd invited him up; he'd knocked Ben around, he wouldn't share the toys, he acted as if he'd never had any other kids to play with. I lit a cigarette, walked out of the bathroom but as I reached for my drink I heard Maury's father call him a little bastard; I set the beer down, walked to the back of the bar, Maury's father looked up, looked down again as if he recognized me, he looked weak, and half drunk, his stringy hair was falling over his face.

—Like to talk to you, man, about Maury.

He leaned toward the woman, as if she could give him some strength, and he looked around quickly, I knew he'd protect himself by staying in the bar. Maury ain't got nothing to do with you, he said. He was right, but I stood there, called him a sonofabitch, said I had a kid I was bringing up alone and doing a damn sight better job than he was, he should give up Maury if he didn't want him.

—I'll do what I want, it's none of your goddam business.

I grabbed his arm and spun him around on the stool, stared at him, felt the tendons in my arm, my teeth grinding together, the cords at the back of my neck—I saw Maury coming up. What are you going to do, I thought, beat him up in front of his little kid? I let go, watched the fear leave his eyes, felt myself shaking, I could hardly talk. You motherfucker, I said, slamming my fist on the bar; he jumped, and I walked out, digging my fingernails into my wrists.

I went home and started drinking, didn't talk to Carol for the first ten minutes, just played with Ben. Seeing him made me feel I'd never let that happen to him, and I began to relax. When I told Carol, she said I'd done a stupid thing, but she'd heard me talk about Maury and she'd seen this coming.

I know it was crazy, but I feel better, I said, losing the good feeling as soon as I'd spoken. Something in me that would always be there, something I couldn't name, had made me call Maury's old man. Maybe Maury was better off for being taken so lightly, maybe he'd learn more than Ben.

On Friday noon, I looked out at the rain I knew would freeze by nightfall, it would stick to the tracks and slow down the train. Carol stood behind me, her arms around my stomach; she'd mostly been quiet these last few days. I thought you'd just take this in stride, like you do everything else, I said.

—Oh, I never take anything that way, it just looks like I do, she said. I sat down at the table, and I waited for a moment I knew would have to come naturally; but nothing seemed familiar, I couldn't talk anymore. If I were alone, if I had a guitar, I'd play until it was time to go, mostly scales, anything mechanical, anything to make noise. The time was going, we were wasting Ben's nap time. Carol was still standing, her fingers shook a little as she lit a cigarette, she crushed it out immediately, I could just reach one of her belt loops, I pulled her toward me, unbuttoned the bottom of her shirt and began kissing her stomach, feeling her fingers tighten, as they always did, at the back of my neck; I unzipped the fly of her jeans and moved down, reaching behind her to pull down her jeans, and she raised her legs slowly, one by one, to step out of her jeans, the scent of her body changing as even her fingers began to relax at my neck, I moved my hands up the back of her legs, she opened her legs as my mouth came down, as my hands slid up her back over her breasts: let's lay down, she said; she unbuttoned her shirt, I undressed, she let me lie down first and then came in next to me, extending her legs as she kissed my stomach and moved down; her mouth was cold and I was tense, a long way from the things her body was doing; I'd never been so awkward with a woman, I wanted her only in my head, I knew there wasn't much time and I'd be gone for better than a week—but she felt like rubber and my hands were as dry and stiff as plaster, she touched me but it didn't make any difference. She was breathing heavily; she lay back, closed her eyes, I could feel her relaxing and we tried again; my arms ached, my flesh was raw and painful against hers and limp and numb at the same time. I thought I could make myself, I thought about it and tried not to think. I sat up; she clenched her teeth, asked me what was wrong.

—I don't know, I said. She didn't get angry as she'd done in the bathroom, but I felt badly when I saw the way she was breathing. We lit cigarettes, and I started to roll away from her; she took my hands, we held hands almost desperately, watching the rain spreading and blowing so we wouldn't look at each other, or at the clock. The skin between my legs was shriveled and cold; I knew I'd hate myself for passing this up. You mad? I asked.

—No, I just wish—was it anything I did—no, I know I guess, what—

She moved first. I lay back and watched her slowly walk into the bathroom. Ben was quiet in his crib, nearly through the second hour of his nap; she came back with the cigarettes, we could hear the wind through the loose sash, the rain driving on the window pane behind us. Let's pretend we're all alone here and we don't have to get out of bed until next week, she said. I smiled at her, leaned over to accept the match she held, feeling good. So we stayed close, not talking much until we somehow began telling each other dirty jokes; she knew more and better ones than I did. As she told the last one, she scratched her fingernails slowly up and down my leg and I put my hand under her, she was laughing when I kissed her and we made love more quickly than we needed to, it wasn't good but it seemed important just to do it. We were up and dressed well before Ben awoke. And his first noises made us remember it was almost time, we began slowly, necessarily, to pull away from each other.

In the last hour Ben was restless, irritable, until we put his jacket on him; when I picked up the suitcases they felt heavier than they had this morning and I wished I hadn't had to bring so much, though I knew there'd be luggage carts in the Chicago train station. Carol said, as she drove north on Charles Street, that she was worried, she'd heard of too many train wrecks when the rails were icy. I told her not to talk like that, a train was safer than a car; better be, she said, we're sliding all over the road.

Outside the car, we felt the raw freezing rain, the cold air blowing up the wide wind alley by the freeway, where the station was, and as I picked Ben up I looked around at the jammed up cars, the blackened buildings and the blurred, looming station and knew I'd always see Baltimore like this in my mind. We got inside as quickly as we could, I looked up at the board, saw the train was on time and said it was good luck. Ben hung on my shoulder, eyes bright, mouth open, this was the biggest room he'd ever seen; already I was tired from carrying him and the suitcases.

—Nothing's settled, Carol said; I said we'd done the best we could. We walked down to the loading platform, and when I looked at her I wished she'd cry, anything to relieve the strain I saw on her face, felt on my own. She kissed both of us, and Ben kissed her, I held the three of us together, said I loved her, and she said something I couldn't hear over the noise of air brakes. She turned away quickly and I watched her walk back up the stairs. In a few minutes we were settled in our train seats and I tried to explain to Ben why Carol couldn't come. He made happy noises when the train began to roll.

PART II

THE TRAIN WAS COLD AND QUIET in the middle of the night, I sat hunched forward on the front right corner of my chair so Ben could sleep across both seats; he was restless and almost fell off a few times, I'd touch his back to soothe him and he'd be still, then, for about fifteen minutes. I kept looking behind me, as if I expected Carol.

I'd seen snow occasionally under the train lights, seen the whole train on the horse shoe curve in western Pennsylvania, barely picking it out through the window reflections; we were nearing Canton, Ohio and the train rhythms made me sleepy, though my position on the chair and my fear that Ben would fall and hurt himself made sleep impossible. I wished I had a beer, I needed a cigarette.

There was one woman awake on the car, and I asked her if she'd take my place so I could go to the washroom; I lit up before I'd closed the door, then I sat down, leaned my head against the train window. I felt good, though I was tired, Ben and I had read and colored, I'd pointed out the cows and barns until it was dark; he'd even gone to sleep easily when I made up a story about our train ride, coming through changes as he's always done, from the hotel in Baltimore to the morning when we'd lost the car; I felt he'd make the trip all right as long as I could give him all my attention. The familiarity of being alone with him sustained me better than conversation or sleep, my love was fierce and hard inside me and I knew it would stay that way, no matter what Nancy might say or try to do.

Remembering last year, it seemed strange to me that I hadn't given him up for adoption, but I must have wanted to quit touring, must have wanted him for a long time without knowing, as I barely knew, tonight, that I couldn't stand to live apart from him. Last summer I begged Nancy to come back, I'd thought mostly for Ben's sake; but now I'd hold him to me stronger than any dreans or memories I'd ever have of women. The steady percussion of the train continued under my feet as I rolled with the train down the aisle, thanked the woman again, and sat down; but I'd take my next smoke here, no matter what the conductor said. I hummed the blues and felt happy with the tunes Ben likes:

> Don't call no doctor, he can't do no good,
> It's my own fault, I didn't do the things I should.

and Ben stirred, maybe hearing the old song in his sleep, and I sang 'Walkin' Blues', the verse he always asks for when I'm on the stand.

We stopped in Canton, two people in our car got out, and I hoped the sudden light wouldn't wake Ben. The snow made things clean in the darkness, but so many towns look good when you're travelling, Canton made me remember how much I hated long car trips; I hadn't worried once on the train, knew we'd make it because I wasn't in charge. In the daylight I'd see the things Ben would make me notice, and this route of tracks would seem more secret than any highway, as if we were the first two people who'd ever seen this countryside. We'd see the Indiana fields and I hoped the day would be bright and cold, the sun rising behind us, further drying and freezing the snow, the snow half covering abandoned cars driven to the edge of railroad property, old cars these farmer kids would pretend to drive in the summer, this flat land would feel like we'd finally left the east, and I'd be imagining Wisconsin, the pine stands on the small hills and the milk trucks way off on the secondary roads.

Ben rolled around, the hump of his diapers showing in the indifferent light; I crushed the cigarette on the sole of my shoe and threw it under the seat ahead of me.

My family moved to the north end of La Crosse when my father got promoted to foreman; before that we lived downtown, on Third Street, and I remember the early morning my friends and I broke into a liquor store and went to the sixth grade drunk. It was rough down there, though not the way a city is rough, and once I'd got beaten up for my paper route money. Sometimes we'd get a rowboat and go out to one of the Mississippi islands, we'd play army and imagine we were George Washington or somebody else who crossed rivers to ambush towns. And I remember asking my seventh grade teacher if I could go to the bathroom, knowing my girl friend would ask right after I did, I'd wait for her and we'd make out in the girl's washroom. My two sisters grew up on the north end, at the dead end of State Street, near the Burlington Station, right under Grandad's Bluff; it was quiet and well lit at night and I missed the fights. My parents seemed confused, afraid the neighbors had more money than they did; those neighbors I never met were the reasons I wasn't supposed to get drunk, stay out all night or get girls "in trouble".

I bought my first car, when I was sixteen, down in the old neighborhood from a man who made me nervous because of his greasy con-man feel; he must have sensed this because, as if to make me feel better about buying the car, he began to use his broken English in a wierd parody of a television used car salesman—how much you think this car worth? such a bargain you can't get anyplace; come on, you just buy yourself a car. By then I was so scared I bought it so he wouldn't shoot me. The transmission burned up in two weeks.

I liked the railroad tracks across the marsh, the Mississippi, in the winter, the unlikely trees on islands flat and white as the frozen water under the snow; I believed the islands had been there long before the river and the water had had to flow around them. Later, going through Trenton to a gig in Philly, I saw the islands on the Delaware and they were long, narrow and sloping toward the water at those places where the river had made them and was wearing them away. And the road along the Delaware was nothing like Highway 14, which runs along the Mississippi, high on the bluffs on the Minnesota side north of La Crosse; I used to drive to Winona where Nancy went to school, look down at the islands and imagine I'd spend each summer living on a different one, moving, that way, all the way down to New Orleans.

As we pulled out of Wisconsin Dells I realized we weren't more than an hour from home; I talked uneasily to my son, imagining how we'd look to my parents. My father would think of the times he'd told me I'd never amount to anything, my mother would remember telling me I was too irresponsible to hold a woman, she'd look at Ben's clothes and uneven haircut and make up her mind that I was disorganized and neglected him, that I'd failed as a father.

I tickled Ben's ribs and felt him squirm and laugh. I remembered suddenly that Nancy was his mother, not just my ex-wife.

—Look, daddy, horses, Ben said, pointing at two brown mares who didn't look up as the train went by. I couldn't remember if horses started at trains. Now I wished we didn't have to leave the train, could just pretend we'd visited my parents. I felt the sleepness night in my nerves, my parents were unimaginable, barely remembered.

The college kids and servicemen stood up and took their bags down, then began forming a line near the door. I saw my whole family, Ben's grandparents and aunts, on the station platform and ducked quickly away from the window, shaking a little; though I'd been thinking about them all day, I realized now that I'd expected Nancy to meet me. My parents could be any parents, could just as well be waiting for this kid who'd just finished boot camp as for me and Ben; but I couldn't be confused if I saw Nancy, there wouldn't be time. As I got Ben ready, I remembered my sisters' voices, my father's habit of touching his ear when he was angry, the smell of the shampoo my mother always used.

Ben was tired, finally cranky, refusing to walk until I squatted down and told him I needed him to walk, I knew I'd want one hand free when I met them. We got out, and they saw us, and their faces stopped as if they'd mistaken me for someone else; but they pushed themselves forward, their tense faces in the cold air moving uneasily into smiles at Ben. I held his hand as tightly as if he were helping me across the street.

The first night, my parents were calm and self-contained, so I knew they were worried, or angry; during dinner, my mother said she hoped I wouldn't be out with my friends every night. I told her that I would see Nancy, but not anyone else, and they looked at each other. My father said I should admit that it was over, there were 'other fish in the sea'.

—No, you don't understand, I said, trying to be careful. By sister Annie, who's eighteen, was sitting at the table with us; she was looking out the window. Susan, the twelve year old, was playing with Ben in the living room, and I could hear them giggling. I knew Ben was tired, and confused, but so far he hadn't been irritable. I looked back at my parents and told them Nancy and I had to work out a definite settlement about Ben. My mother began to criticize Nancy, but I asked her to stop, said none of it'd been easy for Nancy.

My family approached Ben too quickly at first, but by the end of the night everyone felt welcome; we'd all depended on him to pull us together but I knew I'd have to watch him closely, these were strange people who acted differently than I did toward him and I could almost see him trying to understand. He didn't want to go to bed, and I was tired enough so my nerves were short; in the middle of his tantrum, though, I knew I'd have to calm down or he'd never know it was all right to go to sleep here. I was glad, then, for the time alone with him, when I went back downstairs I felt relaxed. They were easing up, too, although my father never relaxes; I'd seen his tension in the way he'd sworn at the drivers on the way home from the train station. He and I stayed up and talked about politics, we split a six pack, which is a lot of beer for him, and he surprised me, he'd become again the socialist he'd been in the thirties; but you have to think of your parents as unchanging for as long as you need something solid to fight against.

Now, sitting around the table for breakfast, I looked around and noticed that they'd papered two of the kitchen walls, they'd painted all the rooms, and Nancy would've hated the neutral colors they'd chosen. But I'd have been disturbed if this house looked like someplace I might live, because I'd always hated it, I'd grown up on my memories of the old house. I had some coffee and listened to my mother tell me I shouldn't let Ben look like an orphan; my father put down his paper, said it was important to look your best, Ben might be held back by his appearance, looks count for a lot in today's world. Just as I was about to react angrily, I saw Annie shake her head so slightly that only I saw her do it. I changed the subject, told them how well Ben was doing in the day care center, feeling Annie's strength and confidence, she'd never argued at home, she'd just quietly done what she thought she wanted to do. She was more real to me than Susan, who seemed, still, the baby I'd changed and put to sleep ten years ago. Even as I kept talking, telling them Julie'd said Ben was a natural leader, I sensed my parent's unspoken question, was I bringing different women home all the time, how did Ben react to that. I didn't like to have that question hanging, but I hoped it wouldn't come up.

Ben came running in and climbed on my father's lap, upsetting the paper. My father hadn't been physically close to us at all, but he bounced Ben on his knee, seemed to know that Ben was really his grandson. You're some boy, he said, ain't he some boy, Arlene?

—Yes and so cute. And so smart, my mother said. Is he always this good? He's hardly made a speck of trouble since he's been here.

I laughed, told her he was excited by all these new people, but he was still tired and she'd find out he was a normal kid as soon as I told him it was time for his nap. Later, while we were doing the dishes, she said that Ben was happy and more secure than she'd expected, she could see I loved him. Then, recovering herself, she said she'd never thought I'd be much of a father. My father said, for the third time since I'd been home, that though I'd flunked out of school years ago, I could still go back and learn a trade if I were willing to work at it. But I didn't care. I could see we'd get along for these four days.

There was a dull feeling in the back of my throat, like a strong memory you refuse to recognize, and I knew I should call Nancy; but I called Carol instead. We talked only a moment, so tense we couldn't say anything, but after I hung up I remembered why I'd come home. I wished Carol were here, then changed my mind, then thought I had to pretend she didn't exist in order to deal with Nancy.

I played with Susan and Ben, trying to draw Susan out and making her even more shy and uncomfortable. She needed time to watch me, I was just somebody who'd never been around much when she was growing up. I began changing Ben's diapers, getting him to stop struggling by talking softly to him. I put him in bed in Susan's room, and he said, daddy I want to go home. I held him, told him home was far away, in Baltimore, but I knew he didn't understand. He didn't cry, looked at me with his questions, said he didn't like it here—where Carol is? and all the kids? An old ache resurfaced; it was as if my brain had dropped by its own weight through the soft part of my skull, just above my neck. My throat was tight; I wished he could tell me better what he was feeling. I said we'd see his mommy soon. Mommy? I know Mommy, he said; he lay down and began his bouncing and I walked slowly out of the room. When I got downstairs I asked Annie to come out and have a drink with me. She drove to a bar I used to hang out in, it was deserted on Christmas eve and I was glad the bartender didn't recognize me. The bar was as familiar as the town, I'd noticed only a few new buildings and already I was beginning to feel as if I still lived here. There was a football game on, as usual; it was the first time I'd ever seen these floors unlittered.

Annie pulled out a pack of cigarettes and lit one. I thought, that's just like her not to smoke at home, not to get into those arguments. Mom and Dad are pretty disappointed in you, she said, you don't write much, or call, and they don't understand what happened between you and Nancy.

—I can't talk about that to them. And the other thing, about the shoe store, well I tried to be a musician and it didn't work out and I never wanted to do anything else. She nodded; she said she knew it'd been hard on Nancy, she'd stopped over there twice when I'd been out on that last tour. I said I'd been a sonofabitch, wished I knew what she was like now, hoped she wouldn't try to take Ben away from me. Then I told her about Carol and she asked how Ben had reacted; the first few months, when we were all alone it was terrible, I said, it hasn't been bad with Carol, she's gone slow and I can sense he's taking his time, you know? She said you never knew about children, and I almost said I know a hell of a lot more about them than you do, but she changed the subject; she told me what she couldn't talk about at home, that her boyfriend was Jewish and she was living with him, she'd gotten pills from the school clinic. I don't like to lie about it so I never say anything when Mom asks me these sort of off-hand questions about men, she said. I said it was more like protecting them than lying, just as they'd protected us. I could answer their questions, but I couldn't volunteer anything. We talked a little about Susan; Annie said she knew Susan was having trouble making friends, that she wasn't sure Susan had adjusted to Mom's going back to work. But I told her about sex, anyway, Annie said, I wish somebody'd told me when I was her age.

We stayed two hours; as soon as I got home I called Nancy. When I heard her voice I felt it all come back, and I knew it'd be worse when I saw her. I said I didn't want to bring Ben over to see her parents, and she said that was all right as long as she didn't have to see my parents. There was no emotion in her voice; I felt she was planning something, she had everything under control. My voice had been shaky on the phone; when I hung up I wondered if I'd even be able to talk to her when I saw her. I didn't think I could wait until tomorrow morning, or I thought I could wait for the rest of my life, as long as I never had to see her again.

Ben liked his Christmas presents, especially the toys, but he wanted to open everything and I'm not sure my parents forgave him for that. I was uncomfortable, as I always am when I look at the endless bright wrapping paper, think of the difference between the presents and each person's feelings about those presents; the presents should suspend the tension but they seem only to increase it, especially when you're Susan's age and you're disappointed because of what you didn't get, sometimes humiliated by presents too young for you. Once Annie'd had an idea, that we should all say something good about each other at meal time. It made everybody too uncomfortable and we never tried it again. I felt everybody except Ben would be happier continuing his or her own isolation, everybody'd given up the sense of family years ago and you can't make it exist one day out of the year.

Ben threw an enormous tantrum when he realized there weren't any more presents, I could see now how badly he'd been confused by the last two days, and as I tried calming him down I imagined my parents' faces when he used words they'd never permitted in their house, I felt their quiet judgment of the way I was handling him as strongly as I would've felt a stranger coming into this room. It was late, I was relieved to take him up to Susan's room and to be alone with him again, I talked to him for a long time, telling him I was tense, that I had things to do here that were important to both of us but I didn't know how to explain them to him. When I'm bigger? he said, wiping his eyes. I nodded, kissed him, and put him down; I felt worse than ever after he was asleep.

Annie had gone out; Susan was getting ready for bed; my parents were watching television in the living room. The memory of Nancy's voice came back to me and I knew I wouldn't get any sleep tonight; how can you say 'hello' to someone you once lived with, just 'hello' like you'd say to anybody? I was trying to get ready in advance, trying to make myself strong; I got another beer out of the refrigerator, I tried but I could imagine only this:

Nancy is in her parents' kitchen, talking to her sister who's been divorced and gone back to school. She has no children; Nancy tells her she's happy with her job, but she misses Ben and she's found a man she'd like to marry, someone who'd be a good father to Ben, she wouldn't have to give up her job because there are good day care centers in the Chicago area. She tells her sister what a bad husband and father I was, how she feels badly for giving Ben up to someone like me.

She'll be reserved and hard with me; her face will be unchanging no matter what I say, her mind will be working on my reactions, maybe she's already seen a lawyer who's told her she has an excellent chance to get Ben back because I was irresponsible when I lived with her, and because I was busted once for possession of marijuana. I see the lawyer, the judge, her new man sitting next to her in court, I see them taking Ben away from me. I see Nancy getting her life back, the one she told me I ruined.

On Christmas morning Susan pulled out her new Monopoly game and asked me if I'd play. Sometimes I held Ben on my lap, let him move my counter, but he'd get bored quickly and jump down. My mother took him into the big chair then and read to him; she'd told me, when I was growing up, that reading to us at bedtime had been her favorite part of the day.

The game calmed me down some but I couldn't really concentrate and Susan laughed at me for losing so badly. I could imagine how she'd look in a couple of years, when her face cleared and her lankiness filled out. We talked about cheerleading, and about a boy she liked, he was the only one who didn't call her 'stilt' or ask her when she'd be going out for basketball. Mostly, she looked down while she talked, played with her counter, messed with her hair. My mother told her, for the fifth time that morning, to take a shower, and she stomped off. I smiled after her, wondering if she'd like to come out and visit for a few weeks.

When my parents and sisters left to go out for Christmas brunch, I tried to play with Ben, but I'd forget and look out the window, or pick up a magazine. He got angry with me, started to cry; I said I'd read to him. He brought his new story book, which unfortunately contained 'The Three Little Pigs'. That's in all of his story books, and he really likes it. I hate that story. As we were finishing I heard someone on the porch, I let a cigarette in that half second before the doorbell rang. Ben ran ahead of me, struggled with the doorknob, stamped his feet; I helped him open it.

We backed away as Nancy walked in, she took her coat off and laid it over the chairs; we showed smiles we had to cut off quickly, and then we didn't look at each other. Ben stood a little apart, stared, but didn't ask who she was. It was as if he knew she was his 'mommy' but he wasn't sure what that meant, it was something people had told him. She neither charged him nor called him, she knew him better than to take an easy dishonest way out, to demand something from him in his confusion. I couldn't say anything. People who've lived together know too much about each other, things impossible to forget, gestures, habits, the sound of Nancy's voice, the strange flatness I'd lost in my own speech. Everything I knew about her was useless, and I'd never lose it. She knelt down and spoke softly to Ben, words I couldn't hear and didn't want to hear, I was looking at her; she'd cut her hair and it fell just to her shoulders, she'd lost weight and she wore these white wool pants and satin shirt as if she felt comfortable in them, as if she'd give up the sloppy clothes she used to wear. I remembered how I'd believed I owned her body, wondered how I could've ever taken her for granted; then I couldn't believe that I'd never see her naked again. I tried to see her as if she were a woman I'd just met, but I'd known her for too long and she was like a woman I'd slept with in some dream, seen later on the street. I felt all the old things, wished I could believe we'd never touched.

She was still talking to Ben and he'd come to her, smiling shyly; she'd carried him, she and I had made love to get him and she'd always be the woman I wanted for his mother, he continued the past we'd left behind and made it real again, and I shook as those days came back, as I knew they'd never leave; she was that whole time to me, the great records and the band coming together, the first dope coming around, the way we'd lived with our friends, one dollar to the next, always enough for beer or smoke, fooling landlords into thinking we were married and moving every six weeks, all of us sure we were hip and superior and close, but especially Nancy and me, for we'd invented each other, and those inventions, now, were as lonely as the anger I'd carried the first few months in Baltimore.

—How are you, Nance?

—Fine, she said. Did you have a nice Christmas? Boy, he's really grown. Her smile was real now, but her face was as vulnerable as it'd been after those nightmares and it hurt to look at her. Ben ran to me and I picked him up automatically, but I saw Nancy's face change, her shoulders seemed to move down a whole inch. She my mommy, Ben said, his left hand moving up my neck, playing with my hair.

—Yes, I said; I didn't look at her. I'd thought she'd be hard and cold, paralyzing my senses and thoughts, making me stumble, say things I didn't mean; but she just looked scared, and I realized how much I still needed her to depend on me, I didn't want to believe I was useless to her. The quiet in the room, my uneasiness was making me panic. I'd never let myself realize, since last year, that she loved him too.

—Can mommy hold you, Ben, she asked, coming up to us; she was so close I could smell her perfume and hair. He looked at me suddenly, held tight and started to cry, as if he believed I was going to leave him. The room was filled with our tension, it must have surrounded him. I talked softly to him, asked her to give him more time.

—But I—he doesn't even know me, she said, her voice dull and hard. Doesn't he even ask about me?

—He did, after your visit, when you first left he asked about you a lot. She looked angry or impatient; I tried to feel some sympathy for her, but I couldn't. She told Ben she was his mommy, then she said what's the use and put her coat on. Nancy, we have to talk, I said.

—Not now, it's—it's too hard with him here. Can't you come over tonight, you know, by yourself, and I'll see him—

—What's wrong with talking—

—Look, I can't do it now, she said, her eyes blurring over, then clearing, except at the corners. Goodbye Ben, I love you.

After she left I told Ben that we'd come out her to visit mommy; I began to imagine what I'd feel like in her place and I told him mommy wanted to see him even though she worked in a faraway place called Chicago. He hadn't asked for any of this, but he listened; then, for the first time since we'd been together he said he was tired, wanted to take his nap. I knew it would be a slow afternoon; I hoped none of my cousins would come to visit, and I thought we could continue the Monopoly game, maybe I could talk my parents into a few games of sheepshead.

I sat in the recreation room I'd helped build, remembering the difficulty Nancy's father and I had had with the runners for the tile ceiling, even now it was easy to find the places where we'd had to cut the paneling into odd shapes to make it fit to the crooked studs. The next summer I'd put a new roof on the garage, replanted some fir trees. Nancy's sister had told me to wait down here when she'd met me at the door; I could hear her and Nancy walking around upstairs, thought I heard a glass break as I walked over to the bar. He still had good whiskey, so I poured out a shot to go with my beer, made Nancy a gin and tonic before realizing that I hadn't asked her if she wanted a drink. But she came down then, took the drink, sipped it and said I always could make a good one. She sat down near the fireplace and asked me to put some logs on, we talked about the weather, how you forget this cold when you don't live here anymore.

Nancy never seemed quite comfortable with her hair; when it was long she used to push it behind her ears, now she pushed it out of her eyes. She asked me if I were playing any and I told her about the coffee house, said I could get other gigs but I didn't want to spend too much time away from Ben, I told her about Marcus, said I thought she'd like him. Her eyes moved as if she's been about to say something, then changed her mind; she smoothed her skirt, got a fresh pack of cigarettes out of her purse, took one out and carefully refolded the paper over the opening; she'd get angry at me when I'd forget and rip the paper off. In the firelight I could hardly see her except for the white spots her knees made. I imagined us together again, I'd been thinking about it all day. She told me she'd been going to concerts, she said the Band had played better, even, than the time we'd seen them.

I got up for another beer; it took me two tries to get it open. When I turned around I asked her if she still liked her job; as she talked she cocked her head, smiled, blinked her eyes, her left hand brushed her cheek, then her breast; I remembered the gestures from the times I'd seen her happy, like the morning we'd awakened in our own house. She leaned forward, her face lighting up on one side, making me think of some pictures a friend had taken of her; she tapped her breast and said she was considering opening a boutique, she was beginning to make the right supply contacts. I love the travelling, she said, I'm not home even as much as you used to be.

We laughed, both embarrassed; then she stopped talking. I wondered whom she's slept with, almost asked her if she were with somebody. The suede skirt kept riding up, and she pulled it down each time; one night, when we'd been out, I'd been high enough to push it back up each time she adjusted it.

—Tell me what else you're doing, I said, the tone of my voice reminding me of the pictures in our wedding album, especially my smiles on the last few. My roommate and I talk French in the apartment, you'd be surprised how well it's coming back, she said. She was relaxing, her fingers had begun to move again when she used her hands to gesture.

—Tarot reading last week and I kept getting the change card—actually it's a death card but it doesn't mean that usually, it's just because, you know, death is sort of the biggest change—I see you're really interested in all this.

—No, no, go on, I'm listening.

—It's all right, we never talked about the things I was into anyway. Ben looks good, she said. She lit a cigarette. How is—is he all right?

I sensed it was too soon to talk about Ben; I wished we could spend weeks talking about unimportant things before getting down to him. I said he'd come through the rough times well and had made an adjustment to the day care center, told her I was working on toilet training him and that I'd decided to let him keep his bottle until he wanted to give it up. She bit her lip, said she'd felt badly about leaving this afternoon.

She asked me to make her another drink, got up with me when I walked over to the bar; as I fixed the drink I told her that Ben really liked to read, we stood talking like a bartender and his customer. She noticed this at the same time I did, and we laughed together; then I came around the bar and we sat on the two stools, our legs not quite touching. She brushed her hair away, leaned her elbow on the bar and turned to me. Ned, I have to see more of him, she said, it's no good like this, he doesn't even know me anymore. She let her hand drop and sipped her drink. I could hear the water heater go on, the pipes rattling from the toilet.

The fire had burned down enough so that I could put on another log. When I came back I put my hand on her shoulder, she leaned her head against my chest. I told her I hoped she didn't think I wanted to keep Ben away from her. She said she hadn't thought so, it was just that we'd gotten along so badly last summer. She sat up again. I pulled my stool a little closer.

—I really miss him—it gets worse instead of better, you know; I cried a lot in the beginning, I got drunk too and I'd tell people about—God, I was awful! But I was mad then, I didn't spend much time feeling sorry I'd done it. Now I just think of him and—

It took me longer than it should've to realize she'd turned her head because she was crying. I put my arm clumsily around her shoulders, this gesture like my tone of voice before, like my wedding smiles. I thought of reassuring things but my mouth seemed to have welded itself together. So I held on to her for awhile; then I lit each of us a cigarette. Thanks, she said, sniffing a little; how're we going to figure this out? I was thinking—I'd like to take him for a month this summer, I've got time off, could take him up to my father's cottage.

I shook my head, saying this trip had upset him too much, that I'd been reading that kids were more affected by changes of place than by strange people; I said she could come to Baltimore. She said I wasn't being realistic, did I expect her to move in with me, look at what happened the last time. I said it hadn't worked last summer because she'd acted so hard, and I saw her face change; I knew I should stop talking like this, but the push to make her believe I was right, the old resentments were strong in me. I don't think you trust me with Ben, she said, that's what it is. She stood up, walked over to the fire and stared at it, saying, very slowly, that I couldn't keep her from seeing Ben, that she had a right to him.

—I was thinking, for Ben's sake, we could maybe try—what do you mean, you have a right, you deserted him.

—Oh, you're into that again—well you wonder why I was hard, you were trying to make me feel

—You should feel guilty, I'd feel guilty if I—

—Yeah you were such a terrific father, you ran around, you

—But at least I'm willing to try it again, but no, you get all this important shit to do in the big city, you just want an easy way out!

—Stop it, I don't have to take that stuff from you any-

—You won't face what you did, that's what you mean

—I listened to you for too long, I tried! I tried so hard to be what—you wanted me to be!

—If you'd ever told me about it we could've—

—I did tell you, don't you remember San Francisco?

—Well, you wouldn't listen!

—Stop it, Stop it!, she said, crying, shaking her fists near the side of her head; I let my hands fall, remembering all of it, hearing her years ago in this basement the first time we ever made love, hearing her on the telephone the nights I'd remember to call her after a gig, seeing her in the doorway of our house, leading me into a three o'clock in the morning big dinner she'd stayed up to make, a dinner I'd been too wasted to eat, hearing my own voice on the telephone, or on that Wyoming morning, or now, in this room, or in San Francisco, when we'd fought and she'd raised her fists and tried to hit me, and I'd told her that I was too good for her, she needed a man who'd beat her up, that was the only thing she'd understand. I came toward her now, and she backed away—Nancy, I swear to God I'm sorry, I never meant to—

She stood still, put her hand against the wall, waved me away when I said, 'you have to listen to me!' See, she said quietly, it can't work, I can't take it, I

—But I still love you, can't you see that?

—I love you too, she said, but it's not—we never knew what we—She couldn't go on, she was crying again. I went to her again but she shook her head. I sensed, horribly, that she had to go through this alone, and I knew I'd feel lonely forever because I couldn't help her now. I didn't want to leave, and I could hardly stand to watch her cry. Finally she got the crying under control. Please go, she whispered, please.

I started an egg for Ben and put some coffee on for myself. It took me a moment to realize that my parents were at work; tonight would be the last chance I'd get to see them. But I had to see Nancy, too, I'd awakened angry at her, and at myself, but mostly scared she'd do something to get Ben away from me. Ben climbed up on the chair so he could watch, he likes to see the yolk break and he likes the popping sound the white makes.

While I was thinking about Nancy, wondering how to get through to her, Annie came down; I started when she said good morning. She bent her knees, held Ben's fingers and let him walk up her body; he hung his legs over her back and laughed with her. I put his eggs in a plastic bowl, and she sat him down.

—Didn't go too well with Nancy, huh?

—No, I really blew it, I said. She pulled her housecoat around her and asked me for a cigarette, seeming to understand that I didn't want to talk about it. Ben was eating well for the first time since we'd been here, so the three of us were quiet; Annie said she'd spent a boring evening with two old friends. As we were clearing the table she told me she'd drive me to Nancy's if I wanted to go, but it would have to be within the hour. I knew Nancy wanted to see Ben, I knew we had to talk, but I was afraid to call her, so as soon as Annie and Ben were dressed we drove over.

Nancy's parents lived on a bluff overlooking the river on the La Crescent side; her father had designed the house and had had it built the year I met her. We drove over the river, and I showed Ben the islands I'd camped on, but he was too short to see out the car window and it took me the rest of the way to Nancy's house to explain to him what an island was. Annie let us off and we walked up the steep driveway; the light snow blew around our faces, it was so cold that my nostrils dried out and seemed to close up. The house had large windows on all sides, and this morning the sun's reflection hid the shape of the house, didn't show anyone watching for us from within. Ben asked me if we were going to live here, if this was where mommy was.

Nancy's mother opened the door, and I saw the strain in her face as she looked from one to the other of us. She let us in, and I saw the unopened presents under the tree, felt I'd been unfair not to come by on Christmas. She shook Ben's hand, though I could tell she wanted to pick him up; I felt it was worse for her than for my mother. She'd been the only one who hadn't opposed our getting married. She asked me if I wanted a cup of coffee, and I nodded, moved fast to save the porcelain angels Ben had just begun to examine. We talked about the weather, and about a fund raising drive she'd gotten involved in; I told her my father was thinking of running for the city council, and she said she thought he'd make a good councilman. She said she'd call Nancy, and walked upstairs.

Nancy came down alone, wearing a knee length housecoat I remembered and a pair of slippers we'd once argued about buying. Her hair was wrapped in a towel, she looked as if she hadn't slept much. Ben smiled at her, she held him and hugged him tight, and when she sat down he stood near her, seemed to be watching me. He said no when she asked him to sit on her lap. I told her I was sorry and she waved me away with her hand, her face as cold and drawn as it always was in my memory, but I was sick of all the things my memories didn't reveal; I thought, the three of us are together in one room again, but it wasn't 'again', the three of us had hardly ever been together, I could barely remember the first year of Ben's life. She asked me if I thought we could talk without getting into another fight, and I nodded; Ben pulled on me, I picked him up, and she asked him if he'd like to color. She took out the crayons and the paper, and during this conversation one or the other of us would draw with him, just managing to keep him interested. Nancy joked with him; she was more sure of him even than Julie was, though she'd been away all these months. When she smiled at him, I remembered how she'd use that smile when we were broke, we'd go into a bar where she knew everybody and she'd squeeze one man's arm, hug another, let someone kiss her on the cheek, and we'd come out with four or five dollars; then we'd go to another bar, or buy a nickel somewhere. I pushed the bread crumbs into small piles on the formica top, hearing her laugh with Ben; I rubbed the side of my face with my hand.

—I don't mean this to be shitty, she said—I realized she'd been watching me—you know, but I never thought you'd be upset like this.

—Well I used to think everything was your fault, but coming back here makes me think I fucked everything up.

Her mother came in, looked at us, and asked Ben if he'd like a story; she said this hesitantly, then relaxed when she saw how happy she'd made him. He ran after her into the living room, we could hear the story and I imagined Ben's face, saw Nancy in his face.

Nancy spoke slowly then, telling me about the months she'd spent thinking, we had to accept what we'd done; she said she too had thought about trying it again, wondered yesterday afternoon if it would work. But I don't want to, she said, all that stuff's still back there and I don't feel strong enough to deal with it—we've started different things. I'm happy, she continued, but I don't think—this is hard to say—I couldn't have what you've got with Ben. He's changed you; I can't explain it, I'd just like us to be friends—and see him a lot.

—I'm sorry about last night—listen, you can see him when you want to, I was just hung up. We'll get papers or something, or have a cheap divorce without any fighting, okay? She nodded; I told her what I'd seen from this time alone with him. I'd come to understand how tied down she'd felt, now I wanted to be with her again because I felt we could do it right. She surprised me, then, by saying it was her own fault that she'd felt so trapped, she could've arranged babysitting and taken some courses, joined something; but I can't talk about us getting back together or anything, she said, if you've got a woman you should—it still makes me sort of jealous, though.

—I'm with somebody. But now I don't know what it's going to be like when I get home.

She nodded; the old feeling that I'd never known her at all came back, then fell away as we went on talking; she said she believed we'd only had ideas and expectations about each other and they'd fallen apart almost as soon as we'd gotten married. I never wanted kids, she said, but I made myself think I did—and I was a bad mother, and I don't know if I can ever—

—I still think it was mostly because of me, if I'd just—I broke off, and she asked me how I thought she felt when she looked at Ben. I lit her cigarette, understanding, though I didn't want to, that this was the best we could do.

We tried putting him to sleep, but he cried, I could see he'd been in one too many strange places and asked Nancy to drive us home. I gathered up his presents and said goodbye to her mother; Nancy and I didn't talk in the car, maybe believing another fight would start if we did. She opened the car door, picked Ben up and held him for a long time in the cold. She kissed him and put him down; I took her hand, told her to take care of herself, and to write. She nodded, looked down at the snow she was moving under her boot.

—You all right?

—Yeah, I think I'll probably cry when I get home, though. Take care of him, she said, hugging me. I stood and watched the car skid to the left, then right itself. I could just see her head through the back window, she had to sit on a pillow to drive. As we walked up the steps the sun moved behind the house and I stopped squinting.

I'd been restless enough when we got on the train so that I didn't want to sit in our seats; we went down and had a coke together. Now we came from the diner, three cars behind ours, and Ben was crying loudly from the rush of compressed air between the cars; I took him into the men's room in our car, to have a cigarette and to calm him down. A middle aged man was sitting on the lounge chair, smoking, facing the window: hey little man, what you crying about, he said, leaning forward to smile at Ben. Big noise, big noise, Ben cried, and he pointed behind us.

—Hey, hey my man, you ain't got to be afraid, you just tell that noise go away or I sock you right on the nose! Hey? Okay, you be all right, he said, laughing, getting Ben to laugh and ask questions. No, I ain't Marcus' daddy, he said; I told him Marcus was a friend of ours, and we got to talking; he said he'd come to Milwaukee to visit his daughter for a few days, she was graduating from college in June; most of his family lived in Milwaukee but he liked Chicago, there's always something going on, man, he said, and a man can always find a job in that town, you know, if he just want to work. When he heard I was from Baltimore, he shook his head and said it was mean and ugly there. His daughter wanted to teach school in the inner city, he'd advised her against it but she'd made up her mind. He smiled, seemed to be remembering a conversation with her, and I could tell he was proud of her, he was touched by her stubbornness and idealism and he believed in her. Well, he said, got to get on back to my old lady. First thing I know, she think I got lost back there in the bar and she come to drag me out. He laughed, told us to have a good trip, said don't forget what I told you, little man, hear? and went out. I remembered, suddenly, that I'd forgotten to call Carol.

Going back on the train was different than coming out had been; Ben was only a little ornery, but I waited tensely for him to do something I'd have to deal with. His confusion was, I felt, as unimaginable as my own; he'd only mentioned Nancy once, cried when I said she wasn't coming, but he'd seemed to be crying mostly because he was uncomfortable and adrift.

The land was changing, becoming flatter, the snow was diry in Illinois and the farm houses were further back from the railroad, as we neared Chicago they disappeared completely behind the shopping centers. Ben squealed at the trains that occasionally passed us, and looked carefully at the trucks passing below us, but nothing looked right to me this time, every town the whole way home reminded me of this first stop over the Wisconsin border, Glen Ellyn, Illinois; you could see all these towns moving outward but I felt closed in by them, even from the train: it was easier to watch Baltimore decay, these towns were still full of promises.

My parents had saved up their questions for last night, and answering or lying to each question had taken something I needed for this trip, I hadn't slept well and this morning, when they took me to the train station, I'd known that none of the talking had done any good.

I touched Ben's face, wondering if I'd be able to let go of him when the time came, and remembered Nancy's face; she'd lost her young wife's face, the gentle believing way young wives speak their husband's names. Then her face moved out of my memory, or merged with Carol's face that first afternoon in the apartment. We were getting close to Chicago, where I'd finally come to believe Nancy's life was, where Ben and I would try to make our connection but would probably miss it because this train was running late, and I wondered how I'd keep Ben busy in the station, I wished Nancy were here to help me take care of him. In the Chicago yards, the switch engine humped boxcars and trailer cars, and an old steam engine stood by the roundhouse terminal. Ben waved to the men in the yardmaster's tower, and I hugged him; he struggled, making me laugh, daddy, he said, I'm busy, see train? Oh, see big houses!

I saw Carol standing on the Baltimore station platform, wearing a short open jacket; she'd tell me later that it'd been warm all week. I thought of our heavy coats and felt tired, though it had been an easy trip; I held Ben up to the window, but he didn't know where to look, and missed her. Since we'd changed trains in Chicago I'd thought constantly about Carol, but it took me a long time to dress Ben, I thought of the time somebody'd told me that guitar players were always good with their hands. It was cold and damp on the platform, we walked slowly, and I felt everything reverse: in La Crosse, I'd been anxious, wondering about my parents, and now Carol was probably wondering how I'd changed. Thinking about her on this train ride had moved me toward her, as if I'd accepted, unconsciously, that Nancy was gone, Carol was now the one thing that'd stayed solid in memory over these eight days, and even while imagining her I couldn't see myself returning to the way we lived, I felt as if I were on tour and realized suddenly, how much I've always hated that feeling.

People kept bumping into us, so I picked Ben up; we'd been at the front of the train, so Carol was probably at the very end of the platform. Maybe she thinks we missed the train, I said, wishing I could run down the platform, catch her before she got back upstairs. She was standing near the ticket window, she saw us and came running, her hair rising and falling in slow dark waves, her yellow skirt waving like a towel around her legs. Ben squirmed in my arms, trying to reach her, she hugged us, put her face between ours, but my arms felt weak and I had to push myself to hold her, as you push yourself out of tangled sheets. The air was stale and dark down here and it was hard to breathe, I lit a cigarette to shake off the tiredness, to give my breathing a rhythm. She suggested we go out for lunch but I said I just wanted to go home. She shrugged, said there was nothing in the house but she could run to the grocery store while I was getting Ben ready for his nap.

The day was bright after the dark platform, Ben squinted and I felt how red my eyes must be, my whole body was reacting slowly to everything. She parked the car. When we got out the breeze blew at us, and Ben looked at the two trees on our block. He said, daddy, the trees give me wind, they make my hair shiny. Yeah, I said, holding his hand up the stairs. The apartment was small, after my parents' house, there seemed hardly room to change Ben's diapers, but he was too tired to struggle. With Carol outside, the apartment made me feel as if we'd always lived here alone; as I made Ben's bottle, I wished Susan were here. Ben went to sleep almost immediately, just as I'd expected, he usually recognizes his own crib after long trips. But when I looked at him he seemed smaller, I remembered him falling asleep in my arms on city buses when I'd been looking for a job, his tired crying in the cafes we'd gone to then, the unheated laundromat where we'd spent one cold day, where he'd slept curled up in my coat on a formica laundry table; then what he'd said about the wind, the longest sentence he'd ever spoken, came back to me, and I began to cry, I tried choking it off, didn't hear Carol come into the room. She put her arms around me from behind and I knew what I'd felt moving in me all three times I'd seen Nancy, I'd needed Nancy and now I had to have Carol, or go back to the drinking I'd done months ago, sitting in this room every night after Ben was asleep, worried, as I'd been then, that it would soon be too much to control, that Ben would find out. I turned around, still choking, I thought, her body's better than Nancy's, and the crying, which I thought had stopped began again and I choked harder, my whole face was running; the room turned under my blurred eyes, the soot on the windows seemed to spread out and drip onto the sash, the yellow ceiling confused itself with Carol's sweater and skirt. She was calm; she led me to the bed, I imagined myself and was embarrassed to be lying curled up against her shoulder, I looked like a woman being held by a man. Later, I told myself, we'd talk, I'd tell her what Nancy and I'd decided, but now I couldn't think through the sound of Ben's breathing, almost as loud as my own, a sound I hadn't listened to, had forgotten about since I'd met Carol.

She asked me gently to make some coffee, and I was glad to be moving around again, I put the hot water on, went into the bathroom and slowly washed my face. When she came into the kitchen she seemed expectant, as if she were still mentally forming her questions; but I didn't really look at her, I was looking at the two rooms and thinking they seemed, after this short time, as if they'd been vacant for years, this was the kind of place Jake Sweetwater must've lived in, and it'd felt this way when we first moved in, though the other tenant had left only that morning.

I poured the coffee, and she carefully set out the sandwiches and condiments, got me a beer, and we sat down.

—You look exhausted. Why don't you let me call in sick for you tomorrow?

I shrugged, said I hadn't thought about the store; but I could see it now, and I knew I'd have to change the window tomorrow, move the old stock up front, put the sale signs out, deal with the sale customers; next week I'd go around with a pad and take inventory. Carol stayed quiet, smoothed her dress down, I wondered why she hadn't asked any questions, then thought she was waiting for me to begin. I told her about my parents and Nancy, as soon as I began talking I wanted to tell her everything, as if the telling would put it behind me. I said I'd been confused most of the time, that Nancy'd had to show me that nothing between us could ever work again, that Nancy'd been honest about Ben. Carol was sitting so that I saw her face in profile, and none of the strength showed; she looked as if all this was bothering her, but she said it wasn't when I asked. There was a distance between us I hadn't wanted to see when I got off the train; but I was too tired to do more than notice it now.

—I know this isn't making much sense, what I'm telling you.

It's okay, she said, I understand; I put my hand over hers, said I was sorry I hadn't called. She eased her hand away, stood up, and leaned against the refrigerator. I don't know, she said, I hope this has—I think you've got to stop playing it safe, maybe you've finally settled something. She lit another cigarette, said we could talk about this tonight, I looked as if I were falling asleep. I went into the bedroom and she followed me, she rubbed my back until I fell asleep, maybe rubbed it for a long time after that.

When I awoke the next morning, Carol and Ben were gone, but Carol seemed still to be somewhere in the apartment; I could see her moving quietly, telling Ben daddy needs to sleep, and I realized this was the first time in months I hadn't felt alone.

As I got dressed for work, I remembered the Chinese food we'd eaten last night, the talking we'd done about Nancy, and the way she'd listened, the fear I'd had of making love after that last time and how quickly that fear had gone, we moved silently, in the dark, single minded, almost determined, for the hours it'd lasted, and I fell asleep almost as soon as I came out of her. Now I read the note she'd left me, stuck it in my pocket, and burned my tongue on the coffee, there was hardly time to drink it.

The warm air I'd hardly noticed yesterday, or hadn't had time to believe in, continued today, dry as San Francisco in early spring—Nancy and I had gone there the April before Ben was born. I walked into the store, nodded to Ira, one of the salesmen, and went to the back room to hang my coat up and punch in. When I couldn't find my time card I walked over to the boss to ask him if he'd mislaid it. The man who'd replaced me over Christmas was looking on, and before the boss began speaking I'd figured it out. He hadn't wanted me to go to La Crosse, he'd given this part-time help my job. You wasn't really happy here anyway, the boss said, writing me out a check, you didn't fit in too good like my new man here, ain't been here but five days and already knows the store.

I took the check, my anger receding almost before it'd begun, and walked out of the store; the new man was changing the window display, and I started to laugh. Early shoppers went by, mostly women in bright dresses, and the rising diesel and wet street smells from the streetcleaner came up around me. I kept walking, looking at the city, the row houses on Chase Street seeming almost to move on invisible hinges, their roof line parallel to the small rises and falls of the land under them, the car tires bouncing hard on the brick streets and dirty streams running through the bricks collecting, hardly moving, in the gutters. A building was going up on the corner, I stood on the corner watching the crane lift casks of wet cement up to the roof. The crane moved back and forth on rails, and I wondered how the soft mud could hold these rails and the weight of the crane, the cement trucks backed into the mud, slipped down almost to their rims. As I turned away, I saw a music store, and decided to go in.

I didn't want to think about what I was doing; in five minutes I put the first payment on a big Gibson acoustic with a good pickup, and a small practice amp I'd have been ashamed to play though before this, I sat in the store and played for awhile, said I'd be back to pick it up, then walked into the bar next door. It felt good to be having a beer when I knew I should be working. We could get a rhythm section, play in bigger clubs, I'd write for a band as I used to, hear a band produce what I already could hear in my head. The bar was cold, so I finished the beer quickly, feeling uneasy when I walked out; there were two employment agencies on this block. I kept moving; if I stopped I might go into one of them, or go back to the music store to get my money back. Ben and I'd have to depend on Carol now and I didn't like it, I'd even have to ask her for cigarette money. You can't do this, I said to myself, you got responsibilities; I remembered that other idiot in the shoe store window and shivered, I couldn't go back there.

The building where Marcus worked was just ahead, and it was almost lunchtime. He slapped me on the back when I told him I'd been fired, grinned when I told him about the guitar; we went across the street to a bar that was supposed to look like an English pub; it had a linoleum cobblestone floor. The beer was warm, and all four waiters were trying to serve us, the place was empty. We ordered hamburgers without looking at the menu, and Marcus talked about the gig tomorrow night, his energy already building, he said we should practice before going on and I agreed with him, but I said I didn't know how I could make it. He didn't say anything, maybe sensing my forced happiness, and we ordered another syrupy beer. Marcus was waiting, his brown eyes moving toward me, then closing off again. What is it, man, the trip home was messed up?

—Yeah, it was but—you know, I don't feel I have any right to go and do the shit I've done this morning.

He said he didn't understand what the problem was, I'd finally got together the money for a guitar and the gig was nothing special, the night club would probably go broke in six months, we were just playing for a good time and a little extra change. I said I could play for fun as long as I had another job, but now I didn't know, I'd tried too hard to make it once and I was afraid I'd get back into trying. He rubbed his hands together as if to warm them, leaned forward, and I got the feeling he'd been waiting a long time to say what he was about to say:

—Look, man, I think you're getting hung up on nothing. You can't stop living because you got that kid, you see what I'm saying, so you made some mistakes and all that shit, don't mean you got to make them again, does it?

He'd convinced me, or I'd convinced myself this morning when I'd bought that guitar, but I didn't let on, I wanted him to talk longer so as to make myself sure inside. He was right; I'd never feel good if I wasn't playing, I had to find out if I could handle it this time. We finished the meal and I said I'd call him; after I dropped him off at his building I bought some perfume for Carol. When I got the guitar home I spent about two hours getting it used to my fingers. I played every tune I knew, worked some others out, and I relaxed, it wasn't that desperate sense I always got when I borrowed Ron's guitar. I remembered how I could stop everything, Nancy's yelling, Ben, the unpaid bills, the landlord, I'd just play and everything would be all right. It even felt good to put it away; I had a beer and looked at the closed case for awhile.

When Carol came in I told her I'd bought a guitar and she said, good;

she seemed distracted, and I wondered if she'd had trouble with Ben today. I told her I'd got fired today, and her face changed, she asked if I'd argued, if I'd thought of going to the labor board. I took a swallow of beer, reminded her that she'd been after me for months to quit that job. She twisted her hands together; she said quietly that she'd only wanted me to move to something I'd enjoy more.

—Oh, now you don't want to work and support us, I suppose.

She looked at the clock. We don't have time for this, she said, I've got to go, Julie and I are going to a lecture on women artists. She started buttoning her coat. I'll leave the car for you so you can get Ben, she said.

—Hey, I just got home yesterday, and you're going *out*?

She walked to the door, her lip trembling a little. She said we'd talk about it later. I said we sure as hell had better. When she closed the door I had the feeling she was never coming back.

Thanks for the perfume, she said the next afternoon, I put some on before I went to sleep last night. She'd come in late, had been sleeping when I awoke with Ben. I'd been waiting for her most of the day, figuring out arguments. Good, I said; she stood holding the teakettle, seeming to forget to put it on the stove. All right, I said, what's going on, you've been acting wierd ever since I got home.

—I'm not acting wierd! Maybe I'm just being myself again for a change, she said. Sunlight kept shifting in the room from the cloud front moving in, changing the grey walls only slightly, and I knew, finally, that it was time to move to another place. She didn't say anything; instead, she began to make tea with the same attention she'd shown to the sandwiches yesterday. I waited, looking at the guitar case. When she turned around, she said Julie was happy being single, she'd gotten over missing Bob and felt relieved that she no longer had to ask him what she could do. And that's what I found out, Carol said, you were gone so I started doing things again. She stubbed out her cigarette, and continued, you know I've hardly seen anybody since I moved in here, all I've done is hang around with you. We might as well be married.

I was afraid to ask her what things she'd been doing; my neck and arms itched, my shoes felt tight, as if my feet were suddenly collecting all my blood. She got herself another cup of tea, said she had a meeting tomorrow and asked me to remind her to get her jacket cleaned. I nodded, and sipped my beer, remembering how I'd believed that Nancy would always wait for me, no matter how long the tour, and I'd been sure Carol would wait, unchanging, for me to come back from La Crosse. Now Julie had changed too; I'd always thought I could go to Julie if I had no other woman, it was as if her husband had been preserving her for me. I cleared my throat, wet my lips, and a whistling sound came out before I heard the question I'd meant to ask, was she leaving, did she have another man? When I looked at her face, just before she answered, I remembered making love to her, I should've known there was something wrong from the smooth, almost careless way she'd been; but I'd only been relieved that we weren't having trouble.

—You would think it was a man, she said, the tone of her voice wearing away the little control I had over my panic. Then her voice changed, became softer and she said she was sorry, she hadn't wanted to talk about this yet but she knew it was time; she asked me to let her think for a few minutes. I got up and went to the front window, the old people were on their porches and across the street students walked back and forth, or stopped to hear the guitar player; there was a lot of wine going around, and some smoke, and I wondered if they'd all forgotten they were in Baltimore. The guitar player was good and I wanted to jam with him, but it was too late; I felt I wouldn't like these people any better than I liked Ron. I thought I could see him over there, but his back was to me, and the woman he was with had dark hair.

The phone rang and Carol answered it, I heard her say something about the meeting but I wasn't listening; I shoved Ben's toys under the crib and thought I'd better look through the want ads tonight. She hung up the phone; as she was about to speak, I pointed to the guitar case, took out the guitar so she could really see it. She said it was beautiful.

—Obviously. But I'll have to take it back.

—Why?

—Well, from what you said about—

—I haven't said anything yet! Now, look, I'm not saying we should split up and I'm glad you bought the guitar, no matter what you think. Ned, please, don't just stand there like that, glaring at me.

She turned away and walked into the kitchen, asked me to unzip her dress when I walked in, and reached for her robe. Seeing her naked made me uncomfortable; she put the robe on quickly, played with the belt as she talked. She said it wasn't going to work this way, we were living through each other, closing everything off, doing it the same boring way everybody else was and it hadn't worked for Julie or me, it wouldn't work for us. She touched my hand, in a way Nancy might've when she wanted to talk me into something; but Carol seemed resigned, or convinced I wouldn't understand. She went on talking about relationships and honesty and meaning and equal responsibility and it all sounded like bullshit, something she'd talk about with Ron or one of her teacher friends. I watched the clock, remembering how I used to wait for eight o'clock so I could put Ben to bed, remembering the time alone. And I'd never asked myself to believe in a woman, I'd only wanted a woman who'd believe in me and understand me.

—You know, I can't play any more gigs if you won't help me out with Ben.

—If you want to, you'll find a way to do it, it hasn't got anything to do with my helping, not really, she said, telling me then that Julie was babysitting for tomorrow night, that sometimes I was going to have to find a sitter for him. I said I wouldn't put that on Ben; she threw up her hands, said don't you even trust Julie? Don't you think anybody's good enough to look after him. I wished there were somewhere in this apartment I could go, she seemed to be everywhere in here and her voice echoed and repeated things I already didn't want to know.

—We've talked about love, she said, nobody even knows what that means. You know, do you realize that? She stopped, lit another cigarette and suddenly her face brightened, her voice sounded the way I remembered it and she began to talk fast, it's like Ben and me, this morning, you know, when we were driving? He asked me if I was his mommy too and I said no but I was his friend, so he said is mommy my friend; I said yes, and luckily he saw a tow truck or something, and I started thinking, well actually I've always known this but I haven't *wanted* to think much about it, I realized that I didn't know what I am to Ben, any more than he does.

Ben and I have to learn that yet, you and I have to learn it? Do you see? I hope?

—Yeah, but it's different.

—Oh, don't just say it's different, think about it. Please!

I said I didn't believe you could sit down and think everything over and that it would make it all right; But in that moment, when she was looking down, trying to figure out what to say next, or wondering whether she should leave, her face drawn tight and her knees banging together, I was more sure of her than I'd ever been of anything, and though I couldn't understand what she saw for us, the feeling that she was honest was stronger than the confusion, the resentment, the old dreams or memories of Nancy.

—Well, I don't really know what you're talking about. But you make me feel like I want to try it.

—You don't sound happy, she said. She scratched her fingers on the table top.

—Look, don't ask me about that now. I don't know anything, it's too soon after—I just want to try.

—Yeah, she said, there isn't anything to know anyway. Her hand closed over my arm; The people were still singing down in the street. Except I know I love you, she said, I guess maybe you had to go away before I could know that. She kissed me on the cheek; I touched the hand she'd laid on my shoulder. Come on, old lady, I said, let's go buy some wine, sit down on the stoop and drink it.

—Watch it, she said, and she slapped my arm. Then she smiled, and looked toward the guitar. You going to play? she asked.

—Yeah, maybe.

Tony Hozeny was born in Madison, Wisconsin in 1946 and has lived in New Jersey, Milwaukee, Baltimore, Pennsylvania and San Francisco. He was principal of a school for emotionally disturbed girls, attended the Johns Hopkins Writing Seminars and taught at three colleges. He did other things too. Presently he lives in Madison and is at work on a new novel.